A Medieval Tale

PALACE INTRIGUE

Lina J. Potter
Translated by Elizabeth Adams
Cover by Marat Gabdrkhmanov

ISBN: 9781717741837
Published by LitHunters, 2018

A Medieval Tale by Lina J. Potter:

First Lessons

The Clearing

Palace Intrigue

The Royal Court

The Price of Happiness

You can connect with Lina on Facebook. Just search for Lina J. Potter

Contents

Astounding travelers! What histories
we read in your eyes, deeper than the ocean there!
Show us the treasures of your rich memories,
marvelous jewels made of stars and air.
We wish to voyage without steam or sails!
Project on our spirits, stretched out, like the sheets,
lightening the tedium of our prison tales,
your past, the horizon's furthest reach completes.
Tell us, what did you see?
　　　　~Charles Baudelaire, "Le Voyage"

Chapter 1
The Brew Comes to a Boil

"'Gammon,'" My Lady."

Lily's eyes flashed, but she had lost fair and square. Hans Tremain had become an expert at backgammon, and he beat her at three out of every five games they played. She was glad they weren't playing for money.

"You have no move."

She studied the simple, unvarnished, wooden board.

Who would have thought a year ago that I would be here playing backgammon with an envoy of the king?

Certainly not Lily; she had been skipping along, enjoying her life and even planningto get married soon, but fate had other things in store for medical student Aliya Skorolenok. Instead of checking off life goals, she had lost consciousness in an automobile accident and awakened in someone else's body in an entirely different world. Neither one—the body or the world—was to her liking. There was no indoor plumbing or decent windows to keep the cold out, and peasants paid their taxes in rutabagas. *Internet? Telephones? Television? For all the locals knew, those are the names of evil spirits.* Her new body was equally shocking. As a young woman reared in the 21st century, Aliya was used to the idea that "thin" and "beautiful" were synonyms. In her new incarnation, however, she weighed as much as a Roman centurion and had several weight-related health issues that worried her.

The dice skittered across the board. Lily glanced at them and shook her head. She wouldn't be escaping Hans' trap any time soon.

The one bright spot in her new world was that she was a noblewoman—Lilian Elizabeth Mariella, the Countess of Earton. It wasn't much of an estate. The castle was a pile of stones, her husband was allergic to her, the manager had been stealing from her, and her only living family—her father—was far away. It was bad business, to be sure, but Lily was making the best of things.

She had expelled the manager and set her peasants to cleaning and repairing the castle. Her husband was a dark spot on the horizon, and she was in no hurry for him to come home. In all honesty, she had her hands full with their one child, his beloved daughter from his second wife.

Lily secretly felt that the little girl could use a spanking, but she was wise enough to see that she was in no position to give it and took to reforming the girl with love and kindness. So far, her approach was successful. In her darker moments, she reflected that Miranda Catherine had grown up a spoiled brat on her father's watch. He obviously knew nothing about children, and that made her even more wary of him and who he might turn out to be. She suspected that she would have a hard time getting along with the earl, and hoped that his travels with the prince kept him away as long as possible.

To add to her troubles, there had been an attempt on her life. Her husband's lover had apparently hired a man to kill her because she thought the earl's emerald bracelet would look better on her own wrist. Lily, however, had no intention of dying that easily. She had always faced problems as they presented themselves, so she squared her shoulders and continued with her work around the estate. In spare moments, she wrote down everything she remembered about medicine and tried to decide what advances she should share with her new world.

One thing was certain; she would tell them nothing about military technology. Her new world had not yet invented gunpowder, and Lily was damned if she would do it for them. She remembered the ingredients (What child didn't fool around with explosives, especially if she lived on a military base?) But she kept it to herself. She wanted her new world's moral capacity to grow faster than its technological prowess, so she kept her innovations simple: glass, lace, ladies' jewelry. And she worked constantly.

Even in her old life, Aliya had never had any patience for people who complained that they didn't know how to do something. With free online classes available on any subject from raising rabbits to tatting lace, she saw no excuse for ignorance.

When Aliya was younger, her mother had signed her up for clubs and classes whenever they moved to a new town. Tatiana Viktorovna believed that a body needed to know as much as possible in order to succeed in Russia, so she filled her daughter's head with knowledge—from wound care and surgery to canning vegetables and embroidery. She was overjoyed when her daughter applied to medical school; a doctor could always find work. Lily was still grateful for her mother's efforts.

A loud bang interrupted her train of thought.

"I believe I've won again!" Hans grinned.

The countess jumped up and went to the window; the children were up to no good.

"Leir Tremain, I admit defeat. Now if you'll excuse me, I must go see what the children are getting into."

Tremain nodded. "Of course, My Lady."

Lily gave a slight bow and sailed out of the room, leaving Hans to put the game pieces away. She reflected that, while the era might not be to her liking, the government was decent enough. Edward VIII seemed to be a sensible and intelligent man, judging by the envoy he sent to get to the bottom of the trouble at Earton. Hans Tremain was whip-smart and a consummate professional. She was even a little afraid of him at times, probably because he rarely smiled.

She pushed open the heavy castle door and walked out into the courtyard, where she barely missed being hit by a small missile. It was a rock, delivered by slingshot; the children were practicing self-defense.

"Lily! Look what I can do!"

The countess smiled down at her stepdaughter. "Let's see."

Another rock went whistling and hit its target with an impressive thump. Miranda looked up at her stepmother, eyes shining.

Lily laughed and nodded. "Keep up the good work. You're my smart girl!"

Miranda Catherine tilted her head to one side and grinned, revealing a gap where she had recently lost a tooth. Lily couldn't accomplish everything she wanted to do in her new world, but she made sure to brush her teeth with Miranda every night before bed. Instead of toothpaste, they used a mixture of nettles, birch bark, and chalk that did the job just fine. At first, Mirrie had protested the new hygiene rules, but after listening to a lecture on cavities and looking around at grown men and woman who were missing half their teeth, the little girl stopped arguing and started brushing her teeth twice a day. To be fair, she would have done anything at all in order to be just like Lily. She was overjoyed to have a kind, fun-loving adult who took the time to listen to her. They argued on occasion, but for the first time in her young life, Mirrie had a mother. The little girl could never have explained it that way, but she knew without words that, finally, someone cared about her.

She threw her arms around Lily's neck, kissed her cheek, and ran off to play with her friends.

Lily smiled as she watched them. There was no sign of the pale, spoiled aristocrat who had arrived in Earton without warning. Now, she saw a tanned little tomboy who was having the time of her life, dressed in comfortable pants that were cut to look like a skirt, and with a slingshot in her pocket wherever she went.

The countess had originally intended to teach the children to use a small catapult, but she then thought better of it. Instead, she gave them all slingshots. True, they had broken quite a few things around the estate while they learned to aim, but Lily noticed that the local children were more mature than what she was used to. They thought ahead of time about the consequences of their actions and tried not to get into trouble. She reflected that this was wise since local parents meted out severe beatings instead of taking away computer privileges for a week.

As a result, the chickens might have been terrorized, but the castle's windows (made of thick, bubbly glass in a variety of unintentional colors) were all still whole.

ഌ ☐ ങ

"My Lady?" Hans came up behind her silently.

Lily turned and graced him with a smile. "Leir Tremain."

"I see you are busy, as always."

"I can set aside my affairs to speak with you," she said sweetly as she petted the mongoose seated on her shoulder. The intelligent little animals stayed close to their master or the countess during the day when there were hordes of children running around the castle, and at night, they hunted rats, bringing back dozens of kills each morning.

Hans studied the countess' face. It was his personal opinion that the earl was lucky beyond all reason. The countess was smart, kind, beautiful, and a good manager. *What else could a man want in a wife?*

"My Lady, I must leave you soon."

"Of course," she nodded. "The things you will be taking with you are almost ready to go. The taxes I owe have been packed separately from the gifts I wish to send to His majesty, the young princesses, and my mother-in-law. I do hope I am not burdening you unduly."

"Of course not. I will make sure that every item reaches its recipient. Will you allow me to take one of the slave traders' ships? I need some way to carry them back to the capital for trial."

Lily nodded. "Certainly. I would like to send Erik with you if you can wait for him to return."

"I will do that, My Lady."

20ℭ

Lily admired Hans. She enjoyed his sense of humor and appreciated his help organizing men to dig out the amber that had been discovered on Earton's coastline.

It isn't truly my amber, though… It belongs to my husband!

Once again, Lily was distracted by the thought that if Jess Earton came to a bad end somewhere out there on the backroads of Ativerna, the king would have to appoint someone to manage the estate until Miranda's second son was born. That would give her plenty of time to accomplish her goals.

She sighed and pushed the thought away. For Mirrie's sake, she was prepared to make nice with her husband. If he wouldn't play along, however, she would make her own plans.

During their long evenings at backgammon, Lily had cautiously probed Hans for information about the laws governing marriage. In the end, she thought she might have found a way out of her predicament. If she gave birth to a son of her own and her husband tragically passed away, her father would act as the child's guardian until he reached adulthood. Meanwhile, Lily would play the role of the grieving widow.

While she would prefer peaceful negotiations, Lily was glad that she had other options, as well. The first step in her plan was to gain the support of those around her—the king, the princesses, her mother-in-law, her father, other courtiers.

Hans had passed along the king's invitation for Lily to come to the palace in the spring. She had every intention of going, and she would outshine everyone there. She was well aware of the rumors circulating about her. It hadn't been difficult to find out. Her loyal housekeeper Emma had struck up a warm friendship with two of Hans' servants, and information was soon forthcoming. To Lily's chagrin, she learned that Lilian Earton was strange and stupid and that everyone at court felt sorry for Jess for having to marry her.

Is that so? We'll see who takes his side once I arrive at court.

It was clear that Lilian had been a disappointment to her husband, but Lily still felt he had behaved badly. Men in her new world were supposed to protect their wives. Instead, her husband went around complaining about her to anyone who would listen.

Shameful!

ജ ര

Jess ran into his cousin's room. Richard looked up in surprise. "What's the matter?"

"Bad news!"

"Sit down and tell me what happened."

"Just look!" Jess tossed a scroll on the table.

Richard raised one eyebrow. "Who is it from?"

"Pastor Simon Leider."

"Did you decide you needed a blessing?"

"No, but he decided I needed to know something! Read it!"

Richard shrugged an unrolled the scroll.

Your Lordship, I fear I must inform you that your wife is behaving strangely. She attends public markets, has dealings with Eveers and Virmans, and even hired a band of the latter to serve as her guards. She trades with Khangans and is up to no good with Baron Avermal. As a servant of Aldonai, I felt it was my duty to let you know.

Pastor Simon Leider.

"What do you think?"

Richard tapped his forehead. "Jess, have you lost your mind?"

"No, but it looks like my wife has."

His cousin sighed, exasperated. "She's pregnant, and she's sitting at home. This man is raving mad."

"That's just it. She isn't pregnant."

A second scroll thumped down on the desk next to the first. "Read it!"

It was from Amalia.

My dearest brother,

I want to tell you the latest news. Your wife has lost the baby. She fired Medicus Craybey—the one I worked so hard to hire—and told him she would have him hung if he showed his face in her presence again. I don't know if you've already heard about this or not. I've asked Uncle to see what he can find out. He promised to send an envoy to Earton. I am worried about Miranda. You should have sent her to stay with us. Peter wants me to return to our estate so that the baby…

Richard scanned the rest of the letter. There was nothing else of interest in it, so he set it aside and looked up at his cousin. "Well?"

"What do you mean 'Well'?' My wife lost the baby and fired the medicus."

"I don't see anything strange in that. He was supposed to ensure that she gave birth to a healthy child. He failed to do so. I would have fired him, too, if I were in her position."

"Why didn't Etor write to me about any of this?"

"Maybe he did, and his letter hasn't reached you yet."

Jess shrugged. "I suppose so."

"You know how the mail slows down the closer it gets to winter."

"True. Etor's letter could be on its way, and she may have been right to fire the medicus, but what about the rest of it?"

"Jess, use your brain for a moment. She's doing exactly what any woman would do after losing a child. She's run off to the market to buy things." He paused. "And to trade with Khangans. By the way, what do you think she could have sold them?"

Jess snorted. "There's nothing to sell in Earton. It's all swamps. Aside from the hunting, I've never even really looked at the place."

"Fine. Maybe she sold the Khangans some of that swampland."

"What about the pastor?"

"Does he know your wife? Has he ever spoken to her in person?"

"I doubt it!"

"There you have it. He's probably mistaken about something. He isn't Aldonai, after all."

"Is that what you really think?" Jess' voice was uncertain. His sister's letter had not surprised him, but the pastor's letter had been a shock.

"Write to him. Better yet, write to Etor.'"

"Yes, Etor."

"Write to him and see what he says. I think the only issue of any interest is why your wife would hire Virmans for protection if she has your manager and the castle guards. Doesn't that strike you as odd?"

"I suppose so."

"See? Some stupid pastor writes you a letter, and you start to panic. Think with your head, Jess."

"You're right. I was being stupid." Jess sat down on the bed next to his cousin and grabbed an apple off the bedside table. He bit into it and grinned.

"You usually are."

"I learned it from you."

Richard didn't want to argue with Jess, even in fun, so he changed the subject. "How is that Adele of yours?"

"I don't really know," said Jess, chewing on the apple.

"Why not?"

"She started to get clingy."

"What does that mean?"

"Everything was good between us in bed, but as soon as we got out of bed, she would start begging me to swear eternal love and whining that she was a fallen woman. And she was always afraid of getting pregnant."

"I hope…"

"I was careful," Jess assured him. "I found an herbalist to take care of her. But her whining was getting on my nerves. She's acting like a wife instead of a mistress."

"Maybe she wants to be your wife."

"I've already got one of those on a rope around my neck." Jess took such a hard bite out of the apple that it split in half.

Richard sighed. "She may be tied to you, and she may not be beautiful, but I think you make too much of your misfortune."

"I just did it for the boatyards…and August."

"I know." Richard reached for his own apple.

The boatyards and August; Jess needed both. That was why he and his father had agreed to the marriage contract. Jess turned to his cousin. "Now, I have to go back to Earton and try to make a new baby with her."

"You'll survive. You can do some hunting while you're there."

"That's the one thing I look forward to, but it won't be until next summer or even the fall."

"I'm afraid you're right."

"Are you going to choose Lidia?"

"Richard lay back and looked up at the ceiling. "I don't know. Anna is a lovely girl, and I can tell she is trying hard, but I have to see them both before I can decide."

"Fair enough."

The prince raised up on one elbow and looked at Jess. "You be careful with that Adele. She's a barracuda."

Jess shrugged. "Barracuda or not, she's a queen next to my wife."

"It's your job to endure."

"I am enduring!" Jess protested. "It's your job to choose a wife that you won't have to endure."

Richard smiled. "That's my plan." He put a hand on his cousin's shoulder. "It's big game season. Enjoy the hunt and try to forget about your problems."

"Don't you want to hunt with me?"

The prince looked away. He did not care for hunting, but he kept that to himself.

How do other men enjoy it? They ride out armed with spears and swords and dogs and beaters. I wouldn't call it hunting; I'd call it murder.

Jess didn't seem to notice. He punched his cousin's shoulder. "We'll have a wonderful time!"

Richard nodded and bit into his apple.

That's why I like apples; when you're eating one, you don't have to say anything.

৪০ ⬜ ୧୫

"My Lady?"

Alicia Weeks turned to face her maid.

"Lord Ivelen is here to see you."

"Show him in."

With a practiced motion, the dowager countess adjusted her dress and ran a hand over her smooth hair. Peter Ivelen walked in and bowed.

"My Lady."

"Dearest son-in-law."

"I hope I find you well?"

"I have no complaints. How is your family?"

"Very well. Amalia asked me to kiss you for her."

Alicia gave a cold smile. "Tell her that I pray for her daily." She was on speaking terms with her daughter, but that did not mean she loved her.

"You look wonderful, as always."

"What brings you here?" she cut him off. Alicia had never enjoyed praise. As a small girl, she had known that people flattered her because of her connection to the royal family.

"I'm getting to that, Mother." Peter smiled with just his lips. Obviously, he didn't think much of his mother-in-law.

Alicia replied with a poisonous smile of her own. "Does my dear daughter need anything? Shall I come hold her hand during the birth?"

"Of course not. Amalia is in Ivelen."

"All the better. The capital is no place for a pregnant woman. How is she?"

"She is concerned about her niece."

Alicia shrugged. "Miranda is in Earton. Alicia would do better to think of her own two children and the one on the way."

"I agree with you, but I was hoping you had some news from Earton."

Alicia shook her head. "You will have to ask the king. I believe Miranda is well. I suppose that is all Amalia wanted to know."

Peter looked at her sharply. he seemed to sense that she was holding something back.

The old woman clasped her hands in her lap. "His majesty places the utmost faith in me, and I have no intention of betraying that faith." Her voice was clear and crisp.

The Earl of Ivelen winced but apparently decided to push the matter no further.

"My Lady…"

"Was there something else you wanted?" Alicia looked up at him, making it clear that she had no time for empty conversation.

"I assume you will see His majesty soon?"

"I will."

"Then tell him about Amalia's concern. He may find time to…"

"I will tell him, but I doubt that will change anything." Alicia stood up, bowed curtly, and showed her son-in-law to the door.

Once he was gone, she frowned darkly. She didn't care for the Ivelens. They were dukes, but they thought entirely too much of themselves. Alicia had known Peter's father, and she remembered clearly how it felt to be an ugly girl without a dowry. Jyce had saved her from the fate of an old maid. She would always be grateful to him, and to the king, and to Jessamine. But that was it. Peter was not on the list of people to whom she owed gratitude.

As she sat back down at her desk, she wondered how long it

would take for Lily to reply to her letter.

Royce Fletch took aside two of his men. "Mick and James, I want you to leave your horses here and walk into the village. Let it be known that you are looking for work. Find out what you can about Earton and about the countess. You know what to do."

The men nodded, knowing exactly what to do. Their job was to find out if murdering the countess would be possible, and if so, how best to get close to her. The village closest to their camp was Appleton. The rest of the men stayed back in the woods, where they would build a fire and wait several days for their two emissaries to return. Once Mick and James brought back news, Royce would decide what to do. They could do the job, or they could tell their employer they did it and take his money. Ivernea was not that far away, and they could always find work there.

"Anna is doing her best, of that I am sure." Altres Lort sat at the king's feet but he kept his eyes on the fire in the hearth.

"But?"

"Richard doesn't look interested."

"Why not?"

"He wants to look at all his options."

"I don't like that. He must leave Wellster wearing Anna's bracelet."

"I agree with you, Gardwig. When should we hold the hunt?"

"In four days."

"Perfect. I have a plan."

"Tell me about it."

Both men stared at the flames. Altres' plan spooled out of him like a spider's thread, ready to grab the trusting fly, Prince Richard of Ativerna.

ԑօ ⌷ ങ

Lily quickly glanced over the document in front of her. "Leir Avels, you're a wonder!"

"I did my best, My Lady." Lons allowed himself a polite smile. It had been no easy business putting the report together, but he had done it well. Lily had asked him to write out a description of the state of affairs in Earton, the estate's income and expenses, and her own actions. Hans Tremain would take the report and present it to His Majesty. It had taken four tries before Lons came up with a format that pleased the countess. In the end, they settled on a report that presented plenty of numbers with little text. When she asked Hans to review the report, he found nothing to change.

Lily turned to Lons. "Can you copy it out one more time in nice handwriting? It is for the king, after all."

"Of course, My Lady."

Lily's face lit up with a smile of gratitude. He could see she expected him to rush off to recopy the report, but he stood there looking at her awkwardly.

"My Lady?"

"Yes?"

"You have been invited to court, haven't you?"

"Is that a matter of public knowledge?"

"The people who need to know are already aware, My Lady." He smiled.

Lily grimaced. "The king invited me to the capital in the spring. I'd rather not go."

"But you must." He paused. "My Lady, can I say something without being considered excessively rude?"

"You may speak openly with me, Leir Avels."

"My Lady, you have very unusual manners."

"I suppose everyone at court will think I've lost my mind."

Lons said nothing, but the look on his face spoke for him.

"I am aware of that, Leir Avels. I am a merchant's daughter, not a born noblewoman, and my upbringing left much to be desired. And, as you can see, there is little call for fine manners here in Earton."

"I would not dream of criticizing you, My Lady. I am a fair teacher if you will allow me to say so, and I could…"

"You could teach me everything I need to know."

"My Lady, I feel I have been too forward." Lons proceeded cautiously, but he could tell that the countess was not offended. In fact, she welcomed his suggestion. If all went according to plan, Lilian Earton would owe him a great deal.

Chevalier Avels had already reached some conclusions

about the countess, and he blushed to recall his plan to become her lover. *How stupid I was!* Lilian Earton was not the type of woman to keep a lover. A man would have to work hard day and night to gain even her notice. She was intelligent, strong, interesting, and even a little bit mysterious.

In truth, it was a relief to know that he wouldn't have to sell his body. Thoughts of Anna still tortured him at night when he lay in his lonely bed.

My poor girl! How is she doing, I wonder?

He would do his best to prepare the countess for her audience with the king. She would be the envy of everyone at court. *She will shine!* Lons knew he could do it. Without altering her personality in the least, he could show her how to behave like the finest noblewoman, and he believed Lilian Earton was a woman who knew how to show gratitude. His salary at Earton was a little less than Gardwig had offered, but she paid him regularly and often presented him with small gifts, such as new clothes, boots, or a lovely silver pen and inkwell the likes of which he had never seen before. In short, Lons hoped to continue his mutually beneficial relationship with Lily as long as possible. Every now and then, he allowed himself to dream about bringing Anna to live with him in Earton. The countess would not mind, and he would live a quiet life with his beloved, teaching at the castle and rearing his own children.

"My Lady, if you can find the time..."

Lily narrowed her eyes at him. "Can you teach me alongside the children?"

"The children?" He didn't understand what she wanted.

"Mirrie, Mark and the Virman children."

"Why in the world do Virman children need to know about etiquette and diplomacy?"

Lily shrugged. "You never know what you'll need in this life."

Lons thought for a moment and nodded. "As you wish, My Lady."

"I believe I will have some time this evening."

"Whenever you wish, My Lady."

"Thank you, Leir Avels. I will not forget this."

Lons had no doubt of that. The countess would not forget him.

∞ ⬚ ∞

"Erik, catch!"

Even through the new panes of window glass, Lily could hear one of the children yelling to another. They certainly were a handful for Emma to manage, she thought.

She knew her housekeeper was running her feet off every day just to keep up. Lily demanded cleanliness, while the servants had only the slightest notions of hygiene, and the band of children running around the castle did little to help matters. Still, Lily felt the children were useful to have around. They saw everything that went on in the castle, and some of them were actually running around doing errands for their parents and other adults. Helke Leitz—an Eveer jeweler—and the other craftsmen were looking at some of the boys and girls as potential apprentices, especially now that most of the Virmans were away working on the coast.

The countess had finally paid a visit to the smokehouse, and she clapped her hands when she saw it. The Virmans had organized a conveyor system; the fish was unloaded, processed, and smoked or salted as quickly as possible. Her salt pits had turned out to be an excellent idea, as well. The salt had a slightly bitter aftertaste, but it would prevent spoilage and keep all of their thyroids functioning. Lily felt like she had scored two big wins with those projects.

When Hans heard that the smokehouse was in operation, he rode down to the beach to examine it thoroughly. Afterward, he bowed most respectfully to the countess and asked for a description of the process. Lily was happy to share her design with other Ativernese, so she wrote it out and gave it to Hans as a scroll.

The king's envoy was almost ready for his return journey. Lily had given him gifts for everyone whose support she would need. Helke was busily polishing a couple of precious stones, and he swore that the recipients would faint when they saw them. When Lily stopped by his workshop, she remembered that she hadn't taught the dressmakers to incorporate glass beads into their lace yet. She also wanted them to make beaded bracelets and other decorative items. The girls were ready to start any day, but the glass blower was taking his time. He wanted to make an impression on the countess.

Lily also had goods that she wanted to send to her father for sale. There weren't enough hours in the day for her to do everything, and as a result, she was rarely able to find time to work on her manners with Lons. Undeterred, he began to work with her when they sat around the dinner table, showing her how to move, how to smile, what to talk about. The countess gained the upper hand, however, once forks were introduced. Nothing like it had ever been seen before, and Lons had not the faintest idea what to do with one. As far as Lily could tell, people in her new world used knives to cut their food and spoons for soup, but everything else they ate with their hands.

It had taken a great deal of trouble to explain to the blacksmith what a fork should look like. Once he got the idea, she handed over boxes of ugly old silver plates for him to melt down to make forks and other tableware. To make sure she got all her silver back, she put a Virman in the forge to keep an eye on things. Soon, Lily had thirty-two full sets of silverware. Her servants stared at her, but she was pleased to see the table finally set with forks, knives, soup spoons and dessert spoons.

When Hans appeared at dinner, he stopped in confusion. After examining the new items, though, he pronounced them both attractive and useful. Lily had secretly set aside a set of silverware for him to take away as a gift, but she decided not to show it to him until the day of his departure.

ജ ഗ

Someone knocked on the door.

"Come in!"

Erik Torvson appeared in the doorway. He smiled, revealing several missing teeth. Lily smiled politely in reply. "I am glad to see you, Erik. How was your trip?"

"It went well, My Lady. I spoke to the mayor and bought everything you asked for, even a little bit more than you asked for. What I mean to say is someone came back with me." He stepped aside, and Lily's smile grew even wider.

"Taris! How good it is to see you, my friend!"

Taris Brok gave a perfectly measured bow, but it was obvious that he was glad to see the countess again.

"My Lady, you are even lovelier than you were when I took my leave. I did not think that was possible."

"Then I suppose I'll be absolutely gorgeous by the time I'm eighty," Lily laughed. "What brings you back to Earton?"

"I brought a letter from your father, My Lady. I also have some carrier pigeons for you and a few other things. Your father asked me to stay here and help you unless you'd rather not have me here."

Lily clapped her hands. "Taris! How could I not want you here? I'm so glad you will be here over the winter. Go get some rest, and later you can tell me all about my father."

Taris handed Lily a letter, bowed and left. Lily knew that Emma would make sure he got the best room. She thanked her lucky stars her father's agent had turned up. She didn't want to make the trip to Altver to sell the things she and Helke were working on, but someone needed to do it. She wanted her inventions to gain traction over the winter so that her name would already be on everyone's lips when she paid her visit to the king's court in the spring. She remembered something people had always said back in medical school: first you work hard for your grades, and then they work hard for you. Lily had every intention of working hard so she would have something to show the king.

ജ ❧ ℭ

With Taris gone, she began to go over her various projects in her head.

Emma was in charge of everything at the castle, and Ingrid was keeping an eye on the villages. Leif was the master down at the smokehouse and salt pits and accompanied Ingrid on periodic tours of the villages. Leis Antrel handled all the guards. That left Lily responsible for all the manufacturing on the estate since no one else could do the job for her. Lons Avels took care of all the estate's books and reports, but she went over all his work. So far, it didn't look like he was lining his own pocket.

Now, what will I do with Taris?

She decided to make him her traveling sales manager. Erik could go with him as both bodyguard and auditor.

The estate now had all the livestock it could hold, and the peasants had stored up a huge amount of peat to use as fuel over the winter.

I'll have them keep bringing it in, though. Earton has plenty of bogs. We could probably find a place for the hound of the Baskervilles if we had to.

Ⅿ Ⅾ

"My Lady?"

Lily turned quickly. It was Erik. He had disappeared somehow when Taris came in, but now he was back.

"Ingrid gave me a little gift for you."

Lily's eyebrows went up. The man was holding a sack, and there was obviously something alive wriggling in it. Erik untied the sack and pulled out a healthy sized dog. She took a step forward. On closer inspection, she saw that it was actually a very large puppy, with huge paws and thick, fluffy fur.

"It's a guard dog from Virma."

"He's gorgeous!" She knelt down and held out a hand. "Let's be friends, little one."

The puppy sniffed her hand and then licked it several times. Erik grinned. "You have a way with dogs, My Lady."

Lily shook her head. "I'm afraid not. I just ate a piece of ham."

Meanwhile, the puppy sniffed around his mistress' skirts. Then he lifted a leg. A yellow puddle began to dribble across the flagstone floor.

Lily laughed out loud. "Call someone to clean this up!"

Erik nodded and ran out. Lily sat down to pet the puppy's head, burying her fingers in his delightfully soft fur. Soon, Ilona and Emma came running in.

"My goodness! What is this?"

"A Virman guard dog."

Emma's hands flew to her face. "I've seen those dogs before. He'll be the size of a horse!"

"Really?"

"Or bigger!"

Lily doubted the puppy would ever be as big as a horse, but he certainly was adorable.

"Emma, have the cook give him something to eat."

"I will do that, My Lady."

"His name is Nanook."

"Nanook, My Lady?"

"Yes. Make him a bed on the floor in my room, and find someone to take him outside every few hours."

Lily handed the puppy to her housekeeper and went back to her desk. She rested her chin on her hand and closed her eyes. A memory from her childhood in her other life came back to her suddenly: A friend of her father had come to visit on his way back to an army base near the Arctic Circle, and he brought with him a giant dog. It was a husky-wolf mix, and its name was Nanook. Little Aliya had fallen in love with him immediately. She spent the whole evening sitting on the floor petting the dog, her small arms buried almost to the elbows in luxurious, thick fur. The dog patiently endured her attentions, every now and then presenting an ear to be scratched and looking at her with keenly intelligent yellow eyes. When he opened his mouth to yawn, she saw giant fangs that would send any bully running to the store for a bag of diapers. Aliya had giggled at the thought.

Lily opened her eyes. She wondered if this Virman dog would grow up to be anything like the one she remembered. She soon learned that he would. Lons swore that the dog would be at least four feet tall at the shoulder once fully grown. Dogs like this one, he told Lily, were used to hunt bears.

Erik had brought back three other puppies as well, a female and two males. Lily told him to give one of them to Miranda. Her nanny, Martha, was vocally opposed, but the little girl squealed and threw herself on Lily's neck. Even Lily's threat that Miranda must train the puppy herself—and that she must do a good job—did nothing to dampen the child's enthusiasm.

My dearest daughter,

I was terribly upset by the news that your life was in danger, even if the danger was but brief. Taris has reassured me that you are well. I am pleased to hear that the family talent has awoken in you. Your mother was always quite adept at managing a household, and she was very good at coming up with new ideas. You look just like her.

Lily smiled. People were always eager to discover that they were the source of positive qualities in their children.

And now let's speak of business. I gave your pen and inkwell to His Majesty. There is a great deal of interest in them at court. Since the guild has ruled that only Helke Leitz can make them, he has at least one hundred new orders coming in from the capital. I will send a list of people wishing to order sets and their specific desires regarding materials, etc., in a separate letter. The princesses were delighted by the earrings. I am likewise sending you a list of ladies who wish to order similar earrings. I suppose you can send the finished goods to me, and I will take them to the palace. His Majesty has invited you to the palace in the spring. Try to make a good show of it. This will be an important meeting.

If you wish, we can collect evidence and request a separation for you from Jerrison Earton under the terms of the marriage agreement and due to the recent threat to your life. Please consider this matter. A separation is entirely possible, but it will hurt my shipbuilding business. However, your wellbeing is of the utmost importance to me. So, please give serious thought to this matter. I will support you, regardless of what you decide to do.

Lily smiled again. That was good to hear.

I am sending Taris Brok to help you. I believe that his experience and knowledge will be of use to you. I have ordered him to provide whatever assistance you require. He also has some small gifts and money for you. Money is always of use in a household as large as yours. What is the condition of your share in the income from the boatyards? Are you managing it yourself?

Lily shook her head. She had forgotten about that share of the income. She would have to investigate right away.

Please write to me in great detail. Taris has a man who is an expert with pigeons. We can exchange short letters frequently.

I am also sending a pair of ships to Altver to provide you with a link to the outside world.

⁊ ⁓

The rest of the letter covered familiar ground, as her father assured her of his love and his prayers for her health and wellbeing. Lily reread the most important parts of the letter and wiped away a tear. Her own father had been just the same. He would have committed barehanded murder for the sake of his little girl. She sat staring at the letter in amazement for a few moments.

Is this for real? Am I truly lucky enough to have someone who cares about me in this world?

A little voice brought her back to the present. "Lily, I've decided to name my puppy Liliona. Do you like it?" The countess turned to look at Mirrie, who wasn't much bigger than her puppy.

"That's a lovely name," she said. "It fits her, that's for sure."

Mirrie beamed. It hit Lily that she actually had two people who loved her.

She turned back to her father's letter.

I won't press for a separation yet. I can always put pressure on the earl if I choose to, but I won't use it just yet.

Lily was confident that she could get rid of her husband if she needed to, but first, she would try to reach a friendly agreement with him.

ဆ ⬚ craft

It had already been a busy day, but there was more excitement in store for the countess. Right after lunch, two young peasants came running to the castle. Leis listened to their story and then went straight to Lily.

"There is trouble, My Lady."

"Of course there is. What now?"

"Some mercenaries are sniffing around Appleton asking questions about you."

"I see."

"Two young men from the village followed their tracks as best they could. They say there is a whole band of them camping in the woods."

"What do you mean they followed their tracks?"

Leis shrugged. "Art trains some of them to hunt."

Lily nodded. That made sense. The peasants in her new world were poorly armed, and a successful hunt would require much patience and tracking skill.

"I see. A band of mercenaries."

"About twenty men, maybe twenty-five."

"What do you think we should do?"

"We can take them out in three minutes."

"Is that necessary?"

As Leis thought for a moment, Lily took a deep breath. He reminded her of a sergeant or perhaps a lieutenant, but he was certainly no general.

"Leis, I believe we would do better to take them alive and question them so we can find out what..." (she almost said "what the hell") "...they are doing here."

"Yes, we could do that."

"Talk to Erik. He will be glad of the exercise."

Leis was visibly glad to have clear instructions: Do not kill the mercenaries. Take them alive and interrogate them. Find Erik.

৪০ ᴄଷ

Royce Fletch gazed at the campfire and pondered life. His scouts had returned earlier that day, but the news they brought gave him pause. As it turned out, Earton was not a crumbling estate with a handful of men guarding it. The countess was a stern taskmaster, and she had at least fifty Virmans working for her, in addition to a militia consisting of local men. It would be suicide to attack the castle. He considered turning back and attempting to dupe his client into paying him as if he had done the job. There was nothing for him to do here. He thought he could probably get through to the countess, but he'd never get away afterward. Virmans were like wolves. Royce knew that his men were no match for them. They would catch them and torture them to find out who was behind the plot. It didn't look good.

"Nice evening, isn't it?"

Royce wheeled around. A giant in battle armor stepped out of the shadows that encircled their camp. The chain mail on his broad chest glinted in the firelight. The other mercenaries leaped up, but 'the Virman raised a hand.

"Be still! If I wanted you dead, you would have been shot an hour ago."

His words were confirmed when an arrow whined from the trees and landed in the campfire. Sparks shot up to the sky.

Royce kept still. He looked up at the man. "Who are you and what do you want from us?"

"I'm Erik Torvson, and that's the wrong question. Why are you here in our land?"

"This is Earton, not Virma."

The man laughed, which made him look truly evil.

"The Countess of Earton hired us to ensure her safety. Will you talk, or should we shoot you all now?"

"You'll fall first," one of the mercenaries hissed.

Erik shrugged. "I haven't fallen yet. I think my luck will hold. I'm not so sure about your luck, though. Anyone who isn't killed outright will be finished off later, and it will go worse for them. Now tell me, what are you doing here?"

Royce wavered. After a moment, he nodded for Erik to sit next to him by the fire.

"Let's talk."

Erik sat down. "I hope you remember we have archers."

"I won't do anything stupid."

"Wonderful. I won't kill you, either. Yet..."

"And later?"

"You may be useful to me later after I learn the truth."

"The truth?"

"You didn't stop here to do some fishing. I want to know why you're here, and I won't put up with lies."

Royce was already trying to decide what to tell the giant when Erik raised his hand. "Stop. Think before you say anything."

"About what?"

"I am just a simple Virman. I know nothing of your intrigues." The smile on the giant's lips betrayed his words. "You won't be explaining anything to me. You will speak to Hans."

"Hans?"

The Virman nodded toward the trees. Royce looked over and saw a shadowy figure.

"He's the one. You will go over there and quietly tell him everything. The rest of your men will do the same, one by one."

"But that…"

"Will take a long time? We are in no hurry."

Royce cursed silently.

The Virman continued. "If your stories are not the same, we will kill everyone who is lying. Theirs will be a slow death."

"We should say what you want to hear?"

"No. Just tell the truth. Hans is a master of asking questions. I am a master of killing, and I will make sure that none of you fix your stories ahead of time."

Royce cursed again, this time out loud. The Virman left him no room for retreat.

"What will you do with those who tell the truth?"

"They will tell their story again in court, and then we will let them go. We will pay them for their time. That's not so bad, is it?"

It wasn't bad if the Virman kept his word. Royce sat still, deep in thought.

ᔕ ᘒ

Erik seemed to read the mercenary's mind. Hans had prepared him for the conversation on their long ride from the castle, providing solutions to various scenarios and telling him exactly what to say in different situations. Erik knew that Hans would have preferred to approach the mercenaries by himself, but Lily had forbidden it. She had said she didn't want to think about what would happen if the king's envoy was injured on her estate.

"The countess has nothing against you. You have done nothing wrong. You have hurt no one. She will not forget about you." When he said those last words, Erik lightly placed a hand on the bag of money that hung on his belt. It was a clear hint, and Royce caught it. He sighed and stood up. After telling his men to stay where they were, he walked over to talk to Hans.

Hans waited for the mercenary under the trees. When the man was close, he waved for him to sit down. "Shall we talk?"

"We shall. Not that I have much choice."

"You could choose to hang. You are in Ativerna, and I am an envoy of His Majesty Edward the Eighth. I have the power to condemn you or pardon you. I answer only to the king."

Royce sighed again. "What will you do with my men?"

"Erik told you. If all of you tell the truth, we will let you go."

"What if I was hired to kill the countess?"

"Can you identify the person who hired you?"

"Yes."

"Then you will hand him over to the law and give evidence against him in court. Then, you will be free. The countess is kind and merciful. She will also be grateful. You have her word and my word."

Royce nodded. He took a deep breath and began to talk. The game was up, that much was clear, but he had to save his men no matter what. As he told what he knew, he wondered who the client was. *Her brother? Someone in her husband's family?* Whoever he was, Royce hoped he burned in hell. Sitting in the dark forest under Hans's' icy stare, the mercenary keenly felt the frailty of human life.

Lily did not go to bed that night. She sat up reading the letter Erik had brought from Baron Avermal. In the most elegant phrases, the Lord Avermal expressed his dismay that Helke was forced to leave the hospitable town of Altver when his life and the lives of his family were threatened.

Of course, he did. He wanted to stay alive!

He also expressed his hope that he and the countess could go on cooperating and reminded her that she could count on his assistance any time she cared to ask for it.

Ha! He doesn't want to leave the food trough, she thought, remembering his partnership with Helke.

Lily scratched the tip of her nose. She would ask Taris to work with Baron Avermal over the winter to sell some of the things she and Helke were making. That still left the question of what to do about sales once the roads dried in the spring.

Someone knocked on the door.

"My Lady?"

"Come in, Taris. I see you can't sleep, either."

"I can't, My Lady." He paused. "Your father spoke very seriously to me about something."

"About what?"

"He says he can obtain a separation that would allow you to live apart from your husband. If you wish, that is..."

"What if I don't wish?"

"He told me that you might not want to write everything down, so he wanted me to find out exactly what your thoughts are."

Lily sighed. Of course, her father was careful. He would not have risked writing out an offer to rip Jess' head off, but Lily could read that very thought in Taris' eyes. It was a tempting offer, but Lily felt she could handle her husband if he turned into a problem. She wouldn't ask her father to take any risks for her.

"Taris, if you had put that question to me over the summer, I would have said that I wish for a separation. I don't know how much of that would have been my own will and how much would have been my misery speaking. Now, however, I have Mirrie to think of. I must do my best to stay friends with her father. I am actually more concerned about something else."

"What is it, My Lady?"

"My men. They depend on me, and I depend on the earl. Do you see?"

Taris understood. "My Lady, that is exactly the sort of thing you should discuss with your father."

"What can he do? I need guards here."

"As your father's agent, I have the right to hire guards for you. Nothing will change, but they will no longer be subordinate to your husband."

"I will still be subordinate to him…"

℘␣℃

"Jerrison Earton is nobody's fool. He won't want to argue with your father," Taris said, seeming to feel his way forward. He watched the countess' face closely. He was sure she had never been in love with Jess. No, Lilian Earton loved her husband in words only. On the outside, she had been a loyal wife. But now that she was relaxed around him, he saw a different face under the mask. Was this the true Lilian, or was she just choosing to show him a little bit more of herself? He could not be sure.

"That is a good solution. Please write to my father to inform him, and ask him to prepare a place for my men…just in case."

"I will do that, My Lady."

"Bring it to me to read before you send it."

"Of course, My Lady."

It was too early for trust, but Taris was not upset. *Trust will come in time.*

℠ ℛ

Hans listened to Royce's tale with focused attention.

"My men are good, but they don't stand a chance against you."

Hans smiled. "You are correct."

"Here we are…"

"Do not jump to conclusions. I will inform the countess of what you have told me, and she will decide what to do. I strongly advise you not to do anything rash. I am going back to the castle, but the archers stay here."

Royce nodded glumly. He had a hard time believing that the countess would deal with them kindly. *A woman!* Even so, he hadn't hesitated to inform on his client. *What else could I say? That we were out for a walk in the middle of nowhere? That we were looking for honest labor without any sort of recommendation?* No, lying would have made matters worse. As it was, he knew he could stand up to a normal interrogation. Especially since he was prepared to give up everything he knew about the man who hired him.

Sorry kid, but I have to save my own skin.

ಹ □ ಚ

When Lilian heard Hans' report, her first reaction was anger, but when she cooled down, she started to think. After a moment, she asked one of the servants to go wake Taris, even though it was after midnight. She was awake, and it wouldn't hurt her father's agent to stay up a bit longer.

Taris appeared before her sooner than she expected, and Lily asked Hans to repeat his story.

Taris shook his head. "What audacity, My Lady!

"Whom do you speak of?"

"The man who hired them, of course."

Hans gave a bloodthirsty grin. "I want to work on them in person once we get them back to the capital."

"Please do. And make sure the king knows that they were ordered to kill Miranda, as well as myself. Dirty bastard!" Lily hadn't meant to swear in front of them, but the men didn't seem to hear her. She hoped that a noblewoman was allowed to swear when someone sent a band of killers after her and her stepdaughter.

I'd like to see how someone else would react in my position!

"Have you written to His Majesty about the first attempt on my life?"

"I have, but only briefly. It went by pigeon. And I'm not sure the soldier's story would hold up."

"What do you mean?"

"It's his word against the word of an aristocrat."

"Well, now you have a whole band of men attesting they were hired to kill me."

"Yes, it certainly looks more serious."

"How could it possibly be more serious? If Miranda or I were lying dead on the floor?"

The countess was furious, but Hans remained calm. "My Lady, I give you my word of honor that this affair will be thoroughly investigated. The person who hired them will be punished. In the meantime, you are in danger. I would strongly advise you to move to the capital as soon as possible."

Lily stared at him. "Right now? What about Mirrie?"

"She could go with you."

"No." Her refusal was swift and decisive. "There is nothing for me to do in the capital. I wouldn't care to go in the spring if His Majesty hadn't called for me."

"He invited you, My Lady."

"What is the difference? I have business to attend to there in the spring, as well. Right now, I need to be here. I will not go, and I will not send Mirrie away."

"She could go with me..."

"Who would she stay with once she arrived? No, Leir Tremain, it's out of the question. My husband sent his daughter here in hopes that I would take care of her. I am trying to do just that if I don't get killed in the process."

"They can't hurt you now. Erik is watching them. If they make a wrong move, they'll be stuck full of arrows," Hans sneered.

Lily smiled gratefully. "Wonderful. But what do we do with them?"

Taris ran a finger across his throat. She pondered his meaning. That was certainly an option, but Lily didn't want to resort to murder. They hadn't actually done anything to her.

"Have they harmed anyone?"

"No."

"Then there is no reason to execute them. They haven't even made an attempt on my life."

Taris spoke up, "Only because they realized they wouldn't be able to escape."

Lily turned to the envoy.

He frowned. "Have them disarmed and bound and send them to me. Once I get to the capital, I will let most of them go."

"What do you mean?"

"I have to take the slave traders. I might as well take these brigands, too."

"What if they don't want to go?"

Taris bared his teeth. Looking at his face, Lily decided the mercenaries would be glad to go with Hans rather than face death at the hands of her father's agent.

An hour later, they had a plan. The mercenaries would go with Hans to Altver and on to the capital. They would be guaranteed their freedom as long as they gave evidence against the man who hired them. Lily's side needed their proof. Hans would leave in two days' time. He would stay in touch with Lily by writing to Baron Avermal. Erik would take his own

Virmans to guard them as far as Altver, and then he would turn back to Earton. Hans promised to keep the countess informed about the investigation.

I have to know where the next blow may come from if I want to stay alive!

ଔ▢୧

The next two days were consumed by packing and preparations. There was cargo for the king, gifts (to Lily's father, the king, the princesses…), and cargo going to Baron Avermal, as well as a small chest of items addressed to Helke's relatives.

When informed of Hans' plan, three of them were killed during the disarmament process, but the others laid down their weapons without argument. They were then loaded into one of the slave traders' sea-going tubs. The surviving slave traders were loaded onto the other ship. Erik uttered a string of terrible Virman oaths, but in the end, he and his men had to take charge of both ships. Leif's men were needed in Earton, and Leis knew nothing of seafaring.

On the third day, Lily saw them all off and waved as the ships pulled away. When no one was looking, she sighed deeply.

Now, I can get a little rest.

Just the thought of it made her happy.

ଔ▢୧

Hans looked out the narrow window of his stateroom as the dark coastline of Earton disappeared. He didn't remember the last time he had felt so dejected. He was sad to leave; his time in Earton had been calm, comfortable and even interesting. No one had looked down on him, and he had been treated as an equal in all things and respected for the work he did.

His eyes turned to a small box on his desk. Lilian Earton had given it to him just as he was getting into the rowboat that carried him to the ship.

"Leir Tremain, you are a wise man. I know you will not mistake this for a bribe. Promise me that you will open it once you are underway."

"We are not allowed to accept gifts."

"It is not a gift; it is a necessity. Do not argue with me, Leir Tremain. I believe that you are utterly impartial and that what I am giving you will have no impact on your report to His Majesty. It is a small thing, of no great value."

Hans had sighed and accepted the box.

Now that the ship was underway, he decided to open it. The lock (he had never seen one like it before, and assumed it must be the work of that clever Helke) clicked open under his finger. He caught his breath. The box alone was valuable enough to be a gift. Inside its lid was one of the new mirrors the craftsmen were making in Earton. For the first time in his life, Hans saw his own face clearly. It was too much. He looked down; the bottom of the box was lined with red velvet and held two simple inkwells, both made of glass. One was greenish in hue, and the other was reddish. There were also several of the countess' new pens. They were very simple, with gold nibs and wooden barrels.

Tucked next to the pens, he found a short note.

With respect and gratitude,

Lilian Earton

Hans sighed. His report to the king would be detailed and wide-ranging. He picked up one of the pens, held it in his hand, and put it down on the desk. Then he carefully poured some ink into one of his new inkwells and took out a sheet of parchment. It was time to get started.

∞ ∞

A royal hunt for wild game—deer, bear, and boar—is a breathtaking sight. Horns blast, huntsmen, and beaters stride through the forest, hounds break away from their packs, flags fly, ladies sit tall on their elegant mares. There is nothing quite like it.

Jess was enjoying the spectacle of the hunt, as always. Richard's emotions were more complicated. Princess Anna was never more than a few steps away from him, and he was beginning to feel like a besieged castle. The man should be the arrow, and the woman should be the target. Here, however, it seemed that the target was flying around trying to run into the arrow. There was something wrong about it.

As if on command, Anna rode over to him. "My dear Prince Richard, what trophy do you hope to bring back today?" She smiled broadly answering her own question, "Me, of course."

Richard wouldn't risk bantering with her. He didn't dare give her an opening. "I'm sure I don't care, madame."

"Your Majesty does not care whom he hunts? Then I must caution you. Some people here have such large horns that you might confuse them with the deer!"

Richard laughed at her joke without meaning to. He glanced

over at Gardwig's jester, the Earl of Lort. The small man was interesting. Richard understood that it took a very intelligent man to play the fool all the time, but he could not tell exactly what the jester was hiding behind his dull eyes. When the man performed for them after dinner each night, he managed to mock the courtiers equally, although Richard felt that he was often spared the worst of it. Only the king, the queen, Princess Anna, and Jess Earton were never teased. The Ativernese nobles in Richard's entourage were already fed up with the jester's poisonous tongue, but Richard noticed that the lords and ladies of Gardwig's court were careful never to betray even a shadow of annoyance. He concluded that the jester was a dangerous man.

Richard saw Altres Lort watching him from astride his shaggy pony. He called out to the jester, "I hope that, as a guest, I'll be allowed to bag a fine deer?"

"We have one guest and plenty of deer," Altres retorted, showing all thirty-two teeth. "They'll never escape you."

Not far away, King Gardwig, dressed in a costume of pale pink velvet, sat on a giant stallion. He raised his right hand to signal the start of the hunt. Horns blasted, and the hounds and huntsmen moved into the woods, followed by the beaters and, finally, the mounted hunters. Everything went according to the ancient rules of the hunt.

Gardwig rode first, looking like a boulder mounted on a horse, his pink cape flapping behind him. The queen chose not to hunt, so next in line was Richard, with Anna holding her horse as close to his as possible. Jess and Altres were also among the first hunters. The rest of the nobles stayed back from the king's chosen companions. Gardwig was not known for his kindness or patience.

He turned to Richard and smiled coldly. "I do not wish to chase after game. That is of interest to you young people."

Jess approached the king, "Your Majesty, I see that beauty and power are aligned today."

Anna blushed. Gardwig waved a hand. "You are a flatterer and a young rogue. Off with you now."

Jerrison bowed graciously and glanced at Richard. "Then I will ride ahead?"

The prince waved at him as if to say "Do as you wish. You aren't any help to me here." He knew that Jess was a passionate hunter, whether his prey was a woman or a pack of wolves, so it would be useless to try to keep him at Richard's side.

With Jess gone, Richard continued to let his horse walk. Most of the other nobles peeled off in other directions. Gardwig galloped ahead for a while, but then turned back and told the prince he could ride ahead of him. This permission was expressed in such a way that there could be no refusal.

ଚ୦ ☐ ଓଃ

Meanwhile, Altres had been leading the hunt, finding various pretexts to send the riders from Richard's entourage in other directions. Jess raced off on his own when he thought he heard something. Two other Ativernese went off after a deer. Three ladies-in-waiting, who had joined the hunt, accepted the jester's suggestion that they turn back to camp. One after another, the prince's retinue melted away like a block of ice on a hot day.

Anna rode alongside Richard and recounted, in a sing-song voice, how much she enjoyed hunting, even though she was such a terrible rider, and how much she loved all the courtiers. "And did you see what the Countess of N was wearing? How shocking…"

ಬಾ☐ಆ

Richard listened to her with half an ear while mulling over his own thoughts. He would have to stay in Wellster for the rest of the autumn, but once the roads froze, he could try to take a sled on to Ivernea. If he had to stay until spring, he would need to be extremely careful. Deep in thought, he was blind to the other riders in sight gradually peeling off. Now, they were all alone, except for three ladies-in-waiting and a few men of no consequence.

Suddenly, Anna's horse whinnied and rose up on its back legs. The princess screamed and tried to hold on. Once all four hooves were on the ground, the horse took off into the trees. Richard cursed inwardly. If they had been completely alone, he wouldn't have raised a finger. There were three women staring at him, however, and he had no desire for them to tell Gardwig that his daughter was in danger and the Prince of Ativerna did nothing. Those thoughts flashed through his head instantly, and he spurred his horse to take off after the princess.

Altres smiled. He had given Anna a signal just a few seconds before. The rest of it would be up to his men.

Anna had played her part well. She had been given a mare that was known to bolt in reaction to pain. When Anna poked her in the side with a pin, the horse took off like an arrow. Yes, it was a dangerous trick, but the princess was actually an excellent horsewoman, and she knew there wouldn't be another chance.

Richard raced through the forest after Anna's horse, leaning out of the way of branches that would have hit him in the face.

I hope I find them before the horse throws her. Maldonaya, take it! Where is everyone? Am I the only person who cares if the princess survives? Where is she?

He soon had an answer to one of those questions. Up ahead, he saw Anna lying on the grass. The horse had apparently thrown her rider and run off.

Is she alive?

Richard dismounted, tied his horse to a tree, and knelt down by the girl. He felt her neck. Her pulse was rapid, like a bird's. She was very much alive. He looked around and saw a creek. Taking a handkerchief from his pocket, he went to wet it.

I hope she hasn't broken anything.

Over an hour passed before Anna "came around". She had

been told to fall by the creek, so she did. She had also been told to take as long as she could to regain consciousness, so she did that, too. Anna would have risked even more foolishness, so great was her fear of the jester. When she opened her eyes, Richard was standing over her with his back to his horse. Suddenly, she saw a long, gray shadow slide between the trees. Her scream stuck in her throat, but all it took was an instant for Richard to turn and grab his dagger.

ᔕ ᙅ

Where's Jess when I need him?

His horse snorted and tried to rear, but its reins were tied tightly. Still, his mount was clearly deathly afraid of the bobcat.

For its part, the bobcat had lived by the creek for several years, and would never have attacked a full-grown man under normal conditions. However, she had been frightened by the hunters and surprised by the two humans and a horse right outside her den.

She leaped to take Richard from behind, but he quickly turned, his dagger outstretched. Man and beast rolled in the grass. The bobcat's claws ripped at his leather tunic. Richard struck several blows with his dagger. In a few minutes, it was all over. The animal's body lay still in the tall grass. Richard got to his knees. His tunic had saved him from much of the bobcat's fury—his chest and abdomen were unharmed—but he had several nasty looking gashes on his arms and legs. He looked around and cursed for what seemed like a long minute.

His horse was gone.

ဆ ❑ ઈ

Earl Altres Lort ran a hand down the horse's side and dropped a pair of gold coins in the palm of the man who held its reins.

"Did anyone see you?"

"No. The prince was distracted. I just cut the reins and let him go. He ran, but I caught up with him soon enough, Your Lordship."

"Good. Bring him to the stable at sundown and tell them you caught the horse running in the woods."

"Yes, Your Lordship."

Altres gave an evil grin. Now, all that was left for him to do was organize a search party. He would make sure that not even a mouse headed in Richard's direction until morning.

ဆ ❑ ઈ

Richard kicked the dead bobcat. *Damned animal!* She had scared his horse away. *How am I supposed to find my way out of the woods with no horse and a stupid girl I can barely stand?* His only hope was that someone would find them, but so far no one had.

He turned to Anna. "Your Highness, are you able to walk?"

The only reply he got was a fresh flood of tears.

Richard nodded. *I see.*

"Your Highness, we must get down to the creek. I can't leave you alone, but I need to wash my wound."

Anna nodded. On the fifth try, with Richard's help, she managed to totter down to the creek. Richard gritted his teeth. His whole body ached, his arm was bleeding, and he needed to bandage his wounds very soon. If he didn't, Anna might end up waiting for help all alone. *That's a sad thought.*

In the end, he had to clean and bandage his wounds on his own. Anna almost fainted as soon as she saw blood. Somehow, he managed to wash the gashes and bandage them with strips of his shirt. While he was at it, he began to wonder why no one was looking for them. He considered trying to walk back, but realized he had lost too much blood.

I can walk, but I can't carry the princess, and I can't leave her here.

There was only one thing to do. He cursed again when he remembered that his tinderbox was in his saddlebag. He stood up heavily and went over to where the bobcat lay. His plan was to drag the body down to the river, butcher it, and try to make a fire. That way, he could cook the meat and send up smoke signals. At the very least, he had to try.

ଔ ଓ

Jess raced through the trees after the deer he had sighted. Altres knew that hunting made Jess feel fully alive, with the sound of the horns in the distance and the hounds calling on both sides. Feeling as free as a bird, Jess had forgotten all about Richard, just as Altres had planned.

Altres had known of Jess' weakness for hunting before the Ativernese delegation arrived in Wellster. Once the Earl of Earton bagged his deer, he would be pointed in the direction of a boar, and he would not be able to refuse. After the boar was dead, some other game would be sent his way. He wouldn't have time to remember his cousin.

The prince was very much in the jester's mind, however. He wanted Richard and Anna to be on their own at least until nightfall, better yet until morning. Gardwig had promised to keep the hunt going until late evening.

It won't kill them to spend the night in the woods, and that way my plan is more likely to work.

෨ ೞ

Richard gazed sullenly at the branches and twigs he had gathered into a pile. They were stubbornly refusing to ignite. It had rained the night before, and all his attempts to start a fire had come to nothing. The recent rain was good for the hunt, but it was bad for anyone facing a night in the woods. He was too weak to skin and butcher the bobcat, so he cut out its liver because it could be eaten raw if necessary. He hoped it wouldn't come to that, but without aid, their prospects were none too good.

He turned his dull gaze to the princess. He realized that it was unfair to be angry with her—she was in the same danger as he was—but that didn't make him feel any more disposed toward her. The situation was going from bad to worse. He wasn't afraid of the cold, as long as someone found them within the next few hours. However, he was worried about what spending the night in the cold forest would do to his health and his reputation.

If I stay out here all night with an unmarried noblewoman, I'm looking at having to marry her or declare war. He disliked both options equally.

Anna sniffled and looked away. Richard felt little in the way of pity for her. *She'll get what she wants, but what will I get? A marriage of diplomacy, void of love?* It sounded sad, and felt even worse the more he thought about it. Anna didn't have any of the qualities he had seen in Jessamine. She didn't even come close.

But…

Moving slowly and painfully, Richard used his sharp knife to cut some fir branches. He piled them up next to Anna and sat down on the pile.

"Come here, Your Highness."

Anna shuddered and stared at him in horror.

Richard grimaced. "All I meant to say is that we will be warmer together."

For a few minutes, the princess sat shivering in silence. Then she moved over and sat down on the fir branches next to Richard. He put an arm around her shoulder and pulled her close.

"Don't be afraid. I won't hurt you. I promise."

The only reply he got was another sniffle.

ଓ ⬜ ଓ

Jess only recalled that he didn't know where his cousin was when he heard the horn calling in all the hunters. He had shot two deer and a small boar and couldn't wait to find out what Richard had scored. Then he looked around. Richard and his entourage were nowhere to be seen. The forest was eerily silent. He looked back at Gardwig, who gestured for him to follow.

When Jess caught up with the king, he saw Richard's horse tied nearby.

"Your Majesty!" His tongue became heavy, and the words came out slowly.

Gardwig shook his head. "He returned without his rider. We are searching."

"May I join the search, Your Majesty?"

"Of course you may, but you do not know our forests. Duke Graves! Put this young man in one of the search parties."

Jess bowed in gratitude. He hoped Richard was still alive. He loved his cousin, despite their dissimilar personalities. And there was another thing; the prince was the only heir to the throne.

If anything happens to him, Uncle Edward will never forgive me.

As he rode off behind the duke, Jess prayed fervently to Aldonai that Richard be found alive and well, and as soon as possible.

༺ ༻

Once he was gone, Gardwig glanced at the jester. Altres looked down. They had chosen Graves for his stupidity and obedience. He would look in all the places they had told him to look and in none of the places they hadn't. There was no chance at all of him finding the lost riders.

Gardwig hadn't mentioned that the princess was also missing, and Jess hadn't thought to ask. The king frowned as he turned back to the castle. He had done his part. The rest was up to Altres.

His jester was adept at planning and intrigue, but sometimes life takes unexpected turns.

Chapter 2
On the Usefulness of Animals

No one would have found them until morning, but Richard was saved—entirely unintentionally—by one of the jester's spies. The prince hadn't noticed he was being observed, and he heard nothing when the spy left.

An hour later, the man stood in front of Altres. "Your lordship, they were attacked by a bobcat."

"A bobcat!"

"The hunt must have stirred her up. Our two were just in her way."

"Are they alive?"

"Yes, but the prince has some nasty gashes."

The jester was about to curse out loud, but caught himself just in time. "Will he survive if he stays out overnight?"

"All he's got is a knife. Those wounds look pretty bad. He could end up with a fever."

Altres nodded. He called for a group of hunters and issued orders on where to search for Richard and Anna. His plan for them to spend the night together wouldn't work. It was a pity. He reflected that shildas and cats were truly servants of Maldonaya. He needed this marriage, but he wouldn't risk letting the prince of a neighboring kingdom die.

It's no great loss. I have other plans I can use.

By the time they were found later that evening, Richard felt extremely ill. He had lost a great deal of blood, and the bobcat's claws had been anything but clean. He looked worse off than Anna, who managed to fall into a dead faint as soon as she heard voices.

The hunters offered Richard a horse. Somehow, he managed to climb into the saddle and take off at a slow walk. He would have liked to go faster, but he could barely stay in the saddle as it was. He never even looked around to see how Anna was.

She'll be fine. They won't leave her here.

Gardwig looked down at Richard with fatherly concern. The prince was not complaining, but His Majesty called for a carriage and a medicus just the same. Just then, Jess came galloping up.

"I'm a fool to have left you!"

Richard agreed wholeheartedly but refrained from saying so in front of everyone.

"It's all right. I am alive, and Princess Anna is alive."

Gardwig shot an angry glance at Altres, who looked down at his shoes. They couldn't very well accuse the prince of insulting Anna's honor given the state he was in. If they tried, all the other bobcats in the forest would fall out of their trees laughing. They would have to wait for another opportunity.

The jester tried to look on the bright side. Now, Anna would have a reason to stay by the wounded hero's bedside day and night, demonstrating her true love. And he would make sure that everyone heard about her devotion.

"I am your debtor, young man. If it weren't for you…" Gardwig paused dramatically, "Never mind. We will praise you loudly once you feel better. Now let's get back to camp!"

When they brought him into the tent that had been set up for the medicus, Richard lay down on the rug. His whole body ached. The medicus immediately began checking his wounds. Jess helped his cousin undress. He cut off the bandages put on in the field, gave Richard a pain-relieving draught and held his head while the medicus cleaned the gashes. Through it all, Richard avoided Jess' eyes.

If it wasn't for you and your love of hunting...

Richard saw very clearly that the bobcat had actually been his savior. If it weren't for the animal, he would have faced an entirely different conversation with Gardwig after spending so much time alone in the forest with Princess Anna. He felt his mind begin to swim under the effects of the medicinal draught. Fighting to keep his thoughts clear, he tried to work out what had happened and what it meant for him.

The two of us were lost in the woods. Anna didn't look too good when they found us, but I probably looked worse. I'm covered with blood, and there wasn't a spot on her. They'll probably say that the bobcat attacked us both and I fought it off to save her. That's no cause for a hurried wedding.

Still, he was worried.

I need to get out of here as soon as I can.

He knew that women fell in love with the men who saved their lives, and Anna would be no exception.

I still haven't seen Lidia.

That was his last coherent thought. Richard fell into a deep sleep in which he lost all consciousness.

ঙ □ ଔ

Baron Donter was in low spirits. His spies had reported to him on the results of the visit by the king's envoy, and jealousy twisted his gut.

A deposit of amber! Glass! And now she has two large ships!

The baron's mind slowly formed a new thought.

Why should the Eartons have so much more money than me?

Then his thoughts took a more precise turn: he needed to grab his share. *But how?*

He would have to ponder that question. He had never paid much attention to Earton before. True, he had often kidnapped peasants to sell to the slave traders, but that was no big deal. No one cared about commoners, anyway. Even if the king's envoy heard about his slave dealings, the baron doubted—hoped, really—that it would all come to nothing. No one would believe a commoner's word against the word of a nobleman.

Now that there was real money to be had, however, he would need a carefully crafted plan. The Earton family was close to the king, and Edward was a man who didn't find lawlessness amusing. If he was caught, Clive Donter knew that his death would be slow and painful. Any attack on the castle would have to go like lightning—he would only get the chance to strike one blow.

Lily did her best to get some rest once Hans and Erik left, but she was soon back at work. She hoped no one else would try to kill her. There were too many things to attend to as it was. She was still working with the apprentices to improve the quality of their glass, but so far nothing was going right. Earton glass was far superior to anything else in Ativerna, but Lily remembered the clear, bubble-free glass of her own world and wasn't satisfied.

We can do better than this!

The apprentices were having a hard time finding the optimal temperature for pouring molten glass, but they kept hoping and kept working.

Lily's dressmakers, on the other hand, were leaping from success to even greater success. Under her watchful eye, they were beginning to work on a "Big Idea". (It was so big that Lily capitalized it whenever she thought about it). And, if she had to drag herself to the capital in the spring, she wanted to shock people by how well dressed she was, not by how much she weighed. The pounds continued to melt away; Lily could tell she was losing weight when she looked in the mirror. Her body would never be slender, but she didn't mind looking like a woman from a Rembrandt…or a Rubens.

The dressmakers were fashioning a dress for her completely out of green lace lined with fine, white silk that she had instructed Baron Avermal to send her. The dress would have ruffled sleeves, a long train, and a flattering low neckline. Best of all, they would be able to take in the silk lining if she lost more weight without affecting the design of the lace layer.

For the bodice, Lily asked Helke to make her buttons of Earton amber. She remembered from chemistry class that you can change the color of amber by cooking it in hot sand or coating it with copper.

I hope we can manage to get green amber for my buttons!

Lily did not consider herself an expert in chemistry. She had studied the subject day and night her first two years in medical school, but after that, had moved on to more interesting subjects and forgotten a lot of what she knew. Still, she remembered that succinic acid was derived from amber and that it could be used to manufacture polymers. *A plan for the future, for sure, but a plan nonetheless.* With a decent laboratory in place, anything was possible.

The countess' laboratory was outfitted with wide tables and a fine set of bottles and test tubes that she had made all by herself. It was also home to her beloved still, which she was using to make moonshine. She had no desire to drink the stuff, but she wanted to have it on hand to serve to undesirable guests and to use as a disinfectant. The infirmary was also in tiptop shape. When Lily showed it to Tahir, he gasped. Her Khangan guest held the countess in the highest regard since the battle with the slave traders, and he followed her around day and night in hopes of learning something new.

Lily was most always happy to share her knowledge with Tahir, Jaimie, and Miranda, as well as Ingrid when she was around. With winter fast approaching, however, Ingrid and Leif spent most of their time overseeing work at the smokehouse. Lily missed talking with them, but she was no longer afraid of going hungry that winter. Earton would survive until spring.

Thinking about winter gave rise to a new question. *I wonder if they have skis here? Or ice skates? Sleds? Snowmen?*

Then her thoughts turned to more serious matters. *What about warm boots, coats, and fur hats? All these layers of skirts are warm enough now, but once there's snow on the ground, I'll need something warmer.*

She had plenty of ideas but forced herself to set them aside. There simply wasn't enough time to do everything.

I've got boots and a shawl. That will have to do. I'll have my chance to shine in new clothes when I go to the palace in the spring.

ಬ ಇ

There was a knock on the door, and Lily smiled when Lons Avels came in.

"Come in, Leir Avels. Is it time for a lesson?"

"Yes, My Lady."

"What do I need to learn today?"

"Dancing, My Lady. Everyone is waiting for you in the small ballroom."

Lily followed him down to the ballroom. When he opened the door, she laughed out loud. Lons' "everyone" turned out to be two dozen children. They all looked up at her with shy smiles. A tall Virman boy took a step forward with a hand out to the countess, and they all spent the next half-hour whirling around the room and laughing as Lons taught them the fine art of dancing, talking, and observing people, all at the same time. Lily was charmed and educated equally, and it was incredibly amusing to watch the children imitate adults.

ಬಿ □ ಛ

Anna was already in bed when her door opened silently. The jester slid in like a ghost. She froze in terror. Altres put up a hand. "Don't get up. Just listen. You did everything right. It isn't your fault that it didn't work."

The princess breathed out.

"But Richard is wounded," he continued.

"Yes."

"You must take care of him."

"Me?"

"He put himself between you and danger. You must go sit with him, at least for a few hours. Do you understand what I'm saying?"

Anna nodded. "Yes, I will do that."

"Good. Because if you don't…"

Her face went pale. "I will! I promise I will!"

"Start tomorrow. Don't go making faces at his wounds, either, or I will find out."

Anna nodded.

"Go to him tomorrow after morning prayers. Ask after his health and beg to be allowed to sit with him."

She nodded again. Altres looked at her sorrowfully, then, turned and left.

ಬಿ □ ಛ

The princess sat motionless for several minutes. Then she

wrapped her blanket around her shivering frame. *But fear is not like the cold, and a blanket cannot make it go away.*

೮೦ ❧ ೞ

Jess sat by his cousin's bed. Richard was pale and shaking, even though there were several blankets on him. However, his eyes were cold and clear.

He looked up at Jess. "That cat saved my life."

"Look at the gashes on you."

"If it weren't for the cat, I would have had to marry Anna."

"Why not go ahead with it? She's good-looking and smart enough, and it looks like Gardwig would like to see the match."

"I have a choice, and I want to use it."

"Fair enough."

"Anna's not bad, but my father told me to choose. I don't want to lose my right to choose because of a stupid mishap. You have to stay right next to me from this moment on. Will you do that for me?"

"I promise."

Richard nodded. He would do everything he could to avoid being alone with the princess. He could lock his door at night, but during the day, he wanted someone with him. Some ploys were as old as time, and Richard realized what he was up against.

"Lie to people, say whatever you have to, but don't leave me."

"How long do we have to do this? I can't be with you day and night until the spring, and it's diplomatically risky to leave before that."

"We're leaving as soon as I can manage it. Who else can sit with me? What about your mistress? Or is she too stupid to understand why I need her here?"

"Adele? She's a whiner, but she certainly isn't stupid."

"Then tell her she'll be doing shifts in my room. Who else can we ask?"

"What about Leihart?"

"He's too old."

"He could sit here and talk to you for a few hours."

"True. He likes to gossip. Tell Rainell, too."

"I don't like that Rainell. He's too religious. I bet Aldonai is tired of hearing from him."

"That doesn't matter. I'll put up with him, and you will, too, if it comes to that."

Jess grimaced but did not object. "Whatever you want. I'll talk to him tomorrow. We'll keep you busy all day."

"Exactly. I don't want to be left alone with her ever again. I might not get as lucky next time."

Jess grinned. "Good on you for planning ahead. Because I doubt there are many bobcats running around the palace." He looked around the room. "Do you want some hot, spiced wine?"

"Sure. I'm shaking with chills."

"I've got to keep you alive," Jess said. His face grew serious as he held out the goblet of wine.

"Do your best," Richard replied. He took several sips of the wine. "Anna isn't bad, but I want to see Lidia before I make up my mind."

Richard succumbed to a bad case of fever the very next day. When Jess woke in the morning (he had taken to sleeping in his cousin's room), he went to wake his friend and immediately noticed that something was wrong. The gashes on his arms and legs were bright red, and heat rose from his body. Jess pulled on his pants and ran off to find the medicus.

Gardwig was still asleep, but Jess found a manservant, who immediately sent for all the healers he knew of. Less than an hour later, six important men, ranging in age from forty to sixty, stood around the prince's bed. They studied his wounds, his urine, the blood on his bandages, and the linings of his nose and ears. Then they embarked on a lively discussion during which each tried to show his colleagues to be uneducated fools.

Richard was too ill to interrupt. After two hours of squabbling, the medical men reached a diagnosis and shared it with Jess. "Bad air" had entered the wounds and spoiled the prince's blood. There was only one possible treatment; they must remove the bad blood so that only healthy blood was left to circulate, and they would give his royal highness an emetic. The only remaining disagreement among them concerned the ingredients for the emetic.

A knife and bowl were prepared for the blood-letting. Richard had been drifting, but he awoke when the room grew quiet.

"Jess?"

"I'm here."

"What is wrong with me?"

"They decided to drain your bad blood."

"Send them to Maldonaya."

Jess froze. "What are you saying?"

Richard took a deep breath and explained. "Get them out of here. Don't let a single one of them touch me."

"But you're very ill!"

"Jessamine was ill, too, and she died after the medicus drained her blood. Get rid of them!"

"Are you sure?"

The prince's gray eyes were stern and cold. Richard was most definitely in his right mind.

"If I die, it will be without their help. Do this for me."

Jess sighed. "I hope you know what you're doing."

"If it makes any difference, I'll leave you everything I have."

Jess cursed quietly and went to find the doctors. They were milling about in the hall.

"Your services are no longer required, gentlemen."

The men looked up in shock. The oldest and most experienced of them tried to resist. "But you don't understand the seriousness of the situation! The prince's body is being poisoned by bad humors and bad blood. His body will begin to rot from the inside out if we don't drain them, and his death will be on your conscience."

Jess put a hand to his steel dagger. His eyes were just as steely in the morning light. "Will you go of your own accord, or must I show you out?"

The healers beat a hasty retreat.

ೞ ⬚ ೮

Half an hour later, Jerrison was called to see Gardwig. He left his cousin under the watchful eyes of Adele—who promised not to leave him no matter what—and another member of the entourage.

ೞ ⬚ ೮

Gardwig looked tired and sick. His swollen legs were elevated on an ottoman. "Good morning, sir," he greeted Jess wearily.

Jess took a deep breath. "Your Majesty, I hope this morning brings you the same joy that you bring to the people of Wellster." He paused. One glance showed that he had taken the right track. Gardwig gave a wan smile.

"How is your cousin?"

"Richard is very ill, Your Majesty. The healers said that he is suffering from bad blood."

"Then it must be drained."

"Richard has declined the procedure, Your Majesty."

"Why is that?" Jess caught a dangerous note in Gardwig's voice. "Does he not trust the art of our healers?"

Jess bowed low before replying. He knew he must tread carefully. After a brief pause, he assured the king that Wellster's healers were worth their weight in gold, and that Richard had the greatest faith in them, but that he had seen his stepmother, Queen Jessamine, die of bloodletting and did not wish to undergo the procedure. If he grew worse, Jess promised, he would insist that his cousin allow the bloodletting. In the meantime, he would be happy to take the emetic to his cousin and, of course, he would spend day and night at his side.

Gardwig nodded regally. "My daughter had much to say about His Highness' courage last night. He risked his life to save her. I expect that she will wish to be of assistance to you."

Jess assured him that the delegation from Ativerna would always be pleased to see his daughter. After another round of compliments, the king let him go.

೮ ೮

When he returned to his post, Anna was already at her hero's bedside. Richard was pretending to be asleep. None of the Ativernese had any intention of leaving her alone with him. This visibly displeased her, but she sensibly said nothing. Jess was politeness itself, but after two hours, he sent her away. At a slight gesture from Richard, he sent the others away, as well.

Once they were alone, he showed the prince the emetic that had been prescribed for him and agreed to toss it down the hole in the privy. Then he gave Richard a bowl of steaming broth and lay down next to his bed on a mattress the servants had brought for him.

The Earl of Earton was feeling resolute. An executioner with an axe couldn't have driven him away from the prince's bed. He loved Richard like a brother. They had grown up together, pairing up in games against Amalia and Edmond, whom Jess had never been able to stand. Jyce was often away from home, and kind Jessamine had always taken in Jess and Amalia for nice, long visits.

Remembering his wonderful childhood, Jess could have kicked himself for his stupidity.

Why did I have to get so carried away during the hunt? I kill enough game when I'm at home. There was no need to set records here.

He thought back to his state of mind the previous day and realized that he had wanted to relax and forget himself because he was getting sick of Wellster and everything in it. He was tired of Gardwig's overbearing hospitality, his jester's cruel jokes, the looks of longing that the younger princesses shot at him, and the false friendship offered by the courtiers.

I feel like a fly right before the spider eats it. That's why I wanted to hunt—so I could forget about everything and enjoy myself for a while. What a stupid mistake!

He rolled over to look at his cousin's sleeping form.

Richard, if you get over this, I swear I'll sell my pack of hounds. Please get better…

ഇ☐ര

"My Lady, there's trouble outside. One of the Virmans got into a fight with one of the grooms." Ilona's eyes were as round as saucers.

"Bloody hell!" Lily exclaimed when she heard the news. "What started it?"

"I don't know."

"What were they saying?"

"They called each other little shits." She covered her mouth. "Pardon me, My Lady!"

"Please continue, Ilona."

"The groom said that he'd like to see all the Virmans drown at sea. The Virman told him that he was village scum."

Lily's first instinct was to curse again, but she held her temper in check this time.

I expected this kind of conflict when I brought the Virmans here. Now, I've got it.

"Is Leis or Erik down there?"

"Both of them, My Lady."

"Then I will go listen."

By the time the countess got to the courtyard, the show was almost over. The two men had been separated, and someone had poured a bucket of cold water over each of them. She could hear Erik roaring before she even opened the heavy door to the outside. Leis was doing his best to keep up. Together, they were roasting their subordinates (since Leis was captain of the castle guards, the grooms were more or less under his command).

"…have to live here…sharing…idiot…" she heard Erik rumble. His tirade was frequently punctuated by expressions he would not have used if he had known the countess could hear him.

"…beat you like a dog…you dolt…sharing…" Leis yelled.

Lily grimaced. She did not want to distract the men, so she beckoned for Helke's sister to come over. Loria quickly gave her the rundown on what had happened. The groom had had too much to drink and had begun complaining that he was no worse than a Virman and that he'd like to see the Virmans all drowned or hung from the nearest tree, like the pirates they were. A Virman named Elg happened to be walking by just then, so he knocked the groom off his seat. The disagreement quickly devolved into a fistfight.

The countess shook her head. This was bad. She knew all about racism and xenophobia from her previous life, and she knew what they could lead to.

Leis caught sight of the countess, and he came over and bowed.

Erik followed. "My Lady," he said and gave a deep bow. When he looked up, Lily caught something strange in his blue eyes. *Was it desire? Who cares? I don't have time to think about that right now.*

Lily raised her eyebrows. "What are we going to do?"

"Whip them both," Erik rumbled. Leis nodded in agreement.

Lily shook her head. "That's easy enough to do, but what started the fight in the first place?"

The men glanced at each other. It was obvious to her that they had not given that question any thought. She sighed, and then she explained that ethnic conflict was a dangerous thing. They would have to prevent it from getting out of hand.

All three were silent for a moment.

Lily spoke first. "Erik, how do Virmans turn a group of men into a strong team?"

"It happens on its own, My Lady, during battle."

That won't do. She shook her head.

"Or when they work hard together," the giant continued.

The three of them smiled. The whipping was canceled, and the guilty parties were assigned to clean out the stables together all week, with the condition that if there were any more fights, the original punishment would be reinstated. Lily quietly asked the Virman children to keep an eye on them and report to her if there were problems.

On the first day, the men were too proud to speak to each other. On the second day, they realized that their work would go faster if they at least communicated. By the end of the week, they were drinking together and slapping each other on the back in the evenings.

Lily sighed with relief. *I managed to keep this conflict from flaring up, but what about next time?*

⍆ ⍅

"I am pleased to see you, Leir Tremain."

"You have my respect, Baron Avermal."

The men bowed, and Hans got down to business. "Lord Avermal, I just arrived here from Earton."

"How is the countess? Isn't she a charming woman?"

"She asked me to bring you some things. I have instructed the sailors to unload the trunk here."

Torius did not particularly care for Virmans, but he could put up with them in the name of trade. He also saw no reason to express his feelings openly in front of the king's envoy. He glanced over at the trunk.

"Is that all?"

"That is what she sent. But there is another thing. I need to use your jail. And I will need a larger ship. I have with me a murderer, several dozen slave traders and a band of mercenaries."

Torius stared at him. "What? Why…"

"I am taking them with me from Earton. The murderer attempted to kill the countess. The slave traders attacked the estate shortly thereafter, and the band of mercenaries was apprehended right before I planned to leave. It seems they were also sent to put an end to the countess' life."

"How horrible! Who would dare do such a thing?"

"There are all sorts of people in the world," Hans said evasively, "for now, at least."

The men commiserated for a few moments on the large numbers of brigands and other undesirables plaguing the kingdom, after which Torius gave his permission to use the jail and promised to outfit a ship as quickly as he could to facilitate Hans' trip back to the capital.

Hans went back to his rooms to rest. Torius, on the other hand, sat down right away to read his letter. As always, Lilian Earton was polite but infuriatingly concise. Her letter informed the mayor that what she had sent him was an entirely new thing she had developed. If the honorable baron found it to be commercially successful, she could send many more of the same. This was followed by a list of materials she would need to continue her work. Torius decided to look at the list in detail later. He turned his attention to the trunk. It wasn't very big. He wondered what on earth of any value the countess could have sent.

When he opened the trunk, what he saw took his breath away. It was a cloud of something pink, the color of the dawn. (Lily had decided to use up her predecessor's large stash of pink silk thread.) Under the countess' direction, the dressmakers had turned the silk thread into a true miracle: lace combs and lace shawls. The box also contained a sketch showing how to wear the various items.

Torius sat back on his heels and called for his wife. He soon regretted it, because she took the best of the combs and—without the need for instructions—put it in her hair. Then she took the largest shawl, wrapped it around her shoulders, and refused to give back either item. Torius begged and wheedled, but his lady was obstinate. It did not take him long to realize that the lost profits would cost him less than war with his wife.

After lifting out the rest of the shawls, he saw several different types of men's lace collars. He tried one on and looked at himself in the polished piece of silver that he used as a mirror. Pleased by what he saw, he realized that the handiwork the countess had sent would sell quite nicely. Local craftsmen knew how to make a narrow braid for trimming coats and dresses, but Torius Avermal suspected he was the first man in the world to see such large expanses of lace, and it was all covered with beads.

People will rip these out of my hands! I must write to the countess immediately and send her as much thread as I can find.

Then he noticed a tightly wrapped package lying under the lace collars. When he opened it, another chunk of his profits disappeared, because his wife grabbed one of the mirrors and announced she would keep it for her very own. There was a note attached to the wrapper, which said that the mirrors were easily broken, but that they would last for many years if handled with care.

Torius shook his head. *A mirror made of glass!* He had never seen himself so clearly before. He could see his own face in great detail, much better than when he gazed into a pool of water or a sheet of polished metal.

I may just keep one of these for myself. I'll make enough in profits to justify the cost.

He looked back at the trunk. *What else is inside?*

ဆ☐ß

As it turned out, the trunk also contained several dozen inkwells made of colored glass and a supply of pens, as well as three simple jewelry boxes. Torius opened one of the jewelry boxes and gasped for what seemed to be the hundredth time that day; it contained several amber brooches. The honey-colored amber shone and sparkled in the sunlight. He noticed that one of the brooches was made of extremely rare red amber. The setting was very simple, tastefully highlighting the priceless stone.

Torius ran a finger over its smooth surface. He took it out of the box and turned it over. The clasp was like nothing he had ever seen before. He looked up at his wife's shining eyes. "No, my dear. This one is too expensive."

"But Torius!"

"You may wear it once to church if you like."

"Torius!"

"My dear, I cannot afford to buy you everything you take a liking to."

Mortally offended, she wrapped her new shawl tighter around her shoulders and ran out of the room. Torius ran a finger over the polished pieces of amber. They were truly beautiful. Lilian Earton was a wonder. Torius never once regretted going into business with her.

An intelligent woman is capable of anything.

Your Majesty,

I must inform you that an accident befell His Highness while hunting. Richard is alive, and the medicus says that he is out of danger. We must remain in Wellster over the winter while he regains his strength.

I am proud to say that he behaved like a true hero. Princess Anna's horse bolted during the hunt, and he pursued her on his own steed. His entourage was not able to keep up with him. Not long afterward, the hunters disturbed a bobcat, and it attacked the princess. Richard was harmed while protecting her. His wounds are healing.

Gardwig has the greatest esteem for His Highness' noble act and has provided all the assistance that is required. The princess spends day and night by Richard's bedside.

Jess dipped his pen in ink, shook off a droplet, and quickly kept writing.

Your Majesty, what happened is largely my fault. I should not have left Richard alone during the hunt. I will accept any punishment you give me. There is no excuse for what I did, and I do not ask for leniency. If my cousin had died, I would have fallen on my sword.

Your devoted servant,

Jerrison, Earl of Earton

He sprinkled the letter with sand. Once it dried, he sealed and sent it. Jess was certain the Duke of Falion, the formal head of the delegation, would write a letter of his own to the king. Jess knew that he deserved punishment, but he still couldn't stand the duke.

Falion is an arrogant old rascal. Why did Uncle Edward put him in charge of the delegation?

It was probably an issue of politics. The Falions were an ancient noble family, and their lands were on the border with Wellster, meaning the duke would be the first to suffer if a conflict broke out. Jess admitted to himself that the duke might be a rascal, but he was nobody's fool. He grimaced.

The duke would have stopped me from bringing Adele along if he could. Thankfully, Uncle Edward gave his personal consent. He remembers what it's like to be young.

Jess knew Richard shared his opinion of the duke. Falion was prone to giving them long talks about honor and proper behavior, and he had ruined many a pleasant evening of drinking. However, he had his uses, and someone had to attend all the official events on behalf of Ativerna. *Why not let the old man do it?*

℠ ℣

Falion did his best to live up to the nickname the other courtiers had given him, which was "shark face". When Jess brought him the sealed letter, the man took it and studied the writing on the outside. Then he looked up with a sneer.

"Is this your confession?"

His barb hit the mark. "Just send it," Jess bristled. "I don't intend to listen to morality lessons from you."

"When I was your age, I knew how to behave responsibly. None of this—"

Jess interrupted him. "I need to see Richard." He

turned to open the door, but old Falion—moving like a true shark—slipped around him and barred the door.

"I'm afraid you'll have to listen, whether you like it or not. Your father was more of a gentleman than you will ever be…"

Two hours later, Jess finally broke through the door, red-faced and sweaty. Falion had raked him over the coals mercilessly.

What a monster! It's hard to believe his sons are decent men with a father like that.

Jess had met the older son several times and knew him to be a fun-loving rogue after the earl's own heart. He had an eye for women, as well.

Strange.

ഏ ⬚ ൠ

Falion smiled as Jess left. He derived no pleasure from lecturing young people, even when they richly deserved it, but he had known Jerrison Earton since he was a boy, and he had heard more about him in recent years from his son. The Earl of Earton was smart enough, but he was too impulsive and at risk of becoming a good-for-nothing unless someone stepped in. Jyce had given him his own way too often, and the result was obvious.

I certainly never made that mistake with my own boys.

Jess needed to be reeled in, especially on an important delegation to Wellster, where he was representing his king. Falion sighed and sat down to continue his letter to His Majesty. The duke had no fear that Jess would be punished too severely. Edward was a fair king, and his response would be just.

Your Majesty…

Anna of Wellster stared at Adele with poorly concealed hate in her eyes.

When will that cow ever leave?

None of the Ativernese would leave her alone with Richard, not even for a second. The prince was always watched over by Jerrison Earton or another of the courtiers. More often than not, it was Adele who sat by his bed. Unfortunately for Anna, she and Adele were more or less the same type of woman; both had thick, dark hair; olive skin; bright eyes; and generous breasts. Anna wasn't worried about losing the prince to this oddly devoted Ativernese woman, but she was concerned that Richard, in his fever, would confuse the two of them.

The role of a nurse did not come naturally to her, either, and the Ativernese kept her from doing anything of significance for the prince. She had hoped for a chance to brush against him with her breasts as she leaned over with a cup of water or a clean rag for his brow, but all they let her do was sit on the other side of the room. Adele had explained that it wasn't fitting for a princess to do the work of a nurse and that Richard was in no shape to be seen by anyone, much less her royal highness. With a tight little smile, Adele reminded the young girl that she was already a widow and therefore allowed to bathe the prince and take out his chamber pot.

Anna was furious, but she restrained her temper until she got back to her room each night. In front of people, she was charming, gentle and ever so slightly sad. Inside, however, she was boiling over with anger.

I would kill that Adele if I thought it would do any good! But I can't kill the entire delegation, and they are plotting to keep me away from the prince.

In all honesty, though—and Anna was always honest with herself—she knew that she meant nothing to Richard. No matter what she did or how gracefully she did it, he was not interested.

She shuddered. I'll have to go talk to the jester.

She needed to go back to the old witch for more of the potion; the jester would understand. And there was something else she needed, too…

ⰆⰓ ⱁⱃ

"Step forward, turn, turn again…" Lons repeated the steps aloud, but he didn't need to. He could tell the countess had already memorized them, and the children were happy to copy her. At first, Lons had thought it was nonsense for the Virman children to take dancing lessons. However, when Ingrid returned to the castle for the rainy season, she explained why her people wanted their children to learn the local ways.

"People think we are barbarians, but they hire our men to serve as bodyguards and soldiers in some of the best houses in the country," she had explained with a smile. "Virma is a poor island, but that doesn't mean we are stupid or that we don't want to learn. We just haven't had the opportunity. I would like to learn to dance. Perhaps when Leif returns…" her voice trailed off.

Lons had been shocked. He had never thought about it that way. Virmans had no teachers. Craftsmen took apprentices, soldiers taught boys to fight, and mothers taught girls to keep house, but there were no formal lessons and no teachers.

When he had put this thought into words, Ingrid nodded her head vigorously. "I wish there were teachers on Virma. That would be a very fine thing."

Lons thought these things over as he danced with Lily. A plan was beginning to take shape.

If I manage to free Anna from her father's house, I can always find work on Virma.

"Ouch!" the countess exclaimed.

The dancing teacher had stepped on her foot. "Be careful with me, Leir Avels!"

Lons begged her forgiveness, but the countess just waved her handkerchief and ordered the dancing to continue. There was no music, just Lons' voice calling out the steps.

"Step forward, turn, turn again…"

Years of experience had taught Lons that most people learned to dance faster if they started without music. Once the feet knew the steps, it was time to hire a musician.

"You're turning into a wonderful dancer, My Lady."

Lily snorted. "I don't enjoy it, but I guess I have to learn."

"Of course you do. You'll be dancing at court."

"Maybe I will, maybe I won't," Lily shrugged. "I make no promises. But if I have to dance, I want to do it well." A few steps later, she added, "I'll need a partner, Leir Avels. Would you consider going with me to the capital?"

"Of course, My Lady." He smiled inwardly.

You never know how the cards will land. I'll dance with her all the way to the palace if she asks me to!

Altres sat back in his chair and glanced over the letter he had just finished writing. He felt satisfied that he had done his best. It was a letter to King Edward, and the jester had walked a fine line between lying and telling the whole truth. He had also managed to slip in a whisper of doubt about Richard's motives. Gardwig would have written it himself, but the ulcers on his legs were giving him trouble so he had taken a sleeping draught and gone to bed.

My dear neighbor and respected friend,

I hasten to inform you that we held a royal hunt a few days back. During the hunt, your son and my daughter rode away from the others. A wild animal attacked them, but, thanks to your Prince Richard's bravery, my daughter is alive and unharmed. Unfortunately, your son was wounded. Our palace healers have ordered him to stay in bed to recover his strength. They expect him to make a full recovery. Anna is always at his side. In her eyes, he is a true hero. I hope you believe me on this. What happened was a tragic accident. I will certainly understand if you wish to recall your delegation, but I hope you will not do so. Neighbors should extend friendship and understanding to each other. For my part, I will follow your instructions regarding the safety of His Royal Highness. I hope that you are well.

Gardwig, by the mercy of Aldonai King of Wellster

The jester smiled. All that remained was to let Gardwig read over the letter before he sent it. He hoped the accident would not affect the outcome of the delegation. If it did, Altres would never forgive himself.

He had always hated cats of all sorts.

❧ ❦ ❧

As a port city, Altver had seen many things. This, however, was something entirely new. The good people of Altver arrived at church for the dawn service as they always did. Everyone was there—Pastor Leider, Torius Avermal, and his wife… People gasped when they saw the baroness—she looked magnificent. Her hair was swept up into a knot on the back of her head, held in place by a lace comb, and there was something fantastic that started at her shoulders and draped elegantly down her back.

What was it? A pink cloud of lace?

Whispers began to circulate. Everyone—men and women alike—kept their eyes on the baroness as she glided down the aisle on her husband's arm. The whispers grew louder when she reached up to adjust her lace shawl and revealed a gorgeous brooch made of blood-red amber. All the women wondered where she got it, and the men wondered how much it cost.

That morning, the service went on as usual but Aldonai received less than his usual share of the attention. Baroness Avermal took up the rest. The questions started as soon as the service was over. Torius was tight-lipped and restricted himself to telling people they could order similar items through him. When asked, he named a sky-high price for the fabulous brooch. His wife smiled and adjusted her shawl. Once everyone was looking, she took out a small mirror and studied her reflection in it. Before he knew what was happening, the baron had enough orders to keep Lily's craftsmen busy for a year. Every man there had a wife, daughter, mother, or mistress who could turn his life into a living hell unless she got her hands on the latest fashions.

Pastor Leider was the only exception, but when the baron offered him the gift of a handsome lace collar, he was highly gratified and stated loud enough for everyone to hear that the new fashions were not the work of Maldonaya. Afterward, he and the mayor moved off to a corner where they could talk in private. Baron Avermal promised to pay for a new roof on the church, and Pastor Leider made it clear that he would not stand in the way of the mayor's profits. The pastor strongly suspected that the Countess of Earton was somehow involved in these strange new fashions, but he had no proof. He decided to keep his mouth shut and gain what he could.

80 ☐ ß

Anna's second visit to the witch went better than the first. She was not as afraid, for one thing. The old woman gave her three small bottles—one potion to charm a man, one potion to reverse the first, and a bottle of a strong sleep remedy.

The princess hoped they worked. She was desperate enough to try anything, but she did not plan to administer any of the portions to Richard. She could still hear his voice in the woods "I won't hurt you. I promise."

Richard had no idea that Anna had played a role in their

misadventure, but she knew he might find out. One thing comforted her; he was kind. She would never have to fear her husband, as long as she stayed within the bounds he set for her.

What were those bounds? Gratitude? Perhaps. Anna didn't really know, but she felt something warm when she thought about Richard. At the moment, that warm feeling was buried under fear for her life, cold calculation, and everyday distractions. But it was still there.

೮ ೮ຈ

Edward put down the letter and cursed aloud. Life was dangerous. It was all too easy for a man to end up without any heirs. Edmund's face flitted through his mind. His older son had put off getting married, always for seemingly minor reasons—he didn't feel well, or the bride wasn't to his liking. Edward knew that he should have put his foot down, but he hadn't, and the young man had died unmarried.

There had been a three-year mourning period after the death of the crown prince, and it had taken longer than the king expected to collect information about potential brides. It was now most definitely time for Richard to marry.

Edward sat with his thoughts for a few moments. Then he took out a sheet of parchment and a pen. He knew what to say; he would balance his anger and his desire for a close relationship with a neighbor. Gardwig would understand that Edward was displeased. *If anything else goes wrong…*

Altres read the report from his agents in Ativerna. Not much had changed. Edward was on the throne and the princesses were growing up, soon to be looking for suitable husbands. The jester hoped they would look toward Wellster. The church did not approve of brides being older than their grooms, but he didn't foresee any trouble. Pastors liked to live in comfort, after all.

Trade was flourishing in Ativerna, the royal fleet was expanding, and there had been some small conflicts with Virman pirates. Altres wondered what that was about; he kept reading. His spies reported the king was very interested in the Countess of Earton. He looked up and scratched his head.

What does that mean? Is Jerrison Earton falling out of favor? Do I know anything about his wife?

He couldn't recall ever hearing of her, except as Jess' wife and the daughter of August Broklend, His Majesty's favorite shipbuilder. Still, any new information concerning Jess Earton was of interest. He would file it away.

The jester wrote *Find out more.* on top of the letter and set it aside. He had many other affairs to attend to.

Time seemed to race away from Lily, so she set herself a schedule and stuck to it. She didn't mind being busy. In her own world, she had worked hard as a medical student all day and then put in several hours as a janitor in the evenings to make extra money. Some days, she only got three hours of sleep. In her new world, she was getting a little bit more sleep, and she didn't have to haul a mop around. *A definite improvement! What else could a woman ask for?* Lily laughed at the thought.

One day in the life of her ladyship looked like this:

Up at five o'clock for the church service downstairs in the chapel. The new church and the pastor's new home were finished, but Pastor Vopler was in no hurry to leave the castle. Lily didn't push him since she generally felt it was safer to have him where she could keep an eye on him. He could be the next Torquemada, for all she knew. So, Pastor Vopler continued to live at the castle, where he tried to engage the Virmans in little chats on religious topics. They ignored him most of the time, but he never took offense and continued his dark—or light, depending on your point of view—deeds. Lily was often amazed by his stubborn dedication and doubted he would ever be able to boast of a Virman convert, but there was no harm in trying.

On occasion, the countess gave him clothes or other small gifts, which kept him happy. Mark, his son, was also enjoying his time at the castle. He and Mirrie were fast friends with all the young Virmans, and the boy excelled at his lessons and his study of manners.

After the morning service, Lily had time for herself. She often spent the hours before breakfast in her laboratory. This precious time was generally divided between trying to complete an experiment and rushing to write down her store of knowledge before she forgot it. Her work with amber was going well. She had sent one of her best pieces to Avermal and continued to heat some of the new pieces in copper. Helke was continually amazed by what the countess showed him; no one in that world had ever tried such things.

Her craftsmen were starting to make decent glass. They had a long way to go, but Lily was already planning to have them make fancy wine glasses.

In other happy news, Earton was chock full of clay, and Lily was picking her memory for what she had once known about ceramics. She knew she could make a potter's wheel and thought she would have the children work on making bowls.

At eight in the morning, the countess went down for breakfast, where she allowed herself no more than half an hour to eat. After that, she attended lessons with the children. All the tutors were pleased with their pupils' progress. Behavior problems were less frequent, especially after the day her ladyship explained to the children that a bullwhip can be an important learning tool. The children took the threat to heart and did their very best.

Only Damis Reis got on Lily's nerves. She attended his lessons because she felt that history and literature were important, but the man annoyed her to no end by staring at her with lovelorn eyes, paying her overblown compliments, or diving to kiss her hand at every turn. She almost wished he would overplay his hand so that she could fire him. As a result, Lily developed an intense dislike for history and literature, which she had never loved, even in her own world.

ೞ ೞ

At noon, the children were free to roam the castle and Lily went to the stable, which was now admirably clean and dry. The Avarian stallion was getting used to his new owner. Lily didn't risk riding him around the estate yet, but she rode in circles around a fenced-in area. She also made a point of feeding him by hand, talking to him softly and cleaning his coat. As the weeks went by, he grew to look forward to her visits. Miranda often went with her stepmother, dreaming of the day when she would have a horse of her own.

Lily intended to keep her promise. As soon as Erik got back, she would ask him to find a good mare for the Avarian to cover. That way, Miranda would have a half-Avarian foal to raise.

∞∞∞

After the noon break, the countess ate lunch. When that was over, she worked with Lons. Some of that time was spent on the estate's business—going over reports, issuing orders—and the rest was spent polishing her manners.

∞∞∞

In the late afternoon, Lily visited her craftsmen—the glassblowers; Helke; the pottery workshop; and the dressmakers, who were now lace-makers, as well. The pottery workshop wasn't much to look at yet, staffed as it was with a pair of the former slaves Erik had given her, but it existed and turned out primitive pottery. The wheel was popular with the children, who ran in at odd hours to work on various projects for use at the castle. The potters had their finished work fired by the blacksmith. Lily also dreamed of firing bricks to repair the wall around the castle, but she was too busy to know where to start.

In the evenings, she had dinner and a bath, then went straight
to bed. Sometimes, she went to the sauna instead of taking a bath.
Getting the sauna built had cost her a great deal of effort and trouble,
and Pastor Vopler still had his doubts. "Why should a decent woman
like the countess sit naked in a sauna with a bunch of Virman women?"
he had asked. Lily explained the health benefits to him, and eventually,
even Martha became a convert once she found that the heat helped
with joint pain. Hoping to gain the pastor as an ally, Lily asked him to
try the sauna just once. He hated it. The heat made him dizzy and
nauseous, both symptoms of overheating. Afterward, Pastor Vopler
decided that anything so unpleasant couldn't possibly be immoral, so
he left Lily alone about it…and never went back.

During her evening sessions in the sauna, Lily saw that her
body was responding well to her new lifestyle. She was still a large
woman, but the rolls of fat were gone. That gave her an infusion of
optimism about the future. She might never be as slender as she had
been in her previous life, but she would be healthy and attractive. The
countess often fell asleep with a smile on her face at that thought.

Many nights, she was joined by Miranda, and sometimes by
the puppies. People in Ativerna did not keep dogs in the house, but one
of the Virmans who knew a lot about training animals told Lily that
keeping the puppies close would improve their personalities. He also
suggested that she give Mirrie a bitch puppy, and the little girl happily
agreed.

Lily knew that, for the first time in her life, Mirrie had a place of her own—a home, a room, a dog, and friends, and hoped she saw Lily as someone like a mother to her. Lily could tell that the little girl still wasn't sure exactly how to feel about her stepmother, but she never pressed her. Instead, she just loved her, spoiled her, and gave her clear boundaries. For the time being, Mirrie respected those boundaries, but Lily had no doubt that—sooner or later—she would test them. Children always test adults.

Sometimes, Martha joined them at night. Martha would stroke her two girls' heads and sing them lullabies. Lily was grateful for Martha's attention, but didn't completely trust her. So, she frequently complained to Martha about how difficult her life was in Earton and asked her for stories about old times when she lived at home with her father.

I'll see him in the capital in the spring, so I'd better be ready.

ᏠᏠ ᏟᏟ

It happened at breakfast.

Everyone at the castle knew Lily ate plain oatmeal every morning. On this particular day, she was late to breakfast. She had been working on an experiment in her laboratory and lost track of time. She was trying to obtain mirabilite, but the mineral was refusing to cooperate.

By the time she reached the dining room, everyone was already at the table. Mirrie was in her place next to Lily's. When the countess walked in, the little girl jumped up to tell her something. "Lily, did you know I can…" She waved an arm, and Lily's plate of oatmeal slid off the table onto the floor. All the puppies ran over to investigate, but the bitch puppy was the fastest.

Lily called for Emma. She was about to ask for a new plate when Mirrie suddenly screamed. Lily turned to see what was wrong. The puppy was vomiting green foam all over the floor. Lily dropped to her knees. She had never treated a dog before, but she had worked on plenty of patients who had been poisoned—children mistaking medications for candy, adults overdosing, etc.

First, induce vomiting, then give water, and then give an antidote.

"Jaimie! Tahir!"

The herbalist was already by her side. He called for the servants to bring milk and water. Ingrid grabbed Miranda and hurried her from the room.

Working together, Jaimie, Tahir, and the countess managed to save the puppy. Jaimie later told Lily that he thought most poisons showed up faster in dogs, but the overall effect was weaker than it would be in a human. If Lily had eaten her breakfast, they never would have saved her. As it was, the puppy spent the next ten days on a strict diet with bed rest and lots of attention from Miranda, who cried whenever she remembered seeing her beloved pet almost die.

Even as Lily sat with her arms around the little girl, her brain was cold and logical. That was my plate—my oatmeal. No one else eats it plain. Mirrie and her puppy saved my life, But who could have poisoned me, and why? Emma swears there have been no strangers in the castle, so it was someone in the household. Who?

Lily was understandably upset, but her logic returned to her about two hours later when Jaimie came to discuss the poisoning.

Thinking quickly, they deduced that her breakfast had contained something like aconitum—wolfsbane. It was easy to prepare and extremely toxic. The countess chewed on her thumbnail.

Who had access to my food?

Helke's sister had cooked breakfast, but Lily saw no reason for any of the Eveers to want her dead. They were living on her estate and were making good money off of her.

Who else had an opportunity?

She made a mental list of everyone who was near her food while it was carried in from the kitchen and put on the table.

Tahir or Jaimie?

They had knowledge of herbs, but both of them were much better off with Lily alive. She also discounted Taris, as her father's trusted agent. Helke and Mirrie were also crossed off the list. Lily wondered about Martha, but she was confident the older woman enjoyed her position as the countess' trusted nanny. Chevalier Avels was a dark horse, but Lily saw no reason he could have to harm her. Ingrid, Pastor Vopler, and his son, Mark, were also above suspicion.

Who brought in the dishes and set the table? Peter, Sara, and Ilona.

Any one of the three could have put poison in Lily's food while carrying it in from the kitchen, but that would have been risky since the children were already in the dining room and would have noticed anything strange. Lily bit her lip.

"My Lady, I would not worry so if I were you," Taris

volunteered. "Just have all three of them tortured until one of them confesses."

Lily snorted. "There is no logic in that, Taris. The one who confesses will be the one who fears pain the most, not necessarily the guilty one."

Taris frowned. "I hadn't thought of that."

She turned to Jaime. "Where could this person have gotten the poison?"

The healer scratched his head. "Wolfsbane is easy enough to find, but you have to know how to prepare it."

"Can you ask the old woman who deals in herbs? What is her name, Moraga?"

"Yes, My Lady."

Leis jumped up from his seat. "I will bring her in for questioning."

Lily waved for him to sit down. There would be no witch-hunts in Earton. "No, Leis. I will not have you interrogating people behind my back."

She turned to Jaimie. "Ride down there quietly, so that no one sees you. I don't want a lot of talk Otherwise people won't leave her in peace."

"Yes, My Lady."

"Find out everything you can. I want to know if anyone came to her to buy wolfsbane or asked where to find it."

Jaimie's face was serious. "I will do my best, My Lady. I promise." He picked up a sack and left the room.

Lily watched him leave. She would have liked to go herself, but that would have looked strange. She turned to Pastor Vopler.

"Pastor, can you question the three servants? I don't want them hurt, but perhaps you could speak to them as a man of the church…"

"That is merciful of you, My Lady."

Lily knew that it was pure calculation, not mercy, but she said nothing to dissuade him.

He's a decent man. We could use more like him in both worlds.

The countess ran her hands through her golden hair and turned to Leis. "Keep all three in the dungeon for now. There is plenty of room with all the slave traders gone. If they are innocent, I will pay them for their trouble."

Something about the whole affair bothered her. *Is my unknown enemy stupid, or did something emboldened him?* None of the three had attempted to run, and the rest of the household was going about its business. *Does that mean that no one has a guilty conscience? None of this makes sense.*

Lily decided to hold off on further steps until Jaimie returned from his visit to the old woman.

Taris cleared his throat. "Shall I write to your father, My Lady?"

She nodded. "Do that, my friend. I may write to him, as well, but not today. My mind is too full to write."

Just then, they heard a muffled noise in the hall. They looked around at each other. Someone was listening at the door. Moving silently, Taris slipped over to the door and opened it, revealing a very dejected little girl.

She ran to the countess. "Will my puppy Liliona be all

right?"

Lily put an arm around the little girl. "Of course she will. I promise."

Mirrie sniffled and buried her face in Lily's shoulder. If her stepmother made a promise, she was inclined to believe it.

80 ❧ 03

Jaimie looked down at the old healer with respect. "Good day, Moraga."

"Be well, my boy. What brings you here?"

"Something has happened. Someone tried to poison the countess."

"Is that so?"

"It was wolfsbane, Moraga."

The old woman turned away and began rummaging through some sacks in the corner of her kitchen.

"Moraga, you know something! Wolfsbane doesn't keep long, and you're the only one who knows how to prepare a strong infusion. Nobody at the castle has that knowledge."

Still, the old woman rummaged through her sacks of dried herbs.

"Moraga, I beg you!"

She turned suddenly. "You should stay out of this, boy."

"Lilian Earton has been kind to me. She is kind to me now. She has given me a home, she pays me, and she feeds me."

"She wasn't always like that."

"Does that matter? She is good now, Moraga. She is good and intelligent."

"Did she send you?"

"Yes. She wanted me to find out what you knew without raising a fuss."

Moraga said nothing, and Jaimie said no more. Silence hung in the room. He knew that the old woman would tell him what she chose, and that pressure would achieve nothing. Five minutes passed, and then ten, fifteen…

Finally, the old woman sighed. "You are right. I sold the infusion. It's fresh, from this year's crop."

"No one else could have done it. I knew it was you. The countess thought the same thing."

"But she sent you instead of her soldiers."

Jaimie was silent. Moraga slapped her hand on the table. "Fine! I sold the infusion. It loses potency quickly and becomes useless after a few weeks."

"Her ladyship says that is because we use the wrong base. She knows of a substance that can keep herbs fresh for a long time."

Moraga raised an eyebrow. "Is that so?"

"I brought a bottle of it with me. I will leave it for you, I promise. Who bought the wolfsbane?"

The old woman winced. "She visits me often; a guest. She started coming back before the countess fell ill. That's when she started."

"How long ago was that?"

"Almost as soon as her ladyship arrived in Earton. This woman knows nothing of the art of herbs, so she paid me handsomely. For the infusions and for keeping my mouth shut."

"What is her name?"

"I don't know, but I can tell you what she looks like."

Jaimie listened intently to the description and nodded. After a pause, he asked, "Why did you decide to give her up to me?"

Moraga shrugged. "I owe a debt to the countess. She has always sent you to visit me…" her voice trailed off.

It was true. Whenever Jaimie paid a visit to Moraga, the countess gave him gifts for her – small things like a bolt of fabric or a basket of fruit. This time, he had a large bottle of alcohol. He poured a little of it into a glass and excitedly told the old woman about its properties. An hour went by before either of them noticed.

"I have to go now. The countess is waiting for me."

"I understand. Describe the girl to her. She won't be hard to find."

"You're right. I just don't understand why anyone would go to all the trouble."

Moraga turned away. That was none of her business. The wealthy people of this world would have to deal with their own problems.

₭ ₰

When he got back to the castle, Jaimie immediately found Lily.

"She used to buy an herb called devil's flower that causes madness, but recently she started buying wolfsbane."

"Why the devil's flower?"

"I believe she was putting it in your food."

Lily frowned. The story she had invented for her father was

quickly starting to look like reality.

"But why? Who was it?"

"Moraga didn't know her name, but she said she lives at the castle. She always came at night, and she wore a cape to cover her head. She's been at it for a long time."

"What else did she say about her?"

"She's young. She started visiting Moraga almost immediately after you arrived here."

"Then it isn't Martha or Tara. How about the servant girls? Mary or Ilona or Sara?"

"Moraga said she had a scar on one hand. A small one, between two fingers."

"Didn't she try to conceal it?"

"She did, but Moraga has sharp eyes."

The countess nodded and turned to Leis, who jumped up and ran from the room. She turned to Taris. "Is it really that simple?"

He shook his head. "It wasn't simple at all. The old woman might have missed that scar. Any number of things could have kept us from finding out who did it."

Lily reflected that criminals were not always as intelligent as they thought they were. The girl had done what she could. She covered her head with a cape and made her visits at night. *How could she know that Moraga would see the scar and, more importantly, tell what she knew?* If the old herbalist had acted out of self-interest, she would have pretended to know nothing. After all, she couldn't be sure that Lily wouldn't punish her for preparing the poison, even if she hadn't known who it was intended for.

Ten minutes later, the three servant girls were brought before the countess. Lily nodded at Leis. Sara had a scar on her hand. Mary and Ilona were released. Sara could tell that her game was over, but she had no intention of giving up easily. Sitting with Leis on one side and Taris on the other, she kept her eyes on Lily. Breathing heavily, she lifted her upper lip, which made her look like a large rat. Lily observed her coolly.

"Will you tell me why you were poisoning me, or do you need help telling the truth?"

"I only wish I had been successful," Sara hissed. "At least I managed to kill your brat!"

Lily bit her lip and put a look of suffering on her face. She didn't care in the least what had happened to her recipient before she woke up in her body, but she couldn't risk showing that.

Time for the waterworks!

"Taris," she whispered, "my handkerchief." Her father's agent quickly handed her the square of lace. She hoped he didn't notice that her eyes were still dry. When he turned away from the countess, he began to rake the guilty servant over the coals. After a good ten minutes of threats and screaming, Sara gave up at least part of her story. Lily was humbled by what she heard.

I can't believe I made such a huge mistake!

When she got rid of the Grismo family, Lily and the others forgot that there was another pigeon coop in Earton…

Sara was the niece of Fred Darcey—his sister's daughter. That was why they had different last names. Still, Lily couldn't understand why Sara had wanted her dead.

Several of the Virmans were sent to bring in Fred and his family, while Leis and Taris continued to work over Sara. Unfortunately, the young woman didn't know much about the plot. All she knew was that her uncle told her to get a job at the castle, which she hadn't minded. Then he told her to put devil's weed in the countess' food, which she was also happy to do. Her uncle was the head of the family, and he had the power to marry her off if she didn't follow his orders. Sara knew herself well, and she understood that any man she married would start beating her before their first month of marriage was over.

After a while, she had taken a true dislike to the countess. To make matters worse, Jess Earton started paying attention to her whenever he stayed at the castle. He was even foolish enough to say things like, "I wish my wife had a nice bottom like yours," and he gave her a cheap ring. That was enough to make Sara go off the deep end. She truly wanted to see the countess dead. Hearing all this, Lily just sighed.

Why do people always think of criminals as being evil geniuses? For every Moriarty out there, I bet there are two thousand idiots who just knock someone upside the head with a frying pan.

The countess kept her view to herself, however, and listened to every detail of Sara's story. She needed to know who was behind this newly uncovered attempt to get rid of her.

Fred Darcey couldn't possibly have anything against me. Someone hired him to do it, and that's the person I have to find.

The interrogation went on until late in the night. Sara, Fred and the rest of his family were taken to the dungeon by the Virmans. Lily had no desire to know what happened to them there. She had already proven that she could watch someone be tortured, but she wouldn't repeat the feat.

It was shortly before midnight when Leis knocked on her door. Lily threw on a warm robe (it was a new one, made by one of the Virman women) and slipped out into the hall.

"Mirrie is asleep in my bed. Have you found anything out?"

Leis nodded. Both he and Taris Brok, who was with him, looked guilty. As Lily soon learned, Fred's weak heart hadn't held up to the Virmans' questioning. Thankfully, he had described his client before he passed away.

Told by Leis, the story was that not long after Lily moved to Earton after her marriage, Fred had to go to Altver to buy some things at the market. While he was there, he met a stranger who offered him good money to report at regular intervals on the countess' doings. The man gave him pigeons and money, and Fred, who could read and write a little, started sending reports. He told Sara to get a job at the castle in order to provide him with information.

He often went to Altver or sent one of his sons to pick up the money, which always appeared on time. Payment was handled by a merchant named Karl Treloney. Fred left most of the money with Treloney to invest in trade since he quite sensibly reasoned that there was not much he could do with cash in Earton.

At some point, the client sent Fred a bottle containing a mysterious liquid, along with instructions to put it in the countess' food. That worried Fred. He tried the potion out on one of his dogs.

The animal stumbled around looking confused but otherwise showed no ill signs. Fred concluded that the potion was some kind of intoxicant and instructed Sara to use it liberally.

Sara did her best, only leaving off when the earl was at home.

Ha! I was suffering from withdrawal symptoms whenever my husband was around. That's just fantastic.

When Lilian got pregnant, Fred's client grew worried. He instructed them to increase the dose, sending a larger bottle of the potion from Altver. When Sara ran out of that, she started buying from the local herbalist.

If they'd managed to kill me, old Moraga would have been next.

Sara did everything her uncle told her and then some.

Leis' face was haggard. "My Lady, she confessed that she rubbed bacon grease on the staircase. That's why you fell. You were pregnant, and your head was thick with an intoxicant."

Lily forced herself to wipe away imagined tears. She had seen enough Mexican soap operas where things like this happened, so she knew how to behave. Inwardly, however, she was ever so slightly grateful to Sara. If the girl hadn't done her darnedest to kill the old Lily, Aliya never would have found her way into this new world.

I could have wound up dead instead of reincarnated. That's a pretty big difference!

"What about the poison?" she asked.

Taris leaned up against the wall. "They had already

been drugging you, so they just asked the old woman in the forest for something stronger—something deadly."

"Why didn't they kill her once they had the poison?"

"They were planning to."

Lily wiped her nose and looked away. I would have gotten rid of her right away, just to be safe.

"What were they waiting for?"

Taris raised an eyebrow. "What if the poison didn't work, My Lady? Where would they have gone for another potion? Nobody in Fred's family knows the ways of herbs. They aren't smart enough. And there's another thing; you weren't the only intended victim."

"Who else were they after?"

"The earl's daughter."

Lily's hands balled into fists. "Mirrie?" she growled. For an instant, both men thought Lily was ready to leap down the stairs and kill the plotters with her bare hands, but they were wrong. She regained control of herself just in time.

"They were thinking ahead, I see," she said gruffly.

In an instant, she saw how it would have played out. In the days after her death, there would have been enough confusion in the castle for the plotters to get to Mirrie. Then they would have mourned the tragedy of the little girl's death. "She followed after her stepmother," they would have said. Lily forced herself to breathe slowly.

"What shall we do with them, My Lady?"

"Did Fred give you the name of the man who hired him?"

"He said his name was something like Kerens, but we have no way to know if that's true or not."

Lily stared at Taris for a moment. "Have you written to my father yet?"

"Yes, My Lady."

"Send another letter with all these details, please. And one more thing…" There was something predatory in her green eyes. "I believe it would be difficult for anyone to get here before spring, wouldn't it?"

Taris and Leis nodded, confused.

"Send the client a letter using one of Fred's pigeons, and sign it from Fred. Does anyone know what he used to write?"

"Yes, My Lady."

"Good. Write that I am at death's door. Then wait to see what happens. I'll smoke the bastard out of his hiding place if it's the last thing I do. And he'll pay me for it, too! You just watch." The men stared at her. "Meanwhile, my father can ask questions while he's in the capital."

Taris blinked. "In the capital, My Lady?"

She sneered. "Taris, use your head. They weren't planning to kill me because I'm blonde. This is the work of my father's enemies or my husband's enemies. I hope my father can learn something over the winter. We're stuck out here, but we can keep playing the game and see how much of the client's money we can get our hands on. I'll write to Torius Avermal. I want to know everything about Karl Treloney—what line of business he is in and who he drinks with.

Leis stared at her as he tried to catch up. Taris had been looking down at the floor during Lily's tirade, but when she was done, he looked up with shining eyes. At that moment, Lily realized she was really and truly in charge. She was the pack leader. She would decide what they did, and the others would follow her. *Why? Because I'm smart.*

ಬ □ ಜ

A letter, supposedly from Fred Darcey, to the unknown client:

"Sir, the cow is near dead, She has no hope to live, but the girl is alive. What should I do?"

Lily read it and approved wholeheartedly. Taris had not wanted to show it to her, for fear that the word "cow" would offend her, but Lily couldn't have cared less. *They can call me a crocodile if they want, as long as I win in the end! I'll write to Torius while I wait for this mystery man to reply.*

The countess had no intention of allowing anyone to hurt her or Mirrie. *Whoever this mysterious enemy is, he's in a heap of trouble.* Lily was confident she would find him and store him away in her laboratory—in little pieces in glass jars! *There will be no appealing the sentence I hand down! People are always hanging the heads of innocent deer on their walls. Why can't I display my enemy's liver in a jar? At least that way, he'll be of use to science.*

ಬ □ ಜ

Pigeon mail for Torius Avermal:

Baron Avermal,

I need you to find out everything you can about Karl Treloney. It's an important matter. I'll explain in a letter.

L. E.

The main question that bothered Lily (other than finding her mysterious enemy) was what to do with the Darcey family. She could send them to their deaths, but there were small children among them. That gave her pause. Lily considered executing the adults and telling the children they were free to go if anyone would have them, but winter was coming, and some of the children would certainly die of exposure. And again, those children that survived would grow up to hate her for killing their parents.

She considered keeping the Darceys in the dungeon over the winter and then letting them go, but that went against one of her fundamental beliefs: if you tried to kill someone, your punishment should be death. In her own world, she had seen too many murderers freed. That would not happen in Earton.

Lily had no problem with executing Sara, as well as Fred's wife since he was already dead. Both women were in on the plot, as were his older sons. But the village elder had a large family, and his youngest child was just three years old.

In the end, Taris suggested a way out. She could keep the family together over the winter, and when spring came, she could execute the adults. The smaller children could be given to other families to raise, and the older children could be given to Ali on his next visit. It wouldn't be slave trading since Lily would have no material gain, and it would ensure that the older Darcey children would be taken far enough away that they would not be able to cause her trouble in the future. Lily didn't like the plan, but she had no better ideas.

❀ ☐ ❀

Richard had every intention of getting better, despite the dire warnings of the healers. His fever still returned sometimes, but less often. His wounds were still infected, but they looked much better after being cleaned and dressed with bandages made of spider webs and moss. Slowly but surely, the prince was regaining his health. True, he was still so weak that he could barely lace up his own pants. Anna sat by him days at a time, wiping away sweat (his) and tears (hers).

Jess was concerned for his friend. The ambassadors were all in a twitter, afraid to find out what Edward would have to say to them. In their minds, it was impossible to keep watch over a red-blooded young man during a royal hunt. He was old enough to watch out for himself, and Gardwig's huntsmen should have chased after the princess. Their reasoning was sound, but it provided them with little comfort. Heads were sure to roll.

When Edward's letter was finally received, Richard was surprised by his father's reaction. True, he was reprimanded for his carelessness and reminded that he was the only hope of the Ativernese dynasty. The king was angry, but Richard could read between the lines. His father felt that, since he had to spend the winter in Wellster anyway, he should put the time to good use and get to know the princess. A man can learn a lot about a woman when he is sick.

Richard followed his father's advice. It wasn't hard since he had little else to do. He saw that Anna did her best to imitate a servant of Aldonai—gentle, sweet and attentive—but that with every passing day she was less and less able to hide her true feelings. As he watched her, he began to notice the occasional angry expression, impatient gesture or look of fear that broke through the mask she wore around him. At times, Anna reminded him of a cornered rat. As he lay in bed and looked out the window, Richard found himself pitying the princess. He suspected Gardwig had not been a good father to her but had no desire to marry her because of it.

ꙮ ꙮ

Edward read Gardwig's reply with great interest. After again apologizing for Richard's hunting accident, the king of Wellster abandoned all subtlety and openly proposed a union between their two houses. He also promised to give Anna the province of Balley as a dowry. The way he described it, such a marriage would be profitable for both kingdoms. As neighbors, they could protect each other from invasions by outsiders. At the end of his letter, Gardwig reminded his dear neighbor and respected friend that both of them were getting on in years and that this matter should be decided as soon as possible.

Edward gave the letter much thought. He was inclined to believe that Richard's mishap was truly an accident. It was impossible that a wild animal was working in the king's hire. He would have heard about it before (Edward had spies of his own, and they did their jobs well).

However, in the end, he decided to write to Richard and suggest he do no more hunting until he got home.

"You're a stupid fool!"

"At least I'm not a cheap whore!"

"Eveer trash!"

"Hussy!"

"What on earth is going on?" This last was said by Lily, who had slipped into the kitchen in hopes of finding a piece of cheese. She knew it wasn't good for her, strictly speaking, but she had decided to give herself a treat. When she opened the door, she found Loria and one of the servant girls in the middle of a loud argument.

"Everything is fine, My Lady. I'm used to it. Nobody cares for Eveers."

"And why is that?"

Lily soon learned that in addition to all the other reasons the locals disliked Eveers, they hated them because it was impossible to steal from them. Loria managed the kitchen with an iron fist. The servant girls were used to helping themselves from the pantry, so they started talking back and causing trouble when Loria punished them for it. Helke's sister had put up with their behavior as long as she could, but her patience had finally run out.

The countess decided her patience had run out, too. The women were not fired, but Lily transferred them to what she called "new opportunities." In such a big castle, she explained, there were always plenty of places in need of a good cleaning. Once the rebellious servants were gone (mops and buckets in hand), Loria chose some of the quieter maids to help her in the kitchen.

That evening, Emma sat down with the newly minted janitors and made sure that they understood they were still better off than if they had been fired or sent to care for the livestock. Grudgingly, they saw the logic in her argument and agreed to make no more trouble.

As an added benefit, the quality of the meals improved and Lily relaxed…but not for long.

ଽ ଔ

Day followed day. Lily worked, cared for Mirrie, waited for news, taught lacemaking, wrote down everything she knew about glass, and spent long evenings talking with Helke and Tahir. She was as close to happy as she had ever been in that world.

Then one day, a letter arrived that shook up her happy state of mind.

"Finish off the cow and kill the girl. Karl will pay you one thousand gold coins." Lily whistled. *I had no idea that a countess and her stepdaughter cost that much.*

She soon sent back Fred's reply:

Sir, I want half upfront for the cow.

And then something else happened…

ଽ ଔ

If you want to hide something, ask an adult; if you want to find something, ask a child. One morning, Lily decided she didn't know her castle well enough. She knew all the official rooms by heart, but she was sure there were secret passages somewhere. *There just have to be.*

She started by gathering the children in the long, dark evenings and telling them mystery stories featuring a hero named Sir Holmes. It didn't take long for the children—who were completely unspoiled by media or devices of any kind—to get hooked on her stories. Even Jaimie sat listening with eyes wide whenever the countess regaled the roomful of children with another episode in the life of Sir Holmes. After a while, other members of the household started to join them for story time. It turned into quite the event.

Soon, the children were spending all their free time running around the castle in search of hidden rooms and passages. They knocked on walls and jumped out at the servants from around blind corners. The servants complained, of course, and Emma reprimanded the wildest of the young detectives, but Lily just smiled and kept telling stories. One day, her work paid off; Mirrie came to her with a downcast face and announced that, "there weren't any skeletons at all in the secret passage…" The child was beyond disappointed.

Lily suggested that Mirrie show her the passage and perhaps, they could look for skeletons together. She soon learned that the children had discovered three secret passages: one from the kitchen to the second floor, another from the family wing to the outside, and a third in the guest wing of the castle. The third passage had caved in. To Lily's mind, all three made perfect sense. The kitchen had a door to the outside, making it an ideal destination for an escape route. The passage from the family wing to the outside served the same purpose. She assumed the passage in the guest wing was used to keep an eye on what visitors were up to, which also made sense.

The passages were such in name only, so narrow and low that

Lily almost got stuck. She also got filthy. Her suffering was richly rewarded, however, when she tripped over something in the passage to the kitchen. Looking down, she saw exactly what she expected—a small barrel. It was new and still shiny.

Of course! A trunk or chest would attract attention, but a barrel looks like something you'd put dried apples in.

It was such an ordinary looking barrel that the children had ignored it.

I wonder what's in it?

Lily soon had her answer when the servants pulled it out of the passage. The lid was on tight, but when they pulled it off…

∞

Silver coins are a strange thing. Even a small handful of them can make people stare. Jaws drop when you have a whole barrel of silver coins mixed with chunks of amber. Etor was a saver. When Lily fired him, he didn't bother to take the largest share of his savings with him. *Why bother? He could always get back into the castle, either through the passage or straight over the crumbling wall.* The barrel would have been easy enough to roll away, too.

When they counted it all, there were over two thousand silver coins and a sizeable quantity of amber. Lily sighed in relief. Now, she was confident they would survive the winter. The weather had already turned cold.

Taris interrupted her pleasant daydreaming with a question. "My Lady, did you ever receive your bride's share?"

Lily could only shrug. She had no idea, but she did have an excuse—the Darceys had been drugging her. That gave rise to another question. *Why didn't the medicus Jess sent notice his patient was under the influence of an intoxicating herb?* The Virmans worked over Sara and soon got an answer—someone paid the medicus to look the other way. Lily wondered who had the time and money to go after her from all sides. She also began to worry about her trip to the capital.

Sounds like survival classes would be more useful than dancing lessons!

For the time being, however, she decided to focus on investing her newly discovered profits. After considering the matter with Helke, she gave him the amber to turn into jewelry and hid the money in the earl's study, where no one would find it.

ෆ ෆ

Erik was soon back from Altver, where he had winterized Lily's new ships. The Virman had accomplished everything she had asked of him, and he brought with him several nice-looking mares. Lily and Mirrie were disappointed when he told them that a mare stays pregnant for almost a year. If the Avarian stallion covered one of the mares that winter, they would still have to wait a long time for a foal. Lily told Mirrie that they wouldn't wait that long; she would order another Avarian from Ali. Mirrie had no doubt that her stepmother would do as she promised. The little girl had grown so attached to Lily that she thought her stepmother had hung the moon in the sky. Lily felt the same about her young charge.

Erik also brought a letter from Torius Avermal. It was politely worded and beautifully written, but the main idea could have been expressed in three words: "Send more goods!"

Lily was gratified that her ideas were selling so well. Her lace-makers had worked for a whole month, only stopping to eat and sleep, but it was worth it in the end. However, she knew they couldn't keep working at such a furious pace so she put out word in the villages that she was looking to hire a couple of girls to learn the trade. She had decided that she would teach the Virman women to knit, but would keep a monopoly on crochet and tatted lace. And if she moved away from Earton, she would take her lace-makers with her.

She had already explained these plans to Taris, who had sent an account of them to her father. They had not heard back from him yet, but they were sure he would help them set up a workshop if Lily had to leave Earton. For the time being, she continued to pay the girls a percentage of the profits from their lace. Marcia and the other lace-makers had never seen that much money in one place, and they were ready to walk through fire and water for Lily. Instead, they worked twelve- and fourteen-hour days with smiles on their faces.

While it took Lily about a week to crochet a lace doily three feet long and about half as wide, Marcia could do the same in three or four days. The countess was amazed by their speed, but she reflected that it made sense since they were working fast to keep their jobs, while she was merely doing it for fun.

The glassblowing workshop continued to expand, and Lily had her workers build two more kilns. Meanwhile, she made notes on everything she remembered about ceramics.

In short, life was busy and good. The only dark spot on the horizon was the official invitation to the palace that spring. It arrived on Lily's desk covered with wax seals and ribbons. When she opened it, she laughed out loud.

I'll need a stiff drink to even try and read this thing!

The long and short of it was that His Majesty wished to see her, and there was no way out of it.

Lily also received a letter from Jess' mother. In her previous life, Aliya had never had trouble with her future mother-in-law. Alex's mother, Galina, was a lovely woman who was overjoyed that her son had found a smart, hard-working girl from a military family. Aliya enjoyed her friendship, and the women often spent time together. In this world, however, Lily could glean little information about her mother-in-law. It was like the woman was a complete stranger who had no interest in her children, much less in Lilian.

That made Alicia's letter all the more surprising:

My dear daughter-in-law,

I heard about your troubles and wanted to write to you. How is your health? Medicus Craybey told us that you lost the baby. Do you need anything? Should I send you a different medicus? How can I be of help to you? You are welcome to stay with me while my son is away. His Majesty the king wishes to see you at court in the spring. I hope you will at least stay with me then. I can provide you with a dressmaker and a hairdresser. We can talk about all of that when you arrive.

I eagerly await your reply.

Alicia, Dowager Countess of Earton

Lily set the letter down on her desk. Her face was blank and her mind deep in thought. *What does the old bitch want?*

She suddenly wished her medical school had offered a course on the art of intrigue instead of the philosophy and ethics she had plowed through. *I'll just have to learn as I go along.*

⁞⁞

His Majesty Edward the Eighth was eager to hear the report Hans Tremain would give him. Curiosity had afflicted him for several months. The envoy's letters from Earton had been too short, and the events they described—murder, slave traders, pirates, amber—were almost too fanciful to be believed. Jess always told people that overfed deer were the only danger in Earton. He was obviously mistaken.

These thoughts ran through the king's head as he endured yet another official reception. It was a small reception, only for the most important nobles, but it was mainly for show, and no matters of significance would be decided. Edward sat bolt upright on his throne and nodded as courtiers approached and bowed. He exchanged a few words with each man before the next one approached and bowed.

Finally, Edward was overjoyed when his chamberlain came in and announced, "Your Majesty! Chevalier Hans Tremain to see the king!"

The nobles all looked around and began to whisper.

Edward waved a hand. "Show him in."

He knew his envoy to be a careful man. The reception

was no place for him to make a confidential report. There must be something else on his mind. (Edward always tried to give his people the autonomy to do their jobs well, and this approach was usually rewarded by excellent performance.)

Hans strode confidently into the room and bowed low. "Your Majesty!"

Edward inclined his head slightly. "How are things in Earton, Hans?"

"All was well when I left, Your Majesty. I have my report with me."

"You may show it to me after the reception."

Edward raised a hand for Hans to leave, but the envoy quickly spoke up. "Your Majesty, can you forgive me my audacity?"

"What is the matter?" the king asked.

"When I heard you were receiving courtiers this evening, I made haste to attend. The Countess of Earton entrusted me with gifts for a number of people, and I hoped to find some of them here. If you will allow it, Your Majesty…" he bowed again.

Edward's eyes glittered. Gifts? How interesting. Especially if they are as fine as the pen and inkwell.

Still, the king thought it a bold move by his envoy. If the gifts were nothing special, he would be the butt of jokes around the capital.

"Of course. Who has the countess sent gifts to?"

"To Your Majesty, of course."

Edward nodded. That was only fitting.

"And to their highnesses Angelina and Joliette."

The king said nothing, but he was curious.

Hans continued. "To her second mother, Dowager Countess

Alicia Earton, and to her sister, Amalia Ivelen."

It took all of Edward's willpower to keep from showing his surprise. *How interesting.*

"Please, Leir Tremain, distribute these gifts to their recipients."

Hans clapped his hands, and the doors to the room flew open. Two servants came in bearing a large trunk between them, followed by four more servants, each with a box. The whispering grew louder. What could be in the boxes, if a single man could carry them? Hans signaled to the servants, and they set the largest trunk in front of the throne. The envoy took a large key from a chain around his neck.

"Your Majesty..."

Edward smiled. "Hans, I may be the king, but I was taught manners like everyone else. Please give the ladies their gifts first, or I fear they may suffer from having to wait."

The princesses were squirming like small children, craning their necks to see the boxes. Hans glanced at them, smiled, and obeyed.

"Your Highness, Princess Angelina." He handed her one of the boxes. Tall and fair-haired like her father, she reached for it with a smile.

"Your Highness, Princess Joliette." The second box was put into the waiting hands of its intended recipient.

The girls immediately opened the boxes, removed the white silk that hid their contents, and gasped in delight. Angelina's slender fingers held up something as lacy and light as a cloud. Her sister lifted something similar, but pink, out of her box.

Lily had been wise enough not to make identical shawls for the two princesses. The elder princess received a white silk shawl embellished with pink and gold flowers. The younger girl's shawl was pink and covered with golden birds. The joins between the threads were decorated with amber beads that Helke had polished to be flat ovals. Together, the two shawls had required hundreds of hours of work by the lace-makers, with Lily's help, but the effect was worth it.

Once they were over their shock, the princesses wrapped the shawls around their shoulders and looked back in their boxes, where they found heavy amber combs for their hair. Never having seen anything like it before, they didn't know what to do with them.

Hans bowed. "Allow me to call for a lady's maid so that I can show you how these combs are worn."

At a nod from Angelina, one of the servants ran from the room. He soon returned, followed by a lady's maid. She did up the elder princess' hair in a knot and, following Hans' instructions, fastened the comb into the thick coil of hair. Soon, both princesses were admiring each other's gifts and laughing like children. Edward smiled down at them, and the other guests clapped their hands. The tedious reception had turned into a party.

The boxes still contained gifts, however, and the princesses sat back down to examine them. They knew what to do with the lace belts they found tucked into the boxes, but the lace fans were strange and new. Hans showed them how to open and hold the fans, and they immediately found them to be both lovely and useful. At the very bottom of their boxes, both girls found small mirrors, no more than four inches across, set in heavy metal frames. When they held them up, only their strict upbringing kept them from squealing in delight as they saw their fresh, young faces.

Suddenly, the whole room was talking at once.

Edward shook his head and leaned over to his envoy. "Hans," he said quietly, "the countess has certainly pleased my girls. Did you tell her what they would like?"

Hans gave a rueful grin. "Not at all, Your Majesty, you must believe me. Lilian Earton is a very charming and inventive woman. Everything you see here was made under her watchful eye. She put her whole heart into these things, not to find favor with yourself, but to give your daughters joy."

Edward raised an eyebrow. Hans pushed on. "Those were her exact words. She said that she does not seek your favor, but she hopes to be treated fairly. The gifts for the girls are very much like her. She adores children, and they adore her, Especially her stepdaughter."

"Is Miranda Catherine well?"

"Very well, Your Majesty. I have never seen a happier child. The countess watches over her and teaches her well, but she also spoils her and gives her every affection."

"How does she combine those things?"

"Your Majesty, all I can say is that she is a very talented young woman. I look forward to telling you all that I have learned about her."

"You intrigue me, Hans." The king smiled. Like any father, he enjoyed seeing his children happy. "Girls, I suppose you would like to take your new things to your rooms where you can look them over?"

The princesses obediently gathered up their gifts, bowed to the courtiers, and disappeared with their ladies-in-waiting. Hans still had tokens of Lily's appreciation to give to Alicia Earton and Amalia Ivelen. Although Amalia was not at the palace, Hans was sure that Alicia—who hadn't taken her eyes off the princesses' gifts—would open hers right away. She wouldn't be disappointed.

⁎ ⁏ ⁎

Alicia Earton left the reception and padded softly down the hallway to her own room, followed by two maids. She had slipped out while the others were still admiring the fanciful things Lily had sent the princesses. She did not want to open her box in front of the others, in case its contents were the same as what their royal highnesses received, which would have offended them. No, Alicia was always cautious in such matters.

As she shut her door, she gave a sigh of relief. Her daughter-in-law had launched herself quite well. Alicia didn't want to spoil it, even with something small. Her fingers ran over the lid of the box and opened it. Inside, she found a short note. It was not a letter, just a few words:

As a sign of my gratitude and sincere affection,
Lilian Earton.

Gratitude? Affection? Alicia shook her head and turned to the gifts. Fifteen minutes later, she admitted to herself that her daughter-in-law was a clever woman. The box revealed a large piece of lightweight lace that Alicia realized was a shawl. She nodded. It was a fitting present. She often found herself needing extra warmth, and she was too old to wear the heavy combs the princesses had received. The shawl was a lovely pale seafoam green and very warm. Lily had plied her finest green wool yarn with a blue silk thread to crochet a simple geometric lace pattern without any amber beads, but with a deep fringe around the edges.

Underneath the shawl was a lace belt in the same color and a simple fan decorated with silver paint. Alicia was pleased to see that she had also been given a mirror, although hers was smaller than the ones Lily sent the princesses. She was about to set aside the box when she saw something white underneath its red velvet lining. She pulled at it with her fingernails and discovered a small silk bag.

How clever of her. She hid it so I wouldn't take it out in front of everyone else.

What she found inside the silk bag was breathtakingly expensive: heavy earrings, a necklace, a brooch, a bracelet, and a ring. All made of amber in a range of shades, from red to honey-colored to pure white. The jewels were truly a royal gift.

The old schemer tried them on and looked at herself in the small mirror. Then she gave a little laugh and put everything away in her jewelry box. She would wear the jewels to a ball someday soon, but not right away. She would also keep a close eye on her daughter-in-law. His Majesty was right; Lilian Earton deserved the closest attention.

ೞ ಚ

Edward looked at Hans. He knew he should ask for the envoy's report, but Lilian Earton had piqued his curiosity. He was dying to know what she had sent him, the king on whom her wellbeing and even her life depended. He nodded at his envoy.

"Well, let's open it," he said, looking at the trunk.

The report wouldn't get lost if it had to wait another ten minutes.

Hans hid a smile as he bowed. "Your Majesty, if you will…" He leaned over the chest.

In just a few minutes, the king decided that Lilian was a most decidedly clever woman. She had sent him a lace collar and cuffs made of white and gold thread and richly embellished with amber beads. Edward had never seen anything quite like it.

I will wear these because I like them, and the countess will make money when other men at court wish to have the same. I see she is making friends before her arrival. Well played.

He looked up at Hans. "Do you think the countess made these things herself?"

"She did, Your Majesty. I saw it with my own eyes. She asked that you accept them as a sign of respect.

Edward smiled. Respect? She will earn a fortune with this lace once I wear it. But I see her hint. The countess is prepared to share her profits in exchange for protection.

"The countess is undoubtedly very talented," he said. Hans bowed and lifted a wooden box from the trunk. "Your Majesty, the countess expressed her hope that you will occasionally have time for this game."

"Game?"

"May I show you, Your Majesty?" Hans put the box on the table. The king saw that it was made of polished oak with a Khangan-style pattern burned into the lid. He squinted at the word above the patterning.

"Back-gamm-on?"

"That is the name, Your Majesty." The envoy opened the box, revealing two smaller boxes inside. When he opened one of them, Edward's eyes grew round. The game pieces—fifteen each—were made of white and red amber. "There is a second set in case any of these are lost," Hans said, pointing to the second small box. Then he showed the king two dice, carved from oak, both with six sides.

"Would you like to play, Your Majesty?"

Edward nodded. He felt as curious as a boy for the first time in many years, and he wanted to get as much enjoyment as he could from this unexpected gift. Hans quickly set out the game pieces and explained the rules. He showed the king the parchment where he had all the rules written out. Edward picked up the dice, and the game started.

The king won the first game because he was the king, and even he could see that Hans had let him have it. He won the second game, too, almost by himself. The third game turned into a true battle of wills, but Edward managed to isolate two of Hans' pieces.

He grinned wolfishly. "This is a nice way to spend time."

"The countess said she hoped it would give you a respite from your cares."

Hans knew Lily had planned to send the king a chessboard with figures but changed her mind. The game was too difficult, and she doubted the king would master it without her there to show him the way. She said it would be difficult to carve the figures so quickly. Chess would have to wait until she visited the palace. Backgammon was an easier game; she had gotten Hans hooked in just two days.

After several more games, Edward pushed the board away and looked over at the trunk. His envoy reached in and pulled out another small box. Inside, was the largest mirror Lily had been able to make— it was about the size of a small computer monitor in her own world. Helke had made the frame and the tripod that held it out of silver. Both bore Lily's red cross. She would have liked to make them out of gold, but she simply did not have enough of the metal. The silver frame was elegant, however, and offset with warmly glinting amber.

Edward studied his face in the mirror for several minutes. It was a vast improvement over polished metal.

"This thing, this…"

"It is glass, Your Majesty. The countess found a description of the process in an old book."

"Glass?"

"Yes, Your Majesty. It will break if you drop it. I had it transported with great care."

The king reflected that few of his subjects would be able to afford such a luxury, at least at first.

"How many of these glass things can be made?"

"As many as you like, given enough material."

"Who knows the secret of their manufacture?"

"Only Her Ladyship and her two craftsmen."

"Wonderful."

"There is something else, Your Majesty."

Helke had outdone himself; the gold cup Hans lifted from the trunk was almost entirely encrusted with amber in red, white, and gold. It was an impressive piece, even for the king's palace.

Yes, it would seem that Jess' wife has me on the hook now.

Hans held out the cup. "Your Majesty, this is just a gift. I already turned over your share of the Earton amber to the treasury."

"I see they have found red and white amber in Earton."

"No, Your Majesty."

"What do you mean?"

"The countess knows a way to turn plain amber, white, or red. It becomes more brittle, but you won't be using the cup as a hammer."

Edward shook his head. "The countess is certainly making sure that people will talk about her."

"She is afraid, Your Majesty."

The king looked up suddenly. "Of what?"

"There have been several attempts on her life." The envoy reached for his bag. "Here, Your Majesty, before I forget."

"Is this your report?"

"I'm afraid not. Forgive me for being so bold, Your Majesty, but I think you will want to see this. It is also from Her Ladyship."

Edward took the parchment, unrolled it with a

practiced hand and started to read. Before long, he looked up at Hans with wide eyes and then back at the parchment. Lilian had sent him a clear and simple description of the technology for obtaining salt from seawater.

Ativerna had a single salt deposit on the border with Wellster, but the salt was contaminated with other elements and tasted strange. Instead, Ativernese merchants imported better salt from Wellster and Avesterra at outrageous prices. Edward laid the parchment on his desk and leaned forward. Hans suddenly noticed that they were alone in the room.

"If the countess truly knows…"

"Believe me, Your Majesty, I have watched her do it. She had her peasants build a salt pit on the coast, where they use the salt they get from the seawater to preserve fish. Salted fish is a true delicacy."

"I see. I shall make inquiries. For now, say nothing about this to anyone." The king looked down at the backgammon board, deep in thought.

Lilian Earton is behaving like a person who intends to be taken seriously. That may be a good thing, or it may not.

He set aside the gold cup and the game and asked Hans for his report. What he heard did not please him in the least. The king's envoy gave a full and accurate accounting of the estate manager's thievery, the condition of the estate, the first attempt on the countess' life, how Lilian hired Virmans to protect herself and her stepdaughter, how the slave traders attacked, and how the countess accidentally learned of the amber deposit on her lands. Edward's face grew grimmer with each new piece of information.

Jerrison told me none of this. He said the castle was not in excellent shape, but we are not at war, either. Who would have thought that a man needed a fortified castle to live in a place like Earton? It appears I have been guilty of an oversight.

Hans continued his report. He showed the king Etor's two sets of accounts. He showed him the statements Pastor Vopler had taken from Leis' turncoat soldier, the slave traders and the Grismo family. He informed the king that he had turned over the guilty parties to the prison as soon as he reached the capital.

When the envoy stopped speaking, Edward gestured for him to remain silent for a moment and began drawing on the back of a piece of parchment with one of the Earton pens Lily's father had given him.

After a while, he looked up. "Tell me, Hans, what was your personal impression of the countess? What can you say about her? Is she stupid and prone to scandals? Edward knew these questions made no sense in the context of all that had happened and that he had learned, but he could not understand why Jess had spoken of his wife that way.

Hans offered a thin smile. "The countess is intelligent and kind. As for scandals, I must tell Your Majesty that I have never even heard her raise her voice."

"Her husband has a different opinion."

೮೦ ೮೪

Hans' face grew serious. He had never liked Jerrison Earton. The earl was arrogant, handsome, and self-satisfied, to the annoyance of those around him. Jerrison Earton was so sure of his superiority that Hans had a habit of imagining him falling off his horse. *True, the earl has cause to be proud—he is young and handsome and very rich. He even has some talent. But even if you outshine everyone else like Aldonai, if you treat other people like worms, you can expect to run into trouble sooner or later.* With that in mind, Hans enjoyed his small moment of triumph.

"Your Majesty, that is a question best put to the countess. I can only tell you what I saw with my own eyes."

Hans kept quite a few things he had seen to himself, however. He told the king nothing about the countess' healers, about how she had stitched up the wounded after the battle with the slave traders, about the Khangans she was friends with, or about her close friendships with the Virmans she had hired. He told himself that those things were not relevant, and focused on praising the countess' wisdom and her careful use of Earton's resources.

Edward's face grew more serious as he listened. Every now and then, he interrupted his envoy to clarify some detail or to ask him to repeat something. When Hans was finally finished, he nodded.

"Tell my secretary that you are to have a room at the palace for now. I will send for you."

ଔ ☐ ଷ

Hans bowed and slipped out the door. The king picked up the gold cup again and looked at it closely. It was almost a work of art.

How beautiful it is, and how well she did to send something that I would want to keep near me.

The game was delightful, and the lace was a simple, elegant gift, fit for a king. He looked down at the mirror and the instructions for evaporating salt from seawater.

Lilian is trying to show me that she knows many useful things. But how can that be? And why did Jess tell me that all was well in Earton if the estate was being robbed and plagued by slave traders? How could he not know about the amber deposit on his lands? Why did he tell me that Lilian was a foolish, hysterical woman?

The king had more faith in his envoy than in the son he called nephew, and Hans had nothing but praise for the countess, and said she was adored by Miranda Catherine. Edward had proof of her intelligence and inventiveness on the desk in front of him. Even if the countess had found old books that explained how to do these wonderful things, she had to be credited for actually doing them, which wasn't easy. The king imagined how long it must have taken her to make all that lace. He knew it was her own work because he had never seen anything like it anywhere in the kingdom or abroad.

What does this mean? Has Jess been lying to me? Is he incapable of seeing the truth, or does he not wish to see it? And what about the attack on his wife? That's an absolute disgrace!

Edward had already decided to place several large orders with August Broklend's boatyard, and he hated to see his strategic plans threatened all because Jess slept with the wrong woman. The king was not disappointed by his son's infidelity—he knew himself to be a sinner in the same way—but his Jessamine would never have dreamed of poisoning Imogene so she could become queen.

If he found a woman to make love to, he should have

told her straight away that he would never marry her, no matter what happened to his wife. Then we wouldn't be in this mess. And who does this woman's cousin think he is? Sending someone to murder the Countess of Earton!

Edward rang the bell on his desk. A servant came in.

"Send the captain of the palace guards to me."

When the man appeared, the king issued one simple order: to grab Adelaide Wells' cousin and beat the truth out of him about the attacks on Lilian Earton, using any means necessary. One way or another, Edward would get to the bottom of the matter. For now, however, he had a letter to write. He took up a fresh sheet of parchment.

You may think you're smart, my boy, but you can't see the diamond right in front of your face. I'll teach you a lesson!

ಬಂ ☐ ೦ಜ

Torius Avermal glared at his wife. "No and, again, no! I told you that you may only keep those things the countess sent us as gifts. The rest of it…"

"But Marietta is angry with me!"

Torius just laughed. "My dear, your Marietta can't afford something like this. I don't care how angry she is. Once we sell it, you'll be able to order a new dress from Marion Alcey."

His wife fumed for a while longer, but eventually, she was appeased by the prospect of buying a lovely new dress that would make her friends green with envy.

"Who bought it from you?"

"A merchant from Wellster, a nobleman from Ivernea, and a

wealthy Khangan."

"What do you mean? Three men at once bought the same mirror?"

"My dear, there is not a single person in this whole town who has enough money to buy one of these new mirrors. Do you realize that they paid me four times its weight in gold? They will take turns using it. What do you think your Marietta could pay me? Or that lazy husband of hers?"

His wife frowned, but the storm was over. Torius had been more than prepared to endure a fight on the home front. He had earned a great deal of money on the transaction, and he still needed to decide how to send Lilian her share. There would be no talk of shortchanging the countess—the baron wouldn't risk trying to deceive a woman like Lilian. She, too, was worth her weight in gold.

૎ ૏

Ten days later, Hans again found himself in a private meeting with the king. Edward was not pleased.

"Where could that bone-setter have gotten to?"

"He seems to have jumped in the ocean, Your Majesty."

Hans had learned that Medicus Craybey had jumped into a body of water, only it wasn't the ocean, and he hadn't exactly jumped. Unsure of Lilian's involvement, he decided to keep the information to himself. The person who had paid Craybey to ignore Lilian's symptoms couldn't risk public disclosure of what the healer knew so, less than a month after his return from Earton, he was invited to treat a private patient at an outlying estate. That was the last he was ever seen. *A lake is just as good a place to hide dead bodies, and fish aren't picky eaters. It's a dangerous world.* Meanwhile, he continued to "help" the king's guards find the medicus, but without success.

ೞ ☐ ೞ

Adelaide Wells' cousin proved easier to locate. In fact, they found him right away and interrogated him using all the most advanced technologies (forceps, hot irons, etc.). Alex was no hero. He started talking before the king's guards had a chance to get rough with him. *Which they could always do later.*

Yes, he had wanted the countess dead. Yes, he had hired a man to do the job. He had even dreamed of success. Why? Because he wanted Jerrison Earton to make Adele an honest woman. That seemed like a lawful enough goal to him. When he had started to voice some ugly opinions about the earl, the guards changed his mind by showing him a hot iron. Still, he said enough to make the king furious with his son. Edward was outraged that Jess would let a woman like Adele harbor hope of becoming his wife. He would have Alex hung, of course, but he didn't know what to do with the scoundrel's fair cousin. There was no evidence that she had wanted Lily dead. Alex had burned their letters, wishing to keep their plot secret.

Edward's first instinct was to recall her from the delegation to Wellster, but that was risky. Outsiders would sniff out his son's disgrace.

Fine. Let her enjoy the trip. But I will write to Jerrison and tell him to keep a close eye on her. If anything else happens, it will be his fault.

As he picked up his pen, he decided that he still might have Adele killed.

After this letter to Jerrison, I'll write to Falion. He will watch the girl like a hawk.

Once the letters were done and sent, he called for his envoy again and raked him over the coals. "Find that medicus. Shake up his family and friends. Find out who his last client was. I shouldn't have to teach you how to do your job!"

Hans swore he would find the man. Then he bowed his way out of the king's study.

ఎం ❏ ☒

Amalia Ivelen studied the box in her lap. It was a gift from Lilian.

She turned to her husband, "What do you think it is?"

He snorted. "Something ridiculous, I'm sure. What else could that cow have sent you?"

Amalia shrugged. "You're right, of course. But I should still send her something in return."

Her husband snorted again but did not object. "As you like, my dear."

Amalia looked bored as she opened the box with one hand. Then she gasped. "Peter!" He turned to see what she was holding, and his eyes grew wide. It was a very long and very wide piece of finely made lace. Peter was not particularly interested in women's finery, but he knew how much something like that would cost. If he had bought it from a merchant, he would have handed over enough gold coins to cover the length of the lace, and even at that price, it would have been a steal.

"What is it?" he asked stupidly.

Amalia held it up. It was a long scarf, light and elegant, with a pattern of flying birds in pink and blue. "How lovely it is," she whispered as it slipped through her fingers. "Peter, where do you suppose she found something so wonderful?"

"You will have to ask August. I think it will look well on you, my dear."

She wrapped the lace around her neck and shoulders. It did flatter her blue eyes and dark hair.

Peter was intrigued despite himself. "Is there anything else in the box?"

Amalia nodded. She reached in and lifted out a small mirror in a heavy frame. "A mirror? Oh, Aldonai! Just look at it, Peter!"

He sat down next to her and looked closely at the mirror. "Are you sure that's what it is?"

"I think it's made of glass!"

Husband and wife were astounded by the clarity of their reflections and the beauty of the frame.

Peter handed the mirror back to his wife. "I've never heard of anything like it."

"Do you think August had it made?"

"I will ask him," Peter promised, still frowning.

Amalia reached into the box and pulled out another item. "This is unbelievable!" It was a brooch made of chunks of red and white amber. "Peter, where could she have gotten this?"

He leaned over his wife's shoulder and looked into the box. "There's a letter, my dear." Amalia took out the rolled parchment.

Dear Amalia,

I am sending you these small things as a gift to mark the birth of your child. I hope they get to you in time. It is my hope that we will see each other at court in the spring. It will be good to talk to you.

With sincere affection and hope of friendship,

Lilian Elizabeth Mariella Earton

This was followed by a seal and Lily's fancy signature.

Amalia blinked. "Peter, I don't understand. Is this from Jess' stupid wife?" Her husband just shrugged. He couldn't make sense of it, either. The whole thing was utterly confusing.

ᘓ ᘔ

From a letter to Erk Grismo:

How is the cow? What is happening in Earton? Has she written to her father? I await your reply.

Chapter 3
Good Neighbors

Time flew imperceptibly. The first snow fell, light and soft, and Lily was happy as a child to see it. Her workshops were making progress, and Mirrie was running around having a wonderful time. Life at the castle was finally on an orderly footing so Lily was surprised one morning when she looked out the dining room window and saw a dozen peasants—men and women—kneeling in the courtyard. They looked like they were ready to put down roots in front of the castle. When they saw her look out, they bent over with their noses almost to the ground.

"What is going on?" Lily asked the nearest guard.

"Don't you know, My Lady? The peasants have come to beg for justice."

"From me?"

Yikes!

Lily was surprised to learn that she had earned quite the reputation with her peasants for being kind and fair, if a little strange. *Why do they think that?*

They had their reasons. First, Lily had already improved the standard of living in the villages. She had bought seed for sowing, meaning that the peasants could keep their harvest for food. She had also done away with the tradition of forcing the peasants to work the earl's land. True, she made them do all sorts of other jobs around the estate, but she fed them well while they worked and even paid them, which was unheard-of in those parts. While the countess may not have given her peasants the livestock she bought at the market, she made sure that every peasant's cow was bred by one of the quality bulls she had brought back with her. She had also drawn up a list of families with small children and made sure that they were given a pail of goat's or cow's milk from her own animals every other day. That was enough to keep the children healthy. The very poorest peasants in Earton were invited to the castle kitchen once every five days, where they were given bread, vegetables, and salted fish. It was not fancy food, but it was enough—when added to what they already had—to see them through the winter.

The peasants owed much of their gratitude for the charity they received to Ingrid and Leif, who had traveled through the villages months earlier and drawn up lists of who would need what over the winter. But since they did not know this, they worshiped the kind countess, who had also hired several orphan girls and a handful of young women from large families to work as seamstresses at the castle. Their families prayed for the countess' continuing health morning and night. It was a fine thing to have a child clothed, fed and taught a profession (and it meant one less mouth to feed). As if that weren't enough, Lily allowed the girls to spend a day at home once every ten days, and the hardest workers were given small gifts of food and other useful items to take to their families. The girls knew how lucky they were, and they worked hard to earn their keep.

The peasants had seen Lily build them a new church, and they had helped with the salt pits and the salting of fish.

They had watched her Virmans hand the slave traders their asses. It was a good year. None of their women had been raped, none of their daughters had been stolen, and none of the men had been killed. Even theft had become a rare occurrence. The peasants were overjoyed.

Two of the villages had lost their elders, to be sure, but the peasants suspected that Grismo and Darcey deserved their fates. Emma did her best to encourage this line of thinking by gossiping with the seamstresses, who took tales back to the villages on their visits home. Soon, even the deafest old man knew that Erk had been cooperating with the slave traders and that Fred had tried to poison the poor, dear countess (who had never done anything but good for her people).

Because they were so pleased with Lily, they decided to come to her for justice. They might not have dared, except that this particular case was complicated: the victim and the accused were from different villages. Art (who had instigated the trip to the castle) suspected that the countess would judge fairly, more or less, and that she would be utterly merciless if she discovered the peasants pursuing lynch law on their own. Heads would roll, and he feared that his own would be the first to go because of his position as elder.

As soon as Lily went out into the courtyard, the peasants swarmed toward her and fell at her feet. She had no choice; she would have to judge their case for them.

ʅ ʘ

The hearing took twenty minutes and was held in the small dining room, which had been rearranged to suit its new purpose. Lily had the servants move the chairs and set up a special place for her to preside. That done, the servants lit the candles, draped her chair in an expensive length of silk (it was pink since that was all they had) and opened the door to admit the parties to the case.

The peasants hung back timidly, so Art stepped forward to explain the matter:

Appleton and Riverton were three hours apart by horseback. If that seemed like enough of a distance to discourage intercourse between the two villages, it was not (at least for one man who had a horse). In Appleton, Art's village, there was a good-looking young widow with three children and a good farm. Several men had their eyes on her, but she took up with a man from Riverton, who rode over every other evening and spent the night. It didn't take long for the widow's neighbors to catch on. They didn't think it was right, and they wanted to make their point by breaking all the bones in the man's body. At this point, the widow had jumped into the discussion and threatened to report her neighbors to the countess if they touched her lover. The crowd cooled off when they heard that. To make things even more interesting, another young woman from Appleton—this one unmarried and living at home—stepped forward and declared she was pregnant by the eager horseback rider. The widow jumped on her and would have ripped her face off, but the girl's parents stepped in and pulled the widow off.

It was a simple question: which woman had a better claim on the man?

The man swore up and down that he had never visited the second girl or participated in any activities that might have gotten her pregnant. Her parents were outraged. The widow was furious at the thought that she might have been sharing her lover the whole time. Passions were boiling over, and the two villages were ready to declare war. Just in time, Art suggested asking the countess to judge the who, where, what and how of the matter.

Lily shook her head. Then she questioned each participant in turn. The widow, named Marianne, was a strong woman who looked to be about thirty-five (which, in that world, meant she was probably ten years younger). She swore on all that was holy that her lover had only visited her, but under questioning admitted that she hadn't followed him everywhere he went. He might have been true to her, or he might not.

The man, a fellow named Tom, was handsome enough for his forty years (or thirty years, since to Lily's eye, the peasants all looked much older than they were). He admitted that he liked Marianne and had been sleeping with her. He swore he would marry her the first chance he got. When asked about the unmarried girl, he declared that he'd never touched, kissed or done anything else to her. She was a skinny fool, and he had no use for her.

Lily sighed and turned to the girl, who was clearly afraid and yet sure of her rights. Tom was the father. It couldn't be anyone else.

The countess sighed again. Someone was lying, but she couldn't see her way to the truth yet. They couldn't just wait for the child to be born and do a DNA test. She needed to come up with an answer here and now. Otherwise, there would be violence, and that was something she would not allow.

How am I supposed to figure this out? I can't ask the Virmans to torture innocent people. If only I had some truth serum, but I don't. Wait a minute!

"Chevalier Avels?"

"Yes, My Lady?"

Lons, who stood at his usual place behind Lilian's shoulder, leaned forward. She whispered something in his ear. He listened, nodded, and gestured for Tom to follow him. Tom looked at the countess. She nodded in encouragement, and he followed Lons out of the room.

Lily turned to the two women. "You go stand in that corner," she pointed at Marianne. "And you," she pointed at the girl, whose name was Iria, "go stand in the other corner. Each of you, in turn, will tell me if your lover has any scars or birthmarks. Tell me quietly, so that the other cannot hear. Then I will inform Chevalier Avels of what you have said, and he will verify your words. If either of you tells a lie, you will only have yourself to blame."

The peasants glanced at each other. It had never occurred to them to decide the question that way. Lily was not surprised. She had noticed that they were very good at certain things and very bad at others. It made sense. Lily would rather not try to milk a cow, and the peasants didn't know how to run an investigation.

The Virmans stood the two women in opposite corners of the room, and Lily, after thinking for a moment, went to the widow first. "Marianne, tell me about Tom's body. Does he have any scars?"

Marianne nodded. "There is one. When he was little, he squatted down outside to do his business, and a snake bit him from behind. His father cut out the poison with a knife.

You can still see the scar on the left side of his…well, below his waist."

"Is that all?"

The widow thought briefly and nodded. She told the countess the man had other small scars, but nothing unlike what the rest of them bore.

Lily turned and went to Iria, who confidently stated that Tom had a single scar on his shoulder. This information was given to Lons Avels, who confirmed that the man had a scar on his backside and none on his shoulder.

The countess frowned. She turned back to the younger girl and offered to let the Virmans work her over (the Virmans in the room grimaced at this), followed by a whipping at the stables and a one-way trip to Altver where she could earn her keep using the only skills she appeared to possess. That was enough of a threat. Through tears, the girl admitted that she had gotten pregnant by one of Erk Grismo's sons. When he was arrested along with his father, she got scared and started looking for someone else to be the child's father.

Lily cursed silently. Then she grinned; she had found a way out. She returned to her ceremonial seat and nodded to Lons.

"Her Ladyship has reached a decision!" he announced.

She looked around the room. "Tom and Marianne, do you want to get married?"

The man and woman glanced at each other. Tom's eyes asked "Will you?" and Marianne's eyes replied affirmatively. Lily saw and understood.

"Pastor Vopler will join you in marriage so you will no longer be fornicating. You can decide where you want to live."

"In my home," Tom spoke up, "in Riverton."

Lily nodded. "Next. Iria is pregnant by a man who committed a crime against myself and against the house of Earton." The grim-looking man standing next to Iria cuffed her upside the head. "But I do not wish to see anyone else die, so here is what I have decided. Marianne, when you go to live in Riverton, what will happen to your house?"

"It will be empty, I suppose, My Lady."

"Then I will buy it from you for a fair price. That will be your dowry." A wide smile appeared on Marianne's face. "And I will give the house to Iria to live in. If she finds someone who wants to marry her, the house will be her dowry. Otherwise, she will live in it on her own. And the village can decide what punishment she deserves for lying about such a serious matter."

Lily had no pity for Iria. As she watched the peasants file out of the small dining room, she felt something like pride—. *My land, my people.*

Mirrie, who stood next to Lily's chair during the entire proceeding, looked up at her stepmother with an expression Lily had never seen before. "Will I have to do that when I grow up?"

"If you don't have a reliable husband, then yes. Watch and learn while I am with you."

Mirrie nodded. She wasn't afraid to learn, and she wanted to be ready for anything.

My...daughter?

The Earl of Earton, ran his eyes over the letter from home and cursed quietly. It was not good news, not good at all.

"What happened?" Richard asked from his bed. He was still weak, but the fever was gone, and the healers were already talking in confident tones about his recovery.

"I already told you that my cow lost the baby, didn't I? My man in town confirmed it. He says that Miranda reached Earton. I suppose that's good news. But I'll have to go down there by next fall."

"Sorry to hear that."

Jess made a face. "A lot of good your pity does me. I'll have to sleep with her again!" He grimaced, remembering his wife. "Disgusting creature!"

"Just grit your teeth and do your duty," Richard snorted. "It's not like you have to stick it in a hot oven."

Jess stared at his friend wide-eyed and went back to the letter. "Miranda is alive and well, thank goodness. My agent in the capital sent money for the estate."

"I don't understand. Why?" Richard asked. He raised himself up on one elbow. "Doesn't your manager collect the taxes for you?"

Jess waved a hand. "The place is a hole, and the taxes don't amount to anything. I always have to send money. Etor collects it in Altver from an agent I use there. Then he buys what he needs and takes it back to Earton."

"Why haven't you ever tried to clean up Earton?" Richard asked. The two friends had never talked about Jess' estate before, and it had never occurred to the prince to ask.

"What for?" Jess shrugged.

"It's your family's estate, isn't it?"

"More like a boil on Maldonaya's ass," Jess shot back rudely. He took a deep breath and continued more calmly. "Look, I have a house in the capital, a small estate right outside town, my shipbuilding business to handle, and my regiment. What the hell do I need with a castle in the woods where my evil grandmother used to live?"

"What about your grandmother?"

"The old bitch couldn't stand my father or me or Amalia. He took us down there one time to see her, but she yelled at him so loud that the gates almost came off their hinges. I still remember his face. He slammed the door, and we got back in the carriage and left."

"Did you ever ask him what it was about?"

Jess gestured impatiently. "All women are fools. Maldonaya would break a leg trying to walk around in a woman's mind."

Richard looked at him thoughtfully. "You shouldn't talk like that," he said softly.

"I'm sure there are exceptions, but I haven't met one yet."

"What about Adele?" Richard smiled.

Jess snorted. "I said all women."

Richard shook his head. He very much wanted to tell his cousin that he was the fool. He had let himself be spoiled by women. He was handsome, young, rich, and connected to the royal house, making him irresistible to a certain sort of woman. But sooner or later, Jess would meet a woman who was a worthy enemy. Richard hoped he would be there when it happened.

❧ ❦ ☙

Edward looked down at the letter on his desk. He tried hard to see beyond the simple words to the person that had written it. In one place, she had pressed too hard with the pen, almost tearing the parchment. Was she nervous? In another, she had obviously picked up too much ink with her pen, and the whole line came out darker. He saw a place where her pen had scratched the parchment. Was she angry? Was she tired of writing? Hans had told him that it took the countess an entire day and then some to write his letter. She had thought about it, choosing the right words, even asking Hans for advice.

Your Majesty,

Allow me to set forth for you the condition of the estate at Earton. I know that Leir Tremain will present his report to you so I will not waste your valuable time. Instead, I will tell you only what it is vital for you to know.

My memories of the time before I lost my child are in a fog. Once I was well and got out of bed, I stopped thinking about my suffering and turned to the business at hand. I saw that the estate manager was a thief. Leir Tremain can show you proof of his guilt. I also saw that Medicus Craybey had almost killed me, whether out of ignorance or on purpose, I know not. He drained much blood from me, even after I suffered a miscarriage.

I learned from my people that pirates and slave traders felt free to visit the estate. Leir Tremain brings some of these men with him.

His advice and assistance in this matter were of the greatest importance to me.

I also wish you to know that a deposit of amber was discovered on the estate. It is impossible to continue digging over the winter, but I hasten to promise that as soon as spring comes, we will renew that work. I have sent the royal portion of what we already recovered with Leir Tremain.

Likewise, I am sending you some small gifts as a sign of my gratitude for your support. I will await your further instructions.

I remain your devoted servant,

Countess Lilian Elizabeth Mariella Earton

It was a simple letter; short and impersonal. All the details had come from Hans, who told the king about life in Earton, about the countess, and even how to wear the lace collar and cuffs properly, and how to wash, dry and starch them so they would retain their shape.

Edward ran a hand absently over one of his lace cuffs. He found that he enjoyed wearing them. The princesses were absolutely delighted to be envied by all the ladies at court. Several dressmakers in the capital had tried to imitate Lily's work but had given up; it was too difficult.

Who are you, Lilian Earton? No hysterical fool could have written a letter like that.

Edward thought back to his son's wedding. He had not seen the bride prior to that day, and she made a less than stellar impression standing at the altar like a haystack. He remembered her: a large girl dressed in white and pink, with long, golden braids hanging down the back of her dress and a round, red face. *Why was she red? Was she embarrassed? Was her dress uncomfortable? Was she just hot?* He decided it could have been anything. At the time, Edward had simply noted that she was not to his taste. She wore too much gold and…well, there was too much of her. She had mumbled something in response to his polite wishes of happiness in marriage.

Edward did not believe that he understood women well, and he would have laughed at any man who claimed to have such knowledge. However, the king knew one thing well: a woman tends to behave strangely on her wedding day. He could clearly remember his own wedding day when he went to see Jessamine and found her fully dressed, from hair to shoes, and sobbing her eyes out. *Why? Because she had never expected to be so happy.*

He wondered if his son could have mistaken shyness for stupidity. That was Jess. Women had always fallen on their backs for Jess without any effort on his part. He was used to being worshiped. He was young, handsome, rich and powerful. Edward remembered himself at the age of twenty, and he was ashamed.

If he could do it all over again, he would build a different relationship with Imogene…and with Edmund. The pain of losing Edmund was always with him. *What did I do wrong with my son? Why did I find in him an enemy instead of a loving child? How much do we lose because we are young and stupid?* Edward knew he could never have turned away from Jessie, but he could have tried harder to be careful with Imogene's feelings. He could have kept his son closer.

I might never have lost him or my best friend, Jyce. Time doesn't really heal all wounds. It just creates a layer of years over something that still pulses and bleeds. When someone cuts a piece out of your heart, it never heals.

Edward wanted to talk to his son in person, but that was not possible. He would write him a very serious letter and speak to him upon his return. *Children should not repeat their parents' mistakes, especially if their parents are around to warn them.*

The king looked back at the letter on his desk. He could sense a steel will behind the decisive, right-slanting letters. If it weren't for the signature at the bottom, he would think the letter had been written by a man. There was no sentiment of any kind, just business. Lilian Earton was nothing like Imogene. She would not sit in a corner and cry.

But what would she do?

Edward suddenly realized with a shock that he was afraid for his son. He picked up his pen and began to write.

∞ ⁒ ∞

A different letter suffered a much different fate. It was balled up in a fit of fatherly rage. Then it was smoothed out and read several more times. August had never been a patient man, and it was hard for him to read about his only daughter's life being in danger.

My daughter! My little buttercup!

The letter was the first to suffer. Then his desk was overturned in a spasm of rage. Once he calmed down, he started to work on a plan.

Jerrison Earton, you'll answer to me for this! You left

my sweet angel in your falling-down castle and forgot her name! Someone was trying to poison her, and they caused her to lose her baby! It's a good thing Lily takes after me. You can't keep her down, and you won't get away with it.

August re-read the letter. His eyes stopped on the name Karl Treloney. He wondered if his daughter had a lover, not that it mattered. She could do what she liked if her husband didn't see fit to live with her and took his whore with him on the trip to Wellster. August laughed. Now everyone would see exactly what that whore had been up to.

∞ ☐ ∞

The king said nothing to August about the new information, of course, but he sent Hans to see him. Hans gave the shipbuilder a note from his daughter and praised her to the skies, assuring August of his affection and respect, and he left August the two carpenter's apprentices Lily had lured away from their master on her trip to Altver. After talking to them, August was beyond pleased.

Well, my girl, you knew exactly what I needed! And their master was right to fear letting go of them. That varnish of his won't be expensive to make, and if I use it judiciously…

That same day, he offered the apprentices a good salary and a guarantee of safety, which they happily accepted. The countess had been generous with them, and her father proved to be the same. *So why not get to work? A boatyard is an excellent place for a carpenter.*

While he was with August, Hans told him everything the king knew. At first, August was angry, but he soon reached an important decision. Lilian might not be ready to leave her husband yet, but he needed to have everything prepared in case that day came—a house, land, workshops. He also needed to collect compromising information on Jess Earton, and the more, the better. August would be damned before anyone got away with treating his precious daughter this way. And whatever his daughter decided, he wanted her to have a safe place to retreat to. He also decided to transfer some of his assets to partners in Avesterra and Wellster. If he had to choose between Jerrison and Lily, he would always take his daughter's side. If they had to, they could run away together. *No one could catch one of his ships on the ocean!*

August knew he could find work wherever he went, and he was confident he could set Lily up and help her raise her children (if she had any). Judging by Lily's latest endeavors, she would have no trouble finding a new husband.

You've got it coming, Jerrison Earton. You didn't love her and didn't care for her, now you'll wish you hadn't lost her...

Seduced by the lyrics to the old ballad, August forgot one thing: Jess wouldn't be sorry to lose Lily. He would only be sorry to lose the income she was bringing in.

℘ ❧

Meanwhile, Lily was talking to Pastor Vopler.

"You have to realize that her unborn child has done nothing wrong..."

"My Lady, your mercy in this matter is beyond what I can understand. Adulteresses must be chased from their villages."

"It's winter, and she has nowhere to go. I believe that Aldonai instructed us to show mercy to others."

"But My Lady, you have already gone above and beyond all of our Lord's commandments. I will not be surprised to see you named a Radiant One in your lifetime."

The kindly smile on the pastor's face hinted that she should not take his words too seriously, so Lily answered in the same vein. "Everything is in the hands of our Lord Aldonai, the merciful and benevolent. All I ask is that you speak to the people in the village. I agree that the girl doesn't have much of a brain to speak of, but she will give birth to a child who has done nothing wrong. Remember, the child did not choose its parents."

The countess knew that Iria was an outcast in her village. No one outside her family would have anything to do with her. Lily wouldn't have cared about that, but Ingrid had sat her down and explained how the situation was likely to develop. In the end, Lily decided that she didn't need any lynchings and she most certainly didn't need another village whore spreading disease. The other women would be upset at the young woman's merciful treatment, but Lily would plow right through them.

"No, the child is not at fault," the pastor admitted.

"Speak to them. Maybe there is a widower with a pack of children who would be glad to have some help. The girl has had enough time to think about her position. She'll be glad to get married."

"I understand, My Lady," Pastor Vopler sighed. "I promise I will do what I can."

Just then, they were interrupted by a maid scratching at the door. "Baron Donter is here, My Lady."

Lily shrugged. "Show him into the hall. I'll be down shortly." This time, she felt calmer about this neighborly visit. If it came down to it, she could run over the baron like a tank. She had almost a hundred Virmans on the estate, as well as Leis' men and the peasants. Earton could win a war if it had to.

She turned to the pastor. "Will you accompany me?"

"Of course," he smiled. "I suppose we should also send for Chevalier Avels and make sure that the children are occupied."

Lily agreed with him on all counts, especially concerning the children. The last thing she needed was for someone to shoot peas at the baron from behind a banister.

Why the hell did I show those kids how to make blowguns? Next thing we know, they'll graduate from peas to poison darts. Step right up and see the Ninjas of Earton!

She laughed to herself and smoothed out her dress. She thought she looked good enough. There were no ink spots on her skirt, and there was nothing sticking out or sticking up anywhere. When at home, the countess almost always wore her special skirts (that were actually very wide pants), along with a blouse and long vest. This outfit of her own design kept her comfortable and decent, and best of all, she was able to wear normal underwear under it all, instead of pantaloons that went to her knees. With careful instructions, her dressmakers had made her some light cotton shorts that tied at the waist and had greatly improved her quality of life.

I'll have time to think about my underwear later. Right

now, I have to deal with the baron.

Lily made her way downstairs slowly, with her entourage behind her. Pastor Vopler and Lons were almost stepping in time with each other (the two men had struck up a friendship right away). The young baron was waiting in the hall. When he saw the countess on the stairs, he leaped up, bowed, and offered his best, most polite greeting. Lily replied in a similar vein, backed up by Lons.

What brought you here, Baron Donter?

ଞ □ ଔ

Clive had been brought to Earton by greed, plain and simple. He was no longer concerned about his possible involvement in the affair of the slave traders. Several of his men had traveled to Altver and done some sniffing around. They learned that many of the pirates had been killed during the battle, including the captain who had been Donter's contact person. Once he knew that no one could incriminate him, the baron was able to breathe easily.

What bothered him was something else entirely: his men had learned of the expensive things Lilian Earton was sending to Altver for Torius Avermal to sell. The baron had a rough idea how much fine handmade lace went for. The usual price was determined by covering the length of the lace with gold coins. *How had the craftswomen in Earton learned to make such exquisite (and expensive) lace?*

The baron had never been particularly interested in Earton. *After all, what good could a woman come up with? Plenty, as it turns out.* He almost fainted dead away when, on his last neighborly visit, he saw real glass in the castle windows. Despite their bubbles and uneven thickness, glass windows made the castle look utterly luxurious. Glass was something few could afford. Clive's informer had told him that the countess' glassblowers were making colored glass and even glass mirrors. Clive had not believed it until the mirrors showed up for sale in Altver.

Now, the baron hoped to reach an agreement with the countess. In fact, he didn't know what he would do if she refused to take him into the business—he had seen her Virmans, and he knew how many of them there were. Given the current state of affairs, it would be madness to go up against Lilian Earton. The Virmans were known to fight like wild animals. The baron could easily imagine losing his head before he had a chance to explain why he was there.

Lily spoke first. "Lord Donter, I am pleased to see you."

The baron bowed again. The countess was a charming woman. She was tall, with a curvy body and a long, golden braid cascading down her back. As she smiled at him, her fabulously expensive emerald earrings and emerald wedding bracelet sparkled at him most appealingly.

Good Lord, just think how rich she is. I wish I could…but no, I'll have to think about that later!

The bowing and scraping took another fifteen minutes, but finally, the baron got down to business. "My Lady, some friends have come to visit me and do some hunting. In the heat of the hunt, we may possibly find ourselves on your land…"

Lily shrugged. "Possibly."

"Would you object…"

Lons was standing off to one side where the baron

could not easily see him. He shook his head ever so slightly.

Lily's face took on a pout. "I don't want a horde of drunk hunters running over my land with their dogs." She wrinkled her nose like a true blonde. "They make so much noise, and I feel so sorry for the poor beasts in my woods. Baron Donter, I'm sure an intelligent, sensitive man like yourself can understand that they suffer when you poke them with your sharp spears."

The baron's eyes were round as saucers. He had never heard such ideas before. "My Lady, we would never hunt your game! I just thought that if one of our own beasts accidentally…"

"No, no, no!" Lily frowned. "Hunting is entirely too bloody. And dirty. And smelly. I am most decisively against it. My husband already harasses the animals in our woods whenever he is here. I expect him home any day now, and it will start up again. Dirty men and baying hounds; it's awful!"

At this mention of the earl, the baron's face fell. Still, he made another attempt; the outcome was the same. Lily stood firm. When Erik ducked into the hall to give the countess a report on his work, Clive recalled the need for caution. That led him to the second item on his agenda.

"My Lady, I saw Baron Avermal not long ago."

"I hope the honorable baron is well?" Lily looked like a woman without any thoughts to weigh her head down.

"He told me about your agreement with him."

Oops!

Lily pricked up her ears.

"I thought that you and I could work together, too. I can always handle negotiations with people you'd rather not be seen talking to."

ॐ □ ಜ

Lily glanced at Lons. Outwardly, she was absolutely calm. Inside, however, her mind was working overtime. *Torius Avermal would never tell anyone about their agreement; he wasn't stupid. Donter has to be lying. But why? The answer is easy: he wants money.*

How did he find out about my agreement with Avermal? That was the important question. Lily didn't want to believe the leak was in her own house, but Torius was too sharp to share that kind of detail with the baron.

She blinked at him. "Lord Donter, what on earth are you talking about? What agreements? I'm just a simple woman living in the country. Perhaps you heard that Baron Avermal helped me when I went to Altver to buy supplies for the winter. That much is certainly true."

Clive squinted at her. "My Lady, he told me…"

Lons stepped forward. "Do you disbelieve what the countess just told you?" His voice was cold and haughty.

The baron backed away. "Of course not; don't think anything like that. I would never dare doubt… Well, I suppose I was misled. That's all."

"That must be what happened," Lily said, looking at peace with the world.

The baron gave up and turned the conversation back to hunting, but Lily was on the alert. As soon as they got rid of their guest, she turned to Lons.

"What is this? How could he have found out?"

Lons' face was thoughtful. "I'll think about it."

Lily didn't stand around waiting for him to finishing thinking. "There are two options," she announced. "Either Torius told him…"

"Which he would never have done," said Taris, who had stayed out of the room until Baron Donter was out of the castle. "Did you ask him to keep your agreement a secret?"

Lily nodded. Torius had promised to tell no one, and she had promised to continue trading with him.

Taris shook his head. "If Avermal didn't tell him, then one of us did."

"One of us?" Lons objected.

"Not you, Chevalier. But this is a large household with many servants. Someone told someone else, a third person overheard, and the gossip made its way to Donter."

Lily bit her lip. "What can we do to keep the information from going further?"

"Nothing." Taris' face was dark.

The countess wanted to curse out loud, but the men would have been shocked by her vocabulary. So, she said nothing.

৪০ ⬚ ୬৪

Clive, meanwhile, was allowing himself to use all the vocabulary at his disposal. *How dare she refuse me everything I asked for?* It killed him that there was nothing he could do about it. Her estate was too well guarded, and the countess was careful.

"Sir!" someone called out. Clive looked up. There was a figure standing in the road. The figure was filthy and wearing stinking clothes, but he was fairly sure it was a woman. He would have ridden right over her, but something urged him to be kind. He raised his whip at her.

The woman jumped out of the way and cried out, "Sir, do you want to know how you can get money out of Lilian Earton? Big money?"

He slowly lowered his whip.

❧   ❦

Calma hated the countess with her whole heart. She had once been governess to the young Miranda Catherine, and now she was assigned to clean the privies. The countess had taken everything away from her: her job, respect, and even her man. Damis Reis had stopped coming to see her. He didn't like how she smelled, so he stayed away. Calma knew exactly what was going on, and she hated the countess for it. All she could think of was revenge. She would get back at everyone who had wronged her, and she knew just how to do it. Baron Donter wanted money so she could use him. *Why not? As long as I'm able to hurt the blonde bitch! The baron is greedy and evil. I know he will listen to what I have to say.*

It didn't take Calma long to explain what she knew. The baron smiled; he had just one question for her. "How much do you want for your assistance?"

❧   ❦

The Duke of Falion re-read the king's letter and frowned. He was supposed to watch Adelaide Wells and make sure she didn't disappear before the delegation returned home. If she tried to run, he was authorized to have her killed.

This is interesting. I wonder what it has to do with Jerrison Earton?

If he had his way, Falion would have kept all women under the age of forty out of the delegation. The king had decided otherwise, however, and now it was up to Falion to deal with the consequences. Not that it would be a problem. For delicate jobs of that sort, the duke always had one or two men he could rely on. They tended to have rank—never more than a chevalier—and pockets full of nothing but lint… For the right price, they would keep all eyes on Adelaide Wells, and if something went wrong, they'd take care of her for good.

ஐ ☐ ஐ

Miranda Catherine lay in ambush. Lately, all the children had been playing at stalking each other: one child would hide, and when the others found him or her, the child would shoot a handful of peas at everyone and run off to hide again. The winner was whoever managed to hide the longest and hit as many enemies as possible with well-aimed peas. Most of the games were won by Loik, an eight-year-old Virman boy, but now it was Mirrie's turn to hide, and she had high hopes of winning.

Lily's teaching had stuck with her: a countess was the first among her people and had to always be the best at everything.

"My Lady!"

Miranda turned angrily to her left, where the whisper had come from.

"What do you want?"

"My Lady, the countess asked me to come find you."

The little girl sighed. "Can't she wait?"

"She said it's a surprise," Calma whispered.

Miranda wavered for a moment and then climbed out of her hiding place. "Fine. Let's go. Where is she?"

"Her ladyship said she would wait for you under the old sycamore tree—the one by the road."

Mirrie never even doubted the woman. Calma was someone she knew, and Lily was capable of coming up with anything. The little girl followed along behind the servant. Nobody tried to stop them.

ᚷ ᚲ

The sycamore tree was not far from the castle. There was no one on the road. There was no one under the tree. Miranda turned to Calma and frowned. "What's going on?"

Suddenly, someone jumped out from behind the old tree. A strong hand covered the girl's mouth.

"Is this the one?"

Calma nodded. "It's her."

They wrapped Miranda in a warm cloak and tied her tightly. Then they gagged her so expertly that the little girl could only blink her eyes.

"Good work. Let's go. The baron will reward you for this."

Mirrie tried to struggle, but it was no use. She was no match for a grown man; the trap snapped shut.

Clive had assumed that the child's absence wouldn't be noticed right away and that he would have time to get far, far away from Lilian Earton. He was almost right. No one would have realized that Mirrie was missing until dinnertime if it weren't for Loik. The small Virman seemed to have a nose for finding anything, anywhere. He had found Mirrie a few minutes before Calma did, but he was taking his time, planning his next move. As a result, he heard every word of Mirrie's conversation with the servant.

Loik never once doubted that the countess had something up her sleeve, but his curiosity drove him to find out what it was. So, he followed at a distance. He knew that the countess had planned to clear out the land around the castle to prevent anyone from sneaking up on her, but she hadn't gotten around to it yet. That meant that there were plenty of bushes and small hillocks for the boy to hide behind. He even saw the actual kidnapping, if from a distance. He watched Mirrie kick and scream as Calma, and the man tied her up. When he thought about what he should do, he saw two options: he could follow the kidnappers or run back to the castle. Loik chose the second. If he followed them and they caught him, they'd kill him outright. And they probably had horses waiting for them not far away so Loik took off running.

He covered the distance to the castle in a few short minutes and was already yelling when he hit the gate. Under a minute later, everyone knew that Miranda Catherine had been kidnapped. The servants gathered around, and Leis' soldiers began to ready their weapons.

Three minutes later, Lily was informed of the event when Emma flew into her study, wild-eyed and holding a Virman boy by the arm.

"My Lady!"

"Yes?"

"Miranda has been kidnapped!"

"WHAT?"

Lily held onto the edge of her desk to keep herself from screaming. She breathed in and breathed out.

You're a surgeon. A surgeon never panics during an operation.

She looked at Loik. "Tell me."

❧ ❧

The boy swallowed. He had seen the countess before, but she had just changed in front of his eyes. Gone was the nice lady who told them stories and spoiled them with candy. In her place, he saw a wild animal with predatory green eyes and sharp teeth. He knew the animal would catch those bad people; they would be sorry.

He shuddered, but Virmans are hardy folk. It didn't take long for him to recount how he had found Mirrie, how Calma drew her away from the castle, how he had followed them to the fork in the road over the hill and seen them tie the girl up.

Lily listened to him in silence. Then she told him he could go.

Once he was gone, she turned to Emma and issued a single order so loudly that Emma almost hit the ceiling. "Leis and Erik! SEND THEM TO ME!"

Emma flew off to do just that. While she waited, Lily paced her study floor. *My child! Kidnapped! I'll eat the heart of whoever is behind this!*

It took less than a minute for Leis and Erik to arrive. They had heard Loik shouting and had been on their way upstairs when Emma found them. They told Lily they wished Leif was there, too, but he was overseeing work at the salt pits. Right behind them was Lons, followed by Taris.

"What happened?"

"Mirrie's been kidnapped."

"Who did it?"

"I don't know. Less than an hour has passed. Can we catch them?"

Before Lily was finished talking, Erik wheeled and ran out the door. His voice could be heard echoing throughout the castle, calling his men to arms.

Lily stopped Leis before he could follow. "I'm coming with you."

"My Lady, that's not…"

She took a deep breath. Don't yell at him. Don't get hysterical. Don't get angry.

"Leis, there may be a situation where you need me. I can protect myself."

Lons spoke up at her side. "I'm coming, too, My Lady." Lily

saw that she couldn't stop him, so she nodded.

"Be ready in five minutes. And call for Jaimie; I want him, too."

"What about your Khangan healer?"

"He's too old to move fast. A ride like this wouldn't be good for him. Let's go!" Lily ran from the room before anyone could object.

Once again, Lily rejoiced that she had insisted on wearing pants that looked like a skirt. All she had to do was grab her medical bag, and she was ready to ride

What about a weapon?

That was a problem. Lily had already lost a great deal of her excess weight, but she wasn't ready for hand-to-hand combat, and the firearms she did know how to use hadn't been invented yet.

What do I have available?

She grabbed the only thing she could think of—three glass vials in a fur-lined pouch—and carefully placed them in her bag. It was just a little something she had been working on in her laboratory. She had requisitioned one of Leif's firebombs when she realized by the smell that it contained oil. Leif had objected, but in the end, he poured out a little of the liquid for her. Lily had split the oil between three vials, which she filled to the top with pure alcohol. Then she attached fuses to the homemade bombs. Lily knew that she could light them and throw them if she had to. She had tested a small amount of the mixture in her laboratory and was pleased with the results.

On her way downstairs, she ran into Martha. "My girl!

Take care of yourself!"

Lily embraced the old woman and kissed her cheek. "Dear Martha, pray for me…and for Miranda."

Martha made the sign of Aldonai.

Just then, Pastor Vopler came running up the stairs. "My Lady, you are a woman…"

"It's my child they kidnapped. Pray for us, Pastor." And she was gone.

≈

Everyone was in the courtyard: two companies of ten men each, half of them on horseback, and around forty Virmans. Erik and Leis glanced at each other when Lily came running up.

Leis spoke first. "My Lady, if you come with us you will have to obey my orders."

She nodded.

Still unsure, he added, "The least disobedience could end up costing you or Mirrie your lives."

Lily nodded again. "Leis, I understand, and I will follow your orders. Let's go. Mirrie's in danger! I promise I will obey you!" With that, she swung herself up onto her Avarian stallion.

Erik measured her with a doubtful look, but he said nothing. Instead, he pulled on the leash he was holding. At the end was Mirrie's puppy. Next to it were several more Virman dogs, all the size of small bears.

Leis shouted at his men, and they moved off. There were not enough horses to go around, so Leis and his men rode ahead as fast as they could, while the Virmans marched behind--almost as fast as an average horse. The kidnappers couldn't number more than twenty, the leaders estimated, or Leif's scouts would have noticed them. Everyone's goal was to catch the evildoers as quickly as possible. Leis had two more Virman dogs with him—a puppy in the saddle with him and a larger one that ran alongside. Once they reached the sycamore tree, they would let the dogs try to catch Mirrie's scent.

The Avarian balked at Lily's commands, but soon he stopped working against her, and Lily breathed a sigh of relief. She was already a more confident horsewoman, and she hoped the horse would manage to keep her aboard, even if the search took hours. She had never ridden the animal for a long period of time because she feared her weight would cause it harm. The stallion was built for speed, not for strength and endurance like the local nags. He was also worth quite a lot of money.

Leis put two men on either side of Lily. They covered the distance to the sycamore in three minutes, and the dogs began sniffing around. In no time, they picked up the scent and began to follow it without barking. Watching them work, Lily understood why the Virmans loved their dogs—none of them barked. They simply raced ahead where the track led them, and only death would stop them from following it wherever it led.

Lily bit her lip. Mirrie, my precious girl! How stupid I was to relax and forget about the danger all around us. This is what I get for forgetting. I'll never make a mistake like this again if I can just have you back! I have to find my girl!

Miranda Catherine Earton was furious. She was so angry that she would have spat if she hadn't been gagged. Strangely enough, the child wasn't frightened for a minute. Mirrie had been raised by people who always took care of her every whim—never raising a hand against her—and all of a sudden, some stranger dared to kidnap her. She knew in her mind that they might kill her, but she didn't feel it in her heart. Like most children, she didn't believe she could die.

Instead of shaking with fear, she calculated her chances of escaping successfully. She knew she couldn't do anything at the moment; she couldn't even scream. She wiggled against the ropes that bound her, and tears came to her eyes. She fought them back; Lily was sure to save her. She was smart; she would find Mirrie, no matter where they took her.

She thought back to Lily's stories about everything under the sun—about the women who worked as spies for their kings. Little by little, using fairy tales, Lily had given the children some very basic ideas about how to survive anywhere, in any world. As soon as Mirrie stopped crying in anger and calmed down, she remembered several important things. First, she needed to pretend to be weak and helpless. *If your enemies think you are weak, they won't expect you to do anything to save yourself, which, of course, is a big mistake.*

Miranda Catherine had been caught unaware, but not unarmed. Like all the rest of the children, she had started carrying a small knife to use in the games they played. It wasn't more than a boot knife, but it was sharp enough to cut through rope, as long as no one knew she had it.

She thought quickly. No one would expect the earl's daughter to have a knife, would they? Calma!

Mirrie almost howled in frustration. She balled her hands into fists.

You stinking traitor! You just wait! When Lily finds out, she'll get you.

Meanwhile, Calma felt quite pleased with herself. Life was full of wonderful and unexpected surprises. On the horizon, she saw the Donter estate, plenty of money and—if all went well—a comfortable role as the baron's lover. *Why not? I'm young, good-looking, well-behaved and an expert in bed.* The baron would also need someone to keep an eye on the little girl. Calma would make herself useful right away, and later on, he wouldn't want to part with her.

If she closed her eyes, Calma could already see the baron's castle, golden jewelry, the envy of other women… Best of all, she would have her revenge on that damned fat woman who had dared to degrade her position. In all honesty, Calma didn't even remember all the times Mirrie had been left to her own devices under her care. She forgot about how, on the way to Earton, she ignored her charge while sneaking off to make love with Damis Reis. She forgot that it was her fault the little girl almost got murdered alongside her stepmother. Like most people, she forgot the things she was ashamed of, but no one ever forgets an insult.

The baron was waiting for them off to the side of the road. He had picked a place where he couldn't be seen from the castle, and none of the local peasants were likely to run into him. The kidnappers were in no hurry. Calma had promised them that no one would notice Mirrie's absence until that evening. She was right. No one would have noticed. Miranda often skipped lunch and, like Lily, ran into the kitchen later to grab a bite. Martha objected strongly to such irregular habits, but it was impossible to control Miranda now that she had a group of friends to play with. The nanny resorted to feeding the little girl lunch whenever she could catch her and hoping that breakfast and dinner made up for the rest. On a regular day, it would be evening before anyone started looking for Mirrie, and they might not have considered kidnapping as a possible explanation until morning came.

❧ ❧

Clive was pleased as he could be. Miranda Catherine Earton's presence meant that he could demand a high price from the Countess of Earton—a very high price. Calma told him that the countess would not write to her husband about the kidnapping since he knew nothing of her latest initiatives on the estate. She had said the last thing the countess would want was for the earl to find out she had let Miranda fall into the hands of kidnappers. Plus, according to Calma, the countess was like a mother to the girl; she would give anything to get her back. There would be no haggling. As soon as the baron reached his home, he would send a runner to name his price to Lilian Earton.

There was a rustling in the bushes, and three people appeared: two soldiers (one of them carrying something wrapped up like a package) and Calma.

Clive, seated comfortably on a cape belonging to one of his

followers, looked up at the man. "You got her?"

"Yes, My Lord." The man placed the package on the ground by the baron. It was sniffling and whining.

Calma placed herself in front of the baron. "My lord, I have done as you wished."

He nodded. "Wonderful. You have done me a good service, woman."

Calma looked down and curtsied, so she missed the look the baron exchanged with one of his followers. They had worked it all out before she got there. The man came up behind her silently and… Calma didn't even have time to cry out when he grabbed her by the neck and stuck something sharp through her back, right next to her shoulder blade. It was done neatly, without too much blood.

The baron grimaced. Calma had been facing him, so her eyes were on his until they closed in death. She saw her true murderer. He did not raise the knife, but he gave the order.

He waved a hand. "Get her away from here."

The men dragged Calma away by the legs and left her in the bushes. The baron looked down at the package. "Open it up. I want to see her."

The soldiers obeyed. He looked down and saw a little girl, about seven or eight years old, her hair sticking up and her face wet with tears. She was pretty, with blue eyes and dark hair, but her clothes were strange: a skirt, blouse and warm jacket, all cut for comfort instead of for fashion. The baron would never have guessed that the skirt was actually a pair of pants, and Calma was no longer around to inform him.

He also had no way of knowing that Miranda wore a boot knife tied to the ankle of one boot and that she could get to it quickly since no one had bothered to tie her hands, just her arms. She might have been tear-stained and disheveled, but her arms and legs would work just fine once she freed them.

Her brain was working just fine, too, so she quickly started crying again.

"Well, well there…" the baron said, patting her awkwardly on the head. "Everything will be fine, my dear, no one will hurt you."

The crying got louder.

"You'll be staying with me at my house for a little bit, and then we'll see how things go…" The baron stopped. He had been thinking about looking for a bride, but there were no fine ladies to be found in that part of the kingdom.

Why ride all the way to Altver if I've got this girl right here?

Then he reflected that Miranda might be more than he could lay claim to. Her father was close to the throne, and the king was very fond of Jerrison Earton for some reason. Clive would have to think it over.

Lily was confident in the saddle. She didn't ride ahead of the group, but she didn't lag behind, either. Her mind was racing, filled with the worst possible images: a child's fingers attached to the ransom note, children kidnapped to force their parents to do something. *Could there be anything worse than blackmail using a child?* Her thoughts jumped from blackmail to the extremists who practice it. She remembered a videotape her father had shown her of how "peaceful Islamists" treated people. She began to shake.

I swear to God, there will never be any of that in this world. I will put a stop to extremism before people even get started. And I will never negotiate with terrorists and blackmailers.

Lily surmised that, so far, the kind of extremism she had seen in her own world did not exist in the Middle Ages of Ativerna. She just remembered the explosions and hostage situations she had seen on television, and she remembered her father saying that the government didn't have the courage to do anything about it. He had used a very short, very bad word to describe the government. Lily had been listening, and what she picked up was that you can't negotiate with terrorists and blackmailers, no matter what they threaten you with, because they are never satisfied.

Lily knew what she would do to the people who had taken her child. She would destroy them and leave their bodies at the crossroads, labeled for all to see. She didn't care if the pastor disapproved. She would do as her father taught her. *When you respond decisively, terrorists stop taking hostages.* He had three rules: never agree to the terrorists' terms, destroy them like rabid animals, and destroy their families and their villages.

It was a terrible, bloody lesson, but Lily—or Aliya Skorolenok—had every intention of following her father's advice. Even if it cost her soul, she would not allow the horror of terrorism to take root in her new world.

If only Mirrie is still alive!

Suddenly, the dogs began to growl. It was a frightening sound.

Leis turned to Lily. "They aren't far away. Stay in the back, My Lady."

The countess nodded. Her hand reached for her knife. She had practiced at the castle—alone, with no one watching— and she knew she could still throw a knife-like Aliya. She would rather not fight for her life against a hardened soldier, but she wasn't completely defenseless, either.

I can do this.

The dogs turned from the road, so the men dismounted. Leis ordered two of them to lead the horses, so Lily stayed back with them. Her Avarian stallion would obey no one but the countess.

When she realized where they were, Lily began to suspect Baron Donter was behind the kidnapping.

Why would he do that? What would he stand to gain? Doesn't he know what will happen to him once we catch him?

Then she remembered that if it weren't for Loik, they wouldn't have noticed Mirrie's absence yet, and the kidnappers would be much farther away. She imagined riding up to the baron's castle and demanding that he give back her child. It wouldn't have gone well. She wanted to ask Leis how people usually treated hostages in this world, but she was afraid to talk to him just then. He was the commander leading the chase, and the men needed to know that he was the only leader. Lily would have to stay out of the way for the time being.

Just then, she heard the sound of swords being drawn. Lily looked at the men who were leading the horses. They hurriedly tied the horses to some nearby trees and reached for their own weapons.

Without hesitating for a moment, the countess tied up her own horse. Jaimie was near her, and Lons was already in the fight. She could hear swords clashing up ahead, but she couldn't see anything because of all the horses and the trees.

₭ ℣

Leis ran right into the baron, who had Miranda in front of him. He instantly sized up the situation in the clearing. The baron had ten men. It was clear he hadn't planned on encountering resistance on his way out of Earton. Leis had at least two dozen men, all of them hardened soldiers. A few former peasants had ridden with him, but they were back with the horses and the countess. Leis was not concerned for her—the baron and his men would never be able to fight through that far.

He also knew that Erik and his men were not far behind. Once they arrived, the baron would look like a bloody rag. For now, Leis wanted to contain Donter and his men in the clearing.

Sword clashed against sword as the baron's men tried to create an opening. Two of Leis' archers stood at the edge of the clearing, bows at the ready, watching the fight. The baron's men were strong and desperate, and none of them turned to run…except the baron. As soon as the first blows were struck, he grabbed Mirrie around the waist and pressed her against the nearest pine tree. If his men won, he still had to keep her from running off. If his enemies won, he would use her as a pawn for securing his safety. Leis knew no one would catch Baron

Donter waving a sword around, risking his life.

⁎ □  

Lons was fighting a dandy in a blue tunic. He waved his sword away and, using his left hand, stuck a dagger into the man's ribcage under his arm. He watched the body fall and pressed on. This was no elegant tournament; men were fighting three against one and striking their opponents in the back, the legs, or anywhere else they could reach. It was ugly and dirty, but no one cared. Each man fought the enemy in front of him, finished him off and ran to help a friend. Swords clashed once more.

It was over soon, and Lons found himself face to face with the baron, who was holding Mirrie. He had a dagger dangerously close to her neck.

"If you take another step forward I'll kill her!"

What can I do?

There was only one thing.

"My Lady!"

⁎ □  

Lily had not been involved in the fighting. She had stayed with the horses, and no one had tried to take them. All ten of the baron's men were kept busy by Leis' two dozen soldiers. It wasn't much of a match, especially considering that the Earton men all wore light chain mail, while the Donter men had nothing over their clothes. The chain mail had cost her dearly, but Lily believed that if you don't take care of your own army, you are essentially taking care of someone else's army.

When she heard Lons' cry, she did not go running to find him. She walked, slowly and calmly. The countess was in no hurry. Her heart fell when she entered the clearing. The ground was covered with bodies. Her eyes scanned the trees on the other side of the clearing. That is when Lily saw her. *Miranda.* The baron had a long, sharp dagger at her throat. His hand was shaking. *Is he unsure of himself, or is he on the verge of hysteria?* Both conditions were dangerous. *Can I do this? I have to!*

The countess turned and saw the archers at their posts. She spoke softly. "Keep your arrows on your strings. Shoot him as soon as he lets go of her."

She was relieved to see they obeyed. Now she had to get the baron to move the knife away from Miranda's throat. She was the only one who could do it.

The countess walked toward the baron. Her men watched her, and it seemed they were under a spell. It was her turn. The fighting was over; it was time for talking.

ဆဝ ❧ ဌ

Clive was terrified. They wanted to kill him, and they would probably succeed very soon. His men were all dead.

No! I won't give up! I'm a baron. How dare they threaten me! They'll have to kill the girl, too! I'll take her with me! They can all go to Maldonaya, for all I care!

He noticed the soldiers hung back, and then he saw her as she came out from between the trees—Her Ladyship Lilian Earton. The tall blonde approached him slowly. Everyone in the clearing could hear the yellow leaves crunching under her feet. They could even hear the baron's heavy breathing.

"I'll kill her! I'll kill her unless you leave!" he screeched. "I swear to Aldonai I will do it!"

The countess was just five paces away from him, just far enough that they could not touch each other. When she spoke, it was in a soft, velvety voice with the words drawn out for effect.

"You won't kill her. What would be the point?"

Clive had expected anything but this. *No point?*

"I'll kill her!"

"Fine. What do you want in order for her to live? A horse? Money? Me?" Her voice drifted over the clearing, calming him, wrapping him in peace, relaxing his muscles. Clive began to regain his faculties. *Truly, what was I afraid of? I am the Baron Donter, and the countess is just a woman—beautiful to look at, but a stupid woman at the end of the day.* He relaxed a bit.

"Have your men give me a horse and then back off. I'll leave with her. I won't kill her, and I won't hurt her."

"Why did you take her?"

"We can talk about that later." Clive gave what he considered to be a wily smile.

Lily sighed. "Is it money you want? Let her go. I'll pay." She slowly unhooked the sack of money from her belt. She held it out, hypnotizing the baron like a snake hypnotizes a bird. With one finger, she removed the loop from around the sack and turned it over. Gold coins and amber fell on the grass at her feet.

"Let the girl go…"

Clive leaned forward. The gold had a powerful effect on him.

The hand that held the knife trembled and moved away from the girl as if it wanted to pick up the gold pieces. It wasn't enough of an opening for a man with a sword, but it was plenty of space for the archers. Leis had not told them to let the baron live, and the archers quite reasonably decided that the countess wouldn't mind if he died. Two arrows twanged.

The baron cried out. One arrow went just wide of the mark and grazed his arm, leaving droplets of blood on the grass. The second arrow hit his shoulder and pinned him to the tree. Mirrie dropped to the ground and rolled over to where Lily stood.

The woman fell to her knees and grabbed the girl. "Mirrie! I was so worried about you! Come here, baby..."

Mirrie buried her face in Lily's shoulder and sobbed, "Mama!"

Lily kept her arms around the child. Where did this maternal love come from? I suppose I shouldn't be surprised. Miranda is the only person who doesn't want anything from me. She just loves me for who I am, not for the old Lilian.

Lily stroked the little girl's hair. More than anything, she wanted to lock her up in the castle and never let her out again. In fact, she wished they could be there right now.

Off to one side, Leis was dressing down the archers, who objected that they were professionals and knew what they were doing. Lily paid none of them any attention. Two soldiers separated the howling baron from his tree, leaving the arrow in his shoulder. One of his arms hung useless at his side. The thought crossed Lily's mind that he had tendon damage. The soldiers tied a tourniquet around his arm but only to keep him from dying before his time came.

Jaimie slipped over to the countess like a shadow. "Give Miranda to me, My Lady. I will watch her for you."

Lily sighed and gratefully put the child in his outstretched arms. Then she turned to the baron. "Shall we talk now, Lord Donter?" At the sound of her voice, the men around her shuddered. She continued, all sweetness and honey. "This nice man here is going to stand next to you," she pointed at Erik, who eagerly took a step forward, "and he is going to hit that arrow every time you lie to me." "The rest of us will be interested to see if you bleed to death or if the pain kills you."

Erik rubbed his hands together. He seemed to agree that this was exactly the right way to deal with people who kidnapped children.

"Let me go!" the baron croaked. "How dare you threaten me! I will complain to the king!"

Lily nodded at Erik, and a howl of pain rose up over the clearing. The Virman hadn't hit the arrow—he had pushed it back and forth in the baron's shoulder, causing as much pain as he could. The horses snorted and stamped. Jaime put his hands over Miranda's ears.

Lily waited a few minutes until the baron stopped screaming. Once he was reduced to whimpering, she inquired politely, "Why did you kidnap Miranda?"

The only reply she got was an ugly oath. Erik didn't bother waiting for an order. Again, the baron's howls went up into the evening sky.

The countess bit her lip and balled her hands into fists, but otherwise, she remained outwardly calm. It was horrible to watch a man being tortured. She felt like something inside her own soul was cracking, something that would never heal.

To hell with it! Miranda matters more to me than anything! For her sake, I would break three men like the baron.

Lily imagined how the bastard could have harmed her little girl, and it made her clench her fists until her nails cut into her palms, drawing blood. Mirrie was accustomed to being safe and loved and given free rein. Evil things were said about the baron. He could have hurt her physically in any number of ways.

I can't think about that. I have the right to torture him until I learn what I want to know.

⋐ ⋑

Like all sadists, the baron couldn't handle the least bit of pain. He cracked like a dry branch. The kidnapping wasn't his idea. It was forced on him. Calma made him do it. She was a witch following orders from Maldonaya. She must have darkened his mind. Acting freely, he would never have risked a falling out with the lovely and charming countess. He tried to kiss her hand, but Erik hauled him back by the neck.

As she listened to the baron's wandering explanation of what happened, Lily's blood pressure began to rise. When she discovered that he had planned to demand all of her craftsmen as a ransom for Miranda, she boiled over. She had spent so much time teaching people how to make useful things, and this big bully thought he could just walk in and take it all from her.

What do I do with him now? I'd like to leave his entrails spread out under the trees, but what does the law say?

"My Lady?"

As always, Lons had quietly taken up his position by her side. Lily looked at him with gratitude, which only doubled when he handed her a flask of cold water.

"Drink. Miranda is fine. She wasn't hurt."

Lily nodded. "I know. What do we do with this louse?"

Lons was surprised by the question. "Execute him," he said shortly.

"But will the king ask me about it later?"

Her advisor shook his head. "No. You are a countess. Miranda can tell anyone who will listen that she was kidnapped. You have my word, as well, and I am a chevalier. Even Leis can be a witness. He comes from a long line of soldiers, six generations back. Erik is a warrior, which puts him at the same level as a chevalier."

Lily nodded. "Then let's do it. Who will take on the job?"

"Erik, of course."

Lons was utterly unflappable as if the torture and death were taking place somewhere else, instead of right in front of him, as if he hadn't just risked his life in a swordfight. Once again, Lily reflected on the difference in mentality and how calm medieval men were in the face of death.

She called for Erik, who came over and bowed so that she could talk to him more easily. "You should rest, My Lady."

"We have been considering what to do with the baron."

"Execute him." It wasn't a question. There were no pacifists in Lily's new world.

"How should it be done? I want every dirty bastard in the area to know that my daughter, my people, and my home are off limits!"

Erik's reply was immediate. "Pull out his ribs and impale him on a stake. That is what we do with those who would hurt a child. Once he's dead, cut off his head, flay the body, salt it well and send it to Altver for Avermal to display in the town square with a notice about what the man tried to do."

Lily shuddered. She would have just killed the baron outright without torturing him further.

"What about his castle?"

"Find out how many men he has and pay them a visit," Erik said, explaining simple truths as he saw them. "Search for whatever he had hidden there. I'm sure we can find plenty of dirt on him."

Lily nodded. That much she understood. "Do I have to go with you?"

Both men shook their heads. "No, My Lady. Leif and I will go. We have done this before. You should write to the king and to Avermal so that the law is on our side."

"I will go, too. I can look through his papers," said Lons. Lily looked around at these men with gratitude. Her new world had no telephones, internet or indoor plumbing. The customs were bloody, and the laws were harsh. A man who tried to hurt a child faced a horrifying death. Women were not allowed to fight, because it wasn't *women's work.* Men were supposed to kill and die. That was what they knew. In the world she had come from, everything was convenient, people felt safe most of the time, and if anyone died protecting a child, it was likely to be a woman.

Which world is more honest?

Lily looked up at Lons, Leis, and Erik. "When do you start?"

"As soon as he's dead," Erik shrugged.

The baron realized they were talking about him. He had stopped screaming and was just whimpering monotonously. A dark, wet spot on his pants was growing larger.

"And Leif?"

"He'll be here by then. I will stay to guard the castle," said Leis.

Lily looked down. There was nothing more for her to do. The men knew these things better than she did. "Then I will go home with Mirrie and write to the king."

Everyone approved that plan.

ଶ □ ଔ

Jamie helped put Miranda on Lily's horse. The little girl huddled close to Lily. "I knew you would save me."

"You knew everything, did you?" the countess teased her. "Perhaps you can tell me, Miranda Catherine, why you left the castle walls. How many times have I told you to stay in the courtyard?"

"But I was with Calma!"

Lily bit her lip. No one was insured against treason. She held the girl tighter. "Promise me something."

"What?"

"That you will never go past the wall without asking me."

"I promise. I was so scared!"

"So was I," Lily admitted.

৪০ ☐ ୡ

At home, they were met by Martha, who looked pale and small, and the pastor, who was smiling and trying to keep his son from jumping on Mirrie. Lily handed the girl over to her nanny in hopes of her getting a bath, eating, and perhaps even sleeping. She promised to come see her after a while. Then she asked Pastor Vopler to follow her to her study, where she answered his cautious question very simply:

"We know everything now. The baron kidnapped Miranda and was planning to demand a ransom."

"I assume he is no longer living, My Lady?"

The countess nodded. "We caught up with them. There was a fight." She said nothing else about what had taken place in the clearing, in case the pastor disapproved.

"You have done well, My Lady. The baron was a doubtful person at best. It was a strange story, but I don't believe he was even a Donter by blood."

Lily shrugged. Then a thought occurred to her. "Did he have a highly-placed protector by chance? I would not like to find myself in conflict with someone important over this."

The pastor shook his head and explained to Lily that the king was the only authority over his nobles. In her new world, there was no system of vassals. A nobleman could hire himself in service to another nobleman, but if he owned his own land, he only answered to the king. Lily had never thought about this before, and she wasn't sure what it meant for her personally.

Just then, there was a knock at the door. Jamie came in, looking pale and disheveled. "I must speak with you, My Lady."

The countess held up a hand. "Let me finish with the pastor first and then..."

Jamie interrupted, "My Lady, I must speak with the pastor, too."

Lily glanced at the pastor, and he nodded in agreement. "Then sit down and tell me what's the matter," she said to Jamie, nodding at a stool in front of her desk.

Jamie sat down and put a small jewelry box on her desk. "Look at this, My Lady." He opened the lid. Lily bent over the box and saw a scroll, three rings, a bracelet bearing a family crest and a small portrait of a woman who looked just like Jamie.

"Yes?"

"Look at the crest, My Lady."

She studied the crest on each ring and on the bracelet. They were the same. She looked up at her young healer in wonder.

"They are old signet rings. One belonged to the old baron, one to his son, and one to his daughter. The bracelet was her engagement gift. That's her portrait. She wrote the account you'll find in the scroll. It was witnessed properly."

The pastor held out his hand for the scroll. Jamie gave it to him, and the room fell silent as the pastor read. Jamie fidgeted with his hands. Lily thought about how many problems it would solve if Jamie really was...

Pastor Vopler looked up from his reading. "My Lady, the statement is clear, and it was, in fact, duly witnessed as the law requires." He handed it to Lily, who scanned its contents.

Someone named Marianna Donter had written a clearly worded account of her life, her marriage to Chevalier Cleins, how he took her last name, how he beat her… Her tale was told in few words, but Lily could feel the pain behind them. Soon the story became more interesting. Marianna stated that Baron Donter (her husband and the father of the man Lily had just executed) killed her family so that he could take over the title. She described how her husband boasted to her of his illicit affair with his own sister, which had been going on for a year, meaning that his sister's son was born through incest.

Lily gave a low whistle. "Pastor?"

"If this is true, My Lady, you have done a holy deed. Aldonai does not approve of incest."

"That may be so, but does he expect us to kill people whose parents committed incest?"

The pastor frowned. Lily frowned back at him and continued reading. When the young woman discovered that she was pregnant, she decided to run away, knowing full well that her life would be worth nothing once the heir was born. She did not describe how she escaped the castle, but Lily suspected she had help from a local herbalist or healer.

God only knows who Jamie's father is…

When she finished reading, she looked up at the pastor. "So that's how it is. We've had the true Baron Donter living here all along." She turned to Jamie. "Couldn't you have told us before?"

"Would you have believed me, My Lady?" Jamie

straightened his back and smiled. Suddenly, Lily could see the noble features in his face.

"What about that story you told me about your grandmother who was an herbal healer?"

"My Lady, can you see now why I withheld the truth?"

Lily did see. She had been a complete stranger to him, and he needed to get out of Altver, so he made up a story to induce her to take him along.

"What do you want me to do now?"

"I want you to write to the king, My Lady."

Lily nodded. She didn't ask him why he couldn't write on his own behalf. It was clear enough: the king was far away, and she still wasn't sure that Donter hadn't had a protector somewhere. Kidnapping Jess Earton's daughter would have been an insane step to take unless he had someone who could gain the king's ear. She would have to be careful.

"I will write," Lily promised. "We must find out if you can recover your title. For now, let's wait to see what the Virmans bring back. If they find compromising information about the baron, everything will be much easier."

Jamie nodded. "May I go now, My Lady?"

"Yes."

The pastor bowed his way out, too. Lily gave up trying to write any important letters right then and went to see Miranda, who was in bed. She got in bed with her and told her a story, and then another...

When did I start to care so deeply about this little girl? I never noticed it happening! I don't know anything at all in this world, but I know that Miranda is mine.

Chapter 4
Why the Hell Am I Writing to You?

Richard had never seen his cousin so upset. "What on earth happened?"

"I got a letter."

"From Aldonai, by the looks of it?"

"From my cow."

"And?"

"Read it for yourself." Jess handed him the letter, and Richard looked it over. The first thing he noticed was the signature—it was firm and even, without the curlicues ladies at court loved to use. It looked to be the handwriting of a man, and a tough one at that. Then he read the letter's contents. When he got to the end, he stared at Jess. He had no idea what to say.

"Is this some kind of joke?"

Instead of a reply, Jess handed him a second letter. This one was from Richard's father.

To the Earl of Earton,

Judging by the conditions of your estate, either you wish to see your wife and daughter dead, or you are incapable of seeing anything past the end of your nose. I will not recall you from the delegation, but I intend to have a serious talk with you when you get back. The countess has sent me a copy of the letter she dispatched to you, and I have verified her every word. My envoy's investigation revealed many other interesting details.

As your king, I hereby order you to refrain from issuing any instructions regarding the management of Earton. The countess will be at court in the spring, and I expect you will wish to meet with her in person when you return from your trip. Until then, I hope you will find time to write and explain to me what caused you to treat your wife this way.

Now, as regards the estate, you have my permission to write to the countess that you are pleased with and completely approve of her decisions, nothing else. The rest we will discuss when I see you again.

Edward the Eighth, by the grace of Aldonai, King of Ativerna.

This was followed by the royal seal and the king's own sprawling signature.

Richard blinked. "What has gotten into Father?"

"I'd like to know what's gotten into my cow!"

Richard snorted. "Did you read the letter? What got into her was a couple of hired killers and a pack of slave traders and contrabanders. Isn't that enough?"

"That's ridiculous. How could people be running contraband in Earton? It's in the middle of nowhere."

"Apparently they found amber there—amber. Looks like you're a fool. All the times you went down there, you couldn't see the truth about your own wife."

"I saw her. She's a cow."

"You should have taken your eyes off her and looked around. What were you doing all those times you visited?"

Jess let loose a string of elaborate oaths. "What do I want with that place? Earton's never been anything but a drain on my finances.

The hunting is decent, but that's all."

"How could you not notice that your manager was stealing from you?"

Jess' face lit up. "Let's look at the accounts!"

Richard stopped him in his tracks. "Are you hoping that the books are in order and your wife got it all mixed up?"

Jess said nothing. That was exactly what he hoped.

ॐ ☐ ೦੩

Richard glared at him. He didn't believe for a minute that Lilian Earton had made a mistake. And it soon became clear that he was correct. The account books had been clearly marked by Etor: "For the earl," "For the syndicate," and "For myself." Their contents were different, as well. In the first book, Earton was prospering. In the second book, it was clear that the manager was a thief. The third book listed in detail how much Etor had taken and from where. Jess read through it and saw that there was no way around it. He had been tricked, fleeced.

That was just half the trouble. "What about this amber?" he looked up at Richard. "Where the hell did it come from?"

"It's a rare thing, but I've heard of people finding it on beaches."

Jess shook his head. "How did she put all this together?"

"You go down there for three days twice a year. She lives there year-round. So she kept her eyes open. What's the surprise about that?"

"But you've *seen* her!" Jess begged, looking up at his cousin.

Richard was merciless. "You know what?" He paused for a moment. "If she managed to figure all this out and put a stop to it, then I'm not sure if she's the cow or you're the donkey." Jess muttered some ugly things, but Richard paid no attention. "You'd be better off thinking about who could have wanted to poison your pregnant wife and then when that didn't work, sent in a hired killer."

"I wish I knew." Jess lifted his eyes to the image of Aldonai in the corner. Unfortunately, his god had no answers for him.

୫ ଓ

Erik and Leif were pleased. The Virman warriors didn't mind working on Lily's projects around the estate, but what they really loved to do was swing their axes.

The Donter estate was not large, and the castle was more like a large, fortified house. The Virmans had no plans to storm the castle, such as it was, because they suspected with the baron gone, the servants had run off to take care of their own business. They expected to find an open gate or unguarded window.

When Ingvar, their spy, returned, he had good news. "There is an unlocked gate. It looks like a back entrance for the servants so that the main gates don't have to be opened every time someone comes or goes."

"Take us there."

They all agreed that Leif would lead the operation. Leif was overjoyed to be going on a raid instead of overseeing work at the salt works on the coast. During the ride to the Donter estate, he told Erik that the process of evaporating sea water to make salt was a good one and that he hoped to take the technology back to Virma one day, but he was bored to death by the monotony of it.

The Virmans made no noise. They carried no torches and spoke not a word as they slipped through the gate. Their chain mail was covered by dark capes, and they held their weapons close to avoid making any noise.

Once inside the gate, they saw that the castle was not exactly imposing. It looked more like a tower with some outbuildings, all surrounded by a wall. They got over the wall easily and split up. Leif pointed to where he wanted the men to go: the stable, the kennel, the barn... The whole operation took all of twenty minutes before the Virmans were inside the castle.

One of the baron's toadies who had survived the battle in the woods—most likely by running away as soon as it started—told them that the servants had been having a wonderful time with wine, women, and food from the baron's table. Erik believed him. The man had seen what happened to Baron Donter, so it never entered his mind to lie to the Virmans, who let him off with an easy death.

Leif and Erik agreed they would have to kill off the baron's guards. Thirty men left without a leader would pose a threat to the surrounding area. Unlikely to look for gainful employment, they would ransack the castle and drink the baron's wine until it was gone. Then they would head to Earton to see what they could steal since there was nowhere else for them to go.

Both men knew the countess would not approve, but they decided not to tell her. The official version would be that the guards died in a pitched battle with Earton's forces. Leif and Erik recognized Lilian Earton's authority over them, but they believed that war was a man's business.

And it was time to get to business.

The operation didn't go off without any casualties, of course. Men on both sides were killed. As it turned out, not all of the guards were drunk, and some of them were even able to find their swords. Still, the Virmans had the upper hand, and they used it mercilessly. In the end, thirty of Donter's soldiers and four Virmans lay dead. Of those, three had died during the battle, and the fourth was mortally wounded by a servant who tossed a cauldron of boiling water on him. They got the servant with a blow to the head and did their own comrade the final honor of ending his suffering.

When it was all over, Leif inspected the castle. He found much to interest him. In the basement, which had been fitted out as a dungeon (much more awful than the one in Earton), he found about forty peasants whom the baron had intended to sell into slavery, supposedly for their debts. In Donter's office, they found a large number of books and scrolls. Erik tossed them all in a trunk and told two of his men to take it all to the countess. They also found weapons and money.

It was not their first time ransacking a castle, so they knew what they were doing. This time, however, they would give everything they found to the countess. None of them doubted that Lilian Earton would turn over their fair share.

The Virmans' attack had started before dawn, and by the time the sun came up, the estate was in new hands. They split into two groups: Erik would stay behind in Donter, while Leif would take the trophies back home to Earton.

∞ ⃞ ∞

Once again, Hans stood before his king. "Your Majesty, it is as we thought. The man and his cousin planned the countess' murder together. She is the earl's mistress, a woman named Adelaide Wells. When she took up with the earl, the two of them decided that it would be a fine thing for her to become the countess. Alex started looking for someone to do the job."

"Do we have any evidence?"

"Of Adelaide's involvement? No, Your Majesty."

"What does that mean?"

"His words are not enough. He says one thing, she will say another... You know how these affairs are, Your Majesty."

Edward did understand. It was a bad business, and Adelaide would deny every bit of it.

"Are there any letters?"

"I'm afraid the rogues were careful, Your Majesty. They knew what would happen if they were caught, so they did their best to leave nothing written down."

Edward frowned. He held a great deal of power, but at that moment he felt powerless. Adelaide was currently acting as a future lady-in-waiting on the delegation. He would have liked to recall her to stand trial, but the scandal would be talked of in three kingdoms. Worse yet, people would wonder why he had allowed his daughters to socialize with a murderer. As much as he hated to admit it, Edward knew that there was little else he could do. The snake had lost her teeth, and he would have to let her be.

I will write to Jerrison and tell him to keep a close eye on that whore of his. I will also warn him that he had better not say as much as a cross word to his wife. I'll work him over until he hiccups whenever anyone says her name! Stupid fool!

"Your Majesty, I have other news. There is a new letter for you from Lilian Earton."

"Is that so? What does she say?"

"Someone tried to poison her after I left."

The king whistled. He couldn't help it. "Does everyone around those parts hate her?"

"No, Your Majesty. But there does seem to be a party whose identity I have yet to discover who would very much like to see her dead. All traces lead back here, to the capital. The countess laid out everything that she was able to learn from the woman who attempted to poison her. If you'll allow me…"

"Allow you? I order you to continue the investigation! Tomorrow you may pick up the execution letter from my secretary."

"For Adelaide Wells' cousin, Your Majesty?"

"Of course."

"Yes, Your Majesty."

"I want you to find out who stands to gain by Lilian Earton's death. There is too much trouble in this world already to allow someone to work this much evil."

Hans bowed. He was in full agreement with his sovereign, and he would be happy to carry out his orders. Especially since his own sympathies lay with the cause of justice, and with Lilian Earton.

ଔ ☐ ଔ

Lily sat working in her laboratory. She had had an interesting idea. Refining oil was well within her capability now, and Ali had promised to bring more crude oil.

Why not refine it into gasoline and make some really simple cigarette lighters? I already have glass, I can make gasoline…well, maybe I don't know what I'm doing, but I can work it out as I go along. I'll just have to talk to Helke about how to attach the flint and the little wheel. It's worth a try.

Someone scratched at the door. "My Lady?"

"Come in!"

"There's a letter from your father, My Lady."

Lily sighed and put down her glass beaker. When she got to her study, she found that Taris had already decrypted the message, which had come by carrier pigeon.

My dearest daughter,

Know that I will help you in all your affairs. We can discuss things in greater detail in the spring. For now, know that I will not forsake you. I have seen Chevalier Tremain. I know everything, and I am assisting him as I can.

Your loving father,

August Broklend

Lily rubbed her eyes to keep from crying. It was a message straight from his heart. Why had she never seen such words from him before? She already knew the answer.

I used to be a stupid fool. Things are different now...

She picked up the letter again. Underneath the emotion, she found important facts: 1) Hans told her father everything he knew; 2) There was something else he didn't want to discuss in a letter; and 3) Lily had her father's unwavering support against her husband and the king, if it came down to it. And there was a fourth piece of important information: they were all working together to find out who wanted her dead. That was a lot to fit into a one-pigeon message, and any outsider who read it would just see a father sympathizing with his daughter. Lily felt optimistic that the two of them would hit it off well.

₮ ₧

Jess sat down to write to his wife:

Dearest wife,

I am pleased with your decisions and completely approve of them.

How is Miranda? Are you in good enough health to try to conceive an heir in the spring? I hope that no one will try to poison you or otherwise harm you before I see you at court.

Your husband,

Jerrison Earton

Jess had tried to write a polite letter, but anger infused every line. His uncle was furious with him, and it was all her fault! Why couldn't his stupid wife sit at home and work on her embroidery? What was all this nonsense about slave traders and thievery?

You just wait, my dearest wife, I'll have plenty to say to you when I see you! And you'll answer for getting me in trouble with the king, you ungrateful bitch!

Meanwhile, the ungrateful bitch was listening to a report from the captain of her guards.

"We have finished, My Lady."

"Finished what, exactly?"

"We buried the bodies and had the pastor perform a funeral service. Baron Donter's head and skin have been salted down."

"Did you find Calma?"

Leis grimaced. "We did, My Lady. She was already dead."

"All the better for her."

"We buried her properly, too."

"Good. The next thing we have to discuss is unpleasant. I want you to watch everyone who lives here in the castle. I also want more guards on the perimeter. If it weren't for Loik, just think what would have happened to Mirrie."

Leis looked down at the floor. He would have preferred a scolding from the countess. It was all his fault. He was the captain of the guards, and he should have thought of the potential for a kidnapping attempt.

"I will do that, My Lady."

"And I will make sure that you do." A heavy sack dropped onto the table in front of him. The clinking sound was pleasant to the ear. "Now for the pleasant part of our conversation. This is for you and your men. You can decide how to divide it up. I'll pay the Virmans separately." She gave him a piercing look. "This is for work done well and quickly."

Leis shook his head. "If we hadn't…I don't deserve it, My Lady."

"That's for me to decide." Her green eyes were cold. "Leis Antrel, you did everything you could, given the circumstances. I especially want you to reward those two archers."

"Yes, My Lady."

"That's more like it." Lily pulled her braid over her shoulder and fingered the ribbon. It was white (there was no pink left in her wardrobe). "When will Erik and Leif return?"

"I expect them back tomorrow morning, My Lady."

"Wonderful. We will wait."

In the end, they had to wait several more days for the Virmans to make it home.

ຂວ □ ໕

Alicia Earton pulled on her new shawl. It was just the sort of thing she liked. She would have been pleased to wear her new jewelry with it, but she restrained herself, even though the pieces were perfectly elegant and did not distract from the person who wore them…

I wonder how on earth she made these lovely things? Or did she buy them somewhere? But how? Earton is so far out in the wilderness that merchants only go there once a year!

It was time to go. Only the king and queen could be late. Alicia had just ten minutes to traverse the palace's many hallways, slip in through one of the doors that only those closest to the throne used, and take her seat in the hall behind the young princesses, who were sure to be wearing their gifts from Lilian Earton. It would not be the first time they had worn them in public, deriving great pleasure from the envy they generated.

As soon as Alicia entered the hall, she was attacked on all sides.

"What a lovely shawl!"

"You look charming today!"

"That color is quite stunning against your hair. Is that from your daughter-in-law?"

Alicia smiled and replied to all the compliments. "Yes, it is a lovely shawl." *Get your hands off it!* "Yes, it is from Lilian." *Keep smiling if you want one* "You'll have to ask her where she gets them from. I might be able to help you get in touch with her."

After several conversations like this, Alicia was getting tired of the attention. She had just told a lady of her acquaintance to write to August Broklend when a man's voice behind her caused her to turn.

Speak of the devil! "I am pleased to see you, Lord Broklend."

"As am I to see you, Countess. You look charming."

"Thanks to your daughter, of course."

August smiled. "Lily's doing well."

"You must tell me, Lord Broklend. Did you help her buy these beautiful and highly unusual things?" She ran her fingertips over the fine lace cascading from her shoulders.

"Of course not, My Lady. I'm afraid to say I have not seen as much of Lily as I would like since she moved to Earton. I feel very guilty about it, actually."

Alicia frowned. "Then how could she have bought such lovely things in Earton?"

"She takes after me," said August with a wide smile. "Now tell me, My Lady, has my son-in-law written to you?"

"No. Has he written to you?"

"No."

"That is strange." The countess and the shipbuilder stood together in silence. Both were thinking along the same lines. *If Jess didn't already know about the things Lily was making in Earton, what would he say when he found out?*

Alicia broke the silence. She might have been mean, but she wasn't stupid. "August... May I call you that?"

"Of course, My Lady."

"And you must call me Alicia. We are relatives, even if we have only seen each other a few times."

"You are always at court, My Lady, and there is nothing for me to do here."

She smiled modestly. "I know. You are at home on your boats. Edward speaks highly of you." Not the king, not His Majesty, just Edward. It was a hint of her friendship with the king and the degree of honor she was conveying on him.

"I'm flattered."

"Now tell me, my son..." Alicia had her reasons for asking about Jess. Lately—ever since he received Lilian's letter—Edward had been angry with Jerrison Earton, and Alicia was concerned that her own position might be at risk. She was an intelligent woman, and she knew that if Lilian shared her secrets with anyone it would be her father.

August saw no reason to hide anything from Alicia. "Your son, My Lady, is an unusual man. He has a creative mind, and he is exceptionally talented in worldly affairs. He is like a bloodhound on a scent when he's tracking down something for the boatyards, and he is doing his best to learn the shipbuilding business. He has good brains, education, and talent. If he is interested in a problem, he will work day and night to solve it."

Alicia looked away. "That isn't all you want to say, is it, August?"

"Of course not. The reverse side of those talents is that he cares little for people. I see it when he is at the boatyards. If he needs a man, he uses him. As soon as he doesn't need him, he throws him away."

"But…"

"I know. Everyone does that to some extent. But he takes it to the extreme. Here is an example." August paused for a breath. "There was an old man who had been working for me for forty years. I valued his skill and his service, so I gave him lighter duties as he got older. Then one day Jess fired him."

"So what?"

"He has a family. Our Lord did not bless him with sons, but he married off all three of his daughters to good men. His sons-in-law are in the shipbuilding trade. One of them worked for me. He wanted to quit in protest, and he's a carpenter with a gift from Aldonai. If I hadn't intervened in time, my business would have gained a bad reputation."

"Jess can be harsh at times."

"Yes, and often to the detriment of his own interests."

"But he is successful, I believe…"

"He is, but he simply gives orders to managers who do his work for him."

"That takes talent, too."

"It does. But your son, My Lady…"

"Alicia."

August took a deep breath. "Alicia, your son ignores other people's interests without even noticing what he's doing." He had done it—used her first name. They were not enemies, not yet.

"Has he ignored your daughter?"

"Lily never complains."

Alicia caught the subtext. Lily doesn't complain, but that doesn't mean she is happy with her position. She doesn't complain, but she could be keeping score against her husband and biding her time.

"Lilian is coming for the spring season, and Edward asked me to take her under my wing."

"I'll be grateful for that, Alicia." His green eyes were serious. The dowager countess reflected that Broklends never forgot anything, good or evil.

What rabid dog bit you, Jess Earton? Why couldn't you treat your wife decently?

August straightened up and held out a hand. "May I invite you to dance, Alicia?"

The old shark blinked. "Me? Dance?"

"You, My Lady. I would like to share a dance with an intelligent, charming woman."

Alicia appreciated the compliment. She also realized that her thoughts were no secret to August.

Jess, you're an idiot! If the daughter is anything like the father...and now, you've made her mad! I'll rip your head off when I see you! No, Edward will rip it off, and I will stand off to one side and applaud!

ᚹ ᚳ

Edward was late for the reception for a very simple reason. He was finishing a game of backgammon with Hans. He was losing, but he wouldn't give up. Backgammon had stuck to him like cloth to a wound. It was one of the few ways he had to relax, moving the amber pieces around the board. When he played the game, his thoughts flowed freely, and on this day, they turned to Earton, as they often had of late.

"The countess' salt works are truly a wonder. I tried the first shipment, and it tastes just as good as rock salt, except for a slight touch of bitterness. The profits from this venture will be royal." He looked up at Hans. "Did the countess really come up with the idea on her own?"

"Yes, Your Majesty. She said it was silly to live on the coast and pay dearly to salt one's soup."

"How long ago did she start the venture?"

"It was already built when I arrived in Earton."

"Why didn't Jess say anything about it?"

"Your Majesty, the countess gave me to understand that his lordship…if you'll forgive my impudence…"

Edward waved a hand to show that any impudence would be forgiven. Then he threw the dice—five and four.

"The earl is interested in nothing but hunting."

"While the countess…"

It was Hans' turn to roll the dice—three and six. "She says she was in a fog from the time she arrived in Earton."

"Were there reasons for that?"

"I do not yet know, Your Majesty. I discovered nothing to explain it while I was there. The countess promised to write to me. I will ask her about it."

"Please do." The king threw the dice—six and six. His Majesty stood up from the table victorious. "I also want you to pay a call on Jerrison's manager here in town. Tell him not a single letter is to go to Earton without my seeing it first."

"Yes, Your Majesty." Hans bowed and made his exit. Edward sighed, checked his reflection in the wonderfully clear mirror, straightened his crown, and went in to see his guests.

Life went on.

ଚ □ ଓ

A letter from Jerrison Earton to His Majesty Edward the Eighth.

Your Most Gracious Majesty,

Allow me to fall at your feet with the smallest of requests.

At this point, Jess dropped the courtly style. He didn't have enough self-control to see it through, and he knew his uncle disliked excessive verbiage.

Uncle, I beg you to write to me in greater detail about what has happened in Earton. I am hearing these things for the first time. Earton is a quiet place. My grandmother lived there for almost twenty years and never saw so much as a horse thief. No sooner did I send my daughter there, however, than the nightmare started. Pirates, slave traders, thieves… I can believe that Etor was dishonest, but the rest of it shocks me. I do not understand!

What you say about my wife is just as surprising. You saw her once, whereas I have seen her many times. She is stupid, hysterical and prone to fits. After reading your letter, I begin to wonder if someone else is behind all of this and telling her what to do. I would like to know who it could be, and what he is after.

I must tell you that I sent Miranda with a large number of servants so that there would be someone to take care of her. Lilian has never shown any capacity for work of any kind. She is only interested in embroidery and food…and prayers. How could she have changed so suddenly? None of this makes sense to me.

What has happened to my daughter? Is she alive and well? Should I have her sent back to the capital?

Uncle, please tell me your thoughts on these things!

I remain your devoted servant,

Jerrison, Earl of Earton

Altres Lort, who made a habit of shamelessly reading all the letters sent by the Ativernan guests, put the letter down and snorted.

I wonder what's going on in this Earton place.

He decided to ask his secretary for all the information he could find on Earton. He would also send someone to Jess' estate to do a little quiet looking around.

Who do I have out that way? Rolf Relamo. He'll do. He's a chevalier, and good-looking. Just what the countess needs to keep her from getting bored over the winter. I'll send him a message by pigeon this very day!

ॐ ☐ ॐ

"I want it!"

Few men can refuse a favorite daughter when she says these awful words while gazing at her face in a wonderful mirror that, while small, reflects her features much clearer than any piece of polished metal. King Leonard looked down at his daughter. Larisia was enraptured by her own reflection and noticed nothing else.

He looked at the merchant. "What miracle made this thing? Is there anything foul about it?"

"I bought it in Altver, Your Majesty," said the merchant, silently counting his profits. "Baron Avermal promised me that there is nothing foul in it. Look at the thing yourself. It bears the mark of Aldonai."

Lily had insisted on that. Helke had made her trademark and his own mark off to one side. In the middle of the mirror's back, he engraved a large, embellished sign of Aldonai. The church approved of such uses.

The king cleared his throat. "That is true. If this thing were the work of Maldonaya, it could not bear our lord's mark." He turned to his daughter. "To be safe, take it to our aldon to have it blessed."

"Yes, Father." Larisia put the mirror back in its box and raced off.

King Leonard turned back to the merchant. "Name your price."

The merchant's price was reasonable, and the king knew it. Later that week, he put the man's name on a list of traders released from paying profit tax for half a year. It was worth the small loss to make Larisia happy.

Leonard loved his daughter. He also loved to spoil her. Some people said she looked like a rat, but in his eyes, she was a beautiful princess.

ଞ □ ଔ

"I beg you, My Lord!"

Things were no better in the Khanganate, where the Great Khangan's favorite wife was stroking a fine piece of lace with trembling fingers and looking up at him with large, tear-filled eyes. The rest of her face was concealed by her head covering, but he could see enough to know how strong her emotion was. She would not forgive him if he refused her this thing. No, there would be no shouting or weeping. On the outside, everything would remain the same. She would only be cooler when she spoke to him. But eventually, a rumor would get out that the Great Khangan had refused his favorite wife a small trinket, and that perhaps his treasury was running low.

The Great Khangan was a wise man. He believed that a wife must be satisfied with her lot in life. If she was, she would go to any lengths to keep her husband happy. There were men in his kingdom who held their wives in line with fear, but the Great Khangan disdained such methods. And he could certainly afford the fine pink cloud of lace and the glossy hair comb.

"How much do you want, merchant?"

The man bowed and named his price. The Khangan frowned, but in the end, he ordered his secretary to pay. It was an expensive gift, but no one else had anything like it.

If she gets tired of it, I'll just take it away and give it to another wife.

The merchant reached into his bag. "I have a scroll here that describes how such a thing is worn, Your Majesty."

That evening, the Great Khangan got a good look at his favorite wife wearing the new lace—and nothing else. Her gratitude gave him immeasurable pleasure that lasted most of the night. In the early morning, he finally fell asleep thinking about how much better life was when his wife was content.

ഽ☐ഗ

Altres ran his eyes over the report. He didn't know what to make of its news. The renowned healer Tahir Djiaman din Dashar was in Earton. The jester frowned. *Why would a wise man like Tahir be staying in the middle of nowhere?*

He put the parchment down and leaned back in his chair. It was obvious that Tahir was hiding from the Great Khangan, but why had he chosen Earton? Rolf Relamo had nothing to offer on that subject.

Altres dashed off a quick note instructing his spy to find out more and report back in detail.

Then he had another thought: *Should I invite the famous healer to Wellster?* The whole world knew that Gardwig was a dangerous man, but very few people knew how sick he really was. There was no guarantee that the learned healer could help, but it was worth a try. Altres loved his brother, and he needed him to stay alive.

ଧ □ ଓ

Just then, the great healer was watching the countess' hand as she moved her pointer around a drawing of the human body. He had studied the art of healing for many years, but always blindly, often guessing. It was pure pleasure for him to learn about such things as muscles and nerves from a professional like Aliya, for it was Aliya, and not Lily, who conducted the lesson.

"That was the path of systemic circulation. Here is the path of pulmonary circulation, which goes through the lungs." She tapped on the parchment. "It begins with the right pulmonary artery in the right ventricle. Blood from the body is carried to the lungs, where the alveoli enrich it with oxygen. After that, the blood returns to the left ventricle."

"My Lady, I understand that blood carries oxygen and that we would die without this oxygen. Can you tell me, then, why a man dies when he inhales smoke? Isn't smoke the same as air?"

Lily took a deep breath and explained about

hemoglobin, erythrocytes and carbon monoxide. Tahir listed raptly as if she were singing his favorite song, taking notes all the while.

When she was done, he looked at her for a long time. Finally, he said, "My Lady, I believe you could heal the Great Khangan's son. In fact, I am sure of it."

"What is wrong with the boy?"

As she listened to his tale, Lily's face grew darker. The Khangan's eldest son—his heir—was sixteen. His symptoms—headaches, nausea, diarrhea, fevers—could signify almost anything. But he was also short of breath, and his gums bled. That was interesting. She asked a few questions about the boy's diet and soon ruled out scurvy.

What else could it be?

Tahir mentioned that the boy complained of a metallic taste in his mouth and of pain upon swallowing.

Lily's eyes grew wide.

"Tell me this, Tahir-jan. Do the tips of his fingers and nose have a pinkish tint?"

"They do, My Lady."

She shook her head. "Then I am afraid for him. There is little anyone can do against the poison that causes these symptoms."

"Poison?" Tahir was aghast.

Lily explained as best she could how mercury slowly poisons the body. She could not, however, answer the question that Tahir immediately posed,"Who is doing it?"

"I have no idea. I might be able to discover the poisoner if I were there, but I can do nothing from here."

Tahir looked down at his hands. "So the boy cannot be saved?"

"I suppose he could be saved if one could stop the poisoner and give him a very long course of treatment. And even that would depend on how much damage has already been done."

"If only they had your knowledge in the Khanganate!"

Lily thought for a moment. She saw no danger to herself in communicating her fears to the Great Khangan. If he found the poisoner, he would be grateful to her. If he did not, it wouldn't be her fault.

"Tahir-jan, can you write directly to your friends in the Khanganate?"

"I would rather not put them at risk."

"Then let's send a letter to Baron Avermal and ask him to send it on with the next merchant ship headed to the Khanganate."

The healer looked up at her. His eyes were shining. "If the heir is still alive, I might have hope…"

Lily gave him a broad smile. "You could go home again."

"And leave you, Lily-jan? Never!" He leaned forward and lowered his voice. "If you want me gone, you will have to drive me from your land, Lilian Earton."

The countess' smile turned bittersweet. "Thank you for that. But you do understand, don't you, that my husband can order the affairs here as he wishes?"

"He would never be so stupid as to stop you from helping people. Your knowledge could save thousands of lives! Even tens of thousands!"

"It is your knowledge, Tahir. I am merely your student."

He put a hand on hers. "As you wish, Lily-jan. Just do not ask me to leave."

She smiled into his kind face, but her thoughts were grim. *What would Tahir do if someone tried to separate him from me? Or if someone tried to stop me from practicing medicine? I believe he would commit murder. He knows how to use poisons that no one here could discover.*

ჯ ✸ ო

Tahir Djiaman din Dashar had never imagined that an opportunity like this one existed. He had spent everything he had to get out of the Khanganate ahead of the palace guards. He was old and tired, and he knew he would need to find a place to live, but he had never expected such good fortune.

When Ali first brought him to Earton, he had looked on the countess with surprise. Here was a woman who was attempting to understand the greatest secrets of the human body. *How could she hope to attain any sort of standing?* She was a woman. That meant she was supposed to adorn a man's home and raise his children while the man made all the important decisions. Life had always worked that way.

And yet, after his first private conversation with Lilian, Tahir realized that he might never know as much as she did about the art of healing. He was confident she was telling him the absolute truth about what she knew. If anything, she tried to make the material easier for him to understand.

Without this absolute faith in the countess, he would not have believed some of the shocking things she told him. For example, there were tiny creatures that lived everywhere, even inside the human body. It was these creatures—and not bad blood—that caused a wound to become infected. They could be defeated through a process she called dis-in-fect-ion. How was a man to believe that?

And what was he to make of her avowal that blood contained tiny beads, each with its own job—white cells, red cells, and platelets? It sounded like nonsense, and yet he believed her. Tahir could tell that Lilian Earton was the recipient of an age-old tradition of healing. This was not the work of a single person, however wise. But when he tried to learn more about her sources, the countess just shook her head and told him she had learned it all from reading old manuscripts.

That part of her story was a lie. Tahir would have liked to press her to get at the truth, but the attack by the slave traders had distracted him. While he and Lily and Jaimie stitched up the wounded, he often glanced over to watch the countess' hands. They were strong and sure, always putting instruments back in a precise order. The more he saw, the more he became convinced that her ladyship was a born healer like himself. *If she had been born a man, she would have accomplished much in this life. She is already doing a great deal, as it is.*

Out of gratitude, he decided not to press her about the sources of her knowledge. Tahir would have given his right hand to study with the people who had taught Lilian Earton, but something whispered to him that that way was closed. He would just have to take what he could get from the countess and thank the Great Mare for the opportunity.

Tahir had never laid eyes on Jess Earton, but if the earl got in the way of his lessons, the Khangan healer would grind him like a snake under his heel, both out of gratitude to Lily and because of what he hoped to learn from her.

The old healer had no children, but if the Mare had given him a daughter, he would have wished her to be just like Lilian: clever, beautiful, and skilled at healing. He was sure the countess deserved to be happy.

ৰে ෴ ৵

The admiration was mutual. Lily spent as much time as she could on her lessons with Tahir and Jaimie. She preferred to sleep less so that she could teach them more. Her new world would not benefit from the invention of gunpowder and cannons, but it could gain a great deal from her medical wisdom.

The snow was blowing hard against the window during one of their lessons when Tahir turned to Lily with a dreamy look on his face. He had remembered a question that had long vexed him. "Why do men die from some head injuries and not from others?"

The countess picked up her pen and began to draw. "Look here. The skull is actually many different bones fused together. Like this." She scratched away on her parchment for a moment and then looked up and smiled at Tahir. "You must also remember that the brain is divided into multiple sections…"

They bent their heads together over the drawing, studying it at great length while the winter sun crawled across the horizon.

Leif was finally back in Earton, and he was visibly pleased with himself as he stood before the countess. "My Lady, the baron's castle and his lands are now fully under our control."

"Excellent. What did you find there?"

"We tossed all his papers in this chest. Would you like to see them?"

"Later. Why did it take you so long to return?"

"The baron had about forty people in his dungeon, My Lady. He was planning to sell them to the slave traders. We thought you'd like to hear their stories. As evidence."

Lily nodded. "Of course. I will question them and send their statements to the king. Was the castle difficult to take?"

"Not in the least. The baron's men had gotten into his wine, so we waited until it was almost light to go in. They were asleep."

"Did we lose any men?"

"Four."

"Wounded?"

"Eight."

"Get them to Jaimie and Tahir, and the sooner, the better. Did you dress their wounds?"

"Yes, My Lady, just how you showed us." Lily taught the Virmans and the castle guards how to dress wounds in the field and gave them bottles of alcohol and clean bandages she had steamed and wrapped in parchment.

"Good. We will take it from here. That is a very small

number of men wounded while taking a castle."

"Yes, My Lady. Erik lost two, and I lost two. Our men did an excellent job."

Lily was pleased to see the pride in Leif's eyes.

"Did any of the men who were killed leave families?"

"One of them had a wife."

"She will continue to receive her husband's pay. It isn't enough, of course, and it won't bring him back, but still..."

All of a sudden, thoughts of the past flitted through Lily's mind and scratched at her heart.

My father. My mother. Alex... Has he forgotten me already?

The countess frowned. This was not the time for such thoughts. She needed to deal with Leif and the other Virmans, who, as she could see from her window, were driving their prisoners into the courtyard like livestock.

"You brought them all here?"

"Yes, My Lady."

Lily stared at him. "Where am I supposed to put them all?"

"Keep the ones you can use, and show the others the gate. They'll settle in the villages."

Lily paused to think. "I suppose you're right. Lons and I will interview them. Go tell Leis to send them in five at a time, and then you may have the rest of the day off. You have earned it."

"Thank you, My Lady." The giant smiled sweetly before turning to leave.

When he was gone, Lily rested her chin on her hand and thought to herself how lovely it was to work with the Virmans.

A brief hour later, the countess was no longer smiling. In fact, she threw a vase against the wall in fury. One of the men the Virmans brought from the baron's dungeon was none other than Etor. Her supposedly dead former estate manager.

Lily was filled with a mixture of anger and excitement, but she was afraid of making the wrong move. She had already dealt hastily with Etor once. After thinking it over, she told the Virmans to hold Etor separately until they located his wife. Then they were to feed the pair and leave them to await their interrogation.

She would deal with the others first. Etor could wait.

ଞ □ ଔ

The others were soon sorted out. It seemed that the baron had seized a random selection of his own peasants – most of them young men and women – to sell. Lily immediately ordered that the women be returned to their families. She offered some of the stronger-looking men jobs at the Earton salt works, which they gladly accepted. The others would be returned to Donter.

All the prisoners sorted, Lily went to see how Jaimie and Tahir were faring. She found them in the infirmary with their patients, all of whose wounds had been cleaned, so she started teaching them how to set a drain tube and what type of stitches to use.

After a short lesson, she stood back to watch them work. *My students are progressing nicely.*

Then it occurred to her that Jaimie—who had every chance of becoming the new Baron Donter—might not wish to continue as her student. She made a mental note to speak to him about it later.

ಬಠ □ ಜ

Jaimie wasted no time. One day, shortly after the lesson on stitches, he sat down in Lily's office and told her his whole story, as far as he knew it.

He hadn't known his pedigree when he asked to travel with Lily. He had only known that there were rumors about his mother. He remembered she always seemed a cut above the people around her and his father (or stepfather, as he now understood), an herbalist, had always paid a neighbor woman to do the heavy work around their house.

Both of his parents died during an epidemic, and after that, his grandmother had taken him in. Jaimie thought she must have known that he wasn't her blood relation, but she gave him a place to live, fed him and taught him what she knew about herbs and treating illnesses.

When his grandmother died, she gave him the box he had shown Lily and Leis.

"Why didn't you open it then?" the countess asked.

Jaimie hung his head. He explained that he had been too busy trying to earn his keep in Altver, and once he arrived in Earton, the countess had kept him on his toes setting up the infirmary.

"I suppose I was afraid of what I would find," he admitted. "So I kept putting it off."

The rings had belonged to his grandfather, his uncle and his mother. The bracelet and the portrait were his mother's. Lily thought Jaimie looked the spitting image of his mother.

She looked at the boy sharply. "You said Pastor Leider didn't like you. How long has he been in Altver?"

"At least ten years, My Lady."

"I wonder what he could have known about you."

Jaimie shrugged his shoulders, showing that he saw no point in guessing.

Lily persisted. "But if you knew you were the rightful heir to the Donter estate, why didn't you tell me before?"

He shrugged again. Lily understood what he wouldn't say. It was highly unlikely that she or anyone else would have declared war on the baron just to restore Jaimie to his rights. But now that the baron was gone, the boy saw an opening for himself. *Why not? My neighbor was my enemy, but now he will be my friend.*

She reflected that it would be prudent to have Jaimie in Donter. If things went badly with the earl, she could always escape and move her manufacturing with Jaimie's help.

It was clear enough what had to be done. The countess sighed and took out another sheet of parchment.

"Let's write a letter, Jaimie."

After much discussion and editing, the following text was born:

Your Majesty,

It is with great sorrow that I write to inform you that Baron Donter, my neighbor, fell prey to incurable insanity that has led to his death. That is the only explanation I can find for his attempt at kidnapping my daughter, Miranda Catherine. All thanks to Aldonai, he was unsuccessful. I believe that this madness was sent to him by Aldonai to punish him for the sins of his father, who had an unnatural union with his sister to sire Lord Donter. This is a strange story, to be sure, and as evidence, I am sending you a copy of the testimony of Lady Marianna Donter, the wife of the old baron, likewise deceased. The original testimony is in my possession and can be produced. I must also inform you that Lady Donter's son, the last of the line of Donters, is currently living here in Earton and awaiting your instructions.

I remain your faithful servant,

Lilian Elizabeth Mariella Earton

It was the best she could do on short notice. She would let Erik run the Donter estate while she waited for word from the king.

Sometimes it seemed to Lily that the Virman looked at her with a hidden passion in his sparkling brown eyes. She was flattered—and she had no intention of living like a nun for the rest of her life—but this was not the time. If she was to have any hope of success in this new world, she would have to reach an arrangement with her husband. Cheating on him with a Virman guard would make that all the more difficult.

It would be a good idea to keep Erik as far from Earton as possible.

හ⃝ౖ⃝ ଔ

Etor was pale and exhausted, but Lily felt no pity for him. She had spent most of her time in Earton cleaning up his mess.

If you can't do the time, don't do the crime!

She looked down at her former manager with one eyebrow raised. "Here we are again, Etor. Shall we talk?"

Her soft tone of voice fooled no one. Etor's face got even whiter, and he did his best not to faint...unsuccessfully. Olaf, who stood behind the prisoner, slapped the back of Etor's head, quickly bringing him to. Etor whimpered and stood up straight.

"My Lady..."

"I'm right here, Etor, and I am eager to hear what you have to tell me."

"About what, My Lady?"

"Start at the beginning."

At this point, Taris stepped out of the corner and stood where Etor could see him. "How long did you manage the estate?" he asked, keeping his voice low. Etor was startled, but Olaf put a fist in his face, and he started to talk. He knew where the Earton castle dungeon was and what they could do to him there.

Of course, he tried to lie, or at least to minimize the truth, but Lily, Lons, Taris, and Leif worked him over for hours. The interrogation moved slowly, but it covered a lot of ground.

Etor had originally managed the estate for Jess' father. Jyce had been a tough master; he kept a close eye on income and expenses, and everyone knew he would hang anyone who tried to steal from him. Etor had despised him. When Jyce died, not long before Jess married Lily, Etor realized he needed a succession plan. Jess was smart, but he was too much of an aristocrat to bother thinking about all the ways his employees might steal from him. In fact, the old earl's son thought that most commoners were too stupid to get the better of him. That opened interesting opportunities for Etor.

He had talked the matter over with his wife's third cousin, Shirvey Lindt, who approved wholeheartedly. They would squeeze all they could out of the land and the people who worked it. The enterprising bastards even talked Baron Donter into introducing them to some pirates. Soon, they were making money hand over fist.

It didn't take long for Etor to discover that the Grismo family was chipping away at a deposit of amber and to demand his share. Soon after that, things began to get interesting.

Jess got married and sent his wife to live on the estate. At first, Etor was prepared to be disappointed. Noblewomen usually took charge of their own estates, or at least, their households. However, Lilian Earton turned out to be a quiet girl who prayed and embroidered and cried instead of looking after the running of the castle. Etor could think of no explanation for her strange behavior, but his wife, Tara, opened his eyes; she had seen Sara putting something in the countess' food. Husband and wife forced the girl to give up her secret, and soon the Darcey family was paying them for their silence.

Taris wanted to know why the medicus had not noticed anything unusual about his patient. Etor explained that the medicus had been in on everything from the beginning and that he had even added some potions of his own. They made the countess sleep for hours on end every day. Martha had tried to intervene, but the medicus told her that sleep was good for the growing baby and that the earl had ordered the treatment.

"What about the earl?"

Etor admitted the earl had known nothing of how Lily was

being drugged. To be safe, the conspirators stopped putting the herbal mixtures in her food whenever the earl came to visit. As a result, she was irritable and angry during those periods. Lily cursed inwardly when she heard this.

When the countess had kicked him out, he had turned his feet toward the Donter estate, hoping to ride back with the baron's men to wreak revenge on Lily. Instead, he and his wife ran into a band of angry peasants, all of whom had lost children to Etor's secret slave trading. The men gave the pair a severe beating. Tara died of her injuries the next day, and Etor spent a month recovering at Erk Grismo's house. By the time he was on his feet again, it was too late; Lily had returned from Altver with her new Virman guards. He was trying to make his way down the Earta to the coast when he was captured by a band of the baron's men. Afraid that the baron would have him killed outright now that he had little to offer, he decided not to reveal his identity and had been sitting quietly in the baron's dungeon, planning his next move.

Etor was pitiful, but Lily's heart was hard. She would let him live because he had value as a witness, but she would keep him under guard day and night.

A new idea occurred to her. "Do you still have any accomplices at the castle?"

He did. There was a stable boy named Alex who had done odd jobs for him. Lily ordered the Virmans to bring him in for questioning. Then she sent Etor back to his cell, where she would leave him until she could take him back to the capital and present him to Hans in the spring.

Damis Reis was furious. The countess continued to ignore him. No matter what he wore or how he looked at her, it was like he didn't even exist. And he was afraid to do more than look since the countess didn't react to him like most of the women he had known. All she did was work from sunup to sundown. Any free time she had was spent with her stepdaughter. *How am I supposed to seduce a woman like that?* Still, he hated to face his client if he was unsuccessful.

He understood that he had been hired because he resembled the Earl of Earton. His client wanted to be able to dispute the legitimacy of any of Lily's future offspring. But alas, the countess had her own plans, and Damis was stuck teaching a rowdy bunch of children. He hated the job more with each passing day. If he didn't manage to get in the countess' bed soon, his client would cut him off.

After much gnashing of teeth, Damis realized he had two options: he could court Lily more aggressively, or he could try to engineer a compromising situation between the two of them…with witnesses.

One evening after dinner, Tahir followed Lily out of the dining room. When they were alone in the hall, he asked, "My Lady, where does mercury come from?"

Lily sighed. "Are you still thinking about the prince? I suppose he could be getting the mercury from anywhere." She thought for a moment. "But since he isn't vomiting every five minutes, I suspect he is either breathing it in or absorbing it through his skin. That is just a guess, Tahir. I am not Aldonai. I can't see all the way to the

Khanganate to tell you what is wrong with him."

The old man put a hand on her arm. "Would you come with me to the Khanganate?"

She stared. "What would I do there? I am a woman, Tahir, and the men in your land think even less of women than they do here."

Tahir sighed. The countess was right. If he took Lilian Earton to the Great Khangan's palace, the courtiers would see her as an attractive woman and a potential bride, but not as a great healer.

"Write to the Great Khangan. Tell him you suspect his son is being slowly poisoned. But I will not go there with you. I have to pay my respects to the King of Ativerna in the spring, and I can't leave Miranda or the estate."

The old man nodded. "I understand, My Lady. I will write in my own name."

He looked very small, with his robe wrapped tightly against the chill. Lily took his hand. "Remember this, my friend. There will always be room for you in my house. You are not a guest here. You are my brother."

Tahir wiped away a tear.

"Thank you, My Lady. I will write to my friends in the Khanganate. Perhaps they will be of some assistance to the prince."

Once Lily was alone in her room, she found she was still thinking about mercury and where it could be found in nature. She sat down on her bed and massaged her aching feet.

I'm a doctor, not a chemist. Someone else will have to

find the poisoner.

ೞ ▢ ೞ

If only she had known what Tahir was planning…

He had studied Lilian Earton at close range for many weeks. He knew that she never turned away a person in need.

ೞ ▢ ೞ

A letter from Lilian Earton to Hans Tremain:

Greetings, Leir Tremain.

I want you to know that my neighbor, Baron Donter, made an attempt to kidnap Miranda. He was unsuccessful and died during the attempt. I have learned that there is a lawful heir to the estate, and he happens to be someone you know: Jaimie, the young herbalist who came with me from Altver. His mother, Marianna Donter, ran away from his father because the man was having an unnatural affair with his own sister and threatening to kill his wife once the heir was born.

I have people keeping watch over the Donter estate for now, and I am prepared to turn it over to the rightful heir once I receive confirmation of the king's will on this matter.

Pastor Vopler has copied out all of the documents, which I am sending for you to give to His Majesty. I hope this question will soon be resolved in Jaimie's favor.

In another interesting development, my men discovered my former estate manager, Etor, in the baron's dungeon. I will not recount here what he told me. You may read it in his own words, which are attached. I will only say that I was astounded by his cunning and villainy.

I await news from you.

As always, I remain your true friend,

Countess Lilian Elizabeth Mariella Earton

Lily re-read the letter and nodded. It would do. She wouldn't show her claws until the time came. *Let them think I'm sweet and soft.*

ೞ □ ೞ

The king received Jerrison's letter on a day that had already proven to be unpleasant. He had just learned of an uprising on the border. It was winter, and people were hungry; it was hard to stop marauders.

Still, he felt he had to answer his son's letter. His pen scratched over the parchment.

To the Earl of Earton,

I have no idea where you got such a poor opinion of your wife. She is perfectly intelligent and in control of herself. I only wish the same could be said of you.

Were you aware that your wife was being poisoned, and that this led to her miscarriage and almost to her death? Did you know about the attempts on her life? And did you know that at least one of the men who tried to kill her almost harmed little Miranda in the process? I suppose you will find it interesting that these attacks were planned by none other than the cousin of your fair Adelaide Wells. Their confessions are attached.

I expect to see you here at court when your trip is over.

In the meantime, question the lady about her involvement and send me a full accounting.

Edward the Eighth, King of Ativerna

He sealed the letter and handed it to his steward. It would be up to Jess to find out what was going on.

Altres watched Anna's face. She was white as a sheet.

"You listen to me. Tonight's ball is your last chance to interest the prince. If you fail, I will take over and do what I must."

"I can do it." Anna's lips trembled.

The jester shook his head. "Can you throw yourself on him at just the right moment?"

Anna nodded.

"I will have two ladies-in-waiting follow you. As soon as you are alone with the prince, they will come find me. That will give you just a few minutes. Use the time as best you can."

Anna nodded more emphatically. The jester frowned. He had little faith in the girl, but his back was to the wall.

"Are you going to the ball?"

"I have to. I've lain around in bed too long as it is."

Jess studied his cousin's face. "And a good thing, too. You look like yourself again." Richard looked royal in his black and gold tunic. "The bitches will faint when they see you."

"Ladies, Jess. Ladies."

Jess made a face. "If you say so. I think they're all whores if you dig deep enough."

"That depends on who you keep company with," Richard shot back.

The earl put his head in his hands. His shoulders shook. At first, Richard thought he was crying, but when his cousin looked up, red-faced, he realized Jess was laughing. He slapped Jess on the back. "Let's go."

"I'll be right there. I got a letter from home. I'd like to read it. No one will notice I'm not there. They'll all be looking at you."

Richard sighed and went out.

Jess turned and went back into his room, shutting the door behind him. He broke the seal on the king's letter and began to read.

After a long silence, the letter dropped from his hand.

After another silence, he picked up the transcribed statements both hired killers had given.

Moments later, his door flew open, and he raced down the hall to find the traitorous Adele.

At the ball. Where else?

ଯ ଓ

Anna had done her best. Her yellow silk dress highlighted her dark hair, and the fine amber necklace around her neck was the same color as her golden-brown eyes. None of her maids could tell that she was terrified. If she couldn't pull off the plan, the jester wouldn't need her anymore.

Once the ball started, Prince Richard was cool and

polite, as always. He complimented her on her dancing and then proceeded to pay as little attention to her as he could.

Anna took a deep breath. It was now or never.

"Your Highness, could you give me a moment of your time?"

"Of course," Richard replied. We are in the middle of a crowded ballroom. What could possibly go wrong?

Anna took him by the hand, and they slid away to a heavy curtain that screened an alcove by one of the large windows. Just then, Jess rounded the corner into the ballroom and saw his cousin's golden head as it disappeared behind the curtain. He wanted Richard to help him pin down Adele's story, so he began to push his way through the crowd of dancers toward the window.

℘ ☐ ℘

No sooner did Anna's lady-in-waiting give the signal than Jess shoved her out of his way. She squawked, but he pulled open the alcove curtain.

"Richard, I need you right away!"

His cousin raised an eyebrow. "Have the courtesy to notice her highness."

Jess swore under his breath and bowed to the princess. "Forgive me, Your Highness."

Anna gave a little nod. She was too upset to speak.

Jess grabbed Richard by the sleeve. "I need to talk to you. It's urgent." He looked over his cousin's shoulder at Anna. "Pardon us, Your Highness. Shall we take you to your father?"

When the princess said nothing, Richard took her by the elbow and led her back through the crowd to where her father sat watching the dancing. He explained that she was feeling unwell before turning and following Jess out of the room.

Once they were alone, he waited patiently for Jess to stop pacing back and forth. Finally, the earl stopped and looked his cousin in the eye. "I had a letter from your father. The attempt on my wife was organized by Adele."

"What?" The two friends stared at each other in shocked silence.

୫୦ ୦ଃ

Altres had been observing the implementation of his plan when he saw Jess burst into the alcove. He had no idea what had upset the earl, so he waved for the lady-in-waiting to stay in position and slipped away after the two young men. Every castle has its secret passages, and the jester knew his brother's castle like the back of his hand. He'd be damned if he didn't find out what the Ativernan guests were up to.

୫୦ ୦ଃ

Richard and Jess flew back to the earl's rooms. Richard's head was spinning.

Did Adele really think Jess would marry her?

As far as he knew, Adele was burning through the money her husband had left her. There was no reason in the world for the Earl of Earton to bring her into his family.

"Jess, could this all be a mistake?"

"Not the way your father tells it," Jess replied grimly.

"But it makes no sense. Adele isn't smart enough to

plan a murder. Someone else is trying to incriminate her."

Jess' face lightened. "Maybe so."

Then Richard read the confessions, and his doubts were dispelled. It was Adele. She might not have devised the plan, but she certainly knew about it. After several days of torture, the cousin had told everything: about his affair of many years with Adele, about their plan to kill Lilian and Miranda, about their hopes of marrying Adele to Jess and then getting rid of him. In the end, Adele would inherit everything and petition the king for permission to marry her first husband's cousin. Richard snorted when he read about how Jess' expensive gifts to Adele had been sold to hire the killers.

When he read through the confession made by Leis' soldier, he looked up at Jess with a face that was gray. "He was one of your men."

Jess slapped his hand on the table as he stood up. "So what? I didn't issue the order!"

"Can you make August believe that?"

"Whether he believes it or not, Lilian is my wife." Jess' eyes flashed. The earl's usual expression of self-satisfaction was gone, and his face actually looked handsome.

"I remember what the marriage contract said. My father witnessed it." Richard gave a little smile. "Your goose is cooked."

"What do you mean?"

"They wouldn't have been able to get to her if she was living with you in the capital."

Jess jerked his head in annoyance.

Richard pressed on. "Didn't you read the letter? My father says she was drugged. There's nothing wrong with her when people aren't feeding her poisonous herbs."

Jess looked over Richard's head. His left eye was twitching.

The prince turned on his cousin. He had had enough. "This is all your fault," he said slowly, with emphasis on each word. "If I were you, I would build a new church in gratitude to Aldonai! Your wife has managed to keep your daughter out of harm's way, and she has done you a good turn cleaning up the estate for you. I don't see what you have to be displeased about."

Jess' shoulders slumped. He looked like a man who had been kicked in public. No matter how he looked at it, the whole awful mess was his fault. He had allowed a pair of thieves to run his estate, and he had put his wife in danger by taking a cold-blooded killer as a lover.

He stood up heavily. "I'll go get Adele while you finish reading."

Richard looked up and nodded. Then he picked up the confessions again. Ten minutes later, Jess stomped back into the room with a weeping Adelaide Wells in tow.

ശ □ ൠ

Adelaide was in shock. Jess had dragged her out of the ballroom in front of everyone. When she had asked him what the matter was, he had growled for her to hold her tongue if she didn't want to get slapped. She hated a scandal, so she said no more.

Her brain was working overtime. What happened? Is he jealous of the marquis I was dancing with? Or is it something else?

Jess opened the door to his room and dragged her inside. She tripped but caught herself. When she straightened up, she found herself looking into the eyes of Prince Richard.

The prince looked disgusted, and when he spoke, his voice was cold. "Adelaide Wells, can you explain to me why your cousin wished to have Jerrison's wife murdered?"

Adele flinched. Alex told everything? Oh, Aldonai…

She had pretended to faint many times in her life, but this time it was for real. Before everything went dark, she noticed that the floor was rushing up to meet her face.

Jess didn't even bother to catch her.

ೞ □ ೞ

Richard looked down at her body on the floor. "You're a dead man," he said quietly, raising his eyes to gaze at his cousin.

"Would you stop that?" Jess felt like he was losing control of his mind.

"I am telling you the truth. I read through everything while you went to find your lady love."

"And?"

"Your song is over."

Jess threw his hands up in the air. "You think I don't know that? I gave her jewelry. I slept with her. Now I have to try and prove that I didn't know anything about it!"

"Exactly. I wish you would think with your head instead of your manhood."

"I do think with my head!" Jess exclaimed. "I've been putting up with that fat fool of a woman all for the sake of August's boatyards!"

"Maybe so, except that she isn't a fool after all. My father says she's gotten rid of the thieves you let in and may even be turning a profit on the estate. That was your job."

Jess made no reply.

Still, on the floor, Adele began to give signs that she was coming around. Richard handed his cousin a cup of wine. Jess poured it over her face.

Adele groaned and opened her eyes. She looked pitiful. With her hair in disarray and her dress stained with wine, she looked more like a sailor's whore than a fine lady. She began to weep, which did nothing for her appearance.

"I...didn't..."

"You didn't what?" Richard interrupted her sniffling.

It took a while for Adelaide's story to come out, and neither man believed a word of it.

Everything was Alex's fault. He had forced the poor widow to sell her husband's estate and move to the capital. Any plotting was his alone. She would never do anything to hurt her dear Jerrison. Alex was trying to blacken her name because she had refused his advances. Her dear Jerrison should remember that she had never refused any of *his* advances...

As Richard listened to her story, he reflected that she would get away with it. There was no proof other than Alex's word. He knew Jess was thinking the same thing. In the end, Jess pushed her out the door and locked it behind her.

Turning to his cousin, he held out his hands, "What do

you think?"

"I think Alex was telling the truth. My father's guards are very good at questioning suspects."

"We can't lay a hand on her here. People would talk."

"Of course. She can wait until we get home…or until Father manages to get rid of her…by accident."

"He could do that," Jess agreed.

For a few minutes, no one spoke. Then Jess sighed. "I feel sorry for her."

"You should feel sorry for your wife," Richard snorted. "I remember how drunk you were at your wedding. I suppose you behaved like a pig on your wedding night."

Jess turned red.

"You didn't even talk to her, did you? You just had your way with her and sent her off to live in Earton."

That was about the size of it, judging by Jess' guilty face.

Richard put a hand on his shoulder. "Then what happened? Did you make it up to her later? Did you ever even talk to her?"

Jess blinked. "How could I? She was always giving me little things she had embroidered. I never knew what to say."

His cousin laughed out loud. "I see how it is! You give expensive presents to your whores, but your wife gets nothing. And when she gives you a gift, you ignore it."

"Maybe I really am the fool you think me," Jess muttered.

"I only hope you see it. Now think. You gave her an awful wedding night. You ignored her whenever you saw her afterward. Did you throw away her gifts?"

Jess hung his head.

"And you sent her off to live alone in Earton. Did you visit her?"

"I did…sometimes. I brought a doctor with me. She seemed insane. She wouldn't even look at me, and she was always yelling at people." Jess was pacing the room at the memory of his wife's strange behavior.

Richard got in his face. "Someone was poisoning her, you idiot. What else was she supposed to do?"

"I didn't know that…"

"And yet she managed to put a stop to it and save your estate for you!"

Jess' face still betrayed anger. Someone who didn't know the earl well would have assumed he was angry at himself, but Richard knew better. He shook his head.

Jess looked up, his eyes desperate. "Now I have to convince my uncle that I wasn't part of the plot."

Richard's eyebrows went up. "I suppose you'll have to beg your wife's forgiveness."

"She'll forgive me," Jess waved away all difficulties. "She is my wife, after all."

Momentarily stunned by his cousin's callousness, Richard said nothing.

Suddenly, Jess looked up, his eyes puzzled. "Wait a moment. I didn't take up with Adele until recently."

Richard frowned, "But someone started poisoning Lilian…"

"A long time ago. What the hell?"

"Does that mean two different people want her dead?"

Jess put a hand on the king's letter. "My uncle says nothing about the medicus."

"They can't find him."

"I wonder why not?"

"If I had hired him, you wouldn't be able to find him, I know that much," Richard said. "Who gave you his name?"

"My sister."

The men looked at each other in silence.

"According to Amalia, he is a good doctor. And he agreed to go see my cow."

Richard put his head down on Jess' desk. It was hopeless. His wife was always a cow, and he felt sorry for the mistress who tried to have her killed.

He looked up at his cousin, eyes twinkling. "Two different people out to get her. Plus the dishonest men you put in charge of the estate. You know what, Jess? If Lilian is anything at all like her father, you'll have to get on your knees to beg forgiveness."

Jess gave his cousin a smile that always won the hearts of the fine ladies at court. "A woman is a woman. She'll forgive me. She'll have to…"

⅓ □ ⅔

Altres agreed with Richard completely: Jess Earton had it coming in the worst way. The jester had no wife or children, but if anyone had treated a daughter of his the way the earl treated Lilian, he would have done something cold and final about it.

From his vantage point looking through a crack in the wall, he couldn't see what women found attractive about Jess, either. He was tall and muscular, with dark hair, blue eyes, and a nice smile. He was smart enough to keep his father's business going, and the jester had heard that he was a good soldier. On the other hand, he was annoyingly sure of himself and acted like women were objects.

Altres wondered if Lilian Earton was the kind of woman who found Jess attractive.

I'll find out when I get the report from Rolf.

෪ ☐ ೞ

Torius Avermal looked like he had just bitten into a lemon after reading a letter from the Countess of Earton. Someone had tried to kill her, and Karl Treloney was involved. That was unfortunate.

I'll have to get to the bottom of this.

And there was another thing: Tahir had sent along a request to forward a letter to the Khanganate. Torius couldn't imagine that any ship captain was planning to cross the gulf at that time of year, but he would send a servant to the harbor to find out. The letter would go out as soon as an opportunity presented.

The lemon of the letter was sweetened by two new pieces of lace that Lily had enclosed. The baron looked forward to showing them to several merchants.

A man could get used to making this kind of money.

෪ ☐ ೞ

Adelaide Wells was not intelligent in the usual sense of

the word. She knew nothing of history, music or politics, and her mental library contained no more than a few dozen jokes and a pair of funny stories she had heard—just enough to make small talk. As a rule, she believed that the less you said, the better off you were. However, she had a rat-like sense of cunning and the rodent's ability to sense danger to herself.

At the moment, she very clearly understood that Jess was her only shield against a dangerous world. So, after tearing up her best handkerchief and slapping her maid, she sent the poor girl to keep an eye on the earl's room and let her know when he was alone.

It was a long wait.

Jess and Richard talked for a long time. Then they opened a bottle of Ivernean wine that was known to cloud the mind without making the body heavy, unlike wine from the Khanganate, which deadened a man's legs while leaving his head clear. They talked some more, and they drank some more. It was midnight before the prince headed to his own rooms.

Adelaide leaped into action.

She undressed down to her nightshirt, rubbed herself all over with a perfume-soaked handkerchief, and padded down the hall. A few minutes later, she was tapping at the earl's door.

There was no answer.

She pushed at the door. It was unlocked.

Jess sat at his table. His head had fallen forward on his chest, and there were at least eight empty wine bottles around him. He raised his eyes to look at Adelaide but had trouble focusing.

"What…do you…want?"

"Jess, please don't chase me away." Before he could move, she fell at his feet. "I love you! I could never live without you! Do what you like—you can kill me if you want to—just don't make me leave you!"

If she had tried it a day earlier, it might have worked. Unfortunately for Adele, Richard's words had made a strong impression on Jess. Now, he was as mad as the devil.

Instead of the caress she expected, Adele got a hard slap in the face.

She cringed away from him. Jess stood up and tried to kick her, but he was too drunk to make contact. As Adele skittered out the door and down the hall, Jess shook a fist at her and let loose a string of oaths that made it clear he did not wish to see her again.

Then he staggered off in the opposite direction to find Richard.

Back in her own room, Adelaide summed up the results of her mission. She would have to stay out of sight until her bruises went away. She would ask her maid to tell the rest of the delegation that she had fallen down some stairs. In a few days' time, she would try again with Jess. She would also look around for another protector—just in case the earl turned against her for good.

Chapter 5
The Plot Thickens, and So Does the Snow…

Richard wasn't asleep when Jess came in. He sat up in bed and listened to his cousin's story with an ironic glint in his eye. When it was over, he made a simple suggestion, "It is time to get rid of Adelaide, once and for all."

Jess disagreed. Adele was a woman; he didn't like the idea of killing her, and he thought it would be easy enough to make her do as he wished.

Richard was only able to get him to agree to write to his wife and his uncle more often. They also agreed that if Adele's guilt was proven, Jess wouldn't try to shield her from her rightful fate.

After Jess was gone, Richard sat watching the candle on his bedside table. He knew it was already early morning, but it was still dark outside the window.

My father taught me that every person, man or woman, acts in his or her own interests. Jess doesn't understand that. He thinks he knows everything about women, but his ignorance puts him in danger.

෮ ⬜ ෧

A night spent sneaking about in the secret passages in the guest wing of the palace had left Altres with much to ponder. He asked two of his men to find out everything they could about Adelaide Wells and to keep a close eye on her movements. She might come in useful if the prince didn't cooperate and fall in love with Anna of his own free will.

The jester also found himself exceedingly interested in another woman, one he had never met: Lilian Earton. He wanted to know more about her, but Rolf had yet to report back.

He would watch and wait, building his plans one step at a time. Intrigue was like hand-to-hand combat, and the jester—always the professional—preferred to finish off his opponent with the first blow.

ꕤ ꕤ

Weeks passed, and snow blanketed the Earton estate. From the window of her study, Lily watched the snow falling in the courtyard, and she observed as Miranda and the other children made snowmen and engaged in wild snowball fights. Winter brought with it a damp, bone-chilling cold. Lily didn't know if the dampness came from the sea or from the bogs. She just knew that she couldn't keep the castle warm, no matter how much peat she burned.

Everyone was cold, but nobody went hungry. There was plenty of salted fish to eat, and Lily continued to distribute grain to those who needed it. Pastor Vopler told her that the people in the villages were praying for the health of their kind countess. And when she made her rounds of the castle, Lily often heard servants commenting that the countess was an odd sort of woman, but a good one…

She was pleased. Earton was her home, and she liked

to have her home in order. Miranda's education was also coming along nicely.

Lily remembered a lecture on psychology from long ago in her other life where the professor had claimed that parents weren't capable of loving an adopted child the way they loved their biological children. Back then, she was too young and too busy studying anatomy to care about her psychology professor. Now that she had more experience, she would have liked to go back and tell that professor a thing or two about love and adopted children.

That said, her love for Miranda never prevented her from teaching the girl a lesson if she needed it.

On one particular day that winter, Lily went to listen in on the history lesson. The servants had hung heavy drapes over the door to keep the classroom warm, so Lily was able to stand behind the drapes and observe the lesson without being seen.

The history teacher asked the children if they remembered who the founder of Ativerna was.

Miranda shouted out "Elor the Great!" and looked very pleased with herself.

A Virman boy frowned and contradicted her. "That isn't right. It was Derek the First!"

Miranda's eyes grew round. "No, it was Elor. I know better than you do!"

"But I'm sure it was Derek!"

The teacher suggested that they consult their history text to resolve the dispute. Lily nodded to herself in approval.

After a moment of silence as the two bent their heads over the scroll, the Virman boy looked up. "I was right! It was Derek, and Elor was his son!"

Then, to Lily's horror, she heard Miranda say, "I'm still going to be a countess, and I can have you whipped at the stable if I want!"

Lily slid out from behind the drapery. "What is going on in here?" Her voice was low and dangerous.

Miranda could have tried to say that she was just joking, but getting the answer wrong had made her angry. "He should keep his mouth shut. I'm the earl's daughter, and he..."

"Knows more than you do," Lily finished her sentence for her. "Miranda Catherine Earton, come with me. You will have to miss the rest of this lesson."

Mirrie ran along behind her, trying to catch her stepmother's hand, but Lily was as cold as the Snow Queen. Once they were in her study, she sat down at her desk and pointed for Mirrie to sit on the chair across from her.

"What do you have to say for yourself, My Lady?"

Mirrie sniffled. "I don't know, Lily."

Sometimes the girl called her "Mama," but Lily never insisted on it. *Everything in time.*

"What do you not know?"

"I don't know why you're mad at me."

Lily looked into the little girl's blue eyes and felt her anger melt away. Mirrie truly did not know what she had done wrong. She was an aristocrat, and she had been watching adults behave that way her whole life.

"Listen to me, my dear," Lily said, her voice softer. "Why did you say you could have that boy whipped?"

"Because he was trying to act better than me." Mirrie was still annoyed.

"Why shouldn't he? He knew the right answer, and you didn't. You wanted to punish him for knowing something you didn't."

The little girl sniffled again. "I didn't like how he talked to me."

"Maybe so, but you really did get the answer wrong. So, even if you're the earl's daughter and he's a Virman, he knows more than you do...at least about history."

"But that's not fair!"

Lily smiled. "Who's stopping you from studying harder? Then, the next time you argue with him about something, you'll be right, and he'll be wrong. That's what I expect from the earl's daughter."

Miranda looked up with a funny look on her face. "Lily, how can he be smarter than me? He's just a Virman."

"How much do you know about Virmans?"

Silence.

"See? Not much," Lily chided her. "Ignorance is no excuse. If you knew more about them, you would know that that boy's father is a shipbuilder."

"So what?"

"Shipbuilders are the most important people on Virma. So, I guess you could say that the boy you were arguing with is the equivalent of a baron's son. That means that your title doesn't put you that much above him." She waited for that to sink in before continuing. "Mirrie, do you know why the Virman boys and girls study so hard? They understand that this is an opportunity for them to bring new learning back to their country. Can you think of a reason why you should be learning?"

Mirrie looked around the room as if she hoped to see the answer written on a wall somewhere. "Because I'm the earl's daughter?" she finally ventured.

Lily snorted. "Think about all the people above you in rank. The dukes, the princes... Won't you ever want to get married someday?"

Mirrie nodded.

"But who will want you? A wife is supposed to run the estate and keep an eye on her husband's managers. She also has to be interesting to talk to. Otherwise, her husband will never want to come home."

Mirrie's eyes got even bigger. "Like Papa?" she asked in a whisper

Lily glanced away. That hurt. Still, the lesson she wanted to impart was more important than her own discomfort.

"Yes. You can ask him about that when you see him. He'll tell you that I used to be fat and stupid and boring. He couldn't even stand to be around me."

"But I'm not fat!" Mirrie exclaimed.

"That may be so, but you are doing your best to grow up stupid and boring." She winked at the girl.

"Lily!"

"Just think. You're all grown up and married someday, and your husband takes you with him to a royal reception. You turn to your neighbor at the banquet table and say 'I believe it was the great founder of our nation, Simon the Eighth, who...'"

"There never was any Simon the Eighth!" Mirrie objected.

"I'm glad to see you know something," Lily said, making a funny face. "But you'll say something else equally ridiculous. Then, when your neighbor at that royal banquet table corrects you, what are you going to do? Jump up and say 'I'll have you whipped for that, sir!'"

Mirrie looked down.

Lily pressed on. "Don't go around showing off in front of people when you don't know what you're talking about, Mirrie. That would make me ashamed of you."

A tear trickled down the little girl's pink cheek. "How am I supposed to do better, Lily?"

"Study. Study your lessons until you know them better than the tutor."

"What if my lessons are boring?"

Lily got down on her knees next to the girl. "My dear, do you think I enjoy taking care of all the estate business?"

"I don't know."

"Then I'll tell you, I don't enjoy it. But I have to do it, and someday you will have to do it, too. If something happens to your father and me, you will be in charge here. How will you make yourself do all the work to run an estate if you can't make yourself learn your lessons?"

Mirrie was quiet for a moment. Then she looked up at her stepmother. "Lily, I want to make you proud."

Lily put her arms around the girl and kissed her. "Good. Because I want to be proud of you. Now, tell me something. Do you think the children will make fun of you when you go back to class?"

"Yes," Mirrie said glumly.

"Then here's what you do…"

❧ ☐ ☙

Later that evening, a glowing Mirrie reported back to Lily on her success in the classroom.

"You were right. When I went back in, Bjorn told me I was too dumb to ever be a countess."

"Did you get upset?"

"No, I didn't! I told him to meet me in the hall a ten night from now to see who's dumb. We're going to compete on our history facts!"

"Good. We'll have to do a lot of work these next ten days."

"Will you help me?"

"Of course."

❧ ☐ ☙

Adelaide Wells was in deep despair. Her plan to seduce Jess again had failed. He was avoiding her. When he saw her at events, he acted as if she didn't exist.

That interfered with her plans, and she began to wonder if her life might be in danger. She was afraid to think what fate awaited her at home in Ativerna if Jess was no longer her protector. Even if the king let her live, she would be banished from polite society and forced to earn her keep as a prostitute; she had to act.

Once her bruises had gone from purple to pale green,

she paid another late-night visit to the earl's rooms.

"Come in," he called in answer to her knock. When he saw who it was, his face turned cold. "What do you want?"

Adelaide fell to her knees. "Listen to me, Jerrison!"

"I don't want to. You should leave."

"But I haven't done anything to you!"

His face turned red. "Didn't you sell my gifts to pay men to kill my wife?"

"I didn't do it! It was Alex! If I hadn't obeyed him, he would have married me off to someone horrible."

Jess sighed. He knew that much could be true. Adelaide's dead husband's cousin would certainly have had the authority to give her away in marriage as he saw fit. If he had demanded her jewelry, she could not have refused.

"Why didn't you tell me?"

"I was afraid of losing you. I love you so much…"

"You've already lost me."

Adelaide looked down and blushed. "Does that mean that our child will never know his father?"

The earl stared at her for a long minute. "Our child?"

"Yes. Our son or daughter."

"But I…"

"We were cautious, but this is the will of Aldonai." She played her role with abandon. "I have lost my connection with the moon, and my breasts are heavy. Look…" She opened the front of her dress. Jess' eyes were drawn to her creamy breasts, but he forced himself to look away.

"I'll give you money for a midwife. And I'll never touch you again." He took a fat wallet out of his desk and tossed it to Adele. She made no move to catch it, so it fell on the floor at her feet. "Poison it before it's too late. You may have slept with other men, for all I know."

Adelaide's eyes shone. "I would rather be an outcast than poison my own child!" She ran from the room, slamming the door behind her.

Once she was alone in her own room, she locked the door and sat down on her bed. She knew she had played the scene well. Jerrison believed that she was pregnant; that was enough for now. He was hard as stone, but she would chip away at him.

ಬ ಲ

Jess poured himself another cup of wine, but he didn't drink it. Instead, he got up and went to find Richard.

He walked in without knocking. "Adele is with child."

"Is it yours?"

The earl thought for a moment. "It could be."

"Do you believe her?"

"I don't know. I bought some herbs to keep this from happening, but maybe they didn't work."

"Idiot. You should have stayed away from her."

"I know." Jess sat down and put his face in his hands.

"What will you do now?"

"If it's mine, I'll have to do something for it."

Richard nodded. He would have done the same. Then he had a thought. "Take her to a midwife before you do anything else. Make sure she really is with child. She's lied to you before."

Jess straightened up. "Excellent idea. Why didn't I think of that?"

"Because you're upset. Have a drink." He poured two cups of wine. They drank together in companionable silence.

⁞⁞

Adele jumped. There was a man in her room.

"Do you have a moment of time for me?" It was Gardwig's jester. Adele didn't know his name, but she had heard rumors that he was close to the king. Normally, she would have screamed at the sudden appearance of a strange man in her room, but she had drunk a large cup of wine after her scene with Jess, so her sense of danger was impaired.

Instead of crying out, she stood up from her bed and gestured at the armchair by the fireplace. "Have a seat, sir."

Altres sneered. "I suppose you're feeling afraid now." Adele tried to look haughty, but he continued without waiting for her to speak. "If you go home, you'll end up in prison or with your head on the block. The best you can hope for is expulsion from the kingdom. Do you think they won't catch you in that lie? You're no more with child than I am."

Adele gasped and put a hand over her mouth.

"If you play nice with me, I'll help you." The jester tried to make his voice friendly. "You won't have to count your pennies or rub paint on your bruises. You won't have to be afraid." He was gratified to see her eyes fill with tears. "Listen to me. I will send a midwife to see you. She will tell the earl that you are pregnant. We can discuss my terms later."

"But…"

"Consider this an advance for your services." The jester unlocked her door and slipped out, closing it softly behind him. (He had entered the room through a secret passage while Adele lay on her bed with her face to the wall, but he had no intention of letting her know that.)

❧ ☐ ☙

Jess brought a midwife to examine Adele. The woman confirmed that she was with child. That put Jess' former lover in a difficult position. On the one hand, Jess was polite and careful around her. On the other hand, however, Prince Richard stared at her with poorly concealed hate whenever he saw her.

The jester said nothing.

❧ ☐ ☙

The children at the castle worked to make the history challenge as hard as possible. Each child wrote a question and placed it in the large gold cup Lily had found for the occasion. Miranda and Bjorn took turns pulling out questions and answering them. A panel of tutors--Damis Reis, Lons Avels, and Maria Reichart—judged whether their answers had merit or not. Lily had warned them to be as strict as possible, so after each child's answer, the tutors unrolled their heavy scrolls and read the relevant passages aloud. The audience, which consisted of servants and Virmans, cheered for the children and sometimes even ventured their own guesses.

In the end, Miranda beat Bjorn by three points.

While the audience good-naturedly cheered, Miranda threw her arms around Lily's neck and whispered, "I love you, Mama!"

Lily stroked her daughter's shiny, dark hair and whispered, "I love you, too, my dear."

⃝ ⃞

The Great Khangan had a fiery temper, but he showed unusual restraint when Tahir's letter was delivered to him by one of the palace healers. He knew that his eldest son--handsome, kind and wise beyond his years--was dying. The young man's condition was dire so, instead of allowing himself to vent his anger that Tahir had run away and left his son in the hands of lesser healers, the Great Khangan took a deep breath, broke the seal and began to read.

After a wordy introduction, Tahir explained that he had not run away out of fear, which the Great Khangan believed was a lie. Tahir informed his lord that he had gone in search of someone or something that could heal the heir to the Khangan throne. And, Tahir rejoiced to announce, he had found her—the Countess of Earton, a woman gifted by the Star Mare to be able to diagnose the boy's trouble without even seeing him.

According to the countess, the boy was being poisoned. She said the poison could be given many ways--applied to the skin or bedclothes, or mixed into food, it was impossible to know. However, she was confident that she knew the name of the poison. It killed slowly, damaging the body as it did its evil work.

If the Great Khangan wanted to see his son healthy again, he would have to discover who the poisoner was or send the boy away from the palace. If he liked, he could send the boy to Earton. It was a long journey, but all the better to put great distance between the heir and his poisoner.

The countess suggested the Great Khangan test her theory by giving the boy extra milk to drink and having him soak in a bath filled with pine needles every day. If he started to feel better—or if he at least stopped getting worse—the answer would be clear.

The Great Khangan set the letter down and considered its contents. He had never heard of a woman healer before, but he would try the milk and the pine baths. Tahir wrote that Ali Akhmet din Tahirjian could confirm that the countess was a great healer, and the din Tahirjians were a wealthy, noble family who valued their ties with the palace.

In all, it was a strange letter, but it gave the Great Khangan something that felt like hope.

ᎳᏅ ᏟᎶ

Much to Torius Avermal's dismay, he had been unable to find out exactly what Karl Treloney was up to. The merchant was obviously doing well for himself, but the people the mayor could rely on to make discreet inquiries didn't know much about him. In the end, his letter to Lily was disappointingly brief.

When she received it, Lily resolved to write and ask

her father and Hans to see what they could discover about the merchant from Altver.

In the meantime, she continued to keep a close eye on the food that was served to her and Miranda. No spices or unfamiliar ingredients were allowed. Everyone at the castle knew the rules at the countess' table.

All would have been well, but Damis Reis continued to hound and annoy her. Lily began to seriously consider sending him on an expedition through the snow to Altver. He was a decent tutor, but he was getting on her nerves. She didn't like how he looked at her, or how he "accidentally" brushed up against her hand, and she didn't appreciate the winter bouquets of greenery he always brought back for her when he went on walks.

She decided to do something about the lovesick tutor at the first opportunity, hopefully before he had a chance to cause trouble.

ᙠ☐ᘓ

Damis Reis thought he was making excellent progress with the countess. She couldn't possibly have failed to notice his attentions. He hoped that when he was able to get her alone, she would drop the show of strength and display more feminine traits. He expected to see embarrassment, timidity, surprise…

What he didn't expect was what actually happened. One afternoon, Lily called for him to come to her study. When he arrived, Lons Avels opened the door for him and then waited outside. Without looking up, Lily said, "Now tell me, Reis, what exactly do you think you're up to?"

Lily had prepared for this meeting. She had chosen the location and her dress very carefully in order to make a strong impression. She wore a loose black dress that hid her curves, and she had had Lons remove the chair that normally faced her desk so that Damis had to stand in front of her like a guilty schoolboy.

When she finally looked up, her eyes were icy.

He was lost. "What do you mean, My Lady?"

"I mean the looks, the bouquets, the brushing up against me. You have been pursuing me for a month. Why?"

Damis was taken aback by her directness, but he decided to play his game as far as it would take him.

"My Lady, forgive me for my impertinence…"

He expected her to say something here, but she just stared at him. He told her how he had looked forward to the trip to Earton, and how delighted he had been to meet her. He recounted how her beauty and intelligence had won him over, eventually causing him to fall in love with her. Since she had shown him no notice, he had started to court her as actively as he dared.

◦◦ ⬚ ◦◦

Lily listened to this nonsense and wondered what it really meant. Of course, she considered herself a good-looking woman, but that didn't explain why this poor man was so love-struck. However, she held her tongue. In her training as a doctor, she had learned that sometimes, the best thing you can do is let a person talk.

Damis, meanwhile, kept talking. He complimented her eyes and her hair, which he compared to a river of gold reflecting the sun's rays.

He's a tutor, Lily thought to herself, just a tutor. In this world, he's got no right whatsoever to even consider falling in love with a countess. He has to know that. What is he really up to? Does he think I'm so lonely out here that I'll fall into his hands like a ripe apple? Or…

At first, the new thought seemed ridiculous. But then she remembered the old saying: just because you're paranoid doesn't mean someone isn't after you. She knew that the law only allowed her to divorce Jerrison Earton if she caught him committing adultery. If the situation was reversed, however, and he found out she had slept with another man, he could send her to a convent, which would actually be more like a prison.

Is my husband trying to set me up?

Once she tried the theory on for size, she decided it fit. Someone—whether or not the earl—wanted to be able to blackmail her.

At that point, Damis ran out of things to say and decided to swing into action. He fell at Lily's knees and started kissing her hand.

Lily jerked her hand away. "Let go of me!"

Unfazed, the man grabbed her knee and tried to move his hand up her thigh.

"Let go!" Lily shouted.

Suddenly, Damis cried out and fell forward. Nanook, Lily's

Virman puppy, had heard the anger in her mistress' voice and decided to take matters into her own paws. She leaped on the tutor from behind and bit him in the shoulder. Once he was down, she stood on his back to keep him from getting up.

"Good dog!" Lily cried. "Hold him there!" She ran to the door and called for her guards.

Ivar was first into the room. "My Lady?"

"Take this man away!"

Lily was too upset to say more, but Ivar knew what to do. He picked up the tutor and held him by the back of his shirt with his feet at least a foot off the floor. Martha had come running when she heard the commotion, and now she stood by Lily's side with a hand over her mouth in horror.

"Did he offend you, My Lady?" Ivar asked.

"He tried to, but Nanook got to him first."

Ivar looked the limp tutor up and down. "Shall I cut off his head, My Lady?" Damis whined something indistinctly. Ivar hit him upside the head. "Where did he get the courage to venture a hand against your person, My Lady?"

"I'd like to know that myself, Ivar. I want to find out what he was promised and who promised it to him."

Ivar hit the tutor again. "Did you hear that, you son-of-a-bitch? Talk, and you may yet live to see tomorrow." Then he let go of the man, and Damis slumped to the floor. At first, he tried to repeat the same old story about how much he loved the countess. After a couple of blows to the head from Ivar, he changed his mind.

Next, he tried to convince them that he was acting out

of self-interest, but alone. When Ivar kicked him hard in the side, he decided to tell the truth.

Lily, Ivar, and Martha listened and shook their heads.

Damis had been hired in Lavery. He really was a tutor, but he couldn't keep his hands off pretty girls. When the father of one of his students came after him with a pair of sheep shears, he ran away and got a job in the capital—where no one knew him—teaching the children of Baron Yerby. Before long, he was enjoying the favors of the baron's wife.

After a few months, the baron told him he was no longer needed in their household, and that he could get him a job teaching little Miranda Catherine Earton.

Lily had never heard of Baron Yerby before.

"Who promised to pay you for seducing me?"

Damis swore it was Baron Yerby that made the offer. The tutor stood to get five hundred gold coins if he managed to get caught in bed with Lily, and three hundred gold coins if he slept with her but was not able to procure witnesses to the fact.

"I'm surprised that a countess' honor costs that much," Lily said grimly. "It would have been cheaper to kill me."

"I wasn't involved in any of that!" Damis exclaimed. He started to shake at the thought that they might suspect him of attempted murder.

Lily continued to press him. "Why try to seduce me when I was already pregnant?"

Damis' face went white. "They told me there wouldn't be a child."

The countess stood up and turned to Ivar. "The miscarriage…

What has he done?" she whispered. She took a deep breath and regained control of her thinking. "Ivar, have someone search his things."

"Yes, My Lady," the Virman replied.

An hour later, Jaimie came in to look at the red powder they had found in Damis' chest.

"I know this weed, My Lady," he said. His eyes were troubled. "Women have always used it to get rid of unwanted children."

Ivar looked over at the tutor and said nothing.

Damis froze, obviously wondering what would happen to him.

Lily winced and looked away from him. She had no desire to see him beheaded. "Put him in the dungeon. I'll deal with him later."

As Ivar dragged the tutor away, he tried to whine something to the countess, but she was no longer thinking about him.

It looks like I have two serious enemies at the same time. One of them is this Yerby. The other one is Adelaide Wells' cousin who sent the hired killers.

She knew from Hans that Alex was in prison awaiting execution.

But who is this Yerby, and who is behind him? Karl Treloney is supposedly connected with someone important in the capital, and I doubt his contact is a lowly baron.

Who wants to get rid of Lilian Earton so badly that they'll try anything? How could a silly young woman with no interests outside of church and embroidery be a target for murder? Why on earth would anyone even know her name?

The whole situation reminded Lily of a subcutaneous abscess that filled with poison before you even noticed it was there.

Not on my watch! I'll write to my mother-in-law and ask her to find out what she can about this Yerby. I'm not the kind of girl to sit around while someone tries to kill me!

めや ☐ ઉજ

Ali Akhmet din Tahirjian obeyed the Great Khangan's request for a meeting as soon as he could. When he entered the richly decorated room of the palace where the ruler saw guests, he knelt down and prepared to go through the elaborate rituals for entering the presence of the exalted one.

"Come, Ali. Sit next to me," the Great Khangan interrupted him.

Ali Akhmet obeyed. "How may I be of service, Your Majesty?"

The ruler's eyes were sad and tired. "Tell me about Earton."

The merchant had not expected such a question, and he wasn't sure how much he should say. "It is a long distance from Altver, Your Majesty."

"I hear there is a great medicus there. Is that so?"

Ali Akhmet looked down at his leg.

"What can you tell me about the Countess of Earton?" the Great Khangan leaned forward. "I hear that she worked a miracle on you."

Ali Akhmet sighed. He looked over at his ruler--who was also his friend--and told the whole story. He recounted how he was gored and tossed by a bull at the fair in Altver, and how a strange woman set his bone and taught him how to care for his leg so that it would heal properly. He even pulled up one pants leg and showed the Great Khangan his scar. The ruler looked incredulous, so Ali Akhmet stood up and jumped on one leg and then on the other leg to show that both were equally sound.

The Great Khangan reached out to touch Ali's leg. He had never heard of a woman healer who could do such work. He knew for certain that there were no such women in the Khanganate. He looked up at Ali Akhmet and saw that his eyes were shining.

"Would you take her as a wife?"

"Never!" Ali Akhmet was emphatic.

"Why not?"

Ali Akhmet thought for a moment before answering. "Because she is a woman with a man's mind. I count her as one of my great friends, but it would be uncomfortable to have her in my house."

The Great Khangan nodded. That was true enough. He interlaced his fingers in front of him and stared at his friend for a long time. Finally, he decided to be open about what was on his mind.

"She sent me a letter with instructions on how to heal my son. The treatment is going well. I would like to invite her to come here."

Ali Akhmet shook his head. "She will not come."

"Why not?"

"She would need her husband's permission."

That made sense to the ruler. "I will write to him, then."

"I believe he is on a diplomatic mission with Prince Richard. They have gone to Wellster."

"Why did she not go with her husband?"

"Your Majesty, it is not the custom in those lands for a woman to travel when she is with child." Ali Akhmet did not mention that Lily had already had a miscarriage.

"I see. I will write to the earl when he returns. We will see what he says." He gestured for Ali Akhmet to go.

࿏ ꕥ

On his way out of the palace, Ali Akhmet thought about Lilian Earton. He owed her his life, and he was more than willing to keep her secrets. He suspected that if Lily did come to the Khanganate, its ruler would do everything in his power to keep her there, like valuable treasure. And knowing the countess, he felt very sure that nothing good would come of forcing her to do that which she did not want to do.

Lilian Earton is an excellent friend, but she is a deadly enemy.

࿏ ꕥ

Unlike Ali Akhmet, the Great Khangan cared little for Lilian Earton's plans and preferences. His thoughts were clear: he loved his son, and he wanted to save his life. If he couldn't get the countess to come to the Khanganate right away, perhaps he should send his son to Earton.

Will he survive the trip?

It was a bad time of year for traveling, but part of the trip could be taken over land. The Great Khangan had already isolated his son from everyone but a chosen few, but somehow the poison continued to find the boy. He would improve for a few days on the countess' treatment, but then he would start to throw up blood again. The ruler suspected that Lilian Earton might be the only person who could save his son.

If I send him, he will go with a handful of soldiers and a few of my most trusted servants to keep him safe.

In truth, the Great Khangan would have sent his son even farther than Earton to get a cure.

ഈ◦◦

Lily found herself enjoying winter in Earton. The children played outside every day after their lessons and before their practical studies in the infirmary with Jaimie. The villages were peaceful, and no one was hungry.

A letter arrived from King Edward informing her that he wanted to see Jaimie in person before giving him title to the Donter estate. For the time being, the king informed her, she should continue to manage the estate in her own name.

ഈ◦◦

Quite conspicuously, there was no word from her husband. Edward had dashed off an angry note informing the earl that he would have to try harder.

To the Earl of Earton,

I am astonished by your wife's patience with you up to now. The letter you wrote her was unacceptable. Write again, this time more sensibly, and send it to me first. If I hear that you are misbehaving in Wellster, you will face a strict reckoning upon your return. Unlike the countess, I do not have unlimited patience.

Edward the Eighth, by the grace of Aldonai King of Ativerna

At the bottom of the letter, there was a scrawl in the king's own handwriting (the rest of the letter had been dictated to a scribe):

Jess, think with your head before you become the first divorced earl in the kingdom. If your wife requests separation from you, I can only support her wishes.

The king's note was torn to pieces by a man tired of hearing and thinking about his wife. Jess was not used to criticism, and it seemed to him that, lately, everyone who walked past him had advice on how he ought to be living his life.

Richard was particularly hard on his cousin. He told Jess he couldn't understand why Jess continued to treat Adelaide with consideration when he ought to hand her some money and tell her to get lost. The truth was, Jess had tried that approach, but it was remarkably unsuccessful and ended with him dodging a vase aimed at his head.

As if the earl didn't have enough trouble, he received a short letter from August Broklend. The first paragraph was all about their business affairs, which were going well, but in the second paragraph, the tone changed. August warned Jess that he would see Lily in the spring. If she had even the tiniest complaint about her husband, August would personally castrate his son-in-law and send him to a monastery, where he suspected the young man's morals and character would be much improved.

His mood was made worse by the fact that Princess Anna told

the ladies at court to keep their distance from the earl. He was reduced to visiting a nearby brothel several times, much to his cousin's horror.

ଚ୦ ଙ୪

For her part, Anna acted on the orders of Altres Lort in his efforts for Adelaide Wells.

ଚ୦ ଙ୪

Richard also had a letter from the king. Edward tactfully reminded his son that Wellster was a good neighbor and that an alliance with Gardwig's daughter would be advantageous for Ativerna. He was still free to choose as he wished, of course, but he could do worse than Princess Anna.

Richard might have been tempted to ignore the letter, but he had also received a portrait of Princess Lidia of Ivernea, which revealed her to be tall, skinny young woman whose expensive gown hung limply on her flat chest. To round out the impression, the look on her face indicated that she might bite if he touched her.

Anna started to look like the more attractive of the two. At the very least, he thought to himself, she is dim-witted enough that I won't have a hard time controlling her.

He had yet to make up his mind when, one bitterly cold morning, Gardwig sent for him.

ଚ୦ ଙ୪

The king's leg had been tormenting him for the past month, and his temper suffered for it. Only his wife and the jester were safe from his wrath; everyone else risked being screamed at, banished from the castle, or even sent to the dungeon. The members of Gardwig's court had taken to walking quickly and quietly through the halls with their heads down.

Milia was expecting another child and could not keep her food down, but she felt she had to stay by her husband's side for his own good and the good of the kingdom. So, she hid her suffering as best she could and stayed close to the king, who hoped to have yet another son before long.

Altres also stayed close to the king, but for entirely different reasons. He was afraid that certain dark forces in the kingdom might take Gardwig's physical weakness as a sign that it was time to act.

ഇൽ ൽ

Prince Richard knew the Lion of Wellster to be a frighteningly unpredictable ruler who still melted at the sight of his wife. In fact, he envied the man his marital happiness.

When Richard entered his room, Gardwig nodded at the seat next to him. "Sit down, young man."

The prince bowed and obeyed.

Without moving, Gardwig looked over at a bottle on the table in front of them. "Will you pour us each a cup of that wine?"

"Of course, Your Majesty."

"Good." He turned to his wife. "My dear, please leave us and make sure that we are not bothered."

Milia smiled, kissed her husband's cheek and left.

When Richard handed the king his cup, he pointed at the door. "She doesn't like for me to drink wine anymore. The healers have told her it is bad for me, and she believes them. Still, I suppose I am a lucky old man to have her."

"Her Majesty is one of the most beautiful women in Wellster, I'm sure," Richard ventured.

"Beauty is skin-deep, young man." Gardwig paused to clear his throat. "Milia is a good woman. She has given me sons, and she loves me with her whole heart. What else could I wish for?"

Richard watched the older man's face as he said this. Then he surprised himself. "I would wish for a love that is mutual."

Gardwig smiled, and the peevish look left his face, making him look almost kind. "You want a lot, young man. Love is a terrible luxury that few kings can afford."

The prince looked down and said nothing.

"Do you want to hear my story? Milia is my seventh wife. I had plenty of sorrow before her. Some of them committed adultery, and one of them even tried to poison me." Gardwig chuckled. "But what I am telling you? Think of your own father." The younger man's face was pained, but Gardwig continued. "Do you even remember your mother?"

"No, Your Majesty."

"I do. She was a lovely woman, and very unhappy. Think what it means to lie in bed with a man and know that he would rather have someone else in your place."

Richard stared at him. He had never considered his

parents' story from that angle. And he really didn't remember his mother. This was the first he had ever heard about her being lovely. Suddenly he remembered words long forgotten.

He looked up at the king. "A cheap whore…" he whispered.

Gardwig leaned back in his chair. "Is that what she said about Jessamine?"

"Yes. Edmund told me that. I was too young to understand."

"That's life," the king sighed and put his cup on the table. "Some people are happy, others are not." He glanced at the prince, his eyes glittering. "Have you thought about Anna?"

"I have."

"What did you decide? To go to Ivernea and look at her competitor?"

"Yes, Your Majesty." Richard was open about his plans because Gardwig seemed to know all about them as if his decision was the most natural thing in the world.

The old man shifted his weight in his chair. "Your father loves you. I can't say that I'd give a son of mine any choice in the matter."

Richard smiled and was about to say something, but the king was not finished. "Now tell me, what do you think about my daughter?" he said quickly. "I know her breasts are more attractive than her brains, but what else have you found?"

Richard started to feel uncomfortable. "Your Majesty, I…"

"Don't be afraid of angering me. I am speaking to you not as a king, but as one man to another. I hope you can see that."

Richard did see, but he was still afraid of angering Gardwig.

The king broke the uncomfortable silence. "I was seventeen years old when I married the daughter of the Duke of Mederin. We had been engaged since we were children, and my father had just died, so I had no choice. Now imagine this: Tisia Mederin was almost fifteen years my senior, and she was already a widow." He let that sink in before continuing. "So we were married."

Richard sighed. He knew parts of this story.

"Tisia was one of the smartest people I have ever known. She sat me down on our wedding night and laid out for me what she knew about the alliances between several of the families around us. She was a friend to me, but she hated her father, who had sold her like a purebred horse. I promised to get rid of old Mederin, and she, in turn, promised to give me my freedom as soon as I cared to ask for it. We were partners."

Richard had never heard these details before. He watched the king's face with increasing interest.

"We never had children. Her previous husband had beaten her. One time, he beat her so badly that she lost the child she was carrying and almost died. She never admitted anything to me, but I suspect she poisoned him in revenge. Tisia was a strong woman, not the kind you can control. She could love powerfully, but she could also hate with a passion. Have you ever met a woman like that?"

Richard shook his head. "Aldonai has been merciful to me."

Gardwig smiled. "Praise be to Aldonai." He rubbed his knee with one hand and grimaced, but his thoughts were still in the distant past. "Tisia was a true friend to me. Once I got rid of her father, we agreed that she would stay with me until I found someone else. Of course, I found someone. I was just nineteen then and too foolish to know what I already had. Lucia was gorgeous. I suppose Anna looks a bit like her, but Lucia had something else, something stronger. When she walked into a room, all the men in the room suddenly remembered that they were men. Tisia saw that I felt it, too, and she told me it was time to part ways. She gave me a divorce, and I bought her an estate. She still lives there, by the way, and she couldn't be happier."

Richard raised his cup and drank a silent toast to Tisia. He was glad things had worked out well for her.

"I married Lucia," Gardwig went on. "We were happy for a year. She gave birth to Anna, who was a tiny copy of her mother. And then…"

The prince was listening attentively.

"I had no idea she was unfaithful. Lucia was smart in her own way. She never had liaisons with any of the nobles at court." Gardwig grimaced. "She sought out my grooms, my huntsmen, my servants. Anyone who would be afraid to talk. But one of the huntsmen saw something and told me."

Gardwig picked up his cup again but did not drink. He was remembering. The huntsman had not actually come to him. He had gone to Altres. Gardwig's adopted brother had convinced him to hide out and spy on Lucia during one of her trysts. That was when he caught her.

"Lucia swore she had never been unfaithful to me before, but when I found out how many men she had been with..." he looked over at Richard, "I had her executed." The room got so quiet that Richard could hear a tree branch tapping against the window. He felt cold.

Gardwig's face darkened. "I have spent very little time with

Anna, but I know that she is mine."

Richard could think of nothing to say.

The old king laughed, "That's right, young man. It's best to keep your mouth shut. But you can believe me on this. Everyone in the Wellster line has a birthmark on the small of the back, right above the buttocks. It's small, the size of a fingernail and shaped like a shield. Anna has it. I have it. My sons have it. You'll forgive an old man for declining to show it to you."

"You're hardly an old man," Richard said diplomatically.

"I am old, and I am tired. I need to know that there will be peace."

Richard nodded. This was safer ground. "As do we. Ativerna has no desire for conflict."

"Your father is a wise man," Gardwig smiled. "He remembers that Wellster has always been a reliable ally against Avesterra and the witless Leonard…"

Richard knew all about his father's foreign affairs. King Leonard of Avesterra was the most religious ruler in those parts, and his neighbors suspected that his policy was dictated by the church. Edward, on the other hand, was a deeply practical man who wanted his aldons to stay behind their alters and let more experienced men govern. Ativernan religious leaders grumbled at being denied power, but they avoided open quarrels.

He looked up at Gardwig. "My father says he would always rather deal with you than with the church."

The old man put a hand on the prince's shoulder. "And he's right. I enjoy my dealings with him." He paused for a moment. "I want to make you an offer, young man."

Richard kept his face still and polite. "What kind of offer?"

"Go see Lidia. You need to be convinced that she isn't the one for you. But after that, come back here. I know Anna is a foolish young woman, but she isn't mean. You'll be able to handle her. And later, if you find a woman for your heart, I won't say anything to you about it…as long as you are discreet."

Richard nodded. It was a generous offer.

"And another thing," the old king continued. "Your father already knows. Did he tell you about Anna's dowry?"

"No, Your Majesty."

"The province of Bali."

It was all Richard could do to keep from whistling. Bali was rich with silver mines.

Gardwig saw the look on his face. "I'm a generous friend, Richard."

The prince nodded. "Very generous, Your Majesty."

Gardwig acknowledged the compliment with a thin smile. Bali had vast natural riches that were the envy of neighboring kingdoms, but it came with its own headaches, as well, and these were problems that Richard did not know about. There were no major towns in Bali, which made moving silver from the mines a dangerous enterprise, and lately, Gardwig had been hearing reports of thieves and bandits in the woods around the province. He didn't have the energy to combat many small enemies dispersed throughout the woods, and he would be glad to hand the whole thing to Richard before the bandits started to make trouble in the more settled areas of Wellster.

"Your Majesty," Richard said quietly, "I have a duty to go to Ivernea, but Princess Anna may be assured of my return."

Gardwig nodded. "You will be a fine king."

"If I live that long," Richard replied wryly.

"You will, and you will prosper. Here, pour me some more of that wine."

ও ∞ ৪

Altres moved away from his peephole and slipped silently through his secret passage. He couldn't help but grin. Gardwig had been masterful. A little sadness, a little talk of love, a little bribery, and the dish was ready to be served.

Richard and his father both wanted to be aligned with Wellster. Furthermore, the jester doubted that Bernard the Second of Ivernea could offer anything near as valuable as Bali's silver mines for his daughter's dowry. Even if he could, his miserly, tight-fisted ways would prevent him from doing it.

Altres sighed. Now that Richard was more or less on the hook, it was time to give Adelaide Wells very clear instructions on what he expected her to do.

ও ∞ ৪

Lily was pleased with her ventures. She had Marcia and two dozen lace-makers working eight hours a day to turn out the most wonderful things. Some of the girls made shawls and flowers, while others specialized in garment pieces like bodices or sleeves. Marcia, Lidia, and Irene took all the pieces and joined them together as finished garments. The results were astounding: floor-length lace dresses, shawls, gloves, collars, cuffs, bolero jackets, veils, and much more, all in a rainbow of colors.

Lily spent most of her time in her laboratory, where she used the acids, bases, and salts she had generated to do experiments on the plant samples the children brought her from their rambles in the woods and bogs. As she ran her experiments, she thought back to her analytical chemistry professor, whose final exam was devastatingly simple: she put a test tube of some unknown substance in front of each student and expected them to perform the necessary reactions to identify it. Anyone who failed was welcome to try again the next semester.

Now, Lily focused her efforts on isolating elements she could use to make different types and colors of glass. Her glassblower was turning out excellent mirrors and colored glass window panes, and he was trying his hand at glasses, vases and small dishes. Some of his experiments worked out, and some of them didn't. Once his results were more consistent, she would talk to her father about selling a line of glassware. As she worked, she thought about what she would call her new venture.

Earton Glass. I like the sound of that, but I'd better choose something else, just in case I have to leave Earton someday.

She reached for a glass beaker and held it over the small flame she kept burning.

Mariella Glass. That's what I'll call it! It sounds fancy, and it uses my middle name.

Her mirrors were already selling for extravagant prices. She would have like to make bigger, better mirrors, but the largest they were able to turn out was two feet square. Even that was unbelievable for the nobles in her new world, who had only ever seen themselves reflected in polished sheets of metal.

Lily had other, more far-reaching plans for her glassworks—reading glasses, or even a simple telescope, like the one Galileo came up with.

With Helke's expert assistance, she had her first prototype lens by mid-winter. Of course, she had an unfair advantage: she already knew about the optical axis and how light bends. Lily felt confident that she would soon have a working telescope. Better yet, she was inspired by the work the blacksmith and the glass blower were doing with their new apprentices. They were already moving beyond what she had taught them and discovering new ways to create useful objects out of glass and metal. It pleased Lily to think that, even when she was gone, her knowledge would live on in this new world.

Lily's other project was printed books. She had already had success making paper: it was grayish green, but definitely paper. Now, she just needed someone to invent a printing press, and she modestly chose herself for the role.

She had asked her craftsmen to come up with some kind of board that could hold letter squares. Meanwhile, the blacksmith was busy making the squares while Lily tried out various kinds of inks in her laboratory. They would soon be ready to print their first text, which the countess had already chosen. Ativerna's first printed words would be an excerpt from the *Life of the Radiant Marialla*. It was a short piece, just ten lines long, in which the holy woman recounted her life before she was visited by the spirit of Aldonai.

Lons Avels and Pastor Vopler were the only other people who knew about the planned printing press. While Lons was too shocked by the project to say a word, Pastor Vopler realized what opportunities a printing press would give the church. As he listened to the countess explain that paper could be made cheaply from hemp and other plants and that a mechanical printing press would reduce the cost of producing a text to almost nothing, he felt the tears come to his eyes.

"My Lady, just think…"

"Yes, pastor. The word of Aldonai will be found in every home. People will be able to read the lives of the radiant ones, the better to imitate them!"

The man sighed and clasped his hands. "My Lady, I believe you must be one of the radiant ones! Such an undertaking!"

Lily looked away, embarrassed. To be honest, she was more concerned about promoting literacy and earning money. The printing press stood to make her a fortune, and Lily had no intention of sharing her profits. If she couldn't reach an understanding with her husband, she would strike out on her own, with her father's support.

I'll found a publishing house that will still be around three hundred years from now!

She knew that she would need a title of her own if she separated from her husband. Expert lacemaking alone was not enough to earn her a title, though. She would have to make herself ever more valuable to the king. Paper, printed books, glass, mirrors… Those were the inventions that would keep her safe.

The countess had been very careful who she shared her experiments with. So far, no one had seen her recipe for making paper, which she had perfected using a blend of nettles, hemp, linen, and hay. Only the blacksmith and the glassblower knew how mirrors were made, and she had explained to them that they would live safer, healthier lives if they kept quiet about all they knew.

Chapter 6
A Visitor Arrives

Rolf Relamo observed Earton Castle from a hill not far away. The castle shone like a diamond on that bright winter morning, in opposition to everything he had been told about the place. What surprised him the most was the glass he could clearly see sparkling in the windows. Glass windows were an incredible luxury because of their extreme fragility *How can a mere countess living in the middle of nowhere afford to have colored glass in all of her windows?*

Rolf slung his lute over his shoulder and started to make his way down from the trees. He had given much thought to how he ought to present himself to the castle guards. Merchants were rare enough in those parts, and he suspected they might not let him in. A soldier might not be welcome, either so he had decided to arrive in the guise of a traveling minstrel.

☙ ❧

As it turned out, the guards had no intention of letting in a traveling minstrel. When Rolf presented himself at the gate, they looked at him darkly and told him he wasn't going anywhere until their commander questioned him. Rolf sat down on his bag and prepared to wait, but he didn't have to wait long. Soon, the gates opened and four people on horseback rode out. He looked up and his heart skipped a beat when he saw the horse that led the others. A purebred Avarian, it stepped carefully on slender legs, the muscles under its fiery red coat rippling in the sunlight. It seemed proud to carry its rider, and Rolf could see why: the woman on the Avarian was a vision of beauty, with thick golden braids hanging down her back and a scarlet cape trimmed with white fur.

Rolf leaped up and gave a low bow, but in his haste, he slipped and fell face-first in the wet snow. He expected to hear laughter, but there was none. Instead, the vision of beauty nodded to her guards, and they helped Rolf stand and brushed off his clothes.

Then, the vision spoke. "Who is this man?"

Her voice fit her appearance, low and warm, from deep in her chest.

"R-r-olf Relamo," he stuttered. Then he whispered, "My Lady?"

Lily smiled. "Yes, I am the Countess of Earton. What brings you to my castle?"

For an instant, Rolf couldn't remember why he was there. Then he focused his thoughts and remembered his story. "My Lady, I am a traveling minstrel, a man of songs and stories. My wandering brought me to Earton."

"That's a long walk," she replied coolly, and her green eyes were expressionless. Rolf generally considered himself a ladies' man, but his charms had no power over the countess. He took no offense, however.

"We walk until our legs give out, My Lady. We sing songs, and people feed us."

"Us? How many are you?"

"I'm alone, My Lady. I parted ways with my

companions several days ago."

He could tell the countess was deciding whether to invite him to the castle or send him to the nearest village when a voice piped up behind her.

"Mama, I want to hear his songs!"

Lily turned to the girl and smiled. He suspected she did not spoil the child, but tried to give way in small matters. "Fine. We will see about having some songs." Then she turned to the guards. "Have him wait here until Leis can speak to him. We will take our ride and decide what to do with him when we return."

Miranda's face shone. "Will you read me a book when we get home?" She was still young enough to believe that one *yes* could be turned into a string of *yeses,* Rolf observed.

"Of course. We will read together after our ride."

Then Lily touched her reins, and all four riders moved off down the road.

The Avarian stallion carried his rider down the snow-covered road toward the forest. Lily noticed that there were no footprints on the fresh snow. The minstrel must have arrived at the castle from over the fields.

Why? What is he up to?

Lily felt she was getting paranoid, but she also felt that someone was watching.

ᘓ ᘐ

For the next half an hour, Rolf was very sorry that he had come to Earton. The castle guards felt the same way. When Leis Antrel arrived at the gate, he raked them over the coals for allowing a stranger to approach the countess. Rolf realized from a few things Leis said that there had been an attempt on the countess' life. He pricked up his ears but learned nothing else. Soon, it was his turn to catch Leis' wrath.

"You! Where are you headed?"

"I just wander the villages, sir, wherever people will feed me in return for a song."

"Where were you before you came to the castle?

"I was east of here. I got lost in the woods, and when I came out on the hill, I saw the castle."

Lons eyed the minstrel's small bag. "What did you eat while you were lost?"

"I had some bread and dried fish, and I caught a rabbit or two," he looked up at the captain of the guards with what was almost a grin. "If you chase me off, at least give me some dry bread. That will last me until the next village..."

Rolf was a convincing liar, and his thin frame and hollow cheeks gave an air of truth to what he said. No matter how much he ate, he had always remained skinny. He could tell Leis felt his dishonesty but couldn't put his finger on what it was.

Finally, Leis told the guards to let the minstrel in and show him to the servants' quarters for a bite to eat.

He turned to Rolf, "If my men find you anywhere but the servants' quarters, they'll snap your neck."

Rolf bowed and followed the two guards who beckoned. Out of the corner of his eye, he got a close-up view of the fine glass in the castle windows.

There was definitely something going on in Earton; he would find out what it was.

What he found in the servants' quarters was even more interesting. Even the scullery windows were fitted out with colored glass that cast rainbow-colored speckles on the clean, white walls. Rolf was shocked. He could understand that the earl sent his wife money and that she probably turned around and spent it on fancy goods, but he couldn't for the life of him understand why she would spend it on fine windows that nobody but the cook and the scullery maids would ever see.

He looked around him. The servants at Earton castle had it good. The tables and benches were solid and polished to a high shine, the floor was cleaner than what he had seen in several royal palaces, and the table was set with pewter dishes. True, it was not the finest tableware, but it was unbelievable to see anything of the sort in the servant's mess hall. In Rolf's experience, servants ate off wooden dishes or scooped their food with a crust of bread. The miniature pitchfork next to his plate gave him pause.

"My Lady came up with that. It's called a fork." whispered the buxom servant girl seated next to him. She proceeded to demonstrate by stealing a piece of fish from the supposed minstrel's plate.

Rolf picked up his fork and gave it a try. Once he got the hang of it, he found it was better than a crust of bread for scooping up food. Even more surprising was the food—it was fresh fish, roasted with just the right amount of salt and other spices.

He winked knowingly at his neighbor. "I think this is her ladyship's food you've brought me. Will she be angry with you?"

Mary shook her head. "My Lady? Eat this food? Never! This is for the servants."

Rolf said nothing, but he took note of Mary's well-made clothes and rosy cheeks. He had seen plenty of servants who worked for wealthy tyrants, and Mary showed none of the signs of hunger or fear that he was used to. It was obvious that she was pleased with her lot.

His eyes went to her plump breasts and the lace flowers that adorned the neckline of her dress. All Rolf knew about lace was that it was sold by the yard for shockingly high prices, but even he could see that Mary's lace flowers were something special. It was unbelievable, like everything else he had seen in Earton. Rolf had never even held a needle so he couldn't tell that half of the petals on Mary's lace flowers were misshapen practice stitches.

He wiped his plate with a piece of bread and listened as Mary praised the countess to the skies. As he chewed, he observed that the bread was real and tasty, made from flour, not the flat meal cakes that most people in those parts ate all winter. Mary told him the countess was very interested in making sure everyone ate well and had gone to great lengths to ensure sufficient stores for the winter. She hadn't always been that way, Mary said. When the countess first arrived in Earton, she spent most of her time sitting in her room. However, after she lost her baby, everything changed.

Mary said the first thing the countess did when she was well again was fire the estate manager. Rolf was confused by Mary's telling of the story—especially regarding whether or not the man was still alive—so he made note to ask someone else when he had the opportunity.

The second thing the countess did, according to Mary, was ride out to the market at Altver, where she sold everything she could—even many of her own dresses—to buy livestock for the estate. While she was there, she hired the Virmans, who were now in charge of catching, salting and smoking fish for the winter.

Rolf listened intently at this point, but Mary knew nothing about the actual process for obtaining salt from seawater. All she knew was that the countess was kind and generous to a fault, as long as the castle was kept clean. Once a ten night, the servants cleaned the castle from top to bottom. There was no way to get out of this ritual. If you were sick or busy, the countess still made you march.

"Why march?" Rolf asked.

"Oh, that's just what the countess likes to say. 'March!'"

He could see that the lady of the castle was much loved by her household. A few of the servants had sullen faces, but Rolf knew from experience that you can't please everyone.

After eating, he made himself comfortable by the fire and played his lute for the servants as they wandered in and out. In between songs, he asked questions.

Forks?

Her ladyship had ordered a fork for herself, and the rest of the household followed her lead.

Glass?

The countess had hired a glassblower in Altver.

Lace?

Skilled dressmakers from the same trip.

The countess was rumored to spend a great deal of time in the workshop with her lace-makers, but none of the servants knew what she did there. And in general, they told Rolf, the countess was strict and frowned on unnecessary curiosity. Anyone caught loafing risked being sent to clean the privy. They all shivered as they remembered the countess' wrath after someone had tried to kill her and the count's young daughter.

Attempted murder?

None of them knew the whole story. They had seen the king's envoy poking around with questions, but whatever he found out he kept to himself. Several of the servants hinted darkly that the Virmans knew more than they were saying. Leis Antrel was another privileged figure whose role the servants could only guess at. He had come to the castle as a simple soldier, and now he was captain of the guards and well paid, by the looks of it. There were even rumors that he had plans to marry one of the lace-makers in the spring.

Rolf turned the talk back to the Virmans. He learned that the locals tolerated them on threat of punishment from the countess, who took the time to resolve any disputes, however minor, involving her Virman guards.

It was not hard to get the servants to talk about their mistress, but Rolf had no way of knowing how much of what they said was true. He picked up his lute and shook his head.

How long will I need to stay in Earton to separate the truth from the fiction in all the stories circulating about the countess? After all, the servants had experienced the events they spoke of gradually, while Rolf was learning of it all in one day. He strongly suspected that no woman in the world was capable of everything Lilian Earton had done, and yet here he was, sitting in servants' quarters with glass windows and eating good bread off pewter dishes.

How did she do it? Instead of an answer, all he had was a blend of rumor and gossip. Rolf felt lost as he sat strumming a tune by the fire. He would have to wait until he could see the countess up close again.

ဆ ⬚ ભ

He didn't have to wait long. A servant came down and informed him that he would be entertaining the countess and her guests at the table that evening. An hour later, he was led upstairs to a modest dining room that was pleasantly warm and comfortable. The table was set for eleven. At the head of the table was the countess. She was surprisingly beautiful, with a long, thick braid of gold hair over one shoulder and her arm around her stepdaughter. The earl's daughter had dark hair and blue eyes, just like her father. At the countess' end of the table sat a man in a priest's green robe and a young boy who looked just like him. Rolf assumed the boy was the priest's son. He bent his head over his lute as he tuned it, all the while stealing glances at the rest of the party. The captain of the castle guards was there, seated next to an elderly Khangan with piercing eyes who looked, to Rolf, to be quite learned. He noticed right away that the countess called the man "Tahir-jan," using the Khangan way of showing respect, and that the man did the same, calling her Lilian-jan. Rolf frowned. He was widely traveled enough to know that the Khangans did not generally speak to women that way. The old scholar must see the countess as his equal. *Strange and stranger!*

Suddenly, Rolf recalled something Mary had said, "There is a foreign healer here who has the greatest respect for her ladyship. He says that people like her are only born once a century…"

The Khangan must be the healer she was talking about.

Next, there was a fair-haired young man in expensive clothes who seemed unsure of himself in the present company. He was followed by two Virmans—a man and a woman. The man was powerfully built and had the face of a sea wolf. The woman was slight and attractive, and her eyes glowed whenever she turned to her husband.

As he stole glances at the table, Rolf saw another man, this one in his middle years. The others called him Taris. Rolf had no idea who he was.

Next to Taris, was a younger man, Chevalier Lons. As he warily watched the young man, Lons happened to glance over at the minstrel and Rolf saw a sudden flash of fear in his eyes. The young chevalier quickly recovered his composure and looked away.

What did that mean? Did I imagine it?

Those were questions for another day. His lute tuned, Rolf struck a chord and began to sing. He ran his fingers up and down the strings while keeping an eye on the countess and her guests. Life had taught him that every powerful woman was backed by a man, but as he watched the flow of conversation, he realized something important: if Lilian Earton had a man supporting her, he was not at the table that night.

The pastor opened the meal with a prayer asking for Aldonai's blessings on the house and the food. Rolf had seen more than his share of pastors. Living in Wellster, Rolf had grown accustomed to looking at men of the church with a critical eye. He could tell that Lilian's pastor was a true believer and that he looked at his benefactor as if she were a holy icon. He was no backstage manipulator, using the countess for his own ends, that much was clear.

Rolf looked up at the flickering candles on the wall as he came to the end of his first song.

Who is supporting her? Could it be that chevalier?

He sang several more songs before stopping to drink the cup of water that one of the servants had placed on the hearth next to him. Keeping his eyes down, he listened to the talk. The atmosphere around the table was most unusual. There was no drunkenness and no loud arguing. The tall Virman and the Khangan spoke quietly about something, the pastor was talking to the countess about church matters, and the children seemed to know it was an honor to sit with the adults and ate slowly and carefully.

When he looked up, he noticed that everyone at the table had a fork.

Rolf could hardly believe his eyes. If anyone had described the diverse group to him, he would have expected the pastor to be spewing brimstone at the heathens, the Virmans to be fighting the locals, and the Khangan to have cursed them all as sons of dogs.

In reality, all of the people around the table were linked by their common interests, and the center holding it all together was Lilian Earton. With each passing minute, Rolf found himself increasingly interested in the countess. She never once raised her voice, and she listened to everyone with a smile on her face. When she spoke, she was brief and to the point. Even so, she was the central figure in the group.

He found it all very strange.

⚜

Lons was desperate for the dinner to be over. He was shaking, and his hands were cold as ice. It was all he could do to keep himself from crying out "Seize that man!" The only thing that stopped him was the fact that Relamo had not recognized him. Lons was sure of that. If the Wellsterite had recognized the former tutor to the king's daughters, he would have killed him on the spot. Lons knew most of the gossip that circulated at the court of Wellster, and he knew that Rolf was a trusted runner for King Gardwig.

What is he doing here?

The chevalier wasn't sure what he should do, but he had survived in the hold of the slave ship, and he had every intention of surviving now.

⚜

Lily listened to the minstrel with one ear. She found the romantic ballads uninspiring, with their lovely ladies, brave knights, dragons, and demons. At one point, even the great and wicked Maldonaya made an appearance. Pastor Vopler frowned, and the minstrel moved back into safer territory.

The countess was even more skilled than Rolf at noticing people without seeming to do so. She saw that he was a good-looking man, and not nearly as starved as his thin frame would have one assume. In fact, he reminded her of Tahir's mongoose—slinking and deadly. That made him a strange minstrel and subject to suspicion. She would ask Leis to keep both eyes on him.

When dinner was over, Lily smiled sweetly at Rolf. "I thank you for providing us with entertainment this evening."

Rolf decided to risk everything. "My Lady, will you allow me to stay here and rest for a few days?" He could have left the next day with plenty to tell the jester, but he had heard too many contradictory things and couldn't make heads or tails of any of it.

Lily nodded. "So long as you promise to entertain us tomorrow evening."

Rolf gave his word, and the countess and her guests left the dining room.

☙ ❧

Lily went no further than Miranda's room, where she put the little girl to bed. That done, she went to her study. Lons knocked on the door before she could even sit down.

"May I come in, My Lady?"

The countess pointed to a chair. "Come in, Leir Lons. What is the matter?"

Lons took a deep breath as if he were about to jump into deep, cold water. "My Lady, that man is no minstrel."

"Is that so?"

"I am not sure, but I fear he may have been sent here after my head."

Lily did some quick calculations. Lons worked for her, and he did his work well; she would protect him.

"Why do you think that?"

Lons looked her in the eye. "I was on that slave ship for a reason."

"I guessed as much."

"I lied to you when I came here. The truth is that I was supposed to be dead."

Lily listened as Lons told her the whole story, how Anna had been interested him, how he had seduced her, how they had been married in secret, and how the king's jester had taken away his marriage papers and ordered some men to kill him. She listened intently, and when he was done, she said nothing for a moment. Then she summed up what both of them were thinking.

"What the hell do we do now?" As always, she was brief and to the point.

Lons looked up at her with eyes full of suffering.

"So you think he's here for you?"

"Perhaps, My Lady, but it doesn't make sense. Why make up that whole story about being a minstrel just to get to me?"

Lily bit her thumbnail. "What else could he be after out here in the middle of nowhere?"

"You, My Lady. Or Tahir."

"Tahir?"

"He is a healer, My Lady, and King Gardwig is very ill."

Lily nodded. "And what about me? I'm just a woman living in the country."

Lons allowed himself a smile but said nothing.

"Fine," Lily continued. "Why shouldn't we deal with this right now?"

"How, My Lady?"

"I'll call him in here and question him."

"But…"

"You will hide behind that cabinet or wherever you want. I'll have Leif come sit with me. He can claim to have seen this man before."

Lons felt something like hope rising in his breast. "It might work."

The countess sighed. She was starting to feel like she needed a Castle Security Committee organized along the lines of the old KGB.

"Leir Lons, go quietly and find Leif. Tell him I need to see him."

With her secretary gone, Lily sat down at her desk.

This minstrel can be gotten rid of, but he will just be followed by other spies. I need a spy network of my own, and I need it yesterday.

છ □ ૬૪

When he heard that the countess wanted to see him, Rolf's first instinct was to run. Unfortunately, he had no way out. There were two Virmans, both the size of bears, standing in the doorway with elbow-length daggers in their hands. He had a premonition that her ladyship didn't want to talk to him about music.

Once in the countess' study, Rolf looked around himself quickly. What he saw was cause for wonder: shelves stacked with scrolls and sheaves of parchment. This was a room intended for work. Lilian Earton, dressed in black, looked at him sternly from behind her desk. Behind her stood the same massive Virman who had sat at her table at dinner, only this time he was without his wife, and his face was dark.

The countess spoke first. "Leir Relamo, is there something you would like to tell me?"

Rolf could tell from her tone of voice that she knew exactly who he was. Still, she couldn't know everything, so he decided to play for time.

"I don't understand, My Lady."

"I want the truth, Leir Relamo. If you don't wish to share it, I will have my Virman guards set their dogs on your trail. What do you think? Will they turn up anything of interest?"

Rolf went cold. Of course, they would.

"Why go to such great lengths, My Lady?"

"Because I have no need of spies in Earton," Lily said quietly. "I don't believe for a minute that you just happened by."

Rolf stared.

She continued. "Leif has seen you before. You would do well to pay more attention to Virmans. I suppose you think they all look alike."

Rolf could have kicked himself. He didn't think they

all looked exactly alike, but there was some truth in the countess' words…

"He saw you in Wellster. Now tell me, Leir Relamo, what does your king want from me?" Her fingers tilted a small silver mirror this way and that.

Rolf shrugged. "Nothing much, My Lady. Your husband…"

"Has accompanied His Highness Prince Richard to Wellster." Lily finished for him.

"Yes. And someone at court was intrigued by your correspondence with him."

℘⃝℘

Lily's eyebrows went up. The letter she had sent her husband was short and unlikely to interest the King of Wellster. Her husband's reply was similarly short and uninteresting to anyone outside the family.

She knew it by heart. It was just five lines:

Dearest wife,

I am pleased with your decisions and completely approve of them.

How is Miranda? Are you in good enough health to try to conceive an heir in the spring? I hope that no one will try to poison you or otherwise harm you before I see you at court.

Your husband,

Jerrison Earton

Rolf seemed uncomfortable as he attempted to explain. "There was an attempt on your life, and the earl's reaction was…"

"Odd," Lily offered. She could imagine the earl's reaction.

The spy smiled gratefully. "Yes, My Lady. The Earl of Lort became interested in Earton—in yourself and in the estate." "What exactly interests the Earl of Lort?"

Her mind was working overtime. She had supposed it was the king who sent the spy. *Who on earth is the Earl of Lort?* Lons had spoken of the king's jester, but he had mentioned no powerful earl by the name of Lort.

Rolf seemed not to see her discomfort.

"He is interested in everything, My Lady. Who, what, how... You see how it is, My Lady. He was in a hurry, so I didn't have time to work up a proper story."

Lily nodded. It would have worked if it hadn't been for Lons and his great confession.

"You wanted information, Leir, so ask."

The man stared.

"Ask your questions. I will answer them. In the morning my people will take you to... Where would you like to go?"

Rolf paused for a brief instant. "Altver, I suppose, My Lady. I can send a letter from there and wait for instructions."

Lily bowed her head in assent. She would take the opportunity to send some goods to Torius and a letter for her father. "My Virmans will accompany you. I promise you will come to no harm, Leir. Do you believe me?"

At this point, Leif spoke up from behind her chair. "I would stick him in the well, My Lady. Or give me three hours with him in the dungeon; that'll keep him from bothering you in the future."

Lily smiled and waited a beat for effect. Then she looked up at Leif. "Thank you, Leif, but I don't think that's necessary. He was simply acting on orders. I would like to meet this Earl of Lort, but that's a matter for another day. In any event, we have no secrets here. The attempts on my life are widely known."

Leif squinted and muttered something in Virman under his breath. Rolf shivered. Lily realized to her delight that she was starting to understand some of the Virman language. She couldn't speak it properly yet, but she could follow the gist of a conversation.

"Now, Leir Relamo, what did you want to know? It's getting late, and I'd like to get on to bed."

℘ ❧ ℘

An hour later, Rolf was led from the countess' study by the same two Virmans who had brought him. The countess had not told him everything he asked, but he had learned enough to make his head spin. Once he was back in his little room, he pulled a piece of parchment out of his bag and began to write down what he knew. Altres would be shocked. Something told Rolf that he would not be the last spy to visit Earton, but he suspected none of them would be as fortunate as he had been. He had escaped the torture chamber and would be escorted to Altver, where he could send his report.

℘ ❧ ℘

"My Lady?"

Lily turned to Lons as he climbed out of the cabinet where he had been hiding.

"You heard everything, didn't you?"

"I did, My Lady." He was grateful, she had talked to the Wellsterite spy for a whole hour without ever mentioning him.

The countess sighed. Her secretary's face was lined with worry and for good reason. "I will not tell anyone about you, but it can't last long. I have to go to the capital in the spring."

"You won't have to introduce me by name to anyone. I can change my appearance. I'll grow a beard and color my hair."

"I suppose so," Lily said doubtfully. "In any case, we will try to let Anna know that you are alive."

"I beg you, My Lady…"

"Don't ever beg, Lons. I want you to think. Will she wish to live with you out here where there is no society to speak of?"

"That's how we always lived before…"

Lily tried to look sympathetic, but she thought Lons' chances were uncertain at best. To a young girl living in the country, Lons might be as good as a prince, but all bets were off once she had a chance to live at court and dance with a real prince.

Once her secretary was gone, Lily put her head in her hands. She was so very tired, and now she faced the prospect of having to learn everything she could about the political situation in Wellster and how it might affect her. Then she could decide what to do with the runaway tutor.

Lily staggered to her bedroom and laid down without

undressing. The last few hours had worn her down to almost nothing. It was no easy feat to converse with a man, getting as much information out of him as you could while weighing every word of your own.

Her stomach rumbled, and Lily wondered how many calories her diplomacy had burned.

She had done her best to send the message that she had nothing against Wellster. There were a few things—like glass and lace—that she was prepared to share, but only after talking to someone more important than Rolf Relamo.

In turn, she had learned that Gardwig was very ill, and that Altres Lort would do anything and kill anyone to help him. She learned that the royal medicus, like everyone else in her new world, believed in the miraculous powers of bloodletting and enemas.

Old Gardwig must have started out strong as an ox if he's still alive after years of that kind of treatment.

There had been an uncomfortable moment when Rolf told her that her husband had earned himself quite the reputation as a gallant ladies' man during his stay in Wellster. The spy naturally supposed that this information would pain her ladyship, and her ladyship did her best not to let on that she couldn't care less.

She had given Rolf a list of questions to ask the king regarding his health. While she couldn't visit the royal patient, she could at least collect his health history and give the matter some thought. In the end, Lily was satisfied that she had shown her interest. What would come of it remained to be seen.

Chapter 7
Winter's Icy Blast

As the year came to a close, Lily was surprised to learn that people in her new world had no mid-winter holiday. She would have liked to put up a tree and decorate it, but she worried that it would raise too many questions. So, in the end, she simply announced that the last day of the year would be a day of rest. Everyone in the castle got the day off, and there was wine and dancing in the evening.

Lily refrained from drinking, but she watched with curiosity as those around her enjoyed the unexpected party. The wine seemed to lift their inhibitions. Even the Virmans looked more relaxed. Lily danced with Tahir, Lons, Taris, and even Leif (with the generous permission of a laughing Ingrid). Erik asked her to dance three times, but Lily was careful not to dance more than twice with the same man. Lons had explained that a noblewoman should not be seen dancing too often with any man other than her husband.

She was doing her best to remember every tiny detail of etiquette so that she would be prepared to attend balls at the palace in the spring. Even so, she was aware there were too many things she didn't know. *I'll stand out like a sore thumb,* she thought glumly.

A letter from Lilian:

My dear husband,

I am sure you will be glad to hear that all is well. Miranda is healthy and sends you her love. I am alive, but my health is a source of constant worry. I have lost much weight because of my recent tragedy and the attempt to poison me. This has been confirmed by an eminent healer who arrived in Earton by a happy twist of fate. I expect you will have heard of Tahir Djiaman din Dashar. In any event, when you arrive, you can talk to him about the proper time to conceive a child. He believes that I will need to undergo lengthy treatment before attempting anything of the kind.

I was pleased to receive your letter of approval and likewise look forward to seeing you in person. I hope you are well and continue to pray for you.

Lilian Elizabeth Mariella Earton

A letter from Miranda Catherine:

Papa!

I'm having a wonderful time! Lily is terrific! I have lots of friends. I also have a dog! And new clothes! Lily promised to get me a horse! I want an Avarian stallion, and Lily says we will order one from the Khanganate. I know how to read and write and count now. Lily says that a woman needs to know lots of things so that people can't steal from her.

Will we see you in the spring?

I love you and pray for you. Lily prays for you, too.

Miranda Catherine Earton

When Jess finished reading the letters, he set them down on the table and turned to his cousin. "Richard, I'm ready to believe that Aldonai walks the earth among us."

"Why's that?" Richard asked, looking up from a scroll.

Jess ran a hand through his dark hair. "Nothing surprises me anymore. Up is down and down is up."

Richard raised an eyebrow.

"Just look," said Jess, handing him the letters. "When I last left Earton, my wife was a fat fool who couldn't even look me in the face. And what do I have now?"

"What?"

"My uncle calls her exceptional, Miranda is happy, the estate has stopped draining me of cash, and my lover..." here his voice faltered, "...well, you know all about it." He looked up at the prince, his face strained. "I must be losing my mind!"

Richard put a hand on his shoulder. "Try to change the way you think about her. She must not be a bad person if Miranda has such good things to say about her."

"She taught the child to write. I didn't even know that Lilian could write. I never saw her read anything."

"Don't forget that she was being drugged."

"True," Jess said, rubbing his chin. "But what about the rest of it? I'm glad for her to buy my daughter some new clothes, but what does she need a dog for? I would expect Lilian to get her a songbird in a cage."

Richard grinned. "Where would she find a caged songbird out in Earton?"

"Exactly!" Jess stood up. "Who are these 'friends' Miranda writes of?"

"The neighbors' children?" Richard ventured a guess.

"It's a ten-day trip to the nearest neighbor!" Jess burst out, not entirely accurately. He paced back and forth. "There's Donter. He's a decent hunter, but he has no wife or children."

"Then I don't know, either," Richard confessed.

"I don't want Miranda playing with commoners."

"Write and tell her so."

"I will, but I don't even know what to expect from her next."

Richard stretched his legs and smiled. "You remember what it says in the Book of Aldonai, don't you?"

"No man knows what to expect from a woman because she does not yet know herself what she will do." Jess recited from memory.

"Exactly."

Jess sat back down, and Richard took up his scroll again. After a few minutes passed, Jess could no longer stand the silence.

"I don't even have a man I could send to Earton now."

Richard set his scroll down. He was used to his cousin's moods. "That's true enough. Go ahead and write, but don't expect a reply until we're already in Ivernea."

Jess knew that without being told. It was the suspense that was killing him. His wife was behaving like a completely different person, and he was forced to rely on other people for information. *It's enough to drive anyone insane.*

৪০ ⬚ ૭৪

The hair on Altres' neck stood up as he read his spy's report. Rolf had learned plenty about Earton. They were making salt from seawater, and the countess had craftsmen manufacturing excellent glass and lace. The jester picked up the small mirror Lily had given Rolf. He didn't particularly enjoy looking at his own face, but the quality made him shake his head. Then he opened the packet of salt and tasted it. It was good, slightly bitter, but good. These things were interesting, but the jester really wanted to know about the Khangan healer, din Dashar.

Rolf wrote that he had invited din Dashar to come to Wellster. The Khangan had refused, saying that there was still much he wanted to teach the countess, who had an uncommon talent for medicine. The jester wondered if there was some way to induce them to come. Gardwig's health was rapidly declining. *If Richard marries Anna, then I will make sure that Lilian Earton is invited to the wedding.*

At the end of the report, he found a list of questions concerning the King of Wellster and his health. He picked up the second letter, which was from Lilian.

To the Earl of Lort.

I expect that your spy has learned quite enough about me and my affairs. In the future, if you wish to know something, please write to me directly. Two intelligent people can always reach an agreement that furthers the interests of both.

I am sending you a list of questions that I would like answers to. It is up to you whether or not to show them to His Majesty.

I am also sending you some samples of the goods we manufacture in Earton. His Majesty Edward the Eighth, by the grace of Aldonai King of Ativerna, is aware of our activities. Any shipments can be ordered through his agents.

Respectfully yours,

Lilian Elizabeth Mariella Earton

The jester whistled under his breath.

To the Earl of Lort. Not "Your Lordship" or even "Kind Sir." No, the countess addressed him as an equal.

Your spy has learned quite enough... More than enough, but no more than she was willing to share, the jester reflected.

Two intelligent people... The countess had caught his spy, but she wasn't angry. More importantly, she was demonstrating an interest in the king's health. Still, Lort wasn't sure whether or not to show his brother the questions.

The jester correctly understood Lilian's mention of King Edward as a mild threat. She wanted him to know that she had a good relationship with the king and that Wellster would not be taking advantage of its proximity to Earton.

On the whole, the letter demanded respect. Altres set it aside to read again that evening. *What to do about her questions?*

He unrolled the scroll. It was covered from edge to edge with the countess' clear, forceful handwriting. The questions covered everything: what the king ate, how much he drank, his age, his clothing, his shoes, how fast his heart beat... *I'm surprised she didn't ask how often he visits his wife's bedroom.*

At the end of the list of questions, there was a note:

"I must warn you that even answers to all these questions may not be sufficient for me to identify His Majesty's malady."

That was all.

Altres suddenly gave a mischievous grin. He knew exactly what he would do.

ഇൻ ⬚ ൚

Jess looked up at Gardwig on his throne. He was every inch the king, and a fearsome tyrant.

Jess bowed. "Your Majesty, I am most gratified to see…"

"There is no need for a lengthy speech, young man. I have a request of you."

Coming from the king, any request was an order. "I will be pleased to hear it, Your Majesty."

"Bring your wife to Wellster. We would like to see her."

That was the last thing Jess had expected to hear. Gardwig worked hard not to laugh as he observed the earl's shocked face. The jester, standing nearby, allowed himself a muffled cough.

"My wife?"

"Yes. The countess. We would be pleased to see her."

At this point, Jess' formal upbringing took over. He assured the king that he would be exceedingly grateful if Lilian were to come to Wellster without delay, but that she was in Earton, and the roads, and the weather… And furthermore, King Edward had expressed a desire to see her ladyship at his own court in the spring.

Gardwig heard him out with a smile playing on his lips. "I understand the difficulties perfectly. Her ladyship may come to Wellster in the summer, once her other obligations have been discharged. I will write to Edward myself."

The Earl of Earton bowed and slid to the side of the room, where he was immediately accosted by Adelaide Wells.

"Jess!"

He turned and scowled at her.

"We need to talk, Jess!"

"I have nothing to say to you," he hissed.

"What about our child?"

The earl kept his voice low. "Your child, not ours. Do what you like with it. Leave me alone, or we'll be having this conversation in a very unpleasant place when we get back to Ativerna. You tried to kill my daughter and my wife. I won't forget that."

"I had nothing to do with it! It was Alex!"

"Alex, the man you slept with," Jess sneered. He put his face close to hers. "If you ever try to speak to me again, I will have you sent back home in chains. Now go!"

Adelaide bit her lip and disappeared into the crowd. Jess sighed with relief and rested his hot forehead against the cold marble of the wall.

His head was literally spinning. His life had always been, if not simple, then at least clear. He had his relationship with King Edward, his diplomatic work, and his estate, which was managed for him. He had a wife, who was an unpleasant consequence of his involvement with the boatyards, and he put up with her only for the sake of his own future financial well-being. He had Miranda to love and spoil. He had Richard as his closest friend. He had various mistresses to spend free time with.

Now, that neat, orderly world was coming down around his ears. He was coming to realize that he wasn't the diplomat he had always assumed himself to be. His estate had been robbed without his knowledge, and now it was doing well without his involvement. And August was angry at him.

Nothing made sense anymore. How could that stupid, fat girl turn into...someone else entirely? Is she, in fact, a different person, or is there someone else telling her what to do? Both theories were equally implausible, but Jess could think of no other explanation.

He briefly considered saddling a horse and making the journey to Earton, leaving Richard on his own in Wellster, but he knew his uncle would never forgive him. *If I did that, I might have to stay in Earton for the next three years.*

There was only one thing Jess could do. He sat down in his room and dashed off letters to everyone at once: his sister, his mother, his sister's husband, August, and his uncle.

Perhaps their replies would shed more light on the mystery of his wife.

ഇ◻ഗ

Lily was pleased to get a letter from her father. He had unearthed quite a bit of information about Karl Treloney, but he didn't know how much importance to assign to each fact. Lily didn't know, either, so she wrote back asking for a list of who traded with whom and who was friends with whom among Ativernan high society.

She also made a more sensitive request—she needed

her father to find someone to engage in espionage; someone who could gather information and present it to her. *Once I have enough information, I'll be able to draw my own conclusions.*

The wind howled outside the castle walls, snow pounded against the windows, and winter marched on.

ঙ □ গ্ন

Your Majesty,

I hasten to inform you that His Majesty King Gardwig of Wellster has taken an interest in the affairs of Earton. He sent a man to make discreet inquiries. I have spoken with him. He left with no information of critical importance, but I expect there to be other visitors of the same sort. I do not see any danger from that direction, but I believe it would be wise to retain the secrets of making glass, salt, and lace within the borders of Your Majesty's kingdom.

With this in mind, I ask your permission to move my manufacturing to another location that my father will select for me. Earton is in a vulnerable position as it is too distant from the capital.

I remain your loyal servant,

Lilian Elizabeth Mariella Earton

Edward was not surprised at Lilian's letter. He knew Gardwig to be no man's fool. The countess was right, as always. He would have to speak with August Broklend.

ঙ □ গ্ন

August hastened himself to the palace when summoned. He bowed low, noting with a smile that, this time, the king's servant offered him a chair, instead of the low stool he had always been given before.

He sat down on the edge of the chair and waited for the king to speak.

Edward wasted no time on formalities. "August, has your daughter asked you to find a place for her workshops?"

"Yes, Your Majesty. She has also asked me to find someone to collect information. She called it," he paused, "a man to head her personal espionage office. She feels that is the only way to combat the spies sent by others."

Edward shook his head with a smile. "Quite unexpected..."

"Your Majesty?"

"Your daughter has the mind of a man."

"She's my own flesh and blood, Your Majesty."

"And I appreciate her loyalty to Ativerna."

August interlaced his fingers in front of his embroidered vest. "We have done well in Ativerna, Your Majesty. We were all born here and love our home."

Edward needed no help hearing the subtext. We will stay here in Ativerna as long as we continue to prosper.

"Have you carried out her request?"

"Yes, Your Majesty."

The two men turned to a discussion of various locations and their defenses. They also considered how best to export the red-cross-stamped goods to other kingdoms. At the end of the half-hour, Edward found himself mightily pleased. Despite all of Jerrison's foolishness, the countess was not demanding that measures be taken against him. She was prepared to meet him in person at court in the spring. *She's a wise woman. How could Jess have so misjudged her?*

ෆ ❧ ﻌ

August was making his way to the palace gate when he heard footsteps from behind. "Lord Broklend?" a man's voice asked.

He turned and gave a broad smile. "Leir Tremain! I am pleased to see you!"

Hans bowed low but wasted no more time on polite chatter. "How are you? How is her ladyship?"

"She is well, so far, and intends to arrive here in the spring. She asked me to give you her very best."

"I will be very happy to see her again."

"I'm sure she feels the same," said August. He felt confident speaking for Lily in this small matter, because he, himself, liked Hans. Suddenly, an idea occurred to him. "Leir Tremain," he continued, "do you know of anyone who would be interested in entering her ladyship's service?"

"In what capacity, Lord Broklend?"

"Like yourself, I suppose. She says she needs someone to be in charge of a small espionage operation for her."

Hans pondered the idea. "What will the job entail? Spying?"

"I believe that's exactly the thing. Rumors, gossip, competitors, collecting information for her. Very much like what you do for His Majesty."

The envoy nodded. "I see. I will have to think on this."

"Please do. How is your investigation into Lily's trouble proceeding?"

Hans looked satisfied. "We recently hung the scoundrel who orchestrated it all."

"What of the woman who was involved?" August had followed news of the intrigue.

"She faces exile. It would be impossible to execute her without outside evidence."

"But what if she just does it again to someone else?"

"I don't believe she will. His Majesty has asked us to come up with an appropriate way to restrain her actions."

"Did you find the person who hired the medicus?"

"I'm afraid not. Whoever he is, he is skilled at cutting off any threads that would lead back in his direction."

Broklend frowned. "Does that mean that this enemy could reach out and kill my daughter and be none the worse for it?"

Hans' eyes flashed. "Of course not! Don't even say that! If I had my way…"

However, both men understood that the unknown enemy who had hired Medicus Craybey would be much more difficult to catch than Adelaide's cousin, Alex.

"I have tried talking to the Iveleans. Peter doesn't know anything, and Amalia is soon to be brought to childbed."

August understood that Hans couldn't jump higher than his own head. He was a smart man and a consummate professional, but he was not the king. And there were certain aristocrats who answered only to the highest authority. The men spoke for a few more minutes and parted ways.

As Hans climbed the many stairs leading to the king's

reception hall, he turned a new idea over in his mind. I've never heard of a king's envoy retiring before, but why not find out if it can be done? After all, His Majesty has an interest in Lilian Earton's wellbeing…

He was afraid to speak his idea out loud, but he held on to it tightly.

৪৹ ☐ ০৪

Torius Avermal was rarely at a loss for words, but he was struck dumb when he saw three ships from the Khanganate standing in the harbor in Altver. For a whole three minutes, he could do no more than open and close his mouth.

The ship captains waited for him to speak first. Finally, Torius bowed. Although he was a baron and they were mere commoners, they were men who had braved the sea in winter, and that fact alone made them worthy of his respect.

"I am pleased to welcome you to Altver. Allow me to introduce myself. I am the mayor of Altver, Baron Torius Avermal."

The men glanced at each other. The most important-looking of the three stepped forward. His importance was not underscored by his clothes. All the men wore almost identical wide pants and fur coats. What set him apart was his beard, which was neatly trimmed and oiled, and the large ruby ring on the first finger of his left hand.

"Lord Avermal, we are grateful for your hospitality," the man said with a bow. "My name is Rashad Omar din Darashaya. I come from a long line of Guards of the Oases."

Torius bowed again. He knew that there were no noble families in the Khanganate, at least not in the Ativernan sense. However, they did have Guards of the Oases, Guards of the Caravan Roads, and Men of the Water. These three tribes were respected above all others. Any Khangan would think long and hard before raising his hand against a man from these tribes.

"May I invite you to my home? My table is humble compared to your own, but you are welcome to share what I have."

The Khangan smiled. "Lord Avermal, at any other time, my friends and I would leap at your offer. Now, however, we are chasing hope, and we are chased by great fear." The man spoke perfect Ativernese, and only his unusual phrasing gave him away as a foreigner. "The Great Khangan has entrusted us with that which he holds most dear—his son. He charged us with delivering the boy to Earton with the utmost speed."

"Earton?" Torius nearly lost his balance. "What for?"

"Our ruler says that in Earton we may find a way to save his son's life. That is where we are headed now."

Avermal let his breath out. "Then, gentleman, I believe you will want to stay here for one more day." The Khangans looked at him expectantly. "I enjoy frequent correspondence with her ladyship."

"The Countess of Earton?" asked Rashad.

"Exactly," said Torius with a small bow of the head. "Two of her men are in my house at this moment. They brought me a letter from her. I am sure you will welcome their help piloting your ships up the Earta River."

Rashad looked closely at the mayor. This man is weak, like all who were not born under the Star Mare. He has no faith in himself, but he intends us no evil. I believe he is trying to help.

Rashad bowed again to show his appreciation for Torius' offer of assistance. "If what you say is true, then we will gain tcn days by delaying a single day. My men will rest and replenish our stores of food and water. Several dozen of our water barrels cracked during the crossing."

Torius shook his head, indicating the brave nature of making that crossing. "I will pray to our lord Aldonai for the success of your mission. And now, please follow me."

Lily was glad to fall into the routine of winter. As the days passed, she grew comfortable in the life she had built for herself. She worked in her laboratory, wrote her books about medicine, helped Miranda with her lessons, and dropped pearls of wisdom on Tahir and Jaimie. Her days were pleasant and productive until a pigeon arrived with a letter from Baron Avermal.

"Tahir!" she announced to her friend. "A group of your countrymen will soon be here with us. Three ships full of them."

"What do you mean, My Lady?"

"One of the ships carries your prince. According to Torius' letter, he is on his deathbed."

Tahir looked alarmed. He reached for the letter. "May I?"

Lily handed him her key for deciphering the message.

My Lady,

Three Khangan ships are coming up the river to Earton bringing the prince of that land, who is near death. I have given them all the things you asked for.

Baron Avermal

"Tahir, what will happen to us if the prince of your people dies here in Earton?"

"I will be put to death."

"What about me?"

"No one will touch you, My Lady. I am the one who wrote to the Great Khangan. The outcome concerns me alone."

A glass vase hit the wall and shattered at Tahir's feet. He jumped.

"Tahir, have you lost your mind?" Lily was past worrying about politeness. "Do you really think I will let a friend of mine be killed just because someone decided to poison your prince? What if it isn't even poison? It could be cancer, for all I know."

"Cancer, My Lady?"

"Cancer is a…never mind. It could be any of a number of maladies, and we don't know which one." She made a fist and pounded on her desk with each word. "If something goes wrong, I don't want to hear a single word about you being responsible. I'll send you to hide in Donter."

Tahir's eyes looked darker than usual as he looked down at his friend and protector. "My Lady, do not take on more than you can handle."

"You've already gotten me involved in this. A little more or a little less makes no difference."

He shrugged. "All roads are chosen by the Star Mare. No one knows which road she will choose."

As Lily watched his face, she felt her anger melt away. *He's a darned pessimist; that's what he is.*

ဆ ☐ ฌ

The Khangans made their way up the Earta at good speed. Soon, Lily was faced with an entire delegation at the castle gates, complete with a curtained palanquin that emitted the fragrant scent of incense. The countess took one look at her visitors and decided there was no point in playing at diplomacy with them since she was sure to lose.

Instead, she simply took a step forward and curtsied with a smile.

Lons spoke for her. "Allow me to introduce you to her ladyship, the Countess of Earton." Lily curtsied again. "And her daughter, Miranda Catherine Earton." Miranda copied Lily's curtsy. She was terribly proud of herself and looked adorable. As usual, stepmother and stepdaughter were dressed in a similar style, wearing blouses and skirts overlaid with fine vests stitched with amber beads. The effect was both simple and very expensive.

The Khangans noticed. The senior member of the delegation took a step forward and bowed. "My Lady, it is a great honor for us to set foot on your land. My name is Rashad Omar din Darashaya. I come from a long line of Guards of the Oases."

Lily turned to Lons. Once again, she sent up silent thanks for the slave ship that had brought him to Earton. He spoke slowly. "We know the traditions of the Khangans. Your visit is an honor for the house of Earton.

The guests seemed pleased by Lons' words, and the atmosphere became a little less stiff. The senior Khangan continued. "My Lady, these men are the ship captains Alim Ramar din Sharradji, another descendant of the Guards of the Oases, and Nazar Khalim din Kharnari, from the Men of the Water."

Lily inclined her head ever so slightly. Lons spoke. "We are pleased to welcome all those who find the path to our home. All men are at the mercy of the Star Mare."

When they were received as friends and given the proper respect, the Khangans relaxed somewhat. Once again, the senior member of the delegation spoke. "The Great Khangan has heard of the beauty and intelligence of the lady of this house. In his infinite wisdom, he ordered us to bring to Earton the light of his eyes, his eldest son by his beloved wife, Gizyar. We were fortunate, and the waves carried us over the terrible gulf, to the port in Altver. There, we found a guide who brought us up the river to this place. Now, we must fall at the feet of the lady of the house."

Lons broke in, "The lady of the house will be happy to do all she can for you. All roads are chosen by the Star Mare, and we have no knowledge of the road she will choose…"

The men bowed and stepped aside for the servants carrying the palanquin. Lily took a step forward. Her hands were shaking. *Can I do this? I remember the symptoms of mercury poisoning, but what if he has something else?*

When the servants pulled open the curtain, she saw a

living skeleton. The boy, who looked to be no more than fifteen or sixteen years old, was pale and hollow-eyed, and his breathing was labored. He had all the obvious signs of poisoning by mercury.

"Get him into the castle and straight to the infirmary!" she cried. She would put everything she had into the fight to save this boy. "Jaimie! Tahir! Let's go!"

The Khangan delegation looked startled. Lons took the senior man by the elbow. "Allow me to show you in. You can be confident that the countess would never harm your prince. You can see for yourself how she cares for her patients after you rest and have something to eat."

ঔ ⬚ ೞ

Lily was already issuing orders. Tahir was drawing a warm bath filled with pine boughs. Jaimie was preparing several adsorbent remedies. *I have to get the poison out of his body! If only we had a hemodialysis machine...* Moving confidently, her hands began to prepare herbal remedies to cleanse the boy's liver and kidneys. *You made it all the way here, young man, and I have every intention of saving you. Just hold on a little bit longer. I promise you will get better!*

When the boy's servants undressed him and laid him in the warm bath, Lily bit her lip to keep from crying. It was clear that someone had been poisoning the boy for many years.

Tahir turned to the countess with hope in his eyes. "My Lady..."

"If he made it all the way to Earton, they must have been giving him only the tiniest of doses of the poison all along. We just don't know how they did it." She lowered her voice to a whisper. "If someone is still poisoning him while we treat him, he won't get better. Tahir, I thought you knew a great deal about poisons."

The man's face was long. "My Lady, many others tried to heal the boy before me. I believe the Great Khangan also hired a medicus for his son."

She turned to Jaimie. He stepped into the hall and came back quickly. "He has three men serving as medicus. They will bring them to us."

"I'm surprised he's still alive," Lily remarked.

It took a long time to bathe the boy. Despite his extreme emaciation, he had a sturdy frame and was fairly heavy. Lily had every stitch of his clothing removed. She didn't know how the mercury was getting to him, but she intended to close off every avenue the poisoner could have used. After that, she gave him a mixture of milk and egg whites, followed by finely sieved charcoal, followed by more milk. *I have to get as much liquid in him as possible. I would give half my estate for an IV and a couple of bags of saline!* It had cost Lily a great deal of effort to obtain activated charcoal for medicinal uses. Her blacksmith and her glassblower had made her a contraption for steam heating charcoal derived from the bark of birch trees. In the end, she used the birch from two whole trees and made a total of five pounds of activated charcoal.

Now, looking down at her suffering patient as he lay in the clean bed she had prepared for him, the countess reflected that she would have to start on a second batch of charcoal immediately. Even five birch trees might not be enough. But it wasn't just mercury that needed to be removed; Lily suspected that the remedies the boy had been given in the Khanganate were only making him worse. *How long will it take me to get the mercury out of him? At least forty days.* She would have to keep the boy until spring, perhaps longer.

Lily only left the prince's room when it was time for dinner. When she reached the dining room, she bowed to her guests and took her place at the head of the table. Miranda materialized at her side. "Mama, how is the patient?"

"He's not well," Lily answered honestly. "If he lives the next two tennights, he has a chance of getting well." She looked around at her Khangan guests. "I believe it must have been more difficult to poison him while he was onboard the ship. Otherwise, he would never have made it here."

The men glanced at each other.

Lons turned to the countess. "My Lady, I have found rooms for your guests in the left wing."

Lily nodded. The Virmans, the Eveers, and all other newcomers were put in the right wing, where there was still plenty of room, but the Khangans were guests of a different sort. She wanted them to have plenty of room to make up their accommodations as they pleased.

"What about the crews?"

"I have called for the village elders. We will find beds for ten men in each village. They will take turns keeping watch on their ships."

"Can we feed them all?" This question was addressed to

Ingrid, who nodded energetically.

"I have not had a chance to send to Altver for supplies, but I believe we can make it to spring."

One of the Khangans spoke up. "Do not concern yourself with our keep, My Lady. We brought plenty of provisions with us. We will not be a burden on your house."

Lily waved a hand. "I beg you not to consider yourselves a burden. If the Star Mare brought you to my house, I will do everything to ensure that you are in need of nothing."

The man's face was still creased with worry. "My Lady, your words are very kind, but we would like to know more about the condition of young Amir Gulim."

Lily realized she hadn't even known the patient's name. "He is alive, but in very poor condition. I cannot know the extent to which his internal organs have been damaged. We will keep watch over him and treat him to the best of our ability." She had no way to explain the effects of mercury on the liver, kidneys, and intestines.

The men listened attentively to each word and asked if they could visit the boy. Lily consented, but with one warning. "The poison did not get into his blood on its own. I will have someone sitting watch by his bed at all times. If you care about his wellbeing, then remember that the first attempt to send away my nurse will be deemed an admission of guilt."

The men's eyes flashed as they glanced at each other.

Lily was obstinate. "He is my patient. I am responsible for his life and health. Anyone who goes against my orders will become my enemy."

The air in the dining room was electrified. Tahir tapped his glass with a fork. "Lilian-jan, please... our guests are not used to being spoken to in this manner." The Khangans were shocked that Tahir din Dashar, one of the greatest healers and scholars in the world, would speak to a woman with such respect. They were even more shocked by her response.

Lily smiled and sat down. "Forgive me my temper, gentlemen. Please understand that my motivation is a good one. I cannot stand to see a young man wither and die at the hands of an enemy when he could have lived for many long years. Tahir, my friend, I beg you to collect the information we need."

Tahir began to pepper the Khangans with questions. What did the boy eat for breakfast, lunch, and dinner while on the boat? What did he drink? How much? How often did he use the privy? What did he wear? Did he have any favorite objects or pets? Who took care of him? What covering was on the walls of his room at home? He asked about symptoms, reactions, the names of men who had treated him. Lily had wanted to invite the Khangan mediuses to the table, but Tahir had told her it would never do—they were ranked too low to eat at her table. Fine. Then I will question them later...in private.

The answers Lily got from the delegation left her with little to go on. The boy preferred simple food and had always eaten little. He was a passionate hunter. He had never been interested in rocks or minerals, and he had never used cosmetics of any kind. So far, there were no leads. *But the poison is coming from somewhere! I thought the mercury was likely to be hidden in his room, but if that were so, he would feel better simply by leaving home. What if he brought it with him?*

While her guests ate and drank, Lily slowly turned over the possibilities and began to put together a list of things she could use to beat back the poison.

ဗာ ☐ ഗ

Leis Antrel had gone out on the wall to check the watchmen. All was well. It was time for him to climb down and check on the gate watches, but he continued to stand in the on top of the wall, his face turned to the dark line of trees in the distance. He enjoyed having a few minutes to breathe the fresh air and think.

He had served under Jyce Earton. It had not been difficult work, but he had always done his best and been paid well. The work had suffered after the old earl's death. Jerrison Earton was no less intelligent than his father, but he lacked his father's intuition and his interest in other people. Old Jyce could have reached an agreement with Maldonaya, herself, if need be. Jerrison, on the other hand, looked down on everyone; Leis had never liked that about the young earl. Jerrison thought his money and his connection to the throne made him better than other people. Under Jerrison's command, Leis had quietly begun to back away from his work. He had saved enough over the years to live comfortably. He was over forty now, no longer a boy...

But everything changed when he arrived in Earton. Leis remembered what he had expected: a falling-down castle, a hysterical woman, and slothful servants. Instead, he found that the castle was being repaired and the servants had forgotten what sloth looked like. And the lady of the castle was something else entirely.

As a boy, Leis had loved fairytales. Now, as a grown man, he often reflected that Lily was the perfect fairytale princess: kind, intelligent, understanding, and always full of energy. He had never seen a woman like her before. *How could Jerrison Earton say such terrible things about his wonderful wife?* He had never heard his master criticize her in public, of course, but servants and soldiers know everything.

After the first attempt on Lily's life, Leis had felt stupid and guilty. He, who had served the Earton family for twenty years, had brought a dangerous murderer into the castle without even knowing it. Still, Lilian Earton laid no blame on him. Instead, she offered him a way to redeem himself. Leis understood what she wanted and decided not to resist fate. As far as he knew, the countess had complete authority to command the guards when her husband was not home unless he had issued other orders. *Did he issue other orders to me? No, he did not.* Moreover, he found her to be a lovely and intelligent woman. She assigned him the title of captain of the castle guards, gave him interesting work to do, paid him handsomely, and invited him to eat at her table.

That was what had won him over. Lilian Earton was equally friendly to Leis, and the Eveers, and the Virmans. She had no favorites, and everyone in the castle benefitted from her attention and care. Leis was no exception. He liked living in Earton, and he also knew that Earton would be nothing without the countess. Lilian Earton had breathed life into the castle and into Leis. He would do what he knew best: serve with honesty and honor. He would serve the one person who saw what he was capable of.

Leis was not blind. He could tell that all was not well between the countess and her husband. Once Jess arrived, there would be fireworks.

What will the earl say when he sees what his wife has been up to? He had no idea. Whose side will I take, if it comes down to it? He thought he already knew the answer.

He shook himself out of his deep thought and climbed down from the wall to see that the gates were properly guarded. He would also remind the men to keep a close eye on those Khangans. *They are the countess' guests, but you could never tell about foreigners…*

ঙ্গ ☐ ৪

Pain twisted Amir's body and settled down as a wave of nausea in his stomach. He was used to it. His pain was as familiar as an old friend. On occasion, he was glad to feel pain. *It means I'm still alive.* He wasn't ready to die. He was much too young for that.

He could barely remember what he had ever wanted to do in life. Everything was clouded by pain and weakness, and the iron hammers that pounded in his head. He vomited and then slipped gratefully into emptiness.

The young man did not know that his healers gave him sleeping remedies and pain remedies every few hours because they were afraid that, otherwise, he would never survive the journey. He simply took the cups they offered him and slipped back into his dreams, where he was healthy and strong.

He had not valued his health until it was gone. The malady had snuck up on him, like a snake sliding into his bed in the night. He fought it as best he could, but he was laid low by attacks of vomiting and weakness. At first, his father thought he would eventually shake off his illness, but after the Great Khangan witnessed an attack of vomiting, he became afraid and called in all the medicuses, herbal healers, and wise women he could find. They gave him herbal tinctures and enemas, they prayed for him, and they let his blood. None of it helped. In fact, he got worse.

The only medicus he remembered clearly was Tahir Djiaman din Dashar. When the great healer entered Amir's room, his first words were "Prince, I do not know how to heal you." Amir was feeling well that day, so he saw the sad look in the man's eyes and understood what it meant.

Tahir sat down by his bed. The conversation between them was carried out in low voices. "I have lived for many years, but there is still much I do not know."

"Will I die?"

"I cannot know that, Your Highness."

"Then you should leave."

Tahir shrugged. "I have considered that, but I am old."

"My father will take your life, and that will not help me." A spasm of pain caused Amir to double over, but he waited for it to pass. Then he continued. "You are the only one who was brave enough to tell me the truth."

The old man's eyes were sorrowful. "I would give my life to save yours if I could."

"But you can't." Amir was silent for a moment. "Write out an order, and I will put my seal on it. With that order, they will let you out of the city. Leave the Khanganate; that way, at least one of us will survive."

৪০ ☐ ೞ

Amir was sick for many weeks after that. Then, he had a period of relative calm. He began to feel better. The servants gave him milk to drink and bathed him in warm water that smelled of pine trees. One day, his father came to him. The Great Khangan sat down on his bed and stroked his hair. The servants slipped away, leaving father and son alone.

"Amir, you are dying."

"I know, Father."

"I received a letter from Tahir Djiaman din Dashar. You let him go. Why did you do that?"

"He knew I was dying, and he refused to lie to me."

"Yes. That is why I did not stop him. We were both right."

A spark of hope leaped up in Amir's chest, only to be beaten back by a wave of nausea. "What do you mean, Father?" he looked up and waited.

"He writes that you are being poisoned. He does not know how, but he has found someone who recognized the poison from its symptoms. This person can help you."

"I am willing to try."

"She is a woman—the Countess of Earton, in Ativerna. I have asked about her. People say she works wonders. I cannot bring her here, however. The distance is too great, and her husband is away on state business."

The boy nodded. He knew he couldn't wait.

"I have decided that you will go to Earton."

"But…"

"If it is poison, the person responsible will have a harder time getting to you on the ship. I know it is winter, and the gulf is treacherous, but we have no choice."

"Father, if I go there…"

"It's a chance—a very small chance, but a chance nonetheless. I will write to King Edward. I will give you gold and men and carrier pigeons. You must write to me, Son."

"I will do everything I can to get better, Father." Amir's face was serious.

The Great Khangan sighed. He had other sons, but none of them were as wise and good as Amir. "You are my son from my most beloved wife, and you are the only one I can trust with the country when I am gone."

"There are those who would not like to hear you say that."

"When you leave, I will announce that Rashad is my heir. Then we will see what happens."

"Don't…"

"The others would be worse."

"What if…"

"I know. Making Rashad my heir puts him at risk. Damn it all…" Amir saw tears on his father's face for the first time. "Come back alive, Son. Just come back."

"I will do my best, Father."

He remembered more thoughts, words, and feelings…
Is it possible that I ever lived a normal life? The pain returned.
He waited. It ebbed away.

There was a crash. Amir opened his eyes. The sunlight
came streaming into his room with an intensity that made his
eyes tear up.

"Who the hell do you think you are and what are you
doing in here?"

The voice belonged to a woman, and she was far from
happy. As she continued venting her anger, Amir listened and
was filled with wonder. He pried his eyes all the way open. He
was no longer on the ship. He was lying in a bright, sunny
room where everything was white and clean and smelled
sharply of something he could not identify. And in the middle
of the room, he saw a woman the likes of which he had never
seen before.

She was tall and dressed in green and white, with a
thick, golden braid over one shoulder. More surprising still,
she was scolding his medical men without any concern for
their rank or their delicate ears.

"Have you lost your minds?" she bellowed. "Burning
incense in a sick room? Stick that pipe up your nose and get
out of here. And take that dirty fur pelt with you."

"But this is the skin of a foal that was never born. It
has been sanctified!" One of the medicuses bleated.

"Get it out! If I see it anywhere near my patient again,
I'll cut it into pieces and feed it to you!"

Lily was in a foul mood. She had been up late, watching the boy while he slept and spoon-feeding him beaten egg whites and activated charcoal. It was almost light out when she finally let a pair of Virman women take over and went to lie down for a few hours. Jaimie had woken her up by banging on her door.

"My Lady, the Khangan mediches are in there. You said not to let anyone near the patient."

"Where is Tahir?"

"With the boy. He won't let them touch him."

Lily slammed the door in his face and began to throw on whatever clothes she could find. She quickly braided her hair as she ran through the halls, bursting into the infirmary just in time. One of the Virman nurses was standing between the boy and his Khangan healers. She had her hands on her hips and looked like she was ready to grab an axe if words failed her.

Tahir was doing his best to keep the three other bearded old men as far as he could from the sickbed. One was waving a heavy bronze censer like a weapon, another was shaking what looked like a dirty rag, and the third had bouquets of herbs and bird feathers hung around his neck. When Lily saw the smoke coming from the censer and the dirt falling from the rag and the bunches of herbs, she lost any tact she might have possessed.

Aldonai had blessed the countess with both height and weight, and over the past several months that weight had turned from fat into muscle. Lily's first move was to grab the censer and slam it against the floor. She would call the maids to clean up when she was done. The Khangan men turned to her with indignation all over their faces, but before any of them could say a word, Lilian Earton launched her attack.

೫ ⸻ ೮

When the storm was over and the opponents utterly cowed, the countess set out her conditions. "Go bathe yourselves and wash your clothes. After that, whenever one of you wishes to visit the patient, you will first obtain permission from myself or Tahir. If any of you is found in here without that permission, I will have you arrested on suspicion of poisoning. Instead of bothering the patient, I want you to write down for me in detail what methods and remedies you have used on the prince. And I want to see samples. Now, get out!"

Her voice was convincing, and the Khangan healers hurried to the door. Once they were gone and the door was shut, Lily turned to assess what needed to be re-cleaned. Just then, she heard a noise from the boy's bed. She knelt down and watched the boy's face.

His eyes were open, and he looked at her with interest. "Who are you?"

"I am Lilian Earton, the Countess of Earton. You are in my home."

"My name is Amir Gulim. I am the eldest son of the Great Khangan."

"Yes, and you're the victim of poisoning, as well. I don't think you're as bad off as I feared, but you will have to stay here for lengthy treatment."

A light filled the boy's eyes. "I did not expect you to

say that my malady could be treated."

"I will not lie to you. You are in great danger, but I will do my best to keep you alive."

"If you help me, my father…"

Lily put her hand over the boy's mouth. "Be quiet. You must get better before there can be any talk of that. Now, I have to examine you. Tell me where it hurts."

The boy nodded. Lily pulled back the blanket and began palpating various parts of his body. "Does it hurt here? What about here? Or here?"

The boy turned pale but answered as best he could. He almost cried out when Lily pulled the blanket completely off and began pressing on his stomach with her long fingers. "I'm sorry," she whispered. "This won't take long."

Then she sneezed. The broken censer was still giving off smoke.

"Open a window," she commanded. The smell was overpowering. It was a blend of sheep's manure and something she couldn't quite put her finger on. *What do they put in those things?*

When she was done examining the boy, she tucked his blanket around him and nodded to the nurse. "Milk, egg whites, and activated charcoal. If he is better, we will try to give him something light to eat tomorrow. I won't risk it today."

The nurse took a clean spoon and began to feed the boy milk and egg whites. Then she gave him a small portion of the adsorbent and reached for the milk again.

Lily picked up the censer, which Tahir had moved to the windowsill and sniffed. *None of this makes sense.* She opened the censer and found the insides caked with a strange, dried substance. *What on earth have they been burning in here?*

She asked Tahir, but he only knew that censers were used to burn holy herbs.

The countess took a towel from the table and wrapped the censer in it. Then, after a pause, she used another towel to collect the bits of herbs and dirt that had fallen to the floor from the foal's skin.

"I'll take these back to my laboratory."

Tahir was curious. "What for, My Lady?"

"I just have an idea…"

80 ☐ 03

No sooner did Lily leave the infirmary than she was accosted by Lons Avels. "My Lady!"

"What is it?"

"I wrote the letter. Will you look at it?"

She reached for it. "You are a miracle, Lons."

He blushed. "I try, My Lady…"

Your Majesty,

I write to inform you that the Great Khangan has sent his eldest son and heir to Earton to undergo treatment with Tahir Djiaman din Dashara. The boy is seriously ill, but I will pray for his recovery.

I remain your faithful servant,

Lilian Earton

The second letter was even more to the point.

Dear Father,

The Great Khangan has sent his son to Earton in hopes of recovering his health. We will do what we can, but I am not assured of success. Keep an eye on your affairs in the Khanganate with this in mind.

Your loving daughter

"Will you send them by pigeon?"

"Yes, My Lady."

The countess threw her braid over her other shoulder. "Fine. Write them out neatly and send them."

Lons bowed and left. Lily reflected that she would be at a loss if she had to leave her secretary at home when she paid her visit to Edward's court. *Still, how can I take him with me without putting him in danger?* There was one idea she had been pondering lately. She smiled. *His own mother won't recognize him!*

ଚୠ ଔଓ

Her laboratory was calm and quiet. Lily looked at the long rows of glass bottles on her shelves and sighed. *So much work went into those.* She had obtained the chlorides from sea salt and purchased the acids and bases from the tanners in Altver. Back home, it had simply been a matter of time and patience to obtain a more or less pure hydroxide.

What do I have that would react with mercury?

If the mercury was divalent, as it usually was in nature, it would produce a yellow residue when mixed with a base. If mixed with potassium iodide, the residue would be red.

Lily suspected that the prince had had a stroke of luck; she didn't know who had been poisoning him at home, but the boy seemed to have improved during the voyage, meaning that the doses were small and infrequent.

Let's figure this out!

She scraped out everything she could from the inside of the censer and divided it into equal portions, which she transferred into jars. Then, she began adding the bases. She could hardly believe her eyes when she spotted yellow residue swimming in the gray liquid of the first jar.

Tahir, who had been watching her movements with increasing interest, looked up to see what this meant. Lily set the jar down on the table. "I don't know how it started, but some of the poison is in the center."

"The censer was prepared by Sulan Mavvar din Sharaya."

"Where is he?"

⁊ ⁓

If it hadn't been for Tahir, Lily would have caused an international incident. Her first instinct was to rip the head off the idiot who had been poisoning the boy with mercury vapors. However, after a talking-to from Tahir, she called Rashad Omar din Darashaya to her laboratory and explained to him what they were looking for. He immediately authorized her to search his ships.

Lily now knew what she sought. All of the censers were removed from the walls of the ships' quarters, along with the rugs and bed sheets in the prince's room.

When opened and tested, all of the censers gave up the

same yellowish residue. Rashad called for Sulan, the medicus who had been swinging the censer, and Lily went to search his room. In no time, she found something that stopped her in her tracks. She opened a richly encrusted box and found a piece of cinnabar—mercury sulfide. To be sure, she applied her base again; the yellow color left no doubt.

The countess was ready to have the man arrested, but Tahir stopped her. "He may not have meant any harm, My Lady."

"Why do you think that?"

"There is an old story that once, the Star Mare came to earth. An evil man tried to harm her, and this stone—cinnabar, as you call it—represents droplets of her blood."

Lily nodded. "I see. Where do you use it?"

"Priests paint their faces with it."

"Do you ever eat it?"

"That would be sacrilege, My Lady."

"What about putting it in censers?"

"That is only done in extreme cases, to call on the Mare's mercy."

The countess shook her head in disgust.

ಬ ⬚ ೕ

The formal investigative committee consisted of Lily, Tahir, Jaimie, Rashad and the two other captains, whose names Lily could not remember, Lons, Taris, and Pastor Vopler. Mirrie sat on her stepmother's lap, and their two dogs lay in the corner. Two Virmans guarded the door. Helke had been invited but claimed to be too busy to attend. Lily knew he disliked Khangans for some reason.

Working together, the group tried to understand how the boy

had been poisoned initially. The mercury vapors from the censers were no more than supporting doses. *Who started the terrible process, and how?*

Rashad gave them as much information as he could. Sulan was not the official court healer. That had been Tahir's job, and Tahir swore he had never used cinnabar as a remedy. In fact, he had seen enough elderly priests—men who had applied cinnabar to their skin throughout their whole lives—to suspect that the substance was not harmless.

After a silence, Jaimie spoke up. "My Lady," he said quietly, turning his face to Lilian, "is this blood of the Star Mare easy to obtain? I must confess I have never seen it before."

Lily played with her braid. He was right. "Tahir-jan?" she asked the healer.

"Lilian-jan, it is a sacred substance. It cannot be bought or sold. It could only be obtained at a temple."

"That does not seem difficult."

Rashad spoke up. "My Lady, there are no temples at the Great Khangan's palace. He does not keep holy men the way that you do," and he looked at Pastor Vopler, who nodded in assent.

"I have heard the same thing," he said.

Lily found that odd. "How do the people who live at the palace pray?"

"They go to the temple in the city once every ten days," Tahir answered.

Lons, who had said nothing up until that point, became

excited. "The easiest way to obtain this poison would be if you had a brother who served at the temple. Or a cousin, uncle, nephew…any relative, really. That way, the culprit would know about the properties of this ci-na…"

"Cinnabar," Lily finished for him.

"Exactly. I expect that the priests are aware of the harm this substance causes," Tahir agreed. He added, "It is the blood from the Mare's wound. It can bring nothing but harm."

Lily felt she no longer understood. "Then why do the priests put it on their faces?" she asked.

"Because the world is not perfect, Lilian-jan." Tahir replied. He looked tired. "I will instruct you in the finer points of our religion some other time."

The countess bowed her head in assent.

They needed to know more about the ties among the Khangan's wives. Tahir had never been interested in such matters, and Rashad was not close enough to the royal family to have such knowledge. They would have to ask the heir.

৪০ ☐ ೦೪

Amir was awake when the committee went in to see him. His nurse was telling him a Virman fairytale and feeding him egg whites. He looked up in surprise when the group crowded into his room.

Rashad spoke for the committee. "Your Highness, we have discovered how the poison was given to you. We know what it is, but we do not know who was behind it."

"Is that so?" Amir was intrigued.

Rashad explained about the substance they had found in the

censers.

Amir thought for a while but finally shook his head. "I do not know. I must write a letter to my Father. I never gave much thought to his harem."

Lily turned to Rashad. "Write for him. Ask your Great Khangan to investigate his own mares."

"My Lady!" Rashad was shocked by such disrespectful language.

The countess stared back at him. "And now, we must leave the sick room. The patient will never get better with all of us in here."

ᚹᛑ ᚲᚳ

Jerrison Earton, a gallant nobleman and dedicated ladies' man, stood in the middle of his room cursing everything under the sun. He would have gone on in the same vein for the rest of the day if his cousin hadn't come in.

"What's wrong with you?"

Instead of an answer, he was handed a scroll.

Richard caught it and examined the seals. "From the Khanganate. Is it about your shipbuilding business?"

"No!"

Impressed by his cousin's emotion, Richard quickly unrolled the scroll and read the first few lines. He soon let loose a string of curses.

It was a personal letter to Jerrison Earton from the Great Khangan. Richard knew a great deal about the Khangans, and he knew that their ruler was both the earthly leader of his people and a representative of their deity. He was not the kind of man to write letters to an earl in Ativerna.

The letter was short, but it was extremely interesting.

Your Lordship,

By this letter, I inform you that my eldest son and heir is on his way to Earton for treatment. Be so kind as to write to your people so that they do not panic, and instead greet the boy and render him all assistance. I will write a separate letter to your manager. If my son dies, I will not hold you responsible. If he recovers, my gratitude will know no bounds.

These unnerving words were followed by a signature and the seal of the Khanganate.

"What nonsense is this? Is there a holy miracle worker on your estate?"

"Not the last time I checked," Jess growled. "I don't know anything about what happens in Earton."

"True enough," Richard agreed. "You were the last to find out that someone tried to kill your wife."

"My wife..." Jess muttered. Then he grabbed the box where he kept his letters. "My wife!" He picked up her last letter.

This has been confirmed by an eminent healer who arrived in Earton by a happy twist of fate. I expect you will have heard of Tahir Djiaman din Dashar.

"Who is this Tahir person?"

"He's her new medicus." Jess snorted.

Richard's face relaxed. "Then it makes sense. They want to take the prince to see him. All you have to do is write to Earton and make sure they're well received."

"Of course I'll write. That's all I can do."

His cousin smiled. "Perhaps you could take the opportunity to write to your wife, as well."

Jess ran a hand through his hair. "Why is everyone interested in that fool?"

"Apparently not everyone thinks she's a fool."

Jess looked away in annoyance. He could see that was the case, but he could not yet believe it. It was easier to believe that Maldonaya had taken possession of his wife's body.

ଚ ଅ

Sulan Mavvar din Sharaya was in shock. No woman could attain the wisdom of a healer. Women were supposed to be silent and look at the floor. Women were supposed to obey men. No woman should behave like the Countess of Earton, yelling at her elders and asking them impertinent questions.

As a matter of fact, Rashad yelled louder than the countess. "Where did you get the cinnabar?"

The old man looked up at him in distress. "What cinnabar?" Then his memory clicked. "Ah, you mean the blood of the Mare? Someone at the temple told me it would help."

"Who? When?"

Slowly, the story came out. Sulan had gone to the temple to pray for success in healing the prince. The youngest priest had promised that he, too, would pray, and had suggested using cinnabar. Sulan did not know his name since the priests did not use regular names like other people. The man had simply called himself Sharadji.

Rashad sighed. He would have to hold onto Sulan until they could get back to the Khanganate and he could identify the helpful young priest.

Lily began to suspect that she would have to take the prince with her when she paid her visit to Edward's court. She couldn't leave him in his current state.

ജ □ ೲ

My Royal Brother,
May the grace of the Star Mare touch your
brow...

The letter was full of poetic images and courtesy, but the main point was delivered perfectly clearly. The Great Khangan was sending his son to Earton for treatment and very much hoped that the treatment would work; his royal brother was not opposed to the treatment, and his royal brother would provide all assistance to the countess and anyone else involved in healing the boy. If the treatment was successful, the Great Khangan would shower Earton with gold.

Edward put his head down on his desk and laughed. *What is that woman up to now?* He began to be sorry that he hadn't sent her to Wellster with the delegation, just to keep Gardwig busy.

He took a deep breath and started to work on two letters. The first was a reply to his "royal brother" and stated that he would certainly do everything within his power to further the boy's treatment. No gold would be necessary, he merely hoped to continue to enjoy the Great Khangan's good graces.

The second letter was to the Countess of Earton, promising all sorts of wonderful things if the Khangan's son recovered. Edward made no threats concerning what he would do if the boy did not recover, but he knew Lilian Earton to be an intelligent woman. She would understand.

Chapter 8
A Prince Underfoot

Amir lay in bed and looked up at the plain, white ceiling without decoration of any kind. It was easy on his eyes. He had been in Earton ten days and liked it there. His room was always quiet, and his nurse cared for him as if he were a small child. Better yet, his awful malady seemed to be releasing its grip on him.

He still had attacks of nausea and pain that were only helped by strong sedatives, but the countess, who spent an hour by his bed each day, said that he was improving. He was no longer receiving the poison, she said, and it was up to his body to complete the process of recovery.

All is the Mare's will, he reflected.

Amir realized that his father had saved his life, even without knowing the source of the danger. When he had received Tahir's letter concerning poison, he had isolated his son from everyone, fired the servants and hired new healers. Apparently, that move had made it impossible for the poisoner to reach him, and his body had begun removing the poison, slowly but surely.

During the trip to Earton, Sulan had subjected him to poisonous vapors, but the dose was much smaller.

Thinking back over the long course of his illness, the boy clenched his fists. *If only I knew who was responsible!*

Suddenly, a voice brought him back to the present. "Hello," it said.

He turned his head to look. Miranda Catherine Earton was standing by his bed. She must have slipped past the guards.

"Hello," he replied with a smile.

"Why aren't you asleep?"

The girl talked to Amir as if he were a normal boy like everyone else. He thought that was curious. He had noticed that her stepmother had the same habit. Everyone else saw him as the son of the Great Khangan, but Lilian Earton saw him as a sick boy. Now, there was Miranda, looking at him with clear, friendly eyes.

"I don't know. Why did you come here?"

"To look at you. I've never seen a prince before."

Amir grinned. "Well? Do you like me?"

"No. You're too skinny."

"Poison never makes you look good."

"I know. Mama Lily explained it to me. Don't worry, she'll fix you. She can fix anything. She saved my dog when someone tried to poison her."

"Why do you call her Mama Lily? How old is she?"

"She's young. I'm not really her daughter. My mother died, and then my father married Lily. I was just a baby."

"And now Lily is your mother?"

The prince was intrigued, but Miranda just giggled and shook her head. "No. I never saw her until last autumn. I always lived with Papa, and Lily lived here."

"Why was that?"

"I don't know. We should ask. Last fall, Papa had to leave, so he needed to send me somewhere. I could choose to come here or go live with my aunt. I chose to come here."

"Why? Is your aunt awful?"

"Very!" came Miranda's emphatic reply. "Her children are awful, and she's awful, and her husband is like a sugar-coated frog!"

"Don't you have other family in the capital?"

Miranda scratched her nose. "I think I do, but Papa doesn't speak to them. So, I just decided to come here."

Amir was thoroughly charmed. "Do you like it here?"

"Of course! I was scared of Lily at first, but then I found out that she's wonderful! I have so many new friends, and I've learned so much. Lily tells the best stories!"

"What kind of stories?" Amir knew more than a few stories, himself.

"All different kinds."

"Do they all end with a wedding?" he asked, jokingly.

"Of course not; they're all different." Miranda informed him. After studying his face critically for a minute, she blurted out, "Do you know how to do anything?"

"What do you mean?" The question was so unexpected that the prince did not know what to say.

"Just that. Do you know how to sew? Or make mirrors? Or weave cloth?"

"No. I'm a prince."

"What do princes know how to do?"

"Run the government."

Miranda measured her new acquaintance with a serious look. "Lily was right. It's no use having a prince underfoot."

It was a good thing for Amir that he was lying down, for otherwise, he would have fallen out of bed laughing. "Why is that?" he asked after he caught his breath.

"Because you can't do anything."

"What about you? What can you do?"

"I'm learning everything! I can sew and knit and make lace and take care of sick people. Lily wants Master Helke to teach Mark and me how to work with precious stones, and the glassblower…"

"But why bother?" Amir interrupted. "You're the daughter of an important man in your kingdom."

Miranda looked down at him with an enormous sense of importance. "So what? Anything could happen tomorrow. You never know where you'll end up. I know a story about that. Want me to tell it to you?"

An hour later, Jaimie walked in to find Miranda curled up on Amir's bed as she told him her favorite story. Amir was listening with great interest and showed no signs of being tired.

"Get off the bed, child," Jaimie scolded her.

Miranda complied but voiced her offense. "You're supposed to call me 'My Lady,' not 'child.'"

Amir smiled. "Do not be harsh with her. She is wonderful."

That same evening, Jaimie told Lilian about the newfound friendship between Amir and Miranda. The countess agreed that they should not let the two young people become too close. Soon, however, she discovered that she was too late. The girl wormed her way into the infirmary whenever she could, and Amir was always pleased to see her. Eventually, Pastor Vopler's son, Mark, began joining them.

After a few days, Lily gave up trying to keep the children away from Amir. Miranda began helping the nurse when she fed the prince and washed his chamber pot. Amir was shocked, but Lily reminded him that there was nothing reproachable about an earl's daughter helping take care of a prince.

"But My Lady, this morning she wanted to help the nurse wash me. She would have seen me…"

Lily stopped herself from smiling. "You should look in the mirror, Prince."

Amir's eyes lit up. "Speaking of these mirrors, I would like to know how your craftsmen make them."

The countess informed him that that was her trade secret. If he wanted to buy some mirrors to take home with him, he would have to speak with King Edward.

"When can I meet your ruler?"

Lily sighed. "I have been asked to pay a visit at court in the spring, once the roads are dry. And that is a problem, Amir, because I doubt that you'll be strong enough by then for me to leave you." After a brief moment, she decided to risk going further. "It would help if your father wrote to His Majesty and asked him to either postpone my visit for one year or allow you to accompany me. That way, I can continue to take care of you."

Amir considered the options. He suspected that his father would not object. Quite the opposite: he would be glad for his son to have a chance to see the world. Later on, when he was the ruler of the Khanganate, such travel would be frowned on.

Amir was intrigued by the countess. He knew enough about Ativernan customs to know that she was breaking all sorts of rules. She had the remarkable ability to make new rules, while the people around her simply followed along as long as the new rules promised enjoyment or profit.

Helke Leitz was intrigued by the countess, as well, but he feared she would work him to death. Once she was confident in her ability to produce glass lenses, she charged Helke with making the metal housing for a device he could barely conceive of. When it was finished, Lily called it a "telescope" and gave it to Leif as a present. The gruff Virman was delighted—the simple spyglass made it possible for him to see three times further than before.

Buoyed by her success, Lily began to plan how she could make the items she would need for intravenous injections. *I know they had IVs long before plastics were invented. The needle is the most important part, plus the line and stop valve.* She thought she could make both things out of the materials she had available in her new world. *It will just be ten times harder!*

For a brief moment, she wished for a grove of rubber trees to be discovered in Earton. Not really, though. *I don't want to see this world fouled up with plastic trash like my own world, where you look up in the sky and see bags flying around instead of birds.*

After spending many an evening thinking and sketching, Lily went to Helke and told him she wanted him to make a device that could provide a continuous flow of medicinal substances through a needle into the patient's body. Helke took one look at her sketches and abandoned his other projects to work on her new idea. He realized that this new plan of the countess' would not necessarily bring profits, but it promised something more valuable: immortality. Five hundred years in the future, people would remember Helke Leitz as the man who saved untold lives with his invention.

Helke could not fail to see the countess' oddities, but he forgave her and said nothing. He was safe in Earton, and he was making money. Those two considerations outweighed everything else. He also appreciated how Lilian Earton judged people by their abilities, instead of by their family tree or rank.

⅒ ◻ ⅓

When she wasn't driving Helke to finish her homemade IV device, Lily was preparing for her trip to the capital. She studied etiquette and dancing and polished her manners. Lons helped her whenever he could.

Now that Lily knew his secret, she realized she was perched on the blade of a knife. She could not possibly know what each of the kings concerned would think about the sudden revelation that Princess Anna already had a husband. If both men wanted Richard and Anna to marry, then they would bury Lons, and perhaps Lily along with him. If not, there was a chance Lons would survive. For now, all she could do was keep her mouth shut. If there was ever an opportunity to whisk the princess away, Lons would have to decide for himself if he still wanted her.

In the meantime, Lons was working on growing a beard.

Lily had hit on the idea of dressing him like a Khangan. She would already have several Khangans traveling with her, one more or one less would make no difference. They had planned that Lons would grow a beard, change the shape of his brows, and wear an eye patch over one eye. He was also learning as much of the Khangan language as he could manage, as were Miranda, Mark, Lilian and all the Virman children. *Why not?* Amir spoke perfectly good Ativernese, but Lily still saw value in teaching the children languages. The more they knew, the more opportunities they would have in life.

When she considered her plans for taking the capital by storm, Lily thought about it as a big show with herself as the star. She wasn't aiming to become the king's mistress. As far as she could guess, Edward was in his late fifties, which made him an old man in that world. Plus, she knew she wasn't mistress material. She could just imagine the shock on the king's face if she rolled over in bed and started talking about the properties of different kinds of glass.

No, her plan was to become so necessary to Edward's kingdom that removing her would cause great damage to the rest of the structure. It was a risky plan, for sure, but she had no choice. Lily never forgot that out there somewhere on the horizon was her husband, who could exercise total control over her life if he chose. And she had no idea what he would choose. That was why she had to make herself irreplaceable.

Medicine? Lilian Earton. Glass? Lilian Earton. Lace, cosmetics, perfume…

If Jess tried to rein her in, the church would stick up for her because she printed their books, sailors would stick up for her because they wanted her spy glasses, medical men would clamor for her knowledge and her new devices, and women… In a word, it would be hard for her husband to go up against the entire kingdom at once.

Plans were all well and good, but her correspondence with her husband did not give Lily a great deal of optimism. His letters were brief, and he often reminded her that he couldn't wait to see her in person. That was worrying.

Lily was still concerned about the plot between Jess' lover and her cousin. She knew that the king had quietly gotten rid of the cousin, and Hans had written to tell her that Adelaide would be married off to some peasant as soon as she returned from Wellster. What she had no way of knowing, however, was how Jess would react to the banishment of his mistress. She hoped he wasn't an idiot. He had to know how bad it looked that the attempted murder of his wife was financed with his own money.

After much thought, Lily wrote to Hans and asked him to find and buy back the jewels that Alex had sold and to send them to her father. She had found some heavy jewelry left behind by the old countess, but she couldn't find the sapphires and pearls that her father had given her upon her marriage. If Jess had taken them, she wanted them back.

The jewels, however, were the least of her worries. She still needed to find out about Baron Yerby and why he had hired Damis Reis to seduce her. *It's almost like he doesn't want Jess to have an heir.*

In her letter to Hans, she asked him to find out what he could about Yerby. The countess did not see the man as a threat—his actions were obviously aimed at her husband—but she would feel safer when she knew what he was up to.

Lily did a great deal of thinking about her husband's family. She knew that illegitimate children could not inherit property and that a man was allowed to marry a maximum of four times in his lifetime. *I'm Jess' third wife, and so far Miranda is his only child. If something happens to him, who will take control of the estate?*

She knew who the possible candidates were: herself, Jess' sister and her husband, his mother, and a number of relatives on the side of his second wife, Magdalena. Since Miranda could not inherit the estate on her own, it would be held and managed by someone else until her second son could step into his inheritance as the new Earl of Earton. During those many long years, the guardian could use the proceeds from the estate however he or she saw fit. The guardian could also choose a husband for Miranda.

As she turned these matters over in her mind, it occurred to her that she and Jess would be in the capital at the same time and that certain parties might be concerned about the possibility of an heir resulting from their meeting no matter how unlikely such an event was in reality. *Will they make an attempt on the earl? It's entirely possible.* She briefly wondered if she should warn him, but waved the thought away. *If I can take care of myself, so can you, my dear!*

What really frightened the countess was the thought that someone had sent Medicus Craybey to get rid of her, and had probably had him killed after he failed in his mission. She had continued to correspond with this shadow enemy through Karl Treloney, writing as if she were Fred Darcy. The previous week, she had received word that the money had arrived—a down payment on her death.

Of course, Lily had no intention of dying. Quite the opposite: she intended to nab the merchant and pick up her money the next time she was in Altver. Once she had Treloney in a room alone with a couple of Virmans, she would ask him her pressing questions. If it took hot irons to get answers, then so be it. *If it's a choice between my life and someone else's, I'll choose me every time…unless the other person is Miranda.*

In sum, Lily figured she had three groups of enemies. She knew who two of the groups were, and one of them had already been dealt with. *Who is in the third group? And what do they want?*

She could only guess, so she continued sending letters signed "Fred" that claimed the countess was on her deathbed, right alongside little Miranda.

In addition to all of her other correspondence, Lily received a letter every two weeks from her mother-in-law, Alicia. The letters were filled with gossip and palace intrigue, and she responded with letters describing Mirrie's health and the weather in Earton. Meanwhile, she began using the letters to draw up a map of the relationships and ties between the people at court.

Setting pen to homemade paper, she wrote out a list of people—the Earl of N., the Countess of M., Baron D.—and filled in everything she knew: husbands and wives, children, lovers, friends, enemies. *Once you have paper, you can do anything!*

ঠ◻ছ

Adelaide Wells was ill and had taken to her bed. A member of the delegation informed Richard immediately. Jess, who was sitting in his cousin's room, frowned. "What's she up to now?'

"I don't know, but I suppose we should go see her."

When they went in, they found Adelaide in bed. She was as pale as a sheet, with blue-tinged lips and hollow eyes.

"What has happened to you?" Richard asked politely. He noticed a heap of bloody rags peeking out from under the bed.

Adelaide sniffled. "I…lost…the baby." She began to cry.

Richard sighed and turned to Jess. "This is your affair to deal with," he said as he left the room.

Jerrison would have happily sent Adele to the devil, but he couldn't. "How did it happen?"

"I was upset. The medicus says that that was the reason…" In fact, Adelaide had simply purchased a powdered herb to cause an increase in her menstrual bleeding.

ℰ ☐ ℭ

Jess sighed. "Don't cry. It's for the best."

That was where he went wrong.

"For the best?" the woman cried. "For the best?"

Jess realized he had made a tactical mistake, but it was too late to retreat. "The child was illegitimate."

"It was your fault! You hated him and wanted him to die. My poor baby!" She fell back against her pillows and began to sob.

Jess' heart was heavy. He knew he should say something to calm her, but he wanted nothing more than to turn and go. Just then, Adelaide's servant came in and gave him the excuse he needed.

"You should leave, My Lord. It's just upsetting her to have you here."

He obeyed.

ℰ ☐ ℭ

Adele cried for another ten minutes, just to be on the safe side, and then made herself comfortable in bed. There was no child—there never had been—but she had successfully made Jess feel guilty of doing something awful. Altres had been right.

The jester had told her that his people would be waiting for her when the delegation reached Ivernea. She would do everything they told her to do. Adelaide wanted to live, and she knew she couldn't go back to Ativerna. If she managed to pull off his plan, the jester had promised to make sure she was well married to a nobleman in Wellster, somewhere in the hinterland. That was far from ideal, but it was her best chance. With Alex gone, she would have to grasp at straws. She would walk through fire, sleep with anyone, even eat a live frog.

She wanted to live...

෨ ෪

Amir was slowly improving. The painful attacks had stopped, and the nausea had left him. He already felt much better.

Lily had questioned Sulan about the priest who gave him the cinnabar. In fact, she went a step further and had one of the other Khangans sketch a portrait of the priest based on Sulan's description. His evidence and the portrait had been sent to the Great Khangan.

The ruler wrote back as soon as he could. They had found Sharadji. The priest's pain tolerance was nothing to speak of, and the whole plot was soon revealed. Gizyar's death and Amir's illness had been plotted by none other than Batita, the Great Khangan's second wife and the mother of Selim. When the illustrious ruler was seventeen, his father had given him five wives. Gizyar was the one he loved best, but once she became pregnant, he spent more time with Batita. Power-hungry Batita never forgave Gizyar for being the favorite wife, and she had her poisoned when Amir was just six years old.

Lily wondered why she hadn't finished off Amir at the same time, and the prince explained. His grief-stricken father had sent him off to live with the family of one of the Guards of the Caravan Roads. There, he had lived in complete safety and learned to love the beauty of the desert. Once he was older, however, he had to return to the palace. The malady struck not long after his return.

Both Batita and Selim were executed.

Even though Amir was doing better, Lily felt it was still too soon for him to return home. To keep his medicuses out of the way, she gave them her notes on the art of healing to read. Soon, she had five dedicated students instead of two. The Khangans were practical men: women were not generally known to possess great wisdom, but Lilian Earton had identified the poison and returned the prince from the edge of the grave. They knew only too well what would have happened to them—not to her—if the boy had died. Sulan studied harder than all the rest.

Whenever he found the Khangans alone, Pastor Vopler attempted to have little chats with them about Aldonai. They were polite but stood firm in their own faith. When she found out about these chats, Lily decided that she would have to take the pastor with her when she left for the capital. He was a little too active to be left alone on the estate. In fact, she had a three-foot-long list of people who couldn't be left alone on the estate. *My craftsmen, the Virmans, the Khangans, the Eveers, my soldiers, Lons, Martha...*

Only Emma, the castle guards, and all but a few servants would be left behind. Lily expected that the estate would continue to run smoothly in her absence. There was plenty of food, and she would send for two more pastors to keep an eye on the villagers while she was gone. The peasants understood crop rotation and were prepared to start using the new system that spring. Her new livestock would soon start bringing forth their offspring. While she was prepared to send Emma money if necessary, she was confident that the estate could prosper on its own.

The only question left to decide was what to do with the village girls who helped with lace making. They were desperate to go to Lavery with the countess. *Why not? I'm sure there will be plenty of work for them.*

⁎ ℙ

One cold winter evening, Emma brought her a letter from Hans. He had gotten a large sum of money from her father and bought back all the jewelry Alex had sold, which was made easier by the fact that the unfortunate schemer had described the jewels and the shops where he sold them. When August Broklend saw the treasure in Hans' hands, he stormed and ranted for a good hour. One of the rings had been his gift to Lilian's mother. It was a simple gold ring set with a single, round sapphire surrounded by tiny flecks of turquoise. It wasn't an expensive piece, but it was the first ring he ever bought his wife, and he had given it to his daughter as a family heirloom.

Lily immediately wrote to her father, imploring him not to kill his son-in-law right away. She suspected that Jess would no longer be welcome at the boatyards.

August, for his part, tore up every letter Jess sent him without opening them. Once he felt he could control his anger, he went to see the king and laid the ring in front of His Majesty, recounting the story of its beginnings and how Jess' mistress had used it to finance an attempt on his daughter's life.

That was the last straw. Edward wrote to the Earl of Earton and informed him that if the countess so much as raised an eyebrow about his behavior, his next posting in the king's service would be to somewhere so far away that Earton would look like the center of high society in comparison.

The letter he wrote to Lilian was very different. His Majesty expressed his confidence in her ability as a healer and his hope for Amir's speedy recovery. Once the crisis had passed, she wrote back to inform him that the boy was on the mend, but that there was no way she could leave him that spring.

His Majesty wrote back to inquire if she could postpone her visit until the summer. Lily gave the matter a great deal of thought. *If I wait until summer, I'll have time to get more people on my side before Jess returns from Ivernea in the autumn. That puts me in a stronger bargaining position.*

What terrified her more than anything was that Jess would do the one thing he had every right to do: remind everyone that he could do as he liked with his own wife, and then lock her up in the castle to start working on conceiving an heir.

She had too many people counting on her and too many ideas to let herself get shut up in the castle like someone's property. Torius Avermal sent frequent pigeon mail from Altver. The local merchants were beating his door down, undeterred by the bad weather or the high prices. Everyone needed all the lace, earrings and mirrors they could get their hands on.

Twice, Leif risked his own ship to take cargo to the mouth of the Earta, but after the second trip, he said he would not make the voyage again until the weather improved.

Lily suspected he had only risked going because he wanted to try out his new spyglass.Upon his return, he told her that any Virman would sell his soul to buy such a useful item. They discussed various schemes for selling the spyglasses in Virma. In the end, they decided that the Virmans would accompany her to Altver, where they would part ways with Erik and his men, who would take a shipment of spyglasses to sell in Virma. Lily and her entourage, housed on six ships (Leif's ship, the two slave ships and three Khangan ships) would proceed on to Lavery to present themselves at the court of Edward the Eighth.

Once the plan was devised, they began to draw up a list of what provisions to take with them. Food and other necessities could always be purchased in Altver, but Lily preferred to save as much of her cash as possible.

"Your Majesty," Jerrison murmured as he bowed his head in front of the queen.

"My Lord, we have enjoyed seeing you here at court." Especially the ladies in waiting, but I shall say nothing of that.

"Your Majesty, my stay here has given me sincere pleasure."

"We have a favor to ask of you."

"My life is in your hands, Majesty."

"The favor is not that great, My Lord."

Jess looked up with perfect attention.

"We have heard rumors concerning your wife."

"I am at a loss, Your Majesty."

"We hear she is very beautiful and talented." Milia was repeating a text she had committed to memory, so she had time to enjoy the look on Jerrison's face. "I would like to meet her and your daughter."

Jess could not hide his dismay. "Y-your Majesty?"

"Yes. We would like to see you, your wife, and your daughter here at court in Wellster."

Jess remembered to bow. "What an honor, Your Majesty. I will certainly do as you wish."

"Yes, that is what we wish, My Lord." Milia nodded and smiled to indicate that the interview was finished. Jess stepped aside to make way for the next person in line. Richard was there and put a hand on his shoulder.

"Jess?"

Jess' eyes were round with shock. "Her Majesty wants me to come back to Wellster."

"A polite nothing," was Richard's opinion.

"She wants me to come back and bring my wife and daughter."

"Whatever for?"

"I have no idea."

"Write to Father. He will know what this is about."

⁝ ⁞

When he received the letter, Edward gave it much thought. What did Gardwig learn about Lilian Earton? He sent a spy to Earton; I wish she had had him hung, but I suppose she's too softhearted.

The king had no intention of letting the countess go to Wellster if his son did not end up marrying Gardwig's daughter. The most convenient excuse would be that Lilian was pregnant, and he wrote a brief note to Jess suggesting that he make it so.

⁝ ⁞

To the Earl of Earton,

Speak to your wife this autumn. If she is amenable, you should talk about children.

At the bottom of the letter, after the king's flowery signature, was a postscript:

Jess, I forbid you to upset your wife. She is of great importance to the kingdom.

Jerrison Earton put his head in his hands after reading this letter. He was no fool. He understood that pregnancy would be an incontrovertible reason to keep Lilian in Ativerna. She would carry the child, give birth to it, and then nurse it. With any luck, at least three years would go by before she was able to travel. Much could change in three years.

All of a sudden, Lily is too important for my uncle to let her leave the kingdom. I don't know why, and I don't have anyone I can ask!

He knew from his mother's and sister's letters that Lily had sent some very fine presents to both women and to others at court. They were delighted by her mirrors and her lace, all made in Earton.

Earton was beginning to seem to its owner like an enchanted land where anything could happen. What frustrated him was that he had no real news directly from the estate and no way to find out quickly what was happening there.

"Richard, do you think we have time to take a detour through Earton before going on to Ivernea?"

"Of course not. Why?"

"I'd like to see with my own eyes what is going on."

Richard stared at him. "We can't do that, Jess."

"What if I just ride down there on my own. I could be back in a ten night if all goes well."

"You'd do better to sit still and avoid angering my father."

Jess' eyes flashed. "I've already felt his wrath, and all because of that…woman," he said, exerting great willpower to control his tongue.

Richard watched Jess through narrowed eyes. He was tired of his cousin's complaining. "What stopped you from running down there before we left? You had plenty of time to check on your household and throw out any thieves or murderers or whoever else was hiding down there. May I remind you that little Miranda came close to getting killed, and all you can think about is how your wife makes you look bad."

Jess sat down heavily. "I sent Miranda with guards. If someone wasn't trying to murder that cow of mine, she would never have been in danger."

"No one ever tried to hurt her while she was Lilian Broklend."

"Are you saying all of this is my fault?"

"Not all of it, but most of it, yes."

Jess leaped up and ran from the room, slamming the door behind him. Richard lay down and thought about what to do next. Spring was around the corner. Soon, it would be time to move on to Ivernea, and Jess was in no shape to continue as a diplomatic member of the delegation. He reflected that his cousin had never had his ears boxed. *He doesn't know how to deal with difficulties.*

He rubbed his eyes with one hand. After spring would come summer, and they would spend it in Ivernea. When the rains came again, he would turn for home and decide his own fate. Anna of Wellster was not to his liking. She was foolish and too flirtatious, and he knew that she would never look at him if he weren't Prince of Ativerna.

However, she did have her good points. She was young—almost half his age—and he could perhaps hope to change her in time. He also gave weight to Gardwig's confession that he cared more for the union of the two kingdoms than for Anna's feelings. As long as Richard had a lawful heir, he would be free to live as he pleased.

He thought about King Bernard of Ivernea. Now there was a man who was unlikely to encourage his son-in-law to keep a mistress. Richard had heard that he adored his daughter, the baby of the family to six older brothers.

When he thought about it, the prince tended to lean toward Anna. *I have to marry someone, and at least she's pretty to look at.* All of a sudden, he wondered what Gardwig would think if his son-and-law dealt with Anna the way he had dealt with his own five wives. He smiled. He was not that man. *If I marry Anna, I will have the freedom to find a woman I can truly love. I'll wait to see what fate has in store for me.*

ഇൗ ര

Sir, I have not been able to get to the child. The cow is almost finished. The medicus has no hope of saving her.

ഇൗ ര

I will pay extra for the child. Write when the cow is dead. You can get your money from Treloney.

Altres frowned when informed of the conversation between the two guests from Ativerna. To his credit, his first thought was to write to the countess. He already thought highly of her and decided he could use her to hedge his own bets. *An intelligent woman's gratitude is a thing very much worth having...*

A few days prior, he had received a short note by pigeon from Rolf, who was still in Altver. He had gone drinking with some of Leif's hotheaded Virmans, who had only been allowed to go on the trip because they needed to blow off steam, and one of them had told him about the Khangan prince and his rapidly improving health. This was all reported to the jester, along with the fact that the Khangan healers now followed Lilian and Tahir around like puppies.

Rolf said he did not know what to make of what he had learned, but he reported it all. He even recalled a conversation he had had in a village not far from the Earton castle, where the peasants told him about the countess with the golden hands who had healed one of their own boys and treated all the wounded men after the battle with the slave traders. Altogether, it was an interesting picture. Rolf wondered if Lilian was like Saint Arlinda, who was said to have healed the sick by laying-on of hands.

The jester, piecing together what he could from his sources, thought it highly likely that Lilian Earton had otherworldly talents that she kept hidden most of the time to avoid attracting unhealthy interest. With each passing day, he felt it was ever more imperative that the countess examine his sovereign lord and brother. *Richard will choose Anna; I'm sure he will. That means a wedding in Ativerna, and Gardwig will have to go. I'll get my hands on the countess once we're there, no matter how I have to do it.*

His pen raced across the parchment that lay on his desk.

My Lady, I hope you were not offended that I sent a man to make inquiries. Rolf had only the most flattering things to say about you. As your admirer, I would like to invite you to pay a visit to Wellster. His Majesty would be very pleased to see you, and I would do everything within my power to ensure that your visit is a success for both parties. It goes without saying that we would obtain King Edward's permission for your visit.

His Majesty read the list of questions you sent regarding his health, but he prefers to provide the answers in person.

Since I am already your great admirer, I feel I must also inform you about the earl's behavior of late. I expect you are aware that his former mistress—the woman who attempted to have you murdered—is traveling with the prince's delegation. I am sorry to say that your husband has learned no lessons from her unmasking, and continues to see yourself as the sole source of his troubles. He continues to be unfaithful. You would be within your rights to demand a formal separation at any time. Because of my position at court, I assure you that I can produce all of the women he has been involved with in Wellster.

I am certainly interested in the glass, mirrors and other items made in Earton, but I am more concerned with people than with things.

I would risk much to ensure friendly relations between two intelligent people.

I remain ever favorably disposed,

Altres Lort

He would send the letter to Rolf to be forwarded. He needed the countess, even if she was not able to bolster Gardwig's health. *I hope she is able to read between the lines. It will be the worse for her if she cannot.*

ᛞ ᚳ

It was mid-spring before the jester's letter reached Lilian. It gave her a great deal to think about. The impression she came away with was extremely unpleasant. *If this Earl of Lort is lying, then there's hope that Jess is a reasonable man and I can reach an agreement with him. In that case, I will have no need of Gardwig's schemer, and he probably knows that.*

If Lort was telling the truth, however, and Jess was furious with her, she would have to get out of Earton as soon as possible. Altres seemed to be hinting that the court of Wellster would always welcome her. *I'll have to discuss it with my father, but I would personally prefer a move to Virma.*

When she considered potential havens, she liked the idea that her father could continue as a shipbuilder in Virma. She could always find work as a healer. *I could marry the head of one of their clans and open a school of healing. People will line up from Virma to the Khanganate.*

Wellster seemed a much less favorable choice, but she would keep her options open for as long as she could. *I have to maintain civil relations with this Lort.* So, she sat down to compose a polite letter in reply. When it was finished, she would typeset it and print it, just to give Lort something to think about.

Looking back over the winter, Lily felt she had done well. She and all of her people had survived with plenty of supplies. She had survived several attempted murders. She knew some of the names of the people who wanted her dead, and she knew which strings to pull to find out the names of her other enemies. She had organized a very successful lace workshop. She was making progress with glass lenses. She was teaching courses for nurses, and the Virman women listened to her with rapt attention. She had made the first paper ever seen in that world, and she had helped her blacksmith make moveable type and print a few trial pages.

However, Earton was no place to expand a printing business, and she needed to find apprentices for her craftsmen. It was time to go to the capital, where she could buy the chemicals she needed and where it didn't take weeks to obtain the most basic supplies.

Also, secrecy was still an issue. She needed a Security Committee of her own. Her father wrote that he had found three potential candidates for the role of chief spy, but that she would have to choose among them.

There's so much I still have to do...

Lily resigned herself to the fact that she needed a day planner and started a new scroll for that purpose. It wasn't as useful as a smartphone, but it would have to do. *I wonder how long it will take for smartphones to appear in this world. I remember back when it was rare to see a cell phone of any kind, and just ten years later, it became strange to see a person without a cell phone. I don't know if the technology is good for us or not, but I'll do my best to introduce innovations that have a positive effect.*

The countess also spent a lot of time thinking about money. Some of the proceeds of her business interests were spent on the Earton estate, but she had asked Torius Avermal to invest the rest in various enterprises. *Whether or not I stay married to the earl, I need to have my own capital that no one else knows about.*

Lily may not have harbored any fondness for the earl, but she was starting to hear the ticking of her biological clock. She wanted to have a family where everyone loved everyone else, and she wanted a husband who would kiss her when they were reunited at the end of the day. She adored Miranda, but she also wanted children of her own to raise. Sometimes she woke up in the night to find that her pillow was wet with tears. *I can't cry now; I can't allow myself to feel anything for now.*

Lily sometimes sensed that there were men among the Virmans who found her attractive, but she was careful never to show any favor or allow anyone to get too close to her. It was tempting to find solace, at least for one night, on someone's strong shoulder, to feel protected and cared for, but she always brushed such thoughts away.

I have to keep moving forward. Sooner or later, I'll find someone to be my safe harbor. But it's all storms for me for now. But they can't break me! Someday, I'll be happy!

In late spring, when the fields were green with new grass, Lily left her home in Earton, bound for Lavery with an entourage of seven ships. Three of the ships were captained by the Khangans, and one of them carried Prince Amir and Miranda. The girl and the prince were fast friends and spent the time on board playing backgammon, checkers, and chess. Tahir and three of the Khangan healers had accommodations on Amir's ship so that they could continue to look after his health.

These were followed by Erik's ship, which was carrying a small but valuable cargo to Virma after stopping in Altver. Leif's ship, carrying the rest of the Virmans, including women and children, came next, followed by the two slaving ships. After much thought, Lily had renamed these two the *Vladimir* and the *Tatiana*, after her parents. The Virmans thought these names sounded just fine. Lily had a small berth on the *Tatiana*, as did Pastor Vopler and his son. Lons, Leis, the Eveers, the blacksmith and the glassblower were sailing on the *Vladimir*, which also carried the tutors, the lace-makers, and Jaimie.

Taris Brok remained behind to manage Earton and the temporarily orphaned Donter estate until August could find someone to take his place. Lily had started digging for more amber as soon as the weather had turned warm, and she didn't trust anyone but Taris to oversee it while she was gone.

Emma also remained behind to run the castle, which was guarded by the men Leis had trained over the winter.

Lily had assigned the job of overseeing the villages to Jan Leig, Art Virdas, and Sherl Ferney. Jan was charged with storing up peat for the next winter. Art would be keeping an eye on the smokehouse, and Sherl would watch over the salt works. With two of her elders gone, she put responsibility for Riverton on Jan and Runstaf on Sherl. Art, who was the smartest of the group, was in charge of helping the peasants get started with three-field rotation, and also would keep watch over the castle's livestock.

Now that the peasants could pay for using the earl's fields with their work instead of their produce, Lily hoped they would all have enough to eat. Just in case, she instructed Taris to issue milk and eggs to families in need.

If all went well, the castle wall would be in perfect condition by the time the countess returned. She had no way of knowing how long she would remain in Earton, but she hoped the wall would serve Miranda well.

ဆ☐ଛ

Lily stood on the deck of the *Tatiana* and glumly watched the coastline slip by. She would have preferred to walk to Lavery, but it would have taken too long and put her cargo at risk of theft. So, she would have to endure the seasickness that already rose in her throat. Lily gulped hard. Once they went around a bend in the river and she could no longer see her estate, she went below to her room and was violently ill. Faithful Martha stroked her hair. The old woman knew how her dear Lily hated being seasick.

At least I'll lose some weight, Lily thought despondently.

Life on board was hard. Her room was tiny and smelly, and she could barely keep food down. Still, she reminded herself how much was at stake.

I can stand it. I can stand anything. I am the Countess Lilian Elizabeth Mariella Earton, and I have many plans to accomplish.

The Earta River carried her ship on to Altver.

End of Book 3.

LitHunters

Hi! We're LitHunters, a digital publishing house that specializes in diamond-in-the-rough book series.

Our selection process is thorough as we choose which book series we want to devote time to and invest in completely. We select books based on their popularity online and their social media following. We publish books that are already famous with the most important people: you, the readers! As well as the book series, we also pay attention to the author's presence in social media and transfer their success on a global scale.

At LitHunters, we focus on the highest quality and most entertaining stories for our readers. That's what you can expect from all of our books! Thanks for checking out our book, and if you like it, we have a few recommendations of some of our other series.

Please consider leaving a review and joining our Facebook page for Lina J Potter and remember you can contact Lina on Facebook or our website: www.lithunters.com

You can find the whole series: https://amzn.to/2WqhY10

We would like to recommend some other books from LitHunters:

If you want to try something darker then we have the book for you. When an innocent and naive girl Arina wanders into an exhibition of an extremely rich and scandalous photograper, Maxim, she got caught by his predatory eyes.

He needs no love, no happiness, no family. Forbidden sensual pleasure, dark passion, and aesthetic beauty are the only things that interest him. And he has an offer she can't refuse. ***Two Months and Three Days*** by Tatiana Vedenska is out now.

Kiran, a flirtatious space cadet, is planning to become one of the most successful starship captains ever. Her life is all about organizing illicit races and gambling. After being kidnapped she is sent to her home planet and is forced to marry the mightiest warrior by the right of the strongest.

She will never accept this. No matter how difficult it might be to confront the whole planet, she is a cadet, after all, and cadets never surrender! Too bad that Eeristan might not survive the changes that she desires strongly. ***Kiran: The Warrior's Daughter*** by Ellen Stellar.